Praise for the novels of Mindy Klasky

How Not to Make a Wish

"Fresh and often hysterically funny, this story
also has a solid emotional core. Heroine Kira's first-person perspective
keeps it all real for the reader."
—*RT Book Reviews*

Girl's Guide to Witchcraft

"What fun! *Girl's Guide to Witchcraft* is a charmer of a story from
start to finish.... With her great characters and delightful prose voice,
Klasky really brought this book alive for me. Recommended highly."
—Catherine Asaro, award-winning author of The Misted Cliffs

"Mindy Klasky's newest work, *Girl's Guide to Witchcraft,* joins a love
story with urban fantasy and just a bit of humor.... Throw in family
troubles, a good friend who bakes Triple-Chocolate Madness, a
familiar who prefers an alternative lifestyle plus a disturbingly
good-looking mentor and you have one very interesting read."
—*SF Revu*

Sorcery and the Single Girl

"Klasky emphasizes the importance of being true to yourself and
having faith in friends and family in her bewitching second romance....
Readers who identify with Jane's remembered
high school social angst will cheer her all the way."
—*Publishers Weekly*

"The entire cast of this book comes to life, making it almost painful
to witness Jane's misplaced trust and inherent naivete. Klasky...
keeps you entranced from start to finish."
—*RT Book Reviews*

Magic and the Modern Girl

"Filled with magic—both of the witch world and the romance world—
complicated family relationships and a heavy dose of chick-lit humor,
this story is the perfect ending to the series."
—*RT Book Reviews*

Also by MINDY KLASKY

Jane Madison series

GIRL'S GUIDE TO WITCHCRAFT
SORCERY AND THE SINGLE GIRL
MAGIC AND THE MODERN GIRL

As You Wish series

HOW NOT TO MAKE A WISH
WHEN GOOD WISHES GO BAD
TO WISH OR NOT TO WISH (available October 2010)

MINDY KLASKY

When Good Wishes Go Bad

MIRA®

Recycling programs
for this product may
not exist in your area.

ISBN-13: 978-0-7783-2821-6

WHEN GOOD WISHES GO BAD

Copyright © 2010 by Mindy L. Klasky.

For questions and comments about the quality of this book please contact us
at Customer_eCare@Harlequin.ca.

www.MIRABooks.com

Printed in U.S.A.

First Printing: April 2010
10 9 8 7 6 5 4 3 2 1

To Jane Leigh, in memory of *Suddenly, Last Summer,*
when the lighting board caught fire.

CHAPTER 1

B— GOTTA RUN. DON'T WAIT UP.

That's what Dean's note said, the one he'd stuck to the refrigerator sometime that Tuesday morning. The one that had obviously been written in haste, his customary tight scrawl spread wide across the sticky note. The one that he'd scratched with a dried-out black marker from our kitchen junk drawer, instead of his customary red-ink fine-point Bic.

After a long day at the Mercer Project, the theater where we both worked, I'd tried to follow his instructions. After all, I knew this was crunch time for Dean. March was the high-water mark for tax season; the Mercer's books had to be balanced, copious obscure documentation needed to be completed, all in time for our April filing. Dean thrived on the detailed requirements; he reveled in the hard-charging challenges of tax time.

I would not survive one single day as director of finance.

Lying in bed, fighting sleep despite the clear instruction

in Dean's note, I tossed and turned, staring first at his night-stand, then at my own. His bedside table was almost completely bare—he had a functional, white gooseneck lamp, precisely angled to shed light on whatever spreadsheet he brought to bed. An alarm clock hunched in stainless-steel solitude, its red numbers winking balefully.

My table was a little more, um, crowded. I hated resetting my alarm clock after power failures, and I could never remember to replace batteries to keep a clock running without fail, so I relied on my cell phone's alarm feature. My phone charger was tangled on my nightstand, looping around one lamp, four books, a bottle of hand lotion, a glass that had held water a week before, a stray earring forever separated from its mate, a notepad, a souvenir pen from the Statue of Liberty that said BECCA in glittery letters, a small stuffed rabbit (gift from my literary associate at work on a day when I'd been in a particularly bad mood), a partridge, and a pear tree.

Yeah. It wasn't readily apparent to people why Dean and I had put up with each other for the past three and a half years. I tried to explain that opposites attract, but I don't know that I was always convincing.

I spent most of the night trying to find a comfortable position, repeatedly punching my pillow. I couldn't remember the last time I'd slept in our bed alone. Or not slept, as the case might be. I woke up over and over again, spending large stretches of the night watching Dean's clock tick through its glaring red paces.

At two in the morning, I administered some emergency chocolate, indulging in the last three pieces from the giant Godiva heart I'd bought myself for Valentine's Day. I'd justified the extravagance by making my purchase on February 15, taking advantage of the postholiday markdown. I was sure Dean would have been proud of my fiscal conservatism, if he'd even noticed. The poor guy had been so busy with Mercer work that Valentine's chocolate had completely slipped his mind nearly three weeks ago.

I finally gave up trying to sleep at 5:00 a.m. After showering, I pulled on black slacks, and I dug out my warmest sweater from the top shelf in our bedroom closet. The calendar might have said that we'd shifted into spring, but the weather hadn't caught up yet. The temperature was well below freezing, and hillocks of dirty snow still held their grips on shaded parts of the sidewalk, left over from a late February squall.

The streets were quiet, at least by Manhattan standards, as I made my way across Greenwich Village, stopping for two of the largest cups of coffee I could find. I arrived at the theater by six, grateful that I had my own key to the office space.

Dean's office light was on. His desk was pristine, not even a Post-it note out of place. A single blank pad of paper was centered on the surface, a single red pen uncapped beside it. The adding machine was a convenient reach away from the telephone, its power switch in the "off" position as it sat like a good soldier, waiting for morning muster.

In other words, Dean had obviously just stepped away for a minute or two. His impeccably organized life was proceeding as usual, even after a night of bleary-eyed number-crunching. I left a cup of coffee on his desk, using his pen to draw a big red heart on the pad of paper, adding a flourished *B* by way of signature.

My own office was down the hall. It was much smaller than Dean's—he *was* the director of finance, after all, and I was just the theater's lowly dramaturg. Dean had also been with the Mercer for two years longer than I had.

Of course, I didn't really mind the size of my office. A lot of people in my position worked at anonymous desks in open spaces, an easy bellow away from their company's artistic director. I was incredibly lucky to have landed the job I had six months earlier; there were maybe a hundred dramaturg positions in the entire country. A lot of theaters weren't financially secure enough to hire a trained scholar solely to provide literary support on each and every production.

Besides, if my office had been the size of Dean's, I would have drowned in the accumulated detritus.

As at home, my professional space was the opposite of Dean's. My single guest chair was piled high with coffee-table books, lushly illustrated volumes that I'd paged through the week before, trying to educate the cast of our upcoming Sam Shepard one-act plays on the eerie beauty of the American Southwest. A dozen banker's boxes were scattered across the floor, each containing a collection of mementos for one play or another, random artifacts that I'd used to explain the significance of various playwrights' sometimes-opaque words.

The bulletin board above my desk was in a similar state of disarray, covered with notes and other memorabilia. I loved the miniature license plate from California, with my name picked out in bold navy letters. Note to self: Insert long, boring story about how my mother still hoped her only daughter would return to the sunny city of San Diego. Insert longer, more boring story about how I was determined to keep an entire continent between my mother and me—for both our sakes. I shook my head and grinned at fortunes from Chinese meals otherwise long forgotten, at cartoons clipped from newspapers, at outrageous headlines from articles printed off the Internet.

My desk was covered in paper, as well. Half a dozen notepads were sandwiched between three-ring binders, manila folders, and scripts. I'd sacrificed at least twenty pens to the chaos; most marked pages that I knew were absolutely, vitally important, ones that I would definitely return to…someday soon. The entire maelstrom was anchored by a stack of manuscripts, plays sent in by hopeful playwrights, despite the fact that the Mercer had a strict submission policy mandating the intermediary of literary agents.

Yeah, we had strict rules, but I still reviewed every manuscript I received. Along with every other dramaturg I'd ever met, I dreamed of the day I discovered America's best and brightest new playwright. I also lived in utter terror of missing the next blockbuster play, overlooking it merely because its author wasn't ready to be bound by silly rules about professional business correspondence, postage, and agent representation.

Staring at the mess on my desk, I comforted myself with the knowledge that this quiet predawn morning would give me a chance to plow through some of the backlog. I fortified myself with a mighty swallow of coffee and settled down to some serious reading. I thought about Dean a half-dozen times, but I made myself stay at my desk. He'd find me when he came up for air, from wherever he was hiding in the Mercer's warren of offices, rehearsal rooms, and storage closets.

He always did.

An hour later, I'd managed to eliminate four new plays from our list of possible blockbusters. Each of the rejects had a different problem. One was written entirely in French— our audiences were generally willing to expand their minds and learn about different cultures, but we'd be pushing things to stage an entire production in a foreign language. Another play was performed completely in the nude—again, we were willing to push some performance envelopes, but we had no desire to become the must-see naughty show for all the tourists from Rubesville. One script might have been the finest play written this century, but it was printed on bright fuchsia paper (the better for me to take notice, I supposed), with each character's lines delineated in a different impossible-to-read font. I just wasn't willing to work that hard. And the fourth script was a cheery and lighthearted musical about bestiality, incest, and pedophilia. Whispers of *Rent*-terror scurried at the back of my mind. That musical had included drug addiction, AIDS, and other upbeat plot twists, and it had gone on to win a Pulitzer and a Tony. But I just couldn't see us staging such a dark new show. Besides, we didn't do musicals. Or at least, we never had in the past.

I took a sip of my now-room-temperature coffee and leaned back, raising a hand to rub the base of my neck. So, maybe this wasn't my day to find a script treasure. I stretched in my chair and decided to head back to Dean's office. He had to be even more exhausted than I was, poor thing.

Before I could move, though, my computer chimed, alerting me to the fact that I had new e-mail. I frowned as I glanced at the incoming message. I didn't recognize the sender—elaine.harcourt@playlaw.com. Puzzled, I clicked on the flashing mail icon.

"Dear Ms. Morris… Regret to inform you… Rights are not currently available to produce Evan Morton's *Crystal Dreams*… Unavoidable litigation… Copyright… Regret any inconvenience… Sincerely, Elaine Harcourt, Attorney at Law."

All of the coffee I had drunk congealed in my belly as one acidic lump. I forced myself to re-read the e-mail, marching my eyes across every single word.

This couldn't be happening to me.

Crystal Dreams was the next play in our production cycle. We were supposed to hold auditions in ten days; the show was going to open in May. The Mercer had been boasting about *Crystal Dreams* for the past year, billing the work as a brilliant new play by Evan Morton, one of America's bravest young playwrights.

Hal Bernson, our artistic director and my direct boss, had been so attracted to the script that he had vowed to direct the show himself. He only took on one play each season, in addition to his artistic director duties, and he'd latched on to *Crystal Dreams* because of the controversy surrounding the play.

Crystal Dreams was based on the journals of a grad student who had starved herself to death four years ago, protesting the imprisonment of her lover for meth distribution, imprisonment that was ultimately found to be based on a corrupt prosecutor's lies. There were rumors at the time that Evan Morton—the lover—had egged the woman on from prison, sending her long letters about how the state had wronged him, about how she was the only one who could redeem him, who could give his life meaning.

Hal had traveled to Florida to meet with Morton as soon as the guy was released. Hal had spent weeks debating the merits of Morton's masterpiece. Ultimately, he had decided that the guy wasn't a murderer. He was just an artist, one who desperately wanted his play produced by the Mercer. One who understood how to use the press to make his project shine. One who could turn a Mercer production into front-page news, even in jaded New York City.

Hal had agreed to produce and direct *Crystal Dreams*. During my first week on the job, Hal had told me that Morton gave him the creeps—the playwright was way too intense. As part of my dramaturg trial by fire, I had been designated the primary correspondent with our difficult artiste. After all, a large part of my job would be coordinating rehearsal-inspired changes in our new play, balancing all of the artistic egos. Morton would be a challenge, but he'd provide great experience for a new dramaturg.

Experience that I was never going to have now, due to legal wrangling.

I read the e-mail again, this time inserting the words between the printed lines. The grad student's family must have sued Evan Morton. There was an electronic attachment to Elaine Harcourt's e-mail. I clicked on it, and a legal document sprang to life on my screen, numbers marching down the left side, setting off each line. My eyes automatically jumped to the title of the document: Order Granting Temporary Restraining Order. I skimmed the legalese. I didn't understand every word, but the overall sense was clear: the United States District Court for the Southern District of New York was prohibiting us, and anyone else, from producing *Crystal Dreams* until the underlying copyright dispute could be resolved.

I felt sick.

Auditions were scheduled to take place in *ten days*. I'd already spent weeks doing background work on the play, research about meth and prosecutorial misconduct and the difficult personal relationship that might—or might not—be at the core of the play.

Forget my work, though. Forget the designers who'd built set models, sketched costumes, planned a lighting grid. Forget the actors who had prepared audition monologues based on our announced show.

We suddenly had a gaping hole in our schedule. A hole that needed to be filled immediately.

I stared at the four rejected scripts I'd read through that morning. There wasn't anything there that we could salvage. And truth be told, all the rest of the over-the-transom scripts on my desk were likely to be the same level of garbage.

I scrambled for my phone, punched in the four-digit extension of my assistant, Jennifer Davis.

"Hey!" she answered, her cheerful greeting the absolute opposite of the dread that chewed at my belly. "I didn't know you were here! Can you come up front for a minute?"

I ignored her question and asked one of my own. "Is Hal in yet?"

Jenn's desk was in the Bullpen, a space she shared with our all-purpose office manager and a couple of interns. She was within easy shouting distance of the Mercer's artistic director. "He's here," she said, obviously a little puzzled by my question, "but he's in a meeting. In the large conference room."

"Damn!"

"Can I help with anything?"

I shook my head, momentarily forgetting that she couldn't

see me. I was going to have to interrupt the meeting. Hal needed to know the bad news immediately. "No," I said, finally remembering to use my words. Then I recalled that she'd asked me to come up to the front. "I'll be out there in a sec."

I hung up the phone and stood, wiping my suddenly sweaty palms down my thighs. My heart was pounding as if I'd run a 10K. I worked my fingers through my hair, automatically twisting its wild waves into a loose knot at my nape. A few strawberry strands twined around my hands; I shook them into my trash can and forced myself to take a steadying breath before heading out my office door.

I glanced toward Dean's office. His light was still on; the door was still open. I walked close enough to see that the cup of coffee I'd left was still on the corner of his desk.

If possible, my heart beat even harder. Where *was* he? Worry for his safety twined between my jangling nerves. I turned on my heel and rushed to the Bullpen.

Jenn stood by her desk, her own obvious anxiety twisting her smile into something painful. Her expression was a direct contrast to the perky cockatiel screensaver that stared out from her computer. Jenn loved the birds; she owned a half-dozen of them. Now, she turned her head to a distinctly parrotlike angle as she asked, "Are you okay?"

I shook my head, but I didn't actually answer her question. "Have you seen Dean?"

"Not since… Wow, Monday, I guess." Day before yesterday. Not good. "Um, Becca—"

I ignored her, glancing toward the large conference room where Hal was holed up. The door was closed and the shades were down, covering the floor-to-ceiling windows. That was strange—meetings around here were always open. "Any chance he's in there?" I nodded toward the room.

Jennifer shrugged apologetically. "I don't know. It's a board meeting."

"A board meeting? Hal didn't mention one yesterday."

"I don't think he knew about it yesterday. Everyone was grumbling as they came in—I think it's some sort of emergency."

Emergency. The word shot another arrow of adrenaline into my heart. Something must have happened to Dean. Hal must have been working late last night, too, must have been here when Dean got sick. Seriously sick, if the board was already in an emergency session to figure out what they were going to do without a functioning director of finance.

But where was Dean? Was he in the hospital? And why hadn't Hal called *me?* Why had he called in the board, but not reached out to me? It wasn't like Dean and I had kept our relationship a secret. I folded my arms around my waist, trying to hold in a rising tide of nausea.

"Um, Becca," Jenn said again. When I surfaced momentarily from my self-recriminations, she nodded toward the corner, toward one of the intern desks.

I followed her movement, only to find that a stranger was sitting in the intern's chair. His winter coat, a ratty beige ski parka that had seen better days, was collapsed across the desk in front of him. The laces on one of his Chuck Taylors were working loose, and the tails of his shirt peeked out from beneath his moss-colored sweater. His dark curls still bore the marks from a comb, although they were struggling to break free.

Before I could say anything, Jenn said pointedly, "Becca,

can I talk to you for a second?" She stalked across the Bullpen, trusting me to follow her into Hal's office. I longed to refuse—I needed to get to the clandestine board meeting— but a tiny part of my mind gibbered that I didn't want to know what was going on behind that closed door. I didn't want to know about the emergency. I followed Jenn because she represented the path of least resistance.

"Don't be angry with me," she said as soon as the door was closed.

"Why would I be angry with you?" I heard the tension in my voice, but I didn't bother to repeat my question, to sound less annoyed.

Jenn started toying with her wedding band, flicking her fingers across the Celtic knotwork. We'd been working together for six months. I knew that fidget meant she was trying to sneak something past me. With her voice pitched half an octave higher than normal, she said, "Oh, forget it. You've obviously got more important things to worry about. I just had a stupid idea. I'll take care of it."

"Take care of *what?*" My nerves made the last word come out a lot louder than I'd intended.

"Shh!" She glanced toward the closed door.

"Jenn, what is going on? Who is that guy?"

"One of the stalking list guys who came by to drop off a script after I told him that he needed to give it to you personally."

"What?" She'd spoken so quickly that I barely caught the gist of what she'd said. "I could have sworn you just said that guy is on the stalking list."

The stalking list. The short list of up-and-coming new playwrights that Jenn and I admired, the authors whose work we thought we might someday produce here at the Mercer. Jenn and I kept an eye on their websites, on their blogs, on ShowTalk, the social networking website for New York theater professionals. Basically, we tracked anyplace they might post online to share their creative process or their personal angst or what they'd eaten for dinner the night before. The important stuff, in other words. The stuff that would let us know when they'd written a new play, when they were ready to unveil a masterpiece-in-waiting to a sympathetic audience.

The whole idea, though, was supposed to be that *we* stalked *them;* we kept an eye on what they were writing. They weren't supposed to come to us. They weren't supposed to show up before the office even officially opened on a random Wednesday morning in the beginning of March. But Jennifer was obviously pretty invested in this whole thing. "Which one is he?" I asked, intrigued despite myself.

Jenn twisted her hands in front of her. "I'm sorry, Becca. I know I should have just sent him away. But he looked so cute, standing there, like a little boy turning in his English homework."

"Jenn, I just read four of the worst plays I've ever seen. You know that we don't accept submissions over the transom."

"But we do, unofficially. And he's on the *list!*"

She had a point. Possibly. "Who is he?" I asked again.

"Ryan Thompson."

I blinked. Ryan wasn't on *my* stalking list. Jenn had found him, just a few weeks before. She'd read some comments he'd posted on a public blog, something about the role of the modern playwright in creating a communal dialogue about social responsibility. She'd been intrigued by what he had to say. (Yeah, we folks in the Mercer's literary department were total theater geeks.) Mostly, though, she'd been impressed with how he'd said it. In fact, she'd been interested enough to track down a copy of his first play, something that had been produced once, at a university in the wilds of Roanoke, Virginia.

And now the guy was sitting in our office, waiting to talk to me. "Jenn, I don't know anything about him!"

She bit her lip and then said, "Trust me. Remember? He's the Peace Corps guy." Peace Corps… Ryan had just returned from a two-year stint abroad—in Africa, somewhere. I nodded slowly, vaguely recalling what Jenn had told me. She apparently interpreted my nod as acquiescence about reading his play. She clasped her hands in front of her, the very picture of riotous joy. "You won't regret this, I'm sure."

"I haven't agreed to do anything yet," I grumbled.

"Please, Becca? Just take his envelope. Tell him you'll read it in the order received, and send him on his way."

"*You* could have done that!"

"Yeah," she said sulkily. "I should have."

Before I could argue with her anymore, a phone started to ring out in the Bullpen. Jenn sighed and opened Hal's office door, rushing to her desk to answer the line. Apparently, the caller wanted to reorganize the United Nations into something only slightly more bureaucratic—at least that's what Jenn implied with her body language. She was clearly too busy to return to the matter at hand. Too busy to talk to Ryan Thompson and send him on his way. Too busy to save me.

I sighed and threw back my shoulders, trying to look professional as I crossed the room. I'd take the stupid manuscript, remind this Ryan guy of our submission policy, and get back to the morning's serious work of tracking down Dean. And then I'd tell Hal about the *Crystal Dreams* disaster. Joy, oh joy— the theater life just didn't get any better than this. My belly churned again as I glanced over my shoulder at the conference room.

Our visitor stood as I approached him. "Ms. Morris, I'm Ryan Thompson," he said. His shoulders hunched, as if he didn't want to frighten me with his full height. He turned his head a little as he introduced himself, smiling shyly and looking at a point somewhere beyond my left ear. "Thank you for taking the time to see me," he said.

Well, technically, I hadn't agreed to take the time. In fact, technically I didn't *have* the time. I had to say something, though, so I introduced myself, even though he obviously knew who I was. "Rebecca Morris." And then I remembered my manners. It wouldn't kill me to be polite, for just a minute. "Jenn said that you've just returned from Africa?"

"I've been back in the States for a couple of months." I glanced at his heavy sweater, at his rumpled coat. Despite their appearance, they must be new—he certainly wouldn't have needed them in Africa. He cleared his throat, drawing my gaze back to his face. When he spoke, his words were slow, as if he were used to thinking in a foreign language. "Jenn was kind enough to read some comments I made on the Internet. She said you wouldn't mind reading my new play. It's called *However Long*."

He looked so nervous, so pitiful, that I had to respond. *"However Long?"* I asked.

"It comes from an African proverb. 'However long the night, the dawn will break.'"

Despite myself, I shivered. What did this guy know about

long nights? I looked down the hallway, toward my office, toward Dean's empty one. It was well past dawn, well past time I should have heard from my absentee boyfriend. Well past time for me to wrap up this conversation and find out what was going on in the conference room.

I reached out for Ryan's envelope. The manila corners were crisp and neat, as if he'd carried his treasure carefully all the way to our office. He'd used a computer to print out his address label, putting both his name and my own in clear, legible type. The plain white square was centered precisely on the envelope.

Given the muck of unsolicited manuscripts I'd already waded through that morning, the condition of Ryan's submission seemed to be a sign from some benevolent heaven.

"I can't promise anything," I warned him. "Ordinarily, we only take submissions through agents, and even then, it can take several weeks for us to get around to reading them."

Again, he gave me that shy grin, and he buried his hands in his pockets, as if he wanted his clothes to swallow him whole. "I completely understand. I wouldn't have bothered you at all, if Jennifer hadn't said…" He trailed off, obviously worried that he was going to get my assistant in trouble.

"Don't worry about it," I said.

His relief was almost palpable. "I won't take any more of your time, Ms. Morris. I enclosed a card with all of my contact information. I really appreciate the chance that you're giving me."

"My pleasure," I said automatically, tucking his envelope under my arm to symbolize that we were done with our conversation. He nodded, taking the hint, and then Jenn magically concluded her phone call. Suddenly suspicious, I wondered if she'd been chattering on a dead line for the past few minutes. "I'm afraid, though, that I'll have to let Jennifer show you out. I'm on my way into a meeting."

Jenn stepped out from behind her desk, a smile broad across her face. She started to walk Ryan toward the door, taking only a moment to look over her shoulder, to mouth a heartfelt, "Thank you!" to me. I nodded and barely waited until they were out of sight before I turned toward the conference room. My hand shook as I opened the door.

Immediately, I was the target of a dozen pairs of eyes as every board member looked up from the table. A heartbeat of a scan, and I could see that Dean wasn't there. Dean wasn't, but a stranger was—a man who sat at the head of the table, shuffling papers as my interruption froze the entire meeting.

My knees trembled, but I wasn't sure if I was relieved or even more afraid. I still had no idea where my boyfriend was, but at least I could pass on the *Crystal Dreams* disaster to Hal. One crisis would be off my plate. "Excuse me," I said, focusing on my boss. "I'm sorry to interrupt, but this is an emergency. Hal, may I speak with you for a minute?"

My boss blinked his sapphire eyes, emphasizing his surprise by running a hand through his short gray hair. His lips were narrow in his immaculate close-trimmed beard. "Whatever it is will have to wait, Becca."

I shook my head. "This can't wait."

He laid his hands flat on the table, as if he were trying to ice his palms. I knew the gesture, even though we'd only worked together for six months. It was an indication that he was out of patience, that he was completely exasperated with the people around him. That he was determined to have his way, then, immediately, without delay.

"It *can* wait," he said, and his voice was as chilly as his gaze. "In fact, I was just about to call you in here about something else entirely. Come in, Rebecca. And close the door behind you."

It took every last ounce of my willpower to step inside that room.

CHAPTER 2

FOR THE RECORD, AN EMERGENCY BOARD MEETING is never fun and games.

It's worse, though, when you weren't even planning on attending. When your boss orders you to have a seat. When everyone looks at you as if you have some supersecret information, or at least some perfectly reasonable explanation, something that they absolutely, positively need in order to resolve whatever crisis is at hand.

And it's one hundred percent the worst when you don't have the faintest idea of what their crisis might be. Especially when you arrived for the sole purpose of handing them a different disaster, one they apparently know absolutely nothing about. One they're apparently not willing to address.

I took a seat at the foot of the table, automatically settling Ryan Thompson's script in front of me, as if the manila envelope could act as some sort of shield. My pulse was skittering around, making me painfully aware of the giant coffee I'd already drunk. Nevertheless, I found myself craving more caffeine. Or, at least, lusting after a comforting mug to fold my hands around.

I settled for curling my fingers in my lap.

"Thank you," Hal said, as if he'd given me a choice about joining the meeting. His voice, though, did not begin to convey thanks. In fact, his words were colder than the sidewalks outside; Hal sounded as if he were furious with me—beyond fury.

Sure, Hal was usually demanding. He wanted things done well, and promptly. He expected me—and everyone else associated with the company—to be on my toes, to anticipate what he needed, what the Mercer needed.

Hal was a theatrical force of nature. He'd carved out our company's mission thirty-one years before. He'd brought together a group of underemployed actors who all believed more in the power of acting than in the lure of computerized bells and whistles, than in the shimmer and shine of a Broadway that had been seduced by new technologies that turned plays into bizarre living movies, into special-effects extravaganzas. Hal and his colleagues believed in the inherent power of words, of passion, of the sheer physical energy that an actor could project onstage, live, within feet of an audience.

The Mercer had started out in the basement of a church, with rented lighting instruments and the simplest of sets. Hal had grown the company, had established the theater I now called home. He had brought together the board of directors, sought out people who knew theater, who understood what we were doing, what made us special. He had insisted that a professional theater mandated a professional dramaturg, and for that I could never thank him enough.

Therefore, I tried not to panic when he pinned me with

his steely eyes. "Rebecca," he said, and just the way he said my name made it sound like an accusation. "Where can we find Dean Marcus?"

Panic took up a steady drumbeat against my lungs, making it difficult for me to draw a full breath. "I—" I started to answer and I had to swallow hard, to crush a sudden, unexpected sob. "I don't know.… I mean, he was working late last night. I thought he was here?"

Everyone shifted uncomfortably. Trying desperately to ratchet down my own concern, I watched them look at each other, look at me, look at the unknown man who sat at the head of the table. I wanted to appear professional. I didn't want them to think that I was the dramaturg who cried, who broke down under pressure. Glancing around for a pad of paper, for a pen, I concentrated on projecting my most mature demeanor and said, "I'll take notes for Dean, if you'd like. I can pass them on to him after the meeting."

Once I found him. Once I figured out where he was, where he'd been for the past forty-eight hours. Calling on my last shred of self-discipline, I kept from leaping out of my chair, from running down the hall, from fleeing back to Jenn's desk to demand that she call every hospital in town.

"That won't be necessary, Ms. Morris."

I whirled to face Clifford Ames, the chairman of the board. He held the position because he was the theater's largest individual donor. During my first week on the job, I'd read his bio in the back of one of our programs. He worked for some huge bank. Or an insurance company. Or something like that. I never was much good with numbers.

I was a little surprised that Mr. Ames knew who I was. We'd been introduced at an opening-night gala, shortly after

I'd joined the Mercer staff. Hal had done the honors himself, summoning me across the room with the intensity of his steely gaze. But Mr. Ames had met dozens of people that night; he'd shaken scores of hands. The other guests at the gala must have impressed him more than I had; they'd certainly known more about the Mercer than I'd been able to glean in my few short weeks on the job.

Nevertheless, Mr. Ames clearly knew me now. "Ms. Morris, Hal asked you to join us because…well, we understand that you… Let me say that it has come to our attention that you and Mr. Marcus, that you…"

Against my will, I blushed. Yeah, like that was something strange. When your skin is paler than the proverbial Irish milkmaid's, you blush. A lot. Even when you're perfectly willing to admit that you live with your boyfriend. The boyfriend who works with you. In your cool, rare theater job.

I swallowed hard and willed my cheeks to cool. Fumbling my fingers around Ryan Thompson's manila envelope, I wished that I could melt into the table, but another board member spoke up before I could figure out a way to respond to Mr. Ames. "Cliff, may I?"

"Please," Mr. Ames said, and I'd never seen a man so anxious to pass the metaphoric buck.

Kira Franklin favored him with a smile and then glanced at Hal, silently seeking—and receiving—his permission to continue. Kira was stage managing the Sam Shepard one-acts that had been my primary focus since I'd joined the Mercer. She was a professional-in-residence; she worked full-time at the Mercer, which gave her a somewhat rare and always welcome stability in the theatrical world.

From what I'd seen so far, she was an excellent stage

manager. She was always prepared; she even anticipated some of the director's quirkiest requests. She was unflappable during rehearsal, keeping her temper no matter what chaos erupted around her. I could see why she sat on the Mercer board—she could advocate effectively for the people who worked in the theater, even as she spoke the language of businessmen and -women, of donors. Rumor had it that her father was some big important lawyer in the Midwest, and it was clear that Kira had mastered the arts of argumentation and persuasion somewhere in her career.

Now, she took a sip from her paper cup of coffee, and I remembered the other major thing I knew about her. Kira liked her coffee *strong,* so strong that everyone else refused to drink the stuff she brewed backstage. During the first rehearsal for the Shepard pieces, Mercer old-timers had taken up a collection and bought her a huge gift card for the Starbucks on the corner, just so that the rest of us could make something drinkable with the in-house machine.

Kira flashed me a professional smile, and I made myself take a deep breath. This couldn't be so terrible. What were they going to ask me about, anyway? Everyone at the Mercer knew that Dean and I lived together. I'd insisted on being up-front about our relationship before I accepted the theater's offer of employment.

So what was I afraid of now? Fielding questions about the deepest, darkest secrets of my love life?

After a firm nod to the rest of the board, Kira turned to me and said, "Becca, were you and Dean together last night?"

Wow. She really *was* going to ask me about my love life.

I didn't think it was possible for my facial capillaries to fill again so quickly. "Excuse me?" I managed to choke out.

Kira sighed, and I could make out a wash of sympathy behind her eyes. "I know that question must seem really intrusive. I'd take more time to explain, but the situation is really urgent. We need to speak with Dean immediately, and we haven't been able to reach him for the past twenty-four hours. He isn't answering his cell or his BlackBerry."

I considered lying. I could say that Dean had come home from the gym yesterday evening. That we'd made a stir-fry for dinner. That we'd slipped into bed after watching the news. That I'd made him a bag lunch that morning and kissed him goodbye before he left, playing my role as the perfect 1950s housewife.

Except the board already knew that Dean wasn't at work. And any lies I told would just delay the moment when I could get help finding my boyfriend. "He didn't come home," I said. "He left the apartment before I did yesterday, but there was a note telling me not to wait up."

Before Kira could ask another question, another board member slammed her perfectly manicured hand down on the table. "I told you!"

Alicia Morton's hair swept back from her face, twin silver wings gleaming against jet black in her corporate bob. A single strand of pearls slashed across her throat. Her severe black jacket managed to emphasize her feminine curves, even as it was cut to make her look like a no-holds-barred advertising executive.

Which she was.

Alicia Morton had recently joined the board as part of Hal's efforts to forge ongoing partnerships with strong, traditional New York businesses. I couldn't imagine what had led Alicia to accept Hal's invitation; she seemed to resent everything about the Mercer.

Everyone in the theater world had heard about her behavior at the Fall Fete, Hal's most important fundraiser of the year. Hal had introduced Alicia from the dais, intending to recognize our newest board member and move on. Alicia had a different plan, though. She'd commandeered the microphone and transformed the dinner into a question-and-answer session, a probing investigation of all Hal's plans for the coming season. In fact, Hal had only succeeded in silencing Alicia when he reminded everyone that the Mercer was going to skyrocket in prominence with its production of *Crystal Dreams*.

Whoops.

"I told you," Alicia repeated, biting off her words with military precision. She flexed her talons toward the stranger at the head of the table. "We shouldn't have a *lawyer* sitting here. We should have the police!"

Well, at least that told me who the unknown guy was. A lawyer. That couldn't be good.

"Bill Rodriguez," he said, inclining his head toward me by way of greeting. I nodded warily. "I'm from Fenter, Grimley, and Swanson. We represent the Mercer Project. We handle tax work, finances in general."

"Pleased to meet you," I said, falling back on the social lubrication of etiquette. Alicia snorted, but at least she held her tongue.

Bill had the courtesy to act as if he hadn't heard her. "What exactly is your job here at the Mercer, Ms. Morris?"

"I'm the dramaturg," I said. I was prepared for the politely blank look he gave me; I encountered it from nearly everyone who wasn't positioned deep inside the theater world. I clarified: "I work behind the scenes. I'm sort of an 'in-house critic.'" I shrugged, as if I were searching for words, even though I knew my little speech by heart. "I'm sort of like a…psychotherapist and career coach for the production itself, helping everyone involved to achieve their full potential. I bring together interested parties, pull whatever strings I can so that a show is the best it can possibly be."

Bill nodded slowly before glancing at his notes. "How involved are you with Mercer Project financials?"

"Financials?"

"Does your job involve your keeping books for the theater?"

I shook my head. "No."

"Do you write checks on any of the Mercer accounts?"

"No." Two simple, straightforward answers. Go, me.

I looked at the board members again. What *was* this all about? Was I in trouble for that reimbursement slip I'd submitted last month? Did they think I'd been too generous with my tip to that cab driver, the one who'd stopped for me in the middle of a deluge at three in the morning, after the first rehearsal for the Shepards? I'd thought the service was worth ten dollars, and if they weren't going to approve the tip, I'd pay for it out of my own damn pocket.

The board members stared back at me. Yeah. This wasn't about any ten-dollar tip. The board of directors didn't give a collective damn about my reimbursement slips.

Bill continued, apparently unaware that every single person in the room was scrutinizing me as if I were some freakish new specimen of bug. Even Hal looked distant, bemused. Bill asked, "What is the maximum amount that you can sign for, here at the theater?"

"Without prior approval?"

"Without prior approval," Bill agreed.

"Two hundred and fifty dollars. But my job doesn't really require me to put out a lot of money up front. I might buy a book or two, or make some copies at the library. Sometimes I download fee-based articles online."

Bill nodded, as if he expected as much. "And just to clarify, Ms. Morris. Are you on the signature cards for any of the Mercer Project bank accounts?"

Signature cards? Like the ones you fill out when you first open up an account? "Um, no." I licked my lips and flattened my fingers on the tabletop. "Why are you asking me all these questions? What exactly do you think I've done?"

Bill looked around at the board members, as if he were requesting permission from them. When both Hal and Mr. Ames had acquiesced with the tiniest of nods, Bill turned back to me. "Ms. Morris, we've been investigating some…irregularities in the Mercer Project's accounts. With an organization of this size, we're accustomed to seeing some fluctuation on a daily basis. The board called this meeting, though, and asked me to attend, because three of the Project's accounts were closed out completely yesterday morning."

Closed. Out. Completely.

The words seemed to echo in the suddenly too-small room. My stomach swooped, as if I were flying down a roller coaster's steepest descent. The board was here. A lawyer was here. And Dean was nowhere to be seen. And money—apparently a lot of money—was missing.

Even as I tried to come up with a benign explanation, I repeated to Bill, "Completely?"

He met my gaze impassively. "Dean Marcus had authority to sign for each of those accounts. He could write checks on them, up to whatever amount he deemed necessary for the Mercer."

I tried to swallow, but my throat was suddenly too dry to complete the motion. I had to be misunderstanding what Bill was saying. There had to be some mistake. "I—I don't know," I stammered, as if someone had asked me a question. "I— How much money are you talking about?"

Bill answered as if he were reciting some obscure clause in the Constitution. "Three million, five hundred thousand, twenty-seven dollars and thirty-two cents."

My lungs froze. "Thirty-two cents?" I managed to chip past the ice crystals, incredulous at the absurd detail when the figure Bill had just named was a quarter of the theater's annual budget.

He nodded curtly. "Thirty-two cents."

I collapsed back in my chair.

Three and a half million dollars.

Dean was good with money. Careful. Precise. When he picked up the check for our dinners out, he tipped an exact fifteen percent, pretax, to the penny, because that was the proper thing to do. That was the *rule*.

I thought back to the Valentine's Day we'd just celebrated. I'd really splurged. Dean had been working so hard; he'd been so stressed. I'd bought him the cell phone that he coveted, the latest model with more bells and whistles than I could even begin to understand. He had been as excited as a little boy when he opened the package—he'd oohed and aahed and made a big ceremony out of opening the box, extracting the phone as if it were some precious religious artifact.

Then, he'd handed me a little envelope. He'd printed my

name on the outside in red ink, a color that might have been romantic if he hadn't used it every day. His tight scrawl had set out the letters of my name, more precise than a type-writer. Inside, I'd found a gift card to Victoria's Secret. Twenty-five bucks. Enough to buy one of the slinky lingerie sets that he'd been drooling over in the store window the week before. On sale.

I'd bought the Godiva chocolates on my own, telling myself that Dean would have gotten them for me, if he'd had time. Note to self: Insert long, boring story about all the other skimpy gifts he'd ever given me the entire time we'd dated—Christmas, birthdays. Insert longer, more boring story about the complete absence of presents for silly dating anniversa-ries. Dean was conservative when it came to money.

But three point five million dollars—that wasn't even in the same world as Christmas presents, as eating out, as worrying about some overworked waitress left with a too-small tip. Three and a half *million* dollars.

And I finally understood why I was sitting at this table, why I was staring at the Mercer Project's lawyer. I understood why Hal had made me come into the room, why he hadn't let me leave when he'd made it clear that he wasn't going to listen to my concerns about *Crystal Dreams*.

I was such an idiot.

Ten months ago, when I'd started interviewing with the Mercer, I'd worried about working in the same theater that employed my boyfriend. I hadn't wanted anyone to think that I was some nepotistic little slut, dependent on my boyfriend to get me my job. But I'd let Dean convince me that the Mercer was one of the finest theaters in the country, the finest theater for *me*.

Eight months ago, when the Mercer offered me a job, I'd been pretty sure it was a bad idea to move in with Dean, once we were both in the city. We'd never lived together before. When he was still up in New Haven, his apartment had resembled a cleaner and neater version of the Crate and Barrel catalog. Mine had resembled Filene's Basement. On a sale day. In the middle of the holiday shopping season. When half the staff was too hungover to come in to work. But I'd let Dean convince me again, believed him when he said that we needed to share an apartment to meet the high cost of living in New York.

Six months ago, I'd been absolutely certain that we shouldn't share a bank account—not while Dean was still nickel-and-diming every waiter we encountered. Not while I was still awed by the generosity of my grandfather, who had written a four-figure check to congratulate me on pursuing my dreams and achieving my master's degree. But Dean had argued that we would be functioning as one household— paying utilities, writing out checks for first and last month's rent, settling into our lives together, forever. Dean was the one who understood money, understood finance. I'd let him convince me again.

I was such an incredibly stupid, naive, idiotic…fool.

I was going to be sick. I was going to cry. I was going to scream.

Instead, I realized that Bill Rodriguez had asked me a question, and everyone in the room was waiting for my answer. "I'm sorry," I said, settling my palms next to the manila envelope that still sat in front of me like a place mat. "I didn't catch that."

"I said, 'Do you know where we can find Dean Marcus?'"

"I have absolutely no idea."

And I really, truly didn't. He'd lied to me. He'd deliberately set me up, left a note so that I wouldn't question his whereabouts until it was too late. Way too late.

Everyone stared at me. Hal was clearly angry; the tendons in his neck looked as if they'd been sculpted into his flesh. I could only hope that his rage was directed at Dean, not at me. A couple of the other board members had pity painted across their faces. Alicia Morton looked blatantly skeptical, as if she thought I could actually snap my fingers and make Dean appear, but I just wasn't willing to try.

"There are computer chips in cell phones, aren't there?" I asked anyone who wanted to listen. "If we call him, the police can locate the phone, can't they?"

Bill nodded and said, "We're already working on that."

"I can go through his desk at home," I said. "I might be able to find more information there. I don't think he has any relatives. He said he doesn't, but maybe…" There was a rustle among the directors, and no one would meet my eyes. I knew what they were thinking: if he'd lied about bank accounts, why wouldn't he lie about family? About anything else? About *everything* else.

Bill spoke to me as if I were a small child. "Your apartment has been sealed off. The police are there now—they're treating it as a crime scene. Once they're through looking for evidence, they'll probably let you back in."

"Probably?" My voice broke on my incredulous question.

"It should only take a week or so for them to finish."

"A week!" This had to be some sort of bad joke. The police never took a week to complete an investigation in the movies.

Bill shrugged, and his tone was apologetic. "If there'd been a murder, they'd move faster. As it is, they're going to want to go through everything. Every single drawer, every last computer file. Financial crimes can be concealed in ways that murders can't."

"Great," I muttered. It sounded like he was saying I'd actually be better off if someone had died.

This couldn't be happening to me. I couldn't be locked out of my own apartment. I couldn't be worried about police going through every last atom of *my* stuff.

But with a final oomph of recognition, I realized that I wasn't actually, completely, one hundred percent surprised.

Oh, I hadn't known that Dean Marcus was a thief. He hadn't told me that he intended to embezzle millions from our employer. He hadn't dropped hints around the house like a naughty eight-year-old, hoping to be caught before he got into really big trouble.

But little things about the past couple of months suddenly crystallized, suddenly collapsed into place. Dean, logging off computer websites a little too quickly when I walked into the room. Dean, pushing off my playful suggestion that we spend an entire Sunday in bed together, saying that he had to finish balancing books for the Mercer. Dean, zoning out while I talked about my pet projects, missing my words so thoroughly that he didn't even hear when I started quoting from Shakespeare, just to test if he was paying attention.

I'd thought that he was just preoccupied. I'd thought that he was just being a guy.

But that bizarre—for Dean's notion of bizarre—note on the fridge: "Gotta run. Don't wait up."

He just didn't say where he was running to. Didn't say how

long he would be gone. And like an idiot, I'd waited up anyway.

My fingers tingled, and I realized that I hadn't drawn a complete breath since Bill had told me what Dean had done. I forced myself to inhale, only to discover that my eyes were burning, stinging. I caught my lower lip between my teeth and made myself count to ten, but nothing got any better.

Slowly, methodically, I picked up my manila envelope. The motion reminded me that we had another problem— the rights issue for *Crystal Dreams*. But somehow, that matter had faded in importance, blotted out by the fact that twenty-five percent of our operating budget had evaporated at the hands of my boyfriend.

Former boyfriend.

I stood up. I sought out Hal's eyes, only to find that he was studying a mess of papers in front of him. I looked at all the other board members, swallowed my relief that everyone had found something else to occupy their apparent attention, something other than me. Only when I knew they weren't staring at me did I trust myself to speak. "Is there anything else you need from me now? Or may I go clean out my office?"

Hal met my eyes. "That won't be necessary, Rebecca. You aren't being fired."

I steadied myself by planting a hand on the table. "I'm not?"

He shook his head. "You haven't done anything wrong."

Except trust a liar. A cheat. A thief.

Alicia Morton tapped a fingernail against the table, the acrylic tip making more noise than I would have thought possible. A quick glance confirmed that *she* would gladly have shown me the door. Made me empty out my office. Empty my office and my bank account, pay back to the Mercer what was rightfully theirs.

As if I'd ever seen a shadow of three and a half million dollars.

I swallowed the sudden acid that coated the back of my throat as I realized that my own bank account—the one I shared with Dean—might very well be as empty as the Mercer's. "I—" I said, but I barely trusted myself to continue. "Let me know if there's anything I can do."

Hal nodded. "We will, Rebecca. We most certainly will."

Bill Rodriguez cleared his throat and spoke before I could leave the room. "The police investigators are going to want to go through your office here, as well. I trust that you'll help them?"

"Yes," I said, pretty certain that I didn't actually have a choice.

"And you'll make yourself available to answer any questions they have as their investigation progresses?"

"Of course," I said. I'd help the nice policemen in any way I could. That's what good girls did, right?

And that was it. There was nothing more for me to say to the board, to their hired attorney. For them to say to me.

I could feel everyone's eyes on me as I pushed back my chair. As I walked to the door. As I slunk out of the room where I'd learned that the past three years of my life had been a terrible, horrible lie. I barely made it to my soon-to-be-invaded office before the stinging in my eyes turned into a full flood of tears.

CHAPTER 3

TWO HOURS LATER, I WAS STILL SITTING IN MY TINY office, still staring at my computer screen, still trying to make sense out of how quickly my perfect grown-up life had come completely unraveled. It had taken almost half an hour of tears before I'd had the courage to turn to my computer. I'd offered up all sorts of prayers when I opened my Internet browser. I'd promised anyone who would listen to my silent soliloquy that I would be good, I'd work hard, I'd follow all the rules. I'd do anything, anything at all, if only…

As I pulled up the bank's website, I interrupted myself. Surely, I was worrying for nothing. There had to be another explanation for what had happened. Dean was going to walk in any minute now. He was going to explain that there'd been a computer glitch at the bank, that the accounts had all been transferred into some high-yield something-or-other, that the Mercer was really better off for whatever it was that he'd done.

Gotta run. Don't wait up.

The lump in my stomach got larger. And colder. And more absolutely certain.

When was the last time that Dean and I had actually had a conversation? He was always too busy, too wired from work.

Forget about conversation. When was the last time we'd even had sex?

Now, I was really going to be sick. I couldn't remember a day, a night, not even a general sense of what had happened, when it had been. Dean was always too tired. He'd brush a kiss somewhere in the general direction of my cheek, tell me to sleep tight. Sometimes, he wouldn't even bother getting up from his desk chair; he was too drawn to his spreadsheets, his graphics, whatever computer files he'd brought home from work, so that he could manage the Mercer's funds late into the night.

But Dean wouldn't do anything to hurt me. He loved me. *He* had pushed *me* to come to the Mercer. He had insisted that I move into his apartment. I had to be making mountains out of molehills. I had to be tempting myself with little lies of disaster, testing my tolerance, like a child watching a horror movie between stiff fingers covering her face.

Dean had to love me. For three and a half years, he'd always said he loved me. I would have known if he'd stopped loving me.

My fingers were shaking so badly that it took me three tries to type in my password on the bank's website. I clicked on the cheerful green square that said *Check balance*.

Zero.

I must have made some mistake. My heart was pounding so hard that I could hear it in my ears. I caught my lower lip between my teeth and navigated back to the home page. My eyes blurred as I clicked on the green square again. *Check balance.*

Still zero.

He'd cleared me out.

Dean Marcus—the love of my life, my theatrical inspiration, my mentor, my love—Dean had taken every last cent in our joint bank account. Including the graduation gift from my grandfather. Including six months of my Mercer paychecks. Including every penny I'd ever saved.

Three and a half million dollars stolen from the theater, and he'd still felt the need to ruin me, as well.

I folded my arms around my belly, rocking back and forth as if the motion could somehow comfort me. My chair squeaked in rhythm with my movement, but I didn't care. I didn't think anyone could hear through my closed office door. And if they did? If they were annoyed? Well, they could just get over it.

It wasn't like anyone was going to seek me out, not until the police moved in, to complete their investigation. I knew the way that gossip spread around the Mercer. Within seconds of the board meeting's end, someone would have started to whisper in the halls. That always happened—no matter how often people were sworn to secrecy, no matter how dire the threats to keep matters confidential. By now, the rumors had probably spawned on ShowTalk, in some discussion group newly created, just for this scandal.

I knew the score. After all, I was part of the theater community. I fed on drama, just like the rest of them, just like all of my peers.

I thought about who I *could* call. There were at least three dozen Yale alums within a three-mile radius. But a lot of them knew Dean. A lot of them had known Dean and me, as a couple. Truth be told, a lot of them had hinted that we might not be a match made in heaven. I could remember a lot of those conversations—every time, I had responded with a smile, a laugh. I had explained that Dean's passion for perfection, his calm, logical, orderly approach to the chaotic world of theater, his ability to be a rock as I tossed around in the often crazy ocean of a professional artist, all of that kept me sane. He was two years older than I was. Older and wiser. Opposites attract.

Well, he'd pretty much proven himself to be an asshole. So what did that make me now? A saint? Somehow, I didn't think my Yale classmates would see things that way.

My college roommate, Linda, was halfway across the country, in Chicago. I'd been ignoring her, though—not on purpose, just by accident. There were too many nights when I came home from rehearsal, from grabbing a couple of drinks with the cast, from long, invigorating conversations with Hal, with Jenn, with all the Mercer folks. (All of them but Dean. Damn. That was another warning sign—we hadn't hung out together with the theater crowd in…months.)

I was pretty sure that Linda had been the one to e-mail first the past dozen times we'd corresponded. Her last message had arrived nearly three weeks ago, and it was still sitting in my inbox. I could hardly break my silence now, just to tell her that my life was collapsing all around me. "Hey, Li—haven't bothered to get in touch for ages because I thought I was too cool, but now that I need you, here I am." Uh-huh. Great way to be a friend.

My parents were in San Diego, three thousand miles away.

Even if they'd been an easy five-minute walk, though, I still wouldn't have called them. We'd fought too many times over the past five years—first, about my being an undergraduate English major, then about my going to Yale Drama. They had hit the roof when I'd chosen the obscure discipline of dramaturgy. Note to self: Insert long, boring story about how I'd tried to bury the hatchet two years before, traveling all the way across country for the extravagant sixtieth birthday party that my mother threw for my father. Insert longer, more boring story about how Dean had been an ass for the entire week we'd visited, repeatedly offending my effusive mother with his standoffishness. Yeah. I wasn't going to reach out to Mom and Dad, to confirm their worst suspicions about Dean.

That left my grandfather, Pop-pop. Pop-pop who had always had faith in me. Pop-pop who had always placed my happiness above more common definitions of success. Pop-pop who had given me my graduation money—money that I'd lost because I'd been stupid and naive and trusting.

"Hi, Pop-pop," I would say. "Becca here. I'm just calling to tell you that Dean is a lying, cheating bastard who has probably been plotting how to bankrupt me and the theater for the entire time I've been shacking up with him."

Yeah, not so much. I wasn't going to tell my grandfather what had happened. Not yet. Maybe not ever.

At least I had three hundred dollars in my wallet—thank God I'd stopped at an ATM on Sunday morning. Money Miser Dean had always advised me to take out the most I could at any one time; we could save on service fees that way. Knowing that my grandfather's gift would easily cover my immediate need for cash, I'd taken my stack of twenties with confidence. Such a luxury, that security. I hadn't even bothered to count the bills.

I'd actually been proud about how well I was managing my life.

That was before I was broke. And homeless. And totally, completely alone.

The bastard. I turned toward my bulletin board, ready to rip down everything that reminded me of Dean—every note he'd ever left me, every card he'd ever given me for my birthday or just because, every menu from every meal we'd shared since I'd started at the Mercer.

Well. That was easy. There wasn't anything there. There wasn't any record of good times together, of shared casual fun. The chaos on my bulletin board was from me, from my life, from my friends and coworkers. But not from the man I'd thought I'd loved.

Huh. What exactly had been going on for the past six months? What lies had I been telling myself, to make our happy, happy home life seem real? Just how much of an idiot *was* I?

I didn't have time for self-pity, though, or self-examination, either. I had to make a plan. The police were going to finish their investigation of the apartment soon enough—a week or two, the precise date didn't really matter. Even when I was allowed back into my home, I knew I couldn't afford to live there on my own. It had been a stretch for the two of us, with Dean's salary, which was half again as much as mine. Unless he'd lied about that. Maybe he'd been earning even more, salting away the difference in some hidden bank account.

Jackass.

It didn't matter. Not now. Not ever again.

The lease required us to give sixty days' notice, and I might as well start the clock now. At least we had put down first and last month when we moved in; Dean couldn't take that security blanket away from me. I only needed to cobble together one month of the completely impossible, utterly exorbitant rent, on a place I couldn't access, with funds I didn't have.

Simple.

I dug around in my purse for my wallet, tugged out a dog-eared business card that our landlord had given me the day that we moved in. Mechanically, I got an outside line, punched in the numbers, got an answering machine.

I pasted a smile on my face so that my voice would seem bright, professional. I said that Dean and I needed to move out immediately, that I'd like to discuss the possibility of paying only one month, if I found someone to move in right away, to take my, er, our place. In any case, I was giving notice. I hung up the phone with a decisive sigh.

If Dean reappeared and had a different plan? That wasn't my problem. Nothing about Dean Marcus was my problem anymore. It was a good thing for him that the police had the place cordoned off. Given half a chance, I'd set every last one of his possessions on the curb, with a giant sign saying Free to a Good Home.

Like he'd really care, multimillionaire that he'd become overnight.

I gritted my teeth and focused on my next problem: a place to live. As if I could afford rent in New York City. I couldn't turn to my friends, to all those people who had questioned my commitment to Dean over the last three and a half years. I was too embarrassed. Too ashamed. And frankly, most theater people in New York were already crammed in small apartments with no extra space.

At least I had a temporary refuge—the Mercer had a large prop room, complete with a half-dozen couches, held in storage until they were next needed onstage. Sure, they ranged in style from unsleepable Empire to overstuffed-and-perfectly-comfortable 1970s rec room. I could turn one into a bed. I could probably even scrounge up blankets, somewhere in the storage bins. The theater had dressing rooms, too, complete with showers.

I didn't *think* Hal would throw me out, if he caught me living backstage.

Despite my determined problem-solving, my brain kept flashing on memories—Dean waiting for me outside a classroom, up in New Haven. Dean getting me drunk on Manhattans, having his entertainingly wicked way with a very willing me, the first time I visited him here in the city. Dean encouraging me through my most difficult classes, my most challenging exams, telling me that I could do it, that I had what it took to be a great dramaturg. Dean waiting for me at Penn Station, each and every time I took a train down to visit him.

It hadn't always been bad. He hadn't always been the rotten guy he'd apparently turned out to be.

No. Not "apparently." The temptation of millions of dollars had unveiled a side of Dean that I'd never imagined existed. Somewhere along the way, he'd changed. I didn't know the man anymore. The sooner I accepted that, the better.

I forced my thoughts away from more fond memories, only to find that my imagination was more than willing to race forward, hurtling toward other disasters. The Mercer wasn't standing still while my personal life crumbled around me.

Crystal Dreams auditions were supposed to take place in ten days. Auditions that weren't going to happen, for a play that we weren't going to stage.

I stared at my desk, at the towering stack of hopeless over-the-transom scripts. I'd tossed Ryan Thompson's on top. At least it was neat, orderly, with its perfectly pasted address label.

Maybe I should read it. Right now. See if it could be the play to save us. Sure, Ryan had seemed like a totally awkward geek. He'd barely been able to string two words together. He seemed uncomfortable in his own skin, uncertain about the most basic social interaction. But Jenn had read *something* online that had made her put the guy on the stalking list. Maybe he could write, put things on the printed page that he couldn't say in person.

And maybe I'd discover a brown paper bag on the street, filled with three and a half million dollars.

Forget it. The Mercer had to pick up something easy to replace *Crystal Dreams*. Something simple to stage on such short notice. Something in the public domain, so that no copyright lawyers ever darkened my e-mail inbox ever again. Ancient Greek drama, stripped down to a skeleton cast. Shakespeare, performed in modern dress on an empty stage. Not some untried author with an unknown script requiring untold resources.

I lifted my chin and squared my shoulders. Okay. I could figure out a play later, maybe stop by the public library to review some possibilities. I forbade myself to even think about the shelves and shelves of plays in my inaccessible apartment.

Next up on the disaster hit parade, then. Clothes. My closet and my dresser were as out-of-bounds as my bookshelves. I took a brief survey of my office, inordinately grateful for my packrat tendencies. Two different gym bags were tossed on the floor. My workout clothes were back in the apartment somewhere, strewn at the bottom of my closet, if I had to make a highly educated guess. The police investigators would have a field day with them.

I regularly changed into my running clothes here at work, getting exercise on the way home, leaving behind what passed for my professional wardrobe. That meant that I had the clothes on my back and two other outfits to wear.

I grimaced as I remembered that one of those outfits consisted of a paint-streaked sweatshirt and torn, holey jeans, remnants from a day when I'd come to work ready to pitch in painting a set. So, I had *one* other outfit—if I had to appear anyplace dressed as a grown-up. Like the police station. Or a court of law.

Great. No end to the fun. I should throw a party, I was having such a good time.

Whoops, that reminded me. One more disaster—food.

At least my starving student days had given me ample practice at stretching a dollar till it tore. First step: taking stock of what I had in storage. I tugged open my desk drawers. Two packets of neon-orange cheese crackers with peanut butter. Half a bag of Hershey's kisses, wrapped in red, pink, and silver. Happy Valentine's Day all over again, on sale. A pack of gum that was so old it might crack my teeth if I tried to mangle a piece. I dumped that in the trash. I couldn't afford to pay a dentist anytime soon.

So, I wasn't looking at the breakfast of champions. Or lunch or dinner, either. The precious bills in my wallet were going to transform into a frightening amount of ramen noodles. My stomach growled in rebellion, but it still ached too much for me to actually think about eating.

I glanced at my calendar. We got paid on the fifteenth and the last day of every month. Direct deposit. And it was just my luck that today was the second. Dean had made off with an entire paycheck, and I had almost two full weeks before I'd see another dime of salary. That reminded me—I needed to cancel my direct deposit. I wasn't about to let the bastard get another penny that belonged to me. I dug out a pay stub, placed another phone call, arranged to receive a live check at the end of the month. While I was at it, I had the bank put a hold on my debit card, issuing me a new one, which Dean would never be able to access.

And then I was through with errands. There wasn't anything else I could do. Nothing that could make things better. Nothing that could change what had happened. Nothing that could keep me busy. Nothing.

Which meant that I had to think about Dean.

Why hadn't I seen what he was doing? Why hadn't I recognized his lying? How desperate had I been to have him, to keep him, to say I had A Boyfriend? How had I never realized just how wrong Dean was for me?

I stifled a sob.

Later. I'd think about him later. I couldn't do it here, not while I was at work, not while I was trying to hold on to the last tattered shreds of my professionalism.

Later, I thought again, a bit more sharply, when I pictured the way he'd grinned at me across our first dinner in our shared apartment—Chinese takeout (one-dollar tip for the delivery guy)—the way he'd reached out with his perfectly balanced chopsticks, feeding me one of his Szechuan shrimp without even a hint of clumsiness, the way he'd laughed when I said that the spicy sauce made my lips tingle.

Later!

I shook my head, determined to make myself pay attention. As if to reinforce my firm command, there was a sharp knock on my office door. I cleared my throat before I answered, determined to sound normal. "Come in!"

The door opened slowly and Kira Franklin poked her head in. "Becca, do you have a minute?"

I shuffled papers on my desk, as if I'd been hard at work being the world's best dramaturg. "Of course."

She hefted a box into the room, grunting slightly as she balanced it on top of the junk that filled my single visitor's chair. Dusting off her hands, she met my gaze with the directness I'd always found likable. "Well, that was pretty brutal."

"Yeah," I said. "I'm sorry. I don't think I said any of the right things in there."

She shrugged. "I don't know that there was any 'right thing' to say. You did better than I could have. I doubt it's any comfort, but we really didn't intend to blindside you. At least, I didn't. And I know Hal would never do that to you on purpose."

She sounded so…normal, so much like a friend, that my eyes teared up again. "I… It's just… I can't believe he did it! I can't believe I was so stupid! I actually thought—"

I stopped myself before I could sound like even more of an idiot. She nodded sympathetically. "You're not the only person who's ever been fooled by a guy with a great line."

"Yeah, right," I said, hunching my shoulders. I pictured Kira's husband, who came to meet her after every rehearsal. He was tall, lanky; if they ever decided to remake Clint Eastwood's early Westerns, he could play the lead. He was more than some stupid cowboy, though—John McRae was an incredibly skilled set designer, so busy that he actually turned away work on a regular basis.

Kira shook her head. "I know you don't want to hear my sob story now, but believe me, I know what I'm talking about." Almost against my will, I gave her a suspicious scowl. "Okay," she said. "I'll spare you the details, but suffice to say, my first fiancé left me at the altar. And he was a director, top of the line in the Twin Cities. I was pretty much blacklisted from every house in town, except for a dumpy little dinner theater that thought *Gypsy* was cutting edge."

I wiped a hand across my eyes. "What happened?" I asked, embarrassed to hear how thick my voice sounded.

She glanced at the cardboard box she'd set on my chair. "Things changed." She shrugged. "Completely unexpectedly, I landed the job of my dreams. Except it wasn't. All that dreamlike, I mean. More like the worst nightmare any stage manager could imagine. But I met John there." Even if I'd been blindfolded, I could have heard the smile behind her words. She trailed her fingers along the edge of the box, rattling her nails across the faint corrugated ridges.

"What's that?" I asked, nodding toward the container.

"Mostly a bunch of clothes, from the costume shop. The Shepard costumes for Lauren, before she started putting on weight."

The lead actress for the one-acts was nervous about her professional debut. In two months of rehearsal, she'd managed to pack on two full sizes. The costume designer had complained bitterly until Kira had taken him aside, told him to stop, reminded him that Lauren was likely even more unhappy about her weight change than anyone else could be.

There'd been something about Kira's tone of voice, something that told me our implacable stage manager spoke from experience, from firsthand knowledge of the never-ending Battle of the Bulge. Kira had smiled as she spoke, though, and reminded all of us that we were lucky—the costumes were normal, everyday street clothes. Nothing hard to find. Nothing that required major tailoring.

Ordinary street clothes. Like the ones that were now locked inside my inaccessible apartment.

The original Lauren and I were about the same size. My available wardrobe had just increased by leaps and bounds. "Thanks," I said, and I meant it.

"And there's one more thing." Kira reached into her magical box of tricks, extracting a plain blue pillowcase that was bunched up around something. She deposited it on my desk, generating a faint metallic clink.

"What's that?" I asked. I reached toward it, but her hands lingered on the wrinkled cloth.

"Something I found a couple of years ago. Before I got that dream job, back in Minneapolis." She smiled, a bit wistfully. "Use it in good health," she said, meeting my gaze with an intensity that was unnerving. Her naturally dark eyes were even more shadowed in my dim office lighting, and for just a moment, I wasn't sure if she was happy to give me her gift, or if it somehow made her sad.

"Kira?" I asked. "Are you okay?"

She shook herself a little, seeming to wake from a dream. "I'm fine." And then she smiled at me—a full, open smile, as if we'd spent the morning talking about ponies and rainbows and other perfectly splendid diversions. "I'm fine. And you will be, too."

Before I could say anything, she hurried out of my office.

I only hesitated a moment before grabbing the pillowcase. Kira had been some sort of guardian angel, dropping off clothes. I couldn't imagine what else she might have left behind, what else would make my newly disgraced status more bearable.

I certainly never thought that she'd give me a brass lantern.

A classic brass lantern, like an oil lamp, one that would have been useful if the Mercer ever decided to stage a night of Turkish one-acts, or *Scheherazade,* or *Ali Baba and the Forty Thieves.*

Something about the metal handle whispered to my hand, as if it hid a magnetic charge and I was made of iron. The spout swooped up gracefully, with a delicate flair that spoke of master craftsmanship. Nevertheless, the brass was tarnished—it looked like the lamp had spent decades buried in the back of some prop closet in a theater very far away from New York City.

I grasped its perfect handle in my left hand and used my right fingers to rub hard at the brass body, trying to clear away some of the dark residue. As my flesh made contact with the metal, though, an electric shock jolted up my arm, burning, jangling with fiery pain. Surprised, I cried out and dropped the lamp.

My fingers tingled viciously, as if I'd tried to grab hold of an electric fence. I shook my hand, snapping my wrist, trying to ease the pain. My heart pounded, and for one insane second, I wondered if Kira had been sent by the board, told to deliver a final blow, a message I couldn't refuse, a brutal execution so that they'd never need to deal with my sorry self ever again.

That was absurd, though. Ridiculous. Absolutely, utterly stupid.

I forced myself to take a steadying breath, to move past the pain that had flash-dried the tears in my eyes. And then I was able to see the fog pouring out of the brass lamp's spout.

Honest-to-God *fog,* swirling around me like I'd been transported to some London street. It poured out of the lamp, a cloud of tiny jewels, brilliant even in my dim office—cobalt and emerald, ruby and topaz, glinting like one of those *Star Trek* transporters gone berserk.

I blinked, and the mist disappeared.

In its place stood a woman—a tall, blonde woman, clad in a perfect navy suit. Her hair was expertly bobbed; her pumps looked like they cost more than my entire longed-for paycheck. Everything about her shouted *professional*—her calfskin briefcase only accentuated the fact that she had to be a lawyer.

Except my eyes were drawn to the hand that held that briefcase, to the woman's creamy wrist. A tattoo blazed there, the ink so brilliant that the design might have been completed only a heartbeat before. A delicate border of black highlighted shimmering tongues of red and gold, individual licks of glittering flame. The design reached out to something deep inside me, burrowing into memories I'd never known I had.

I gaped, speechless, as the woman smiled. She extended one perfectly manicured hand, which made the captivating tattoo dance with an energy all its own. "Let me guess," she said, with a nod toward a sheaf of papers that had suddenly materialized in her manicured, tattooed hand. "You're the party of the first part, aren't you?"

CHAPTER 4

THE PARTY OF THE FIRST PART.

"I—" I wanted to answer. I really did. I wanted to say something calm, cool, and collected, something that would drag me back to my safe, little, normal corner of the world, one where I only had to worry about failed romance, economic disaster, and copyright law.

But I couldn't keep my gaze from slipping back and forth, from the lamp to the genie.

She had to be a genie, right? If she'd come out of the lamp? Even if she didn't look like one? Even if she seemed miles and centuries away from magic carpets and turbans and abracadabra and open sesame and all that?

The woman clicked her tongue and rolled her eyes, the perfect picture of corporate exasperation. "It wasn't that difficult a question. If this were a real deposition, I'd be asking the court reporter to let the record reflect your speechlessness."

"You're a lawyer?" I gasped.

She shrugged, a perfectly controlled little roll of her shoulders, eloquently dismissing my boggle-eyed amazement. "I'm not a lawyer, but I play one in my lamp."

"In your lamp," I repeated. Suddenly, I glanced at my office door. Was this all a joke? Was Kira standing out there, listening to every word I said? Or didn't say, as the case might be? But if this was a trick, how had Kira done it? How had she made the fog, summoned a living, speaking body out of nothingness? I forced myself to choke out, "So you really are a genie?"

"That's right," she said. "I'm Teel." She gave me a single firm nod, as if she were checking an item off on some mental list. She delivered the unfamiliar name as smoothly as if she were announcing that I should call her Tiffany or Madison or Crystal. "At your service." She placed her right hand across her heart in a gesture that an ordinary human would use if she were pledging allegiance. That is, if I were the flag. I found myself unable to look away from the sparkling tattoo on her wrist.

"What is that?" I asked, stretching my own fingers toward the fresh-inked flames. My hands tingled with a diluted version of the same compulsion that had led me to rub the lamp.

That movement was enough to make faint shadows leap to life on my own fingertips. I tilted my hand in front of me, making out the vaguest echo of flames on my own flesh, as if my fingerprints had been magically transformed from police-procedural arches and whorls into pulsating works of art. Fascinated, I pressed my thumb to my index finger and squeezed, half expecting to see color leak out from the crease. I started to ask a question, but I needed to clear my throat.

Then, I realized that the impossible creature in front of me—the *genie?*—had started to root around in her briefcase. Trying to smother an almost incapacitating wave of shyness, I pressed my fingers together even more tightly and raised my voice to get her attention. "Teel?" I asked.

As I spoke, the genie's own fingers flew to her temples. She shook her head queasily, as if I'd shouted through a bullhorn the morning after an opening-night gala sponsored by Dom Pérignon, Jack Daniel's, and a half-dozen other purveyors of alcoholic temptation. "I'm right here," she croaked. "No need to shout."

As she groaned, the flames on her wrist stood out even more sharply than they had before. Mystified, I reached toward her, more than a little worried that my simply repeating her name had caused her such distress. As soon as I opened my hand, though, revealing the marks on my own fingertips, Teel's tattoo faded back to its original compelling glint. Unable to resist a little test, I clenched my fingers together again, watching the parallel marks on the genie's wrist surge back to full brilliance. I managed, however, to squelch the impulse to say her name out loud. Better not to cripple my genie with a permanent migraine before I even learned what this strange magic was all about.

Eyeing me balefully, Teel swallowed hard, grimacing like a person knocking back a fistful of aspirin. Then, she reached for her briefcase. "Well," she said, her efficient smile turned brittle, "I usually *end* a first session by telling people how to get my attention. At least we have that all taken care of."

"I'm sorry," I said, trying to force a bit of meek apology past my fascination.

"Why don't we just go through the paperwork?" She

flourished her extensive set of documents. "You'll find everything's in order—the newest boilerplate is already incorporated."

"Boilerplate?" I felt like I was scrambling a few steps behind as Teel led me along some tangled forest path. One part of my brain was frantically fighting to catch up, to accept that a creature had just coalesced out of fog in the middle of my office, a magical being who seemed intent on handing me a ream of paper that was thicker than most scripts that I read. Another part of my brain had already accepted what was going on here—after all, I'd absorbed more shocks in this one day than I'd ever thought possible, going from beloved, financially secure, well-housed theater professional to a jilted, broke, homeless…theater professional.

I still had my life as a dramaturg.

Dean couldn't take that away from me.

"Boilerplate," Teel repeated, as if I hadn't just lost myself in further contemplation of my disastrous morning. "Legal terms that are standard for all contracts. Term and termination. Choice of law. Blah-de-blah-de-blah and all the rest of the boring stuff." She yawned.

Okay. Maybe she wasn't actually the severe lawyer that she appeared to be. I didn't think that Bill Rodriguez, the attorney who had crushed my morning in the conference room, would yawn as he quoted chapter and verse at me. I took Teel's stack of paper and started glancing through the pages.

Every single sheet was crammed with tiny writing. The minute text was broken up with boldface headings and with outlined indents that led to paragraph numbers like V.A.iii.h.(iv).(q). The more that I examined the words, the more they danced before my eyes.

I blinked hard, then tried again. The words stayed stable this time, but I still didn't understand them. One passage, printed in bold, stated: "Where any wisher stands to be seized, or at any time hereafter shall happen to be seized, of any lands, tenements, rents, services, reversions, remainders, or other hereditaments, to the use, confidence, or trust of any other person or persons, or any body politic, by reason of any conveyance, contract, agreement, will or otherwise…"

I dropped the pages onto my desk. "This doesn't make any sense at all."

Teel sniffed in annoyance. "Nineteen out of twenty wishers said the exact same thing. That's why we simplified the terms. We've just completed our review of all the paperwork. It's *much* more basic now than if you'd summoned me a month ago."

"'We' reviewed the paperwork?" I couldn't smother my suspicious tone. "Who's we?" I pictured a bunch of women who looked like clones of Teel, all gathered in a huge conference room, masquerading as the Lawyers of the Round Table.

Teel didn't change my mental image substantially when she said, "Magic."

"Magic?"

She clicked her tongue. "MAGIC," she repeated, a bit more forcefully. "The Multijurisdictional Association of Genies and Imaginary Creatures. We just concluded our Decadium last week."

"Decadium?" I parroted, as if I'd forgotten how to speak a full sentence.

"Our group meeting? Every ten years?" She rolled her eyes, and I was pretty sure she was saying that only an idiot would be unfamiliar with the concept. "All the genies in the Northern Hemisphere get together to discuss important things like case distribution and wish escalation. And simplification of contract terms."

She made it sound so simple. So normal. So absolutely, positively commonplace. Still, I couldn't quite picture the meeting. "You get together? You mean, like a conference? In a hotel?"

She pursed her lips. "Not exactly. MAGIC doesn't convene on your plane of existence. Or in your time, for that matter. It can be a little complicated."

"Complicated…" I repeated, my eyes straying back to the brass lantern. Somehow, I could see that my entire life had just become a *lot* more complicated. "Wait a second. You said genies and imaginary creatures. So am I only imagining you?"

"Well, everyone would *think* you were imagining me if you ever told them about this conversation."

"That's not really an answer," I pointed out.

"That's as much of an answer as I can give. Isn't it enough to know that you're talking to me? And I'm answering? And I'm offering you a wish contract with the most current terms?"

I reached behind me for my desk chair, locating the familiar padded arms without too much fumbling. As I sank onto its seat, I shook my head. This was crazy. Absolutely nuts. Sure, my morning had been a disaster, but had it been so stressful that I was actually hallucinating? Imagining a genie? One who spouted words that sounded like the sort of institutional technospeak that every human trade association gives itself? I recognized self-aggrandizing babble when I heard it—*I* had a masters degree.

I reached out to touch the contract again. The paper was

real enough—a little heavier than the cheap stuff the Mercer used in its laser printers, but absolutely, unqualifiedly real. If I were hallucinating, I wouldn't be able to *feel* the paper, right? I mean, hearing was one thing, and seeing nonexistent creatures was probably relatively commonplace. But if the contract on my desk was a pure figment of my overstressed imagination, would I really be able to *feel* it?

I reached a shaky hand toward my office telephone. 9-1-1. I could place the call, even in my compromised state. An ambulance could be here in minutes. They'd take me to the hospital; they'd make sure that I got whatever care I needed. They'd protect me until my obviously overtaxed brain could stabilize.

Which hospital was closest to the theater? I glanced at my bulletin board, at a neat printed sheet that I'd received during my very first rehearsal for my very first Mercer play. Kira had typed up the list of hospitals, along with a summary of local drugstores, bodegas, and late-serving restaurants. She took her stage manager duties seriously. As seriously as she'd taken our conversation, just a few minutes before. When she had given me the lantern.

She'd known exactly what it was. She'd known what would happen. That was why she had looked so strange after handing over the blue pillowcase. That was why she had told me that she was fine, and that I would be, too.

"Kira knows about all this, doesn't she?"

"Kira Franklin?" Teel narrowed her eyes, as if she were searching through a gigantic filing cabinet in her mind. I nodded. "Kira doesn't know about the Decadium. It never came up while she and I were working together. We finished our business relationship before I left for MAGIC."

"No," I said, frustrated that I hadn't made myself clear. "She knew about *you*. About genies in general."

"Well, I should certainly think so. Didn't she say anything about what we accomplished the last time I was out and about in this godforsaken place?"

"Godforsaken place?" I was surprised at the scorn in the genie's voice. "What do you have against New York?"

"Well, shine my lamp! She finally left that frozen pit!" Minneapolis. Where Kira had landed her dream job. Where she had met John McRae. And, apparently, where she had met Teel. Met our genie.

"Um, Kira moved here about three years ago."

"Three! Well, it took her long enough, then, to pass along the lantern." Teel clicked her tongue. "Seven out of ten wishers pass on their lamp within one month. Remember that."

"Um, I will." What? Was I going to be quizzed on these statistics? Or was I just supposed to feel a little pressure, an obligation to conform to everyone else who'd been granted magic wishes?

Like Kira, apparently. Maybe I wasn't crazy after all.

I picked up the contract again, seriously considering signing on the proverbial dotted line, even though I couldn't begin to comprehend the document. Beggars couldn't afford to be choosers.

Of course, Dean would have handled all this differently. He would have taken all day and all night to mark up the pages, scribbling minute notes in the margin with his fine-point red Bic, asking endless questions. Well, I wasn't Dean. In fact, screw Dean.

I waved the pages at the genie. "What's in here? What are my obligations to you?"

For an instant, she got a crafty look in her eye. She turned her head to one side, arching one expressive eyebrow. I could *feel* her measuring me, trying to decide if I would buy whatever answer she made up. "You have to make all of your wishes within a twenty-four-hour period?" she said.

That sounded like a question, though. Not an answer. "How many wishers do that?"

Teel frowned. I suspected that she was accustomed to using statistics to her own advantage. "Some?"

Another question. I wasn't willing to push for actual numbers, though. Instead, I asked, "Did Kira make all of her wishes in a single day?"

Teel pouted, and I could see with perfect clarity the petulant teenager that the blond woman once had been. "No," she admitted. I could almost imagine her digging the toe of her pumps into my office floor before she flounced out of the room mid-temper-tantrum. "She took a lot longer than that."

"So, what was Kira's deal? She signed the contract, got her three wishes, and then you waltzed off to your conference?"

"Four," Teel said.

"Excuse me?"

"*Four* wishes."

That didn't make much sense. "Every book I've ever read says genies grant three wishes. Isn't that in all the fairy tales?"

Teel seemed a bit put out. "It's a good thing life isn't a fairy tale, then, isn't it? You get four wishes, okay? I'm bound to you until I've granted all four."

I actually felt a little sorry for her. It had to be a drag, waiting around to grant that one extra wish to every single person who rubbed the lamp. I suspected that the delay could really screw up her completion statistics.

But four wishes? All mine? Who was I to insist that the standard was three? Gift horse, and all that.

I turned to the last page of the agreement and signed my name, looping the letters with a little more authority than I customarily used.

"Wonderful," Teel said. "And initial here. And there. And at the bottom of that page, there." What did I have to worry about, really? It was the devil who stole souls, right? Not genies. As I finished adding my last scribble and set down my pen, my attention was drawn back to Teel's fiery tattoo. All of a sudden, the ink wasn't quite as fascinating, now that I'd spoiled it by thinking about demons.

"So?" she said, as if she were afraid I'd change my mind. "What's your first wish?"

I thought about everything that had happened that day. Kira had given me the lantern because she had known just how absolutely, completely, irredeemably miserable I was. But now I had the power to act. I had the power to change things.

What should I wish for? Information about Dean's whereabouts, so that I could turn him in and get back everything he owed me? Me, and the Mercer, too?

But that was sort of petty, in the big scheme of things. Sure, my day had been a disaster. Absolutely, my personal life had fallen apart at the seams. Beyond doubt, the Mercer was in trouble. But the world had even bigger problems.

Universal health care. Equal rights for all people. Genocide in countries I could barely name. How could I pass up solving such major problems for so many others?

I rolled global crises around in my head for a few minutes. And then, I said, "Global warming."

"Excuse me?" Teel's words sounded liked they'd been punched out of a sheet of frozen metal.

I tried to project an air of confidence. "I'd like to solve global warming. Climate change. You know, polar bears drowning in the Arctic, drought in Australia, ecological disasters around the world."

Teel closed her eyes and brought her hands together in a gesture of prayer. Her tattoo pulsed as she inhaled, then exhaled. Four times, she repeated the breathing exercises. Each time that she filled her lungs, the flames on her wrist glowed a little brighter, as if she were pumping a bellows, breathing fresh life into the tattoo. On the final exhale, Teel opened her eyes and stared at me levelly.

"Was that it?" I whispered, awed. "Global warming is solved?"

She snorted, scattering any semblance of peace and harmony. "Of course not. You'll *know* when I grant one of your wishes."

"But what were you doing?" I heard the wail behind my words, realized that I sounded like a spoiled child.

"I was calming myself. We had an entire afternoon seminar on that at MAGIC. On how to handle the Grand Wishes."

"Grand Wishes?" I repeated.

"Ninety-eight out of one hundred first-timers try to save the world. Make a better planet." She drew out that last phrase into a mocking sing-song.

I started to argue even before I wondered about those other two, the pair who didn't have altruism running in their veins. "But you said—"

She cut me off. "You can ask me to solve global warming. And I can grant your wish. But I'm only one genie. And the globe is a very large place. Climate change is especially tricky—I have to balance everything, from one region to another, and every adjustment I make in one place will have an effect somewhere else. You know—butterflies, flapping wings, hurricanes, all that garbage."

"So you can't do it?" I was astonished to hear the disappointment in my voice. Half an hour before, I hadn't even known that genies were real, and now I was sulking because mine was backing off from her promises.

"I can do it, but I wouldn't finish up for…" she trailed off, staring at my office wall and moving her lips as she made some mental calculation. "Six hundred and forty-three years, twenty-seven days, four hours, and oh, give or take twenty minutes."

"Wow." I felt like I had to say something else, so I tried, "You can be that precise?"

"That's one of the new requirements, in the revised contract. Page thirty-one?" She pointed a perfectly manicured nail toward the document that I'd signed. "Fulfillment delay for any wish that will take longer than twenty-four hours to grant must be disclosed in full to the wisher. Prior *written* notice must be provided in cases of time variance stemming from high Ethical Interference Quotient, extended Physical Impact Vector, or substantial Time Adjustment Factor. No written notice necessary here, though." When I merely stared, stunned into submission by all the jargon, Teel dusted off her hands. "Of course, the actual contract language is a little more complex, but those are the general ideas that we covered in our breakout session at MAGIC."

I was beginning to gain a little more respect for the administrative nightmare that must have taken place at that conference. I sighed. Bottom line, if most wishes could be granted in less than a day, and my climate change wish would take six and half centuries, give or take… "Okay," I said. "Forget about global warming."

"Thank you." Teel nodded firmly. "Do you want to try something a little more manageable?"

I chewed on my lip. Money. That was the root of all my problems. If I wished for enough money, I could pay back the Mercer, buy myself a condo, replace all of my possessions, and guarantee that I'd have a diet more satisfying than flash-fried noodles in oversalted broth.

But money would get Dean off the hook.

Sure, the cops would still track him down. They'd arrest him. He'd go to trial. But any lawyer worth his astronomical hourly rate would get Dean off if no one could prove any lasting financial impact from his misdeeds. I didn't want to do anything to help that lying, cheating sack of…

I cut my mental tirade short. For now, I'd use my wishes to take care of myself. Of my immediate problems.

"Okay, then. I need a place to live." I started to suggest a rent-controlled apartment, the Holy Grail of Manhattan tenants, but I could be a *little* more extravagant than that, couldn't I? I mean, genies had to have some way of covering up their actions, right? Teel had to have some secret magic that would make everyone forget that I'd been terrified and homeless only an hour before.

I steeled myself and elaborated: "A condo." No negative reaction from the genie, so I must still be on track. "Two bedrooms? And an actual kitchen, not just a galley?" She still

wasn't saying anything, wasn't shutting me down. I decided
to push for even more. After all, this *was* one of my wishes,
one of the four total. If I could have asked Teel to invest centuries managing climate change, I could certainly elaborate
a little bit on my new home. Couldn't I? "And could it have
a view of the river? And a doorman? And, um, two bathrooms, do I have to specify that?"

"I get the idea," Teel said dryly. "You have to phrase your
request in the form of a wish."

I felt like I was a contestant on some obscure new game
show. Any moment, there would be flashing lights and blar-
ing music, and a secret studio audience would be revealed
behind a curtain. "You're kidding, right?"

"Do I look like the type of genie who kids?"

Not with that perfect haircut. Not with those pumps and
that expertly tailored suit.

I took a deep breath and said, "I wish that I had a condo
with two bedrooms, two bathrooms, a kitchen, and a view
of the river, all in a doorman building." I barely remembered
to exhale as I waited to see what Teel would do.

She nodded once, and then raised perfectly shaped fingers
to her right earlobe. Flawless nail polish highlighted her pearl
earring. I watched, hypnotized, as my genie's tattooed flames
caught the light. "As you wish," she enunciated, as if she were
speaking to a judge, a jury, and a courtroom full of specta-
tors. Then, she tugged at her ear twice, hard enough that I
winced in reaction.

An electric shock jolted through my body, stronger even
than the current I had felt when Teel had manifested from
the lamp. My lungs were frozen between breathing and
coughing; my heart bucked in my chest as if I were a patient

in some lousy television medical drama. The jagged electricity *hurt,* and tears sprang to my eyes.

And then all of the jangling power dissipated, flowing into the space around me as harmlessly as wine pouring from a bottle. Teel nodded, a satisfied smile turning the corners of her lips.

"You've done it?" I croaked. "You granted my wish?" I looked around, half expecting to find us transported to my dream apartment.

"Just...one...mo-ment..." Teel said, drawing out the last syllable.

And then my phone rang. A quick glance at the built-in caller ID showed that the call came from outside the Mercer, from somewhere else in Manhattan's 212 area code. One ring. I stared at it. Two. My fingers froze. Three. I was afraid to answer.

With an annoyed harrumph, Teel grabbed the handset before the call could roll over to voice mail. "Rebecca Morris's office." All of a sudden, she was chomping on a wad of gum. The minty stuff had materialized from thin air; I certainly hadn't seen her unwrap a stick. Her lawyer-modulated voice was gone, replaced by the nasal stereotype of bad secretaries everywhere, each phrase punctuated with a hearty Doublemint smack. "Just a moment, ma'am. I'll see if she's available."

She extended the phone to me.

I gave her a curious glance, but she refused to say anything, to give me any more to go on. I forced myself to take the instrument, to put on my most businesslike voice. "Rebecca Morris," I said, trying not to sound as puzzled as I felt.

"Maureen Schultz here," said a crisp voice. When I didn't respond immediately, she added, "With Empire Realty? Over at the Bentley."

"The Bentley?" I repeated.

"I just wanted you to know that we're ready for you to move in at any time. Per your contract, the painting was completed last week, and the floors were refinished over the weekend. Your furniture all arrived this morning, and I had the men place it where you indicated in your sketches."

"My…sketches." I swallowed hard and watched Teel's smile grow broader.

"I have to say, Ms. Morris, I was quite impressed with the information packet that you sent over. So many of our new owners don't plan ahead, and we end up needing to reserve the elevators for another round of furniture removal and re-delivery."

"Well, yes," I said. I'd never lived in a building where elevators needed to be reserved. When Dean and I had moved into our place together, we'd just traded off pressing the call button, doing our best to keep the too-small elevator on the floor where we needed it. I shook my head. "My assistant, um, Teel, takes care of those details for me."

My genie beamed as Maureen made approving noises. "So can we expect you this afternoon?"

I glanced at my shabby surroundings. I wasn't going to get anything else done today. Not with rumors from the board meeting still metastasizing in the hallways. Besides, the cops were likely going to show up soon, to go through my every professional possession. "I'll be there in about an hour," I said.

"Wonderful!" Maureen's enthusiasm made me believe I'd just perfected her afternoon. "I'll see you then!"

"Oh!" I said before she could hang up, and then I improvised, "I don't have my papers in front of me, and I need to fill out a change-of-address form here at the office. What's the exact address?"

Teel nodded in approval as Maureen recited a street number that placed me in prime West Village real estate. The real estate agent laughed as she added, "Of course, your unit is 8D."

"Of course," I said. "I'll see you soon."

After I hung up, Teel said dryly, "I took the liberty of having furniture delivered for you. I'm sure you would have thought of that, if I'd let you go on with your wish-making."

"The liberty…" I stared at the address that I'd scribbled down. "How does this work? I mean, how much is the mortgage on a place like this?"

"Nothing," Teel said.

"Nothing?"

"Nada. Zip. Zero. Zilch. You wished for a condo, and your wish was my command."

"I bought it outright?"

"That's what the paperwork will say."

"And taxes? Insurance?" I remembered my grandfather ranting about his real estate taxes. Even after he'd paid off his home, he'd complained bitterly that San Diego was trying to bury him with annual levies.

"Everything's wrapped up for as long as you own the property." She clicked her tongue. "Honestly, all of this is in the contract that you signed. Real estate obligations are there on page seventy-four, in simple black and white."

I could barely process what she was saying. An hour ago, I'd been homeless. Now I owned a home that was probably worth more than my parents' and my grandfather's houses combined.

Teel allowed a very lawyerly frown to crease her brow. "You should start over there. You don't want to keep Maureen waiting."

I heard the dismissal in her voice. "And you?" I asked. "Aren't you coming with me?"

Teel's carefully glossed lips came close to mocking me. "*I* already know what the condo looks like." She shook her head and raised her fingers to her ear. This time when she tugged, I didn't feel anything, didn't suffer the electric shock. When she lowered her arm, she wore a stunning wool coat over her suit, a fitted garment with a belt that accented every curve of her figure. A cashmere muffler draped over her shoulders with casual élan, and a pair of fur-lined leather gloves covered her fingers, palms, and tattooed wrist. "You go ahead," Teel said. "I'm going to spend a little time visiting some old haunts."

"Are you allowed to do that?" I blurted, glancing at the lamp, which still lay on my desk.

"Of course," Teel said with a sweetness that made me just a little suspicious. "That's the bargain. You have however much time it takes to make your wishes. And I have my freedom."

"But how am I going to find you? What about when I'm ready to make my next wish?"

She nodded toward my hand, the one that was embossed with my own faintly flickering flames. "We already went over that. Just press your fingers together and call my name." She tossed one end of her scarf around her neck and breezed over to my office door.

"Teel!" I called, before she could open it, before she could disappear into the Mercer hallways, into the New York City streets. She turned back with one eyebrow arched into a question. "Thanks," I said. "Thanks for everything."

"Oh." She chortled, and her stern lawyerly facade crumbled before my eyes. "You ain't seen nothing yet."

CHAPTER 5

AND TEEL WAS RIGHT.

I'd had an image in my mind when I'd described my dream apartment. I'd pictured enough space to move, a little open air to breathe, enough room for a couch *and* a love seat in the living room.

But I had never, even in my wildest dreams, imagined living in the incredible condo that I now, um, owned.

Picture the coolest apartment you've ever seen in a movie, the most incredible airy Manhattan loft. Make sure to include floor-to-ceiling windows. Toss in unbelievable furniture, fresh from the catalog of your choice—just make sure that there are a few hints of the softest teal, of dusty rose, of wintergreen, all used as perfect accent colors to offset the classic upholstery of the couch, the love seat, two chairs, matching ottomans, side tables, and a full-size coffee table. Yes, all of that furniture—picture it!—just in the living room!

Add a kitchen, and a couple of bedrooms, and a view of

the river, and you'll soon understand why I was unable to summon two consecutive sentences as Maureen Schultz showed me around my new home. I'm sure she thought I was nuts—Teel's magic somehow had her believing that she and I had met many times before, that we'd actually weathered a long business relationship with plenty of failed visits to other buildings before I'd set my heart on the Bentley.

I tried to remember basic English sentence structure as one part of my mind gibbered, "Mine, mine, mine!" and another chanted, "Eat your heart out, Dean Marcus!" I was still grinning like an asylum escapee when I stood in my doorway, waving Maureen toward the elevators. Yes, *elevators*. Plural. "Thank you!" I said, pumping her hand once again.

"No," she said with a throaty chuckle. "Thank *you!*"

I barely kept from squealing as I gazed down the carpeted hallway (carpet!) and watched the whisper-quiet doors whisk away my fairy real estate godmother. Before I could turn back to explore my domain further, the door across the hall opened. Still reeling at my personal good fortune, I grinned and took a step forward, forgetting New York City's un-spoken Good Neighbor Rules, the ones that mandated silence and polite disinterest in all public interaction with strangers. "Hi!" I said, extending my hand.

The woman in the doorway could have been the cover model for the debut issue of Earth Mother magazine. Her elaborately embroidered blue cotton workshirt hung loose over faded jeans. The pants were too long for her; she'd rolled them up in cuffs that displayed beat-up Birkenstock sandals. Bright red socks peeped out between the shoes' leather straps. Her face was weathered, as if she'd spent long hours in the sun, and her eyes were the color of well-watered earth. A long braid hung down to her waist, generous strands of gray twining around dark chestnut.

"Hello," she said, and her voice was soft, like a brown paper bag that had been reused so many times it felt like cloth. "You're the new neighbor?"

"Becca," I said.

She shook my hand firmly, and I felt the rasp of calluses on her palms. "Dani. We were wondering who would move in here."

"We?" I looked behind her, into the violet-tinged shadows of her apartment. From the hallway, it looked much smaller than mine.

"My son and I." She sighed, sifting a layer of sweet fondness across her placid features. "He's new to the building, but I've lived here forever. The Bentley is a perfect place for gorilla gardening."

Okay… What was that supposed to mean? Did she raise primates for the Bronx Zoo? I resisted the urge to take a deep sniff in the direction of her apartment. Nothing *seemed* too strange there, no bizarre noises, no caged-animal stink. There *was* the slight flicker of the purplish lights, though…. I tried to smile. "Um, gorilla gardening?"

"Guerilla," Dani repeated. When I still stared at her without comprehension, she enunciated the word with care, trilling an exaggerated Spanish accent: "Guer-ee-ya. As in 'warfare'?"

"Guerilla gardening," I repeated, a little relieved that I wasn't going to have giant apes across the hall. The purple cast must be from grow lights. But growing what? My pulse surged momentarily, and I wondered if Teel had dropped me into the middle of some clandestine West Village marijuana-growing cooperative. "I'm sorry," I said. "I don't know what that is."

Dani nodded patiently, as if she were accustomed to people admitting such ignorance. Her earthen eyes twinkled as she said, "It's my passion."

"Passion?" The psychedelic embroidery on her blouse made my throat seize up. I pictured police raids throughout the building, being thrown out of my new home before I'd even settled into it. Out of the frying pan, into the fire... I fought to swallow my panic.

Obviously unaware of my reaction, Dani elaborated with a rapturous smile. "We call ourselves the Gray Guerillas. Most of us are over seventy—who else has time to do this sort of thing?" She shook her head. "There's so much space that goes unused in the City—on rooftops and fire escapes, in those cutouts of dirt by trees on the sidewalk." Her sing-song voice told me she'd recited her words a thousand times. "We can reclaim that space. We can *use* it. Guerilla gardeners create little havens, right here in the middle of Manhattan. Today, we might be growing a few sprigs of parsley, some basil, some sage. But tomorrow, we'll have peppers! Tomatoes! Flowers of all kinds! Treasures you don't even realize you're missing!"

Her enthusiastic words melted into laughter, an infectious joyousness. She wasn't trying to break the law. She wasn't going to attract police raids. She was talking about regular plants, legal plants, perfectly ordinary, everyday, green, grow-ing plants.

I couldn't help but look over my shoulder, blinking grate-fully at the golden flood of an early-spring sunset splashed across my living room. "Oh, my!" Dani exclaimed. "Just look at that light! You could start seedlings right now, have everything ready for a mid-April planting! It's such a joy to see things sprout, to see new life begin!"

And when she said it, I believed her. Me—I thought about joy. Me—the woman who had spent the entire day wallowing in doom, disaster, and the breakup from Hell.

I had a fresh beginning. Courtesies of Kira and Teel—and Dani now, too—I had a chance at something new.

Before I could say anything, though, my cell phone trilled from the pocket of my black trousers. Jenn's ringtone, probably alerting me to some disaster back at the Mercer. Er, some *new* disaster back at the Mercer, I amended to myself. I clenched my teeth as all of the day's disgraces swept back to the front of my consciousness.

"I'm sorry," I said to Dani, torn between answering the phone and learning more about guerilla gardening.

"Go," my new neighbor said, sharing another smile that warmed me to my bones. "We'll talk more. Welcome to the building."

I grinned and managed to grab the call just before it rolled over to voice mail. "Hey," I said, slipping into my condo (my! condo!) and closing the door.

"So," Jenn said without preamble, as if we were already in the middle of a conversation. "You rushed out of here so fast, I didn't have a chance to ask if you're coming to the Pharm."

The Pharmacy. The neighborhood bar that regularly provided the Mercer cast and crew with whatever form of liquid medicine they needed.

I sucked a regretful breath between my teeth. I knew that Hal had conducted rehearsal for the Shepard one-acts that afternoon, even though I hadn't bothered to attend. In fact, he had integrated some substantial changes to the blocking, to where the actors stood when they said their lines. I'd actually been the one to recommend the changes—the new blocking emphasized the common elements among all three of the short plays. Hal had agreed with my suggestions the day before—a lifetime ago, or so it seemed. Nevertheless, he'd predicted that the cast would be on edge, would have a hard time handling so much transition this close to opening night.

I owed it to him to show up at the Pharm at least. I could take the cast's temperature, figure out just how traumatic the changes had been. I could explain Hal's vision again, make clear the reason for modifying things, reassure everyone that the extra effort was worth it so that we could realize the full potential of the production.

That sort of psychological jiggering was one of my informal, but vital roles. I never would have shirked it, on a normal day.

"Bec?" Jenn said. "We really need you. This afternoon was rough on everyone." I blinked hard, thinking about the trauma of the rehearsal, how it must have been compounded by the gossip about Dean. About me. I shivered and tugged at the collar of my sweater. The golden sunset had winked out over the horizon; my incredible new home was now chilly in the grey of early-spring twilight.

"Yeah," I said, before Jenn could think that I'd gone mad. Or any madder than I'd already proven myself to be. "I'll be there."

"Great! We're heading out in about fifteen! Ciao!"

"Ciao," I said, but I was already speaking to the static of an empty line.

The Pharmacy was even more crowded than usual. Mercer folks were gathered around three tables in the back, and from the sound of things, they were already well into their second round. At least. Pete, the ever-patient bartender, nodded a greeting from behind his long stretch of polished mahogany. "The usual?" he asked, already reaching for a cocktail glass and a bottle of rye.

My usual. A Manhattan. Dean had bought me my first Manhattan.

I shook my head. "Let's try something new," I said. I didn't need Dean. I was infinitely better off without him. I had my fairy godmothers instead. Kira. And Teel. And Maureen Shultz.

That reminded me of a drink I'd had at a cast party once, for Steven Sondheim's *Into the Woods,* a musical about fairy tales gone nightmarishly bad. There. That was a perfect antidote to Dean-driven memories, a great reminder that there was no such thing as a Prince Charming. Ever. Anywhere.

I said to Pete, "How about a Godmother?"

Always the perfect bartender, Pete nodded, without my needing to define the drink. If he realized the importance of my decision to change my poison, he hid it well. He grabbed a highball glass and poured a generous amount of vodka. As he swirled in the requisite Amaretto, I couldn't help but remember the cascading fog that had billowed out of Teel's lamp. I glanced down at my fingertips, but it was too dark to make out my subtle flame tattoo. *I* knew the mark was there, though. *I* knew that I still had three wishes to harvest.

Pete handed over my drink with a professional nod. He'd run a tab for me. He always did. I tried not to think about the lonely twenties in my wallet, the three hundred dollars that weren't going to see any companions until my next pay check. I picked up my drink. Some splurges were worth it. Necessary, in fact, for the preservation of mental health.

"Becca!" Jenn exclaimed in an overloud voice as I made my way back to the Mercer crowd. A momentary silence flickered over the gathering, just enough to make me certain that they'd been talking about me. They were actors, though, trained professionals. It only took an instant for them to ad-lib new lines, to exclaim about the bitter wind outside, about some actor's total embarrassment in an audition the day before. No one even mentioned the blocking change from the afternoon's rehearsal—it must not have been too traumatic, after all.

Jenn waved me to her side. She was sitting with a couple of long-time Mercer performers, Kelly Reilly and Rob Cornell.

"Here, Becca," Kelly said, rolling to her feet. She was hugely pregnant; she looked like she might deliver triplets right there in the Pharm. "Rob and I are heading home. Steal a chair while you can!"

I appreciated the cheerful way she addressed me, looking me directly in the eye, as if I weren't the scum of the theatrical earth. Maybe those were the type of good manners that Kelly had mastered in her native Minnesota. Rumor had it, her father ran a great bar for the theater crowd there—that was where she'd met Kira Franklin, how Kira had ended up at the Mercer, way back when. The theater world truly was as small as a frontier village.

Not that that boded well for anyone disgraced, the way I was.

Rob pushed Kelly's chair toward me. I was grateful, given how crowded the Pharm was. "Thanks," I said, but I was spared more small talk as Kelly and Rob made their way to the door.

Jenn watched them leave before she clinked her glass of beer against my Godmother. She said, "I'm glad you came."

I looked at the remaining actors wryly, pitching my voice so that only my assistant could hear. "You made it sound like they were desperate for me. Like they were prostrate with grief over the old blocking."

She shrugged. "I figured you needed to get out. Spend some time with friends, instead of holed up home alone." She obviously thought that I'd been at my old home, at the place I'd shared with Dean. Well, no time like the present to share my incredible news.

"That's the thing," I said. "That's why I rushed out of the office today."

"What?"

I took a healthy swallow of my drink, fortifying myself before I said the words out loud, words that would have made *me* think I was crazy if I just happened to overhear someone else saying them. "I know this is going to sound nuts," I said, hunching over my glass so that Jenn had to lean closer. She cocked her head at an angle that mirrored one of her beloved cockatiels. "You know what happened in the meeting this morning, right? You know about Dean?"

I could see her start to lie, start to say that she had no idea what had taken place behind the closed conference room door. But we both knew that was absurd. We both knew the Mercer had no secrets. She nodded and looked sympathetic, but I hurried on before she could say anything. "Well, you know that Kira came in to my office afterward, right?"

"I saw her walk down the hall. With a box or something, right?"

"Right." My heart pounded as I remembered the moment I'd picked up the brass lamp. I barely resisted the urge to rub my marked fingertips together. Jenn waited expectantly as I counted out three beats, applying the perfect sense of timing that I'd built in a lifetime of watching rehearsals. "One of the things in Kira's box was a—"

My voice cracked and my words faded away, as if I were a teenage boy.

Jenn leaned closer. "What?"

I cleared my throat and raised my voice. "There was a—"

Again, my voice broke. I'd spoken loudly enough that the people closest to us turned to look at me. I flashed them a smile, acutely aware of the fact that they'd think I was talking about Dean, think that I'd been silenced because I was overcome with emotion about that bastard. They looked away, embarrassed for me.

I wiped my sweaty palms against my pants and tried again, precisely measuring out each word. "Kira." So far, so good. "Gave." No problem. "Me." I was fine. "A." Okay, so I must have imagined the entire thing, dreamed up the whole inability-to-talk thing.

Except I couldn't say the next word.

Lamp wasn't coming out. I tried *lantern,* but that stuck just as firmly. I reached out for adjectives, as if I could sneak up on the concept, sort of like a graduate student padding out a late-night paper with extra words. *Magic* was a no-go. *Genie* wasn't going to happen, either. I sputtered, angry with myself, my cheeks flushing as Jenn waited, as our nearby eavesdroppers pretended not to be waiting with bated breath for whatever I was going to choke out.

Finally, Jenn reached across to pat my hand. "It's okay, Bec. I know what Kira brought you."

"You do?" My relief was like a cashmere wave.

She nodded. "I went into your office after you left. I saw

the box on your desk. Don't worry! They totally look like normal clothes. No one will know that you're wearing costumes. I mean, no one who isn't working on the show."

Clothes. She thought I was getting all choked up about clothes.

"That isn't—" I started to say. But then I thought better about my protest. Something strange was going on here. I'd have to ask Kira, or Teel, the next time I summoned the genie. Some sort of magic—or was it MAGIC, the trade association?—was keeping me from talking. I forced myself to laugh, and then I said, "That beer isn't going to last you the rest of the night. Can I get you another?"

"Just a sec." Jenn glanced around at the cast, obviously making sure that everyone else was distracted. (Not that distraction was difficult with this group—they'd already forgotten my near-confession about Teel and had moved on to chattering about some flubbed line from the afternoon's rehearsal.) When Jenn was satisfied that no one was paying attention, she leaned down and pulled a cardboard banker's box between our chairs.

"What's that?" I asked.

"ShowTalk has been nuts all afternoon." ShowTalk. The Internet gossip mill. The theater community's discussion boards must be red-hot.

"Has anyone seen Dean?" I asked bitterly.

Jenn shrugged. "That's not the biggest story today."

"What do you mean?"

"Everyone's talking about *Crystal Dreams*."

"*Crystal*—!" How did they hear about that? I hadn't told anyone about our copyright disaster—not even Hal. I knew I'd have to face *that* spectacular crisis tomorrow.

Jenn scowled. "That lawyer, Elaine Harcourt? When she didn't hear back from you this morning, she called Hal."

"Oh, God!" I gulped half of my Godmother.

"Don't worry," Jenn reassured me. "He was still tied up with that lawyer and the bank and Clifford Ames. The call rolled over to my phone, and I took the message. Don't *worry*," she said again. "I went into your e-mail and forwarded Elaine's message to him. As far as he knows, you sent it to him before you left the building."

I forced myself to take a deep breath, to exhale slowly, spreading my fingers on the tabletop to dissipate a little of the anxiety constricting my heart. "Thanks. What did he say when he read the e-mail?"

Jenn's mouth twisted into something that might have been a smile if she'd actually been amused. "I'm not allowed to use those words in public."

I downed the rest of my drink. "What happened?"

"He made a bunch of phone calls. He was trying to find out who Elaine Harcourt really is. Whether she's really serious. Whether we should be worried."

"And?"

"We should be worried."

I slumped back in my chair. "We are totally screwed."

Jenn's smile was pure mischief. "That all depends on how you look at it."

"What do you mean?" I rattled my bare ice cubes in my glass.

Jenn lifted the lid off the box. "You and I are making out like bandits."

I looked down. "Holy crap!"

That exclamation was loud enough to regain the cast's attention. The three actors nearest to us looked up expectantly, as if they thought I was going to deliver a monologue on love, embezzlement, and the devastation of betrayal. "Sorry," I muttered, waving a hand toward the box. "Jenn just brought me some unsolicited scripts."

They laughed understandingly and looked away.

But the box didn't contain manuscripts.

No. The box contained a bottle of red wine, a Burgundy, if my French was any good at all. A bottle of single malt nestled beneath it. A bright pink box cradled a half-dozen vanilla cupcakes, each perfectly frosted with fondant Easter bunnies. My mouth started to water when I saw a gigantic gold box of Godiva chocolates. I reached out a tentative hand and quickly revealed other treats—a stash of giant cashews, a bag of Blue Jamaican coffee, a package of venison jerky, a half-dozen canisters from Republic of Tea, a trio of French milled soaps, and a bag stuffed with Sephora cosmetics.

I looked up at Jenn, mystified. "From friends?"

She shook her head. "From playwrights. From people who want to get their respective feet in the Mercer door. People who want you to select their plays to fill the gap in the schedule."

"You have got to be kidding."

"All of this arrived this afternoon. With cards, all delicately phrased. You know—'Hoping to ease your loss during this difficult time.'"

"That sounds like someone died!"

She grinned. "It does, doesn't it?"

"We can't keep these, Jenn. They're bribes!"

She shook her head and clicked her tongue. "Now, now…

I'm your loyal assistant, and I've assisted you out of that problem."

"What did you do?"

"I threw out all the cards. If you don't know who sent the gifts, then you can't reward the givers. You can't be corrupted."

Wow. She had a point. "But what about you?" I asked, my sense of professionalism surging reluctantly back to the surface.

"Weeeeeellll…" She sighed. "If you take half the things and leave half for me, without my actually choosing anything…and if I keep my mouth totally, completely, one hundred percent shut about what play should replace *Crystal Dreams*… Then I wouldn't be guilty either."

"Did you tell Hal about all this?"

She frowned. "He was a little busy today, Bec."

Yeah. I guess he had been.

So. We had ten playwrights so eager to get their works staged by the Mercer that they were willing to invest in some pretty serious bribes. Ten playwrights who my ethical dramaturg's heart would immediately strike from the rolls of possible works. If I knew who they were.

But Hal wasn't going to make a decision about a replacement play based on alcohol, or sugar, or cosmetics. He—and I—would look at the merits of all the possibilities. We'd find something simple, something stable, something we could pull together on our very abbreviated schedule.

The bribes were immaterial.

I darted a glance at Jenn. "How about if I take the wine, the Godiva, the coffee, cashews, and soap?"

"Sounds perfect!" She laughed. "But I'm keeping the box to carry my stash home."

"Deal," I said, offering my hand for a quick shake.

"Another drink?" she asked, looking at the lonely ice cubes in my glass.

"Might as well."

I stared at our loot and shook my head, suddenly overwhelmed with exhaustion from my insane day. And tomorrow was only going to be worse, as we moved full steam ahead to find a replacement for *Crystal Dreams*. I'd better enjoy tonight—it was likely to be the last break I'd have in a long, long time. I waved my hand to get Jenn's attention, and then I mouthed clearly, "Make mine a double!" She laughed and nodded and turned to update Pete about his bartending responsibilities.

In retrospect, I should have stopped at one drink.

The workday had been emotionally exhausting, and I *had* hardly slept the night before, worrying about Dear Departed Dean. (After a couple of Godmothers, though, Dean's deserting me was looking a lot less terrible—especially when I silently factored both a magic genie and a new apartment into the deal.)

One drink should have been enough, but I had Jenn sitting beside me—Jenn who was feeling unusually generous. Or maybe just solicitous.

That double drink she retrieved left me pleasantly buzzed. My next one left me feeling loose, extravagant—I almost broke out the box of Godiva, almost shared the chocolates with the ravenous hordes of the Shepard cast. Common sense prevailed (by that point in the evening, no one would have appreciated the treat, at least not as much as I'd appreciate having the chocolates in my otherwise foodless kitchen.)

That same common sense should have kept me from ordering yet another drink. At least it kept me from finishing the damn thing.

By the time I got to my new front door, I was proud just to be able to extricate my keys from my pocket. I tumbled my collection of bribes onto the floor, fully aware that I would need both hands to work the intricate magic of opening my door. I nodded confidently as the upper lock turned precisely. Maybe I wasn't as drunk as I thought I was. I eased the middle one open with a satisfying click. That left the bottom one.

The key stuttered as I put it in. At first, it wouldn't turn at all. I tried edging it out just a little, tried twisting it hard enough that I grew afraid it would break off inside the stubborn mechanism. I nudged my bottle of wine with my toe, forcing it to one side so that I could station myself more precisely in front of the lock. I took the key out altogether and started again, trying to find the sweet spot where it would work.

"Need some help?"

I caught a shriek at the back of my throat. I'd been so intent on manipulating the stubborn lock that I hadn't heard anyone come up behind me. Hadn't heard a *man* come up behind me. Hadn't heard a man who sounded distinctly amused at my predicament come up behind me.

I turned around to see Ryan Thompson.

That Ryan Thompson, the guy from Jenn's stalking list. The playwright who'd been in my office—was it only that morning? It seemed like a lifetime ago.

I glanced at my illicit treasures, spread on the carpet at my feet. Had Ryan sent any of them? Had he tried to bribe me as soon as news of the Mercer's dilemma hit ShowTalk?

"Hi," I said, because the silence had stretched so long that even *I* was uncomfortable. My conversational skills were apparently as much on the blink as my key-turning abilities.

"Rebecca Morris?" He looked as startled as I felt. If possible, his hair was more rumpled than it had been that morning. His coat hung open, barely held in place across his shoulders by a messenger bag that was slung across his chest like a bandolier. The bag's flap gaped open, too, revealing a laptop computer.

"What are you doing here?" I managed to say.

"I live here. With my mother." He nodded toward Dani's door, looking down at his shoes like a bashful schoolboy. His eyelashes were long enough—or I was drunk enough—that his admission seemed endearing, not creepy at all. "Just until I get my act together, get settled back here in the States."

He waited for me to say something, but my mind was as sticky as the Amaretto I'd been downing all night. Ryan Thompson was my neighbor. The guy I'd just met that morning, through a miniature cascade of coincidences—his getting on the stalking list, delivering a play to the office, getting past Jenn's usually ferocious barriers.

I believed in coincidence as much as the next superstitious theater professional, but this one was a little difficult to accept. Apparently Ryan thought so, too. He sounded incredulous as he prompted, "Mom said someone had moved in, but she didn't tell me your name."

"It didn't mean anything to her, I'm sure," I said.

But what did all this mean to *me*? What did it mean that my world was spinning in tighter and tighter circles? Or was that just the alcohol making the hallway seem like it tilted on an unreliable axis?

Ryan nodded toward my keys. "Is that lock sticking again? Mr. Greenbaum used to complain to the super about it all the time. Want me to try?"

I shrugged and stepped back, fighting to smother a sudden Godmother-induced yawn. As Ryan leaned over my keys, I closed my eyes, suddenly exhausted by the accumulated weight of my day. I could picture my computer at work, Elaine Harcourt's e-mail flashing on the screen. I could see the giant stack of scripts on my desk, still waiting for my attention. I could imagine Teel's lamp, glinting where I'd first dropped it amid the rubble.

Teel. Teel had stood in that same office. She had looked at the same desk. She had seen Ryan's script, right on top of the stack, where I'd dropped it after the disaster in the conference room.

She must have read Ryan's address label—the neat, perfectly-centered label that had impressed me that morning. Teel must have somehow used the address label to trigger her magic, to provide a concrete place for me to live. I thought about the genie's sly smile as she'd left my office. "You ain't seen nothing yet," she'd said. Had she known that Ryan lived across the hall? Had she planned our meeting, all along? And what if she had? Why should it make any difference who my neighbors were?

As I speculated furiously, Ryan managed to spring the bottom lock. He extricated my key and handed it over. "There you go," he said. And then he eyed the ill-gotten booty spread around my feet. "Um, do you need help with that?"

I blushed, guilt speeding blood into my cheeks. "They're just, um, gifts. From a couple of playwrights." I said it as a sort of test, to see if he admitted to having sent anything. As

soon as the words were out of my mouth, though, I knew I'd
made a mistake. I shouldn't have mentioned the theater at all,
shouldn't have planted even a seed of doubt about bribes. I
could have said that they were all birthday presents—he had
no way of knowing that my actual birthday was in June. Desperate to say something, anything, to wipe away the disbelief
that peaked his eyebrows, I said, "You know. Guerilla dramaturgy."

I tried to smile as I trilled the *r* in *guerilla,* but he wasn't
amused. His volume increased with the shock in his expression. "People are actually bribing you to fill in with their
plays?"

"Hush!" I said automatically, even though our neighbors
were probably sound asleep behind their well-locked doors.
Of course Ryan knew about my *Crystal Dreams* disaster—he
had to be plugged into ShowTalk like everyone else in the
theater world. I nudged the box of chocolates with my toe.
"I promise," I said, "I don't even know who sent these!"

"Sure," he said, but he clearly thought I was lying.

"Seriously," I said. Suddenly it was really important that he
believe me, the most important thing in the world. I drew
myself up to my full height and settled my right hand over the
approximate area of my heart, before I enunciated very carefully, "Jenn just passed them on. Anonymously. I have absolutely
no idea who sent them. Honest. Cross my heart and hope to
die." I matched action to words, and then I had a brilliant inspiration. "Hey, why don't you come in? Have a glass of wine!"

He shook his head, easing his hands into his pockets. "I
don't think that's a good idea."

"Why not?" Belligerence rose inside me, fueled by vodka
and Amaretto.

"I can think of three good reasons, without even trying."
I glared a challenge, but he kept his voice even. Light. "One,
it's after midnight on a work night. Two, you look like you
don't need a glass of wine, or anything else alcoholic. Three,
you don't know anything about me. I could be an axe
murderer."

"Are you an axe murderer?"

A shadow of a smile flicked across his lips before his earnest
expression returned. "No."

I turned my head at an angle, trying to see Dani's placid
face reflected in his. He had her calm eyes, dark and reassuring. His chin echoed hers, coming to a point. But his flat
cheekbones were all his own. And those lips—those mascu-
line lips, dusky in the soft hallway light…

Dean's lips had always been chapped. He chewed on them
whenever he was deep in thought. It was his one failing. Aside
from being an embezzler and all.

I blinked hard, hoping that I hadn't lost too much time responding. Ryan seemed not to have noticed that my attention had strayed. I said, "But an axe murderer would lie to
me, wouldn't he?"

"Yeah," Ryan said. "He probably would." He leaned over
and collected my treats, passing them to me as if he were an
earnest young clerk at an all-night grocery store. "Go to bed,
Rebecca Morris. And drink a glass of water before you fall
asleep. Take an aspirin or two."

My fingers brushed against his as I took the golden box of
chocolates. His hands were warm, a little rough, like a man
who'd done more than sit at a computer for days and weeks
and months on end. I wondered how much time he spent
working with Dani, helping her with her secret gardening

projects. I wanted to ask him how much time he'd invested in Africa, building villages, bringing new life to desperate folks.

As I hesitated, an awkwardness bloomed between us, the sort of gawky uncertainty that I hadn't felt since my parents were driving me on dates with underage junior high class-mates. A part of me thought that I should lean forward and kiss Ryan on the cheek. Another part of me thought that I should juggle my unethical gifts, adjust my grip so that I could shake his hand. An astonishing third part of me considered dragging him into my home, axe murderer or not, luring him across the threshold to test out the new king-size bed that Teel had so thoughtfully provided.

That was the Godmothers talking.

"Good night," I said.

He met my eyes, as if he'd heard the entire battle that had just raged inside my skull. "Good night." As I took a single tentative step forward, he smiled again, shook his head just slightly. "Sleep well." And then he turned back to his own door, working his own three locks with ease.

Safely inside my apartment, I slid to the floor like a melted ice sculpture of the goddess Embarrassment. What had Teel done? How had she placed me in an apartment across the hall from a potential business colleague, from someone who had practically begged me to give him a break in the brutal world of the theater? What had Teel been thinking?

I caught a whiff of the delicate soaps that were balanced in the crook of my arm. What high horse was *I* sitting on? What right did I have to chastise my genie, when I was clearly not above having *some* outside communication with playwrights? At least when it benefited me, personally.

Shaking my head, I clambered to my feet. Crossing to the kitchen, I deposited my treasures on the granite counter. I opened the cabinet to the right of the sink, discovering a dazzling array of glasses. Leaning against the counter, I ran the tap for a minute before filling a tumbler with water, drinking it down, filling it again.

As for aspirin, that would have to wait. Unless Teel had filled my medicine chest, as well. I shuffled back to the bedroom to find out.

CHAPTER 6

IN THE MIDDLE OF THE NIGHT, I BOLTED UPRIGHT IN BED.

I didn't know what had awakened me—one moment, I'd been sound asleep, the next, I was absolutely, completely, one hundred percent awake. I caught my breath, listening for strange noises coming from the front of the apartment.

Nothing.

I winced as I remembered the Godmothers I had consumed. Swallowing hard, I expected to be rewarded with the parched nausea of an incipient hangover. Somehow, though, I'd lucked out. Or else Ryan's recommended water and aspirin (Teel had, in fact, provided for me) had served me well.

Ryan.

Flushing with sudden embarrassment, I tossed off my duvet. I squeezed my eyes shut in the darkness, but the image of Ryan's face remained before me—his earnest eyes, his goofy grin. His quiet, firm decision to send me off to bed, alone.

No. I couldn't think about that. I didn't even know the

guy. Why had I considered inviting him into my home? Um, into my bed.

Sure, Dean had abandoned me, left me high and dry, but there were better ways to declare my emotional independence than throwing myself at the first thing in pants that crossed my drunken path. Moaning about my alcohol-inspired stupidity, I rolled over onto my stomach, covering my head with my pillow.

Not that smothering myself helped much. I could still see Ryan, picture him as he'd stood in the Mercer's Bullpen, gawky and uncomfortable. I could envision the script that he'd handed to me, the sleek envelope that Teel had obviously used to manipulate her magic.

That envelope glinted in my mind, sparkling as if it were lit from within. Yesterday had been so crazy that I hadn't even opened the thing. Hadn't even glanced at the manuscript inside. Hadn't even considered it.

Despite the fact that we were desperate to replace *Crystal Dreams*.

What had I been thinking? I needed to read Ryan's play. *Now.*

Consumed with a sudden compulsion, I leaped out of my warm bed. I washed my face and brushed my teeth, not worrying when I flung water around my marble-finished bathroom. I tugged on the same clothes that I'd worn the day before, grabbing for my coat with an overwhelming sense of urgency.

So what if it was dark outside? So what if it had started to rain, one of those freezing early-March downpours that would have been snow a few weeks before? So what if I was the only person in the entire Mercer Project complex, as I unlocked the glass door to the lobby, as I walked down the dark hallway to my office?

There! The envelope rested on top of my to-be-read stack, as perfect and pristine as I'd remembered. I didn't bother looking for a letter opener; I just tore the thing open, like a starving dog ripping through a bag of kibble. The pages gleamed, pure white with strong black ink printed in an easy-to-read font.

However Long. By Ryan Thompson.

Gathering my coat close around me, I huddled against myself for warmth in the cool nighttime office and started to read.

An hour later, I came up for air, gasping as if I'd completed a marathon.

Ryan's play was incredible. Every line was perfect. Each character was whole, complete. The story—the struggle of second wife Fanta to feed her family and herself in the face of near-starvation—was heart-wrenching, overwhelming. True.

The Mercer needed to produce *However Long. I* needed to work on the play. I needed to teach audiences the truths behind its words. I needed to share Ryan's intricate vision, to bring it to full life. I needed to redeem myself from the *Crystal Dreams* fiasco, from the Dean debacle—and *However Long* was strong enough, magical enough to offer me that new lease on my theatrical life.

It wasn't the replacement play I'd envisioned the day before, something simple and stripped down. Ryan's play was challenging. Intricate. There was a dream sequence that filled half of the second act, a swirling sea of words and motions that were detailed in Ryan's meticulous, magical stage directions.

However Long wouldn't be easy. But it would be *right*. For me. For the Mercer. For all the women in Africa who needed a voice to tell their stories.

I scrambled for my cell phone, squinting at the time. 5:15 a.m. Hal would be up in another hour. I'd awakened him once before, my second week on the job, and I'd learned my lesson. He wouldn't be able to hear me, wouldn't be able to understand a word that I was saying, if I buzzed him out of sleep a full forty-five minutes before his alarm normally went off. Sighing in frustration, I ran my fingers through my hair, knotting it haphazardly to keep it out of my way. I forced myself to lean back in my chair, to pick up the pages, to tap them into a clean, neat, straight-edged pile.

And then I read through the entire play once again, from start to finish, savoring every single word as if it were a feast laid before a ravenous woman.

That second reading carried me deeper than I'd expected, took me further away. When I finished, I blinked at the cold light that sifted down the hallway, a wintry reminder of the windows in the reception area. I scrambled for my phone— 7:30 a.m. I dialed Hal from memory. "Hey," I said, as soon as he answered.

"What's wrong?"

"Nothing." I hurried to reassure him. Oh, he had every reason to expect a disaster, after all the cards he'd been dealt the day before.

"Are you with Dean? Is he threatening you? If you're with Dean, give me a number between one and ten."

I had to hand it to him—Hal thought quickly on his feet. "I have no idea where Dean is," I said. "I didn't even try to find him last night. I figure the police are going to be better at that than I could ever be."

After all, I barely knew the guy. Apparently. I expected that thought to burn, but I barely noticed it as I drummed my fingers against Ryan's script.

Hal sounded a little annoyed. "What's up, then?" I could hear a whirring sound in the background. He must be training on his elliptical.

"I have a play for us. Something to replace *Crystal Dreams*."

The whirring stopped. "What is it?"

"It's new. You haven't heard anything about it. It's called *However Long*—it's by Ryan Thompson."

"Who the hell is Ryan Thompson?"

"He's on our stalking list. Jenn introduced him to me the other day." I flipped to the one-page biography that Ryan had thoughtfully included at the back of his play. "Ryan Thompson graduated from Princeton University with a degree from the Woodrow Wilson School of Public Policy and International Affairs. After completing four years with a prominent New York consulting firm, he joined the Peace Corps. Assigned to Burkina Faso, he was instrumental in the development of an education and empowerment program for girls. Having returned to the United States, Ryan hopes to use his plays to educate the developed world about the plight of women in Africa."

"Sounds like a real upbeat guy. That play should be a laugh a minute."

My heart clenched at the dismissal in Hal's voice. He didn't understand. He couldn't. He hadn't read the script. Yet. I forced my voice to stay steady. "*Crystal Dreams* wasn't exactly a 'laugh a minute'—starvation, death, emotional blackmail?"

"What does this guy Thompson's play have that other scripts don't?"

"Everything," I said, not even a little ashamed by the passion in my voice, by the way my heart beat a little faster as I thought of how perfect Ryan's words had been. "Please, Hal. It'll only take you an hour to read it."

"Leave it on my desk. I'll take a look as soon as I get in."

"Thanks. You won't be sorry."

Filled with nervous energy, I marched the script down to Hal's office. I set the pages in the center of his desk, lining them up precisely with the wooden edge. I rummaged in the old coffee mug that held his pens, digging out one of the Rollerballs that he preferred, setting it at a jaunty angle across Ryan's masterpiece. The display was perfect, like a stock photograph of "Director at Work."

No. Wait. It needed something else.... I turned my head to one side, squinting for a better perspective.

Scones.

The bakery around the corner had blueberry-orange scones. Hal loved them—just the other day, he'd said that they were his favorite breakfast treat. I'd set one out for him—he'd appreciate the thought, and he wouldn't even recognize the compelling irony until he got to the end of Ryan's incredible play, until he finished the story of Fanta and her struggle for peace, for food, for survival.

Yeah, it was bribery. Plain and simple. I seemed to have become an expert in less than twenty-four hours.

All the way to the bakery, I grappled with that thought. There were definite ethical considerations that went along with being a dramaturg. My value to the production was directly tied to my ability to distance myself, to serve in a dis-

interested capacity. That function was infinitely more important when I was working on a play that had never been performed before, one that was still evolving for the stage.

It was a disastrous idea for me to recommend a play when
I had a personal relationship with the playwright.

But Ryan and I didn't really know each other. Not well.
Sure, I'd almost made a fool out of myself the night before, but
that had been the Godmothers talking. The Godmothers, and
Teel, that meddlesome genie. And my bastard of a former boyfriend, abandoning me without a single thought to my welfare.

But Ryan's play was more important than any of that.
More important than a belly-swooping moment of alcoholic
longing. *However Long* had to be shared with the world at
large. If staging the play meant that I had to put my feelings
for Ryan Thompson—whatever they actually were—under
lock and key, then that's what I would do.

Easy. No contest. Hell, the guy was nervous enough that
any personal attention from me was likely to send him skittering all the way back to Africa.

Half an hour later, I was pacing my own office, waiting
for Hal to arrive, to read, to confirm my absolute certainty
that *However Long* would be our replacement play. I was
checking the clock for the one hundredth time in fifteen
minutes when there was a light knock on my door. "Kira!"
I gasped when I looked up.

The stage manager's eyes gleamed, and a smile brightened
her face. She edged into my office and closed the door,
hunching forward a little. Immediately, I felt like we were
conspirators in some grand scheme. "So?" she asked.

"I can't believe it! Did you get the wishes, too? All four of
them?"

WHEN GOOD WISHES GO BAD   105

She smiled wryly. "Yep. How many have you made so far?"

"Just one." I was suddenly shy. "I asked for a new place to live. You know, since I wasn't able to fix global warming...."

"I *know*," she said, and she sounded almost indignant. The expression on her face made me laugh. "Or bring about world peace, or end hunger, or cure all diseases..."

She'd obviously stuck with the Grand Wish attempts for longer than I had. I said, "Teel guided me away from all of that pretty quickly." Huh. It was easy to say the genie's name now. None of that strange throat-locking silence that had taken over at the Pharm the night before. "Um, Kira? How come I can talk to you about this? Why wasn't I able to tell Jenn what happened?"

She rolled her eyes. "There's something about the magic that keeps us from telling other people, people who've never met a genie. I'm not sure how that works—I'm not sure how *any* of it works. Teel just manages to make outsiders forget about whatever wishes he's granted. He makes them accept things, like nothing ever changed."

He? Teel? Was Kira talking about the female genie-lawyer who had manifested in my office the day before? Before I could ask, though, everything around me disappeared.

Yeah. It was pretty strange for me, too.

One minute, I was surrounded by the clutter of my office, standing across from Kira. The next instant, I was nowhere. No place. No time.

It wasn't like I'd gone blind. I raised my hand in front of my face—I could make out my wiggling fingers just fine. I could hear my heart beating, suddenly fast in my ears. I could feel my fingernails digging into my palms.

But there was nothing around me—the air was the exact

same temperature as my skin, no breezes, no currents. My feet were there—I looked down and saw them. I curled my toes inside my shoes. But I couldn't see any ground, any floor. No ceiling above, either.

"Teel, you *know* I hate this!"

I whirled around. Kira was standing behind me, her hands firmly planted on her hips. A clown stood between us.

Yep—a clown. Just like the ones from all the circus nightmares of my childhood. My throat grew dry as I ordered myself not to panic.

He wore a rainbow fright wig, and his face was painted white, with gigantic red lips outlined in black. His nose was a red ball, and his eyes were highlighted by yellow stars. Blue-and-gold suspenders held up patchwork pants that were at least ten sizes too large, and his shoes looked like massive neon-pink frying pans.

"Ta-da!" the clown said when he saw that I was gaping. He thrust one arm forward, as if he were showing off the entrance to the Taj Mahal. The motion made his sleeve ride up, and I could see flames tattooed around his wrist, brilliant gold, outlined in black. "Welcome to the Garden!"

"Teel?" I said, rocking on my heels as I turned around to face…my genie head-on. All of a sudden, Kira's choice of pronouns made much more sense. I shouldn't be so surprised that my genie could change her, um, his appearance. She, um, *he* worked magical miracles every single day. What was a little gender bending on the side?

"At your service," Teel said, sweeping a dramatic bow. Despite the outrageous clown makeup, despite the crimson lips that filled the lower half of his face, I could see the genuine wistfulness in his eyes as he straightened up and looked beyond me, into the grey nothingness. He sighed, as if he were staring at something stunningly beautiful.

Kira was distinctly less enchanted. "Teel, I thought we had an agreement. You promised never to take me here again."

"I didn't take you," the clown pouted. "I took Rebecca. You just happened to be standing close enough to be dragged along."

Kira snorted. "That doesn't make sense! You never dragged along my housemates, or anyone at rehearsal, the entire time we were working together."

Teel clucked his tongue and shook his head in an exaggerated motion made even broader by his bouncing hair. "Those people were different, Kira. They were *ordinary*. You've rubbed my lamp—you're attuned to magic now. I couldn't *help* but carry you along." Kira harrumphed and crossed her arms over her chest. Teel ignored her obvious exasperation and said, "Just because *you* didn't like coming to the Garden doesn't mean Rebecca won't like it." He blinked at me with those enormous star-studded eyes.

"Becca," I said, eager to buy a few seconds, to figure out just what the "Garden" was that they were talking about. I certainly didn't see anything in the shapeless, spaceless nothingness around me that would qualify. "All my friends call me Becca."

"Becca," Teel said happily. He inhaled deeply, throwing his head back so vigorously that I expected his ghastly rainbow wig to plummet to the ground.

Kira was also staring at the hairpiece, with her own expression of horror. "Let me guess. You were left free to roam New York, and the first thing you thought about was breaking into a Ringling Brothers show."

Teel snorted. "Who's to say I wasn't entertaining children in the hospital? In the orphans' home?"

"I don't think we even *have* orphans' homes anymore," Kira complained.

"Let's just say that I wanted to amuse some old friends. And what's more amusing than a clown?" Kira didn't look convinced, but Teel didn't seem to notice. "Except the Garden, of course. It's definitely more amusing." He whirled on me. "Isn't it fabulous?"

"Um, yes," I improvised. "It's definitely...fabulous."

Teel jutted his head forward on his neck, as abruptly as a bird. "Just seven more wishes, your three, and the next wisher's four, and I get to go in."

"Go in?" I had no idea what he was talking about. "What do you mean?"

"As soon as I grant seven more wishes, I get to take my first sabbatical, my first extended visit to the Garden."

I nodded, reflexively falling back on my dramaturgy skills. I was accustomed to working with artists, with directors who got so wrapped up in their productions that they forgot the parameters of normal, everyday life. That was actually one of my job responsibilities, channeling that type of passion, helping people share their dearest, most closely held beliefs.

Using one of my tried and true techniques, I repeated, "Extended visit to the Garden..."

And it worked. Teel rushed on, "Every genie gets rewarded after granting a certain number of wishes. We all dream of the time that we can spend in the Garden, the time that we can be away from the cares and demands of the everyday world. I thought that if I brought you here, if you actually saw what I'm waiting for, *you'd hurry up and make your three remaining wishes.*"

He said the last clause so quickly, with so much vehemence, that I felt like I'd been caught by whiplash. I turned to Kira to see how she was responding to this sudden demand.

But Kira didn't look too concerned. In fact, she raised a hand to her mouth, covering an elaborate yawn. She made a point of studying her fingernails when she was done, broadcasting "boredom" so transparently that I would have protested her lack of creativity if she'd been an actor in any production where I was involved.

So. Kira clearly wasn't worried about my delay in making my three wishes. And if she wasn't concerned, then I wouldn't be, either. I started to run my fingers through my hair, only to find that it was still held against my neck in a loose knot. I settled for shoving my hands into my pockets.

My defiance was all well and good, but I should still *try* to keep on Teel's good side. After all, I had no idea how much trouble an annoyed genie could cause.

I closed my eyes and took a deep breath, filling my lungs and rolling my head back until I stared at the nonexistent ceiling. Sky. Whatever. I exhaled slowly. "I can't believe it," I said, threading my words with pretend fascination. "I have never smelled…what is it? It's so intense!"

Teel beamed. "Lilacs!" He shot a vindictive glare toward Kira. "You can smell the lilacs!"

I nodded slowly. "But there's something else there… Something more subtle."

"Freesia! They're just starting to bloom!"

"That's it!" I exclaimed. Kira's eyes widened, and I caught her flaring her own nostrils, trying to make out the scents that Teel described. I felt a little guilty for pretending.

But then I saw Teel's excitement. He practically skipped

forward, tripping over the magenta monstrosity of his shoes. Raising his gloved hands, he folded his oversize clown fingers around something vertical, clutching something tight at the level of his heart. "You understand!" he said to me. "You can see how important it is for me to get inside the Garden."

With sudden comprehension, I realized that he had to be touching a fence, or a gate, some sort of barrier. I raised a finger and placed it just above his Bozo hands. "What's that sound?" I said, taking something of a chance. "Do they even *have* those birds here in New York?"

Teel laughed. "It's a nightingale! You've probably never heard one before, live."

I hadn't heard one in the dream-space of the Garden, either, but I nodded. "That's incredible," I said. "It sounds so…pure."

"So you'll help me?" Teel wheedled. His pout looked even more pitiful beneath his exaggerated face-paint. "You'll get me in as soon as possible, by making the rest of your wishes?"

I forced regret into my voice, harvesting everything I'd ever learned in the theater, all the skills I'd ever glommed on to from the finest actors I'd ever met. "I want to, Teel. I really do. I'm just not ready yet. I'm not certain. But I see how much the Garden means to you. I'll let you know as soon as I've made up my mind."

Teel flashed a triumphant smile at Kira. "See?" he said. "That's all I ever wanted. Just someone who understands what's important to me. Ninety-nine out of one hundred wishers say *kind* things to their genies."

Kira gritted her teeth. "I'm sure they do, when they can get a word in edgewise. When they're not being harangued and harassed to make up their minds." She sighed with something that might have been nostalgia. "I said kind things, too, Teel. Every once in a while." She looked around uncomfortably, looking distinctly queasy as she struggled to find some stable point to settle her eyes. "You got your answer from Becca then, right? She'll make her wishes as quickly as possible. Will you please take us back now? And will you please make sure you don't drag me along again?"

Teel's real smile beamed inside his painted clown one. "I can't make any promises!"

"You can say that again," Kira muttered.

Teel turned to me. "You'll summon me, then? For your second wish? Soon?"

"I will," I agreed.

"Six out of ten wishers make their second wish within twenty-four hours of their first."

I was going to be part of the outlying group of four. But there was no point telling Teel that. "Thanks for the information," I said, trying to sound sincere.

Teel looked at both Kira and me. He stripped off one of his huge white gloves, raised his seemingly tiny human (genie?) fingers to his earlobe. He cast one last, wistful glance toward the invisible fence, and then he tugged once, hard.

And Kira and I were back in my office, with Teel nowhere in sight.

Kira stomped her right foot on the floor, as if she were trying to restore circulation after sitting still for a long time. "Ah," she said. "Terra firma. I *hate* it there! Could you really see the Garden? Could you really smell it, and hear the birds?"

"God, no!" I admitted. Kira gaped, and I rushed on, "I figured it wouldn't do either of us any good to be stranded in the literal middle of nowhere, with an angry genie who was dressed up like a clown. I lied about the entire thing."

Kira's laugh was refreshing. "Well, that's a relief. I thought *I* was stranded with two people who could see the exact same hallucinations."

"So, I guess the whole wish thing is really important to her. Er, him."

"Whatever," Kira agreed. "You'll probably get pressured even more than I did—he's that much closer to his goal. Just remember that the choice is always yours. Don't let him railroad you into anything. I think he makes up most of those statistics, anyway." She started to turn back to my office door. "Oh, and don't worry. You'll get used to the whole gender thing. The gender and the costumes…" She shook her head and turned to leave.

"Kira?" I said, before she could disappear down the hallway. "Thanks."

As Kira smiled and walked away, the phone on my desk rang. I glanced at the caller ID. It was him. Hal. And he'd had long enough to read *However Long*. My hand shook as I picked up the receiver. "Hey," I barely managed to say.

"Call Ryan Thompson. Tell him I want to meet the author of the Mercer's next production."

I barely remembered to hang up the phone before I pumped my fist and cried out, "Yippee!"

CHAPTER 7

EVERY DRAMATURG DREAMS OF THE MOMENT—THE instant when all those years of professional training merge into an indefinable something, a soul-felt understanding, a perfect *yes*. That's what it feels like when a new playwright is discovered.

Sure, I could have called Ryan to tell him that we were choosing his play. As he'd mentioned when he left his envelope, he'd included his business card with his manuscript, and that card had listed a home phone, a cell phone, an e-mail address, and an IM address. I had plenty of ways to reach him electronically.

But news this big required a personal touch. Besides, I'd already put in a long morning reading *However Long*—twice, no less. I deserved a break. I shrugged on my coat and headed toward the Mercer's front door.

Glancing at Jenn's desk, I saw that her computer was off; no amusing screensaver of cockatiels danced across her monitor. I winced as I thought about how much she'd drunk the night before. How bad was her hangover today? Had her husband reminded her to drink some water? Had he shaken out a handful of aspirin for her?

Oh, well. Under other circumstances, I would have invited Jenn to join me in sharing the good news with Ryan. After all, she'd originally placed him on the stalking list. But she had introduced the two of us the day before; she'd asked me to get involved with his future.

And I couldn't delay delivering my message. Not when there was so much to do in so short a time. And not when we'd promised each other that she would stay totally disconnected from the decision-making process, lest the bribes that we'd received corrupt our selection.

Not that Ryan had bribed anyone, I thought. I hoped. I didn't really care. *However Long* was too strong a play for me to worry about who had given the gifts that Jenn and I had received the day before. Especially when we'd already worked out a system to avoid corruption.

I barely felt the cold as I raced back to the Bentley. Pushing the button in the elevator repeatedly, I was frustrated that it took so long to arrive. (It didn't actually take any longer than it had the day before, and it certainly wasn't slower than the ancient machinery in the building I'd shared with Dean. It just *seemed* to take forever.) On the eighth floor at last, I bounded up to Ryan's door.

And then, I stopped.

I wasn't a shy person by nature. I'd spent most of my life around actors—I was used to fighting to be heard in a small, crowded room. I knew how to express myself, how to get people's attention.

But I suddenly wasn't sure that I wanted Ryan's attention.

Oh, I *wanted* it. My belly did a little flip-flop as I remembered that brief moment between us the night before, the instant when I'd almost invited him in, the split second when he'd thought better for both of us. What had *that* been about?

Of course, I knew what it was about. It was about Dean. It was about the fact that I'd had a boyfriend every day of my life, ever since I'd turned ten and Timmy Dayton had given me a friendship bracelet twined out of red and white lanyard. Note to self: Insert long, boring story about boyfriends I had known and loved through the years. Insert longer, more boring story about how I'd thought every single one of those guys was The One.

The simple fact was, I *always* had a boyfriend. Someone always wanted me. I was always special. Popular.

And in the midst of my personal disaster, in the midst of Dean walking out on me, leaving me holding the bag for our apartment, for the theater, for every aspect of our life together, there was a teeny, tiny part of me that was already shouting, already demanding that I hook up with someone new.

That little voice was totally sick. I knew that.

I absolutely understood that women could be strong and independent. I was a vocal advocate for women standing on their own two feet, for professionals carving out their own places in the world. I completely, one hundred percent supported women who broke down barriers, who built up their own accomplishments into towering edifices of independent success.

I just didn't know how to live my own life like that. I didn't know how to wake up alone, morning after morning after morning. I didn't know how to succeed without immediately turning around to share that success with the special guy in my life.

All of which pretty much underscored why it was a bad idea for me to be the dramaturg on Ryan's play. It was one thing for me to wrestle with my own personal demons, but my professional obligation to the Mercer went beyond those feelings, was bigger than those fears.

But what choice did I really have?

However Long was good. It was beyond good—it was magnificent, easily one of the top ten plays I'd ever read. And that was saying something. By a conservative estimate, I'd read about a thousand plays in the past five years. Ryan's voice was going to reach the Mercer's audience. It would open up the hearts and minds of theatergoers, make them see a world—a real world—so completely different from their own that their lives would never again be the same.

So why was I hesitating? Why wasn't I pounding on Ryan's door, shouting out the good news? Why wasn't I giving a struggling artist the break that he'd worked for, for years? What was I afraid of?

Good questions, all of them. Especially that last one.

The rap of my knuckles on Ryan's door seemed louder than it should. I half expected our neighbors to peer out of their own doors, to shout down my disturbance. (Of course, I'd expected them to stare at me after midnight, too, when I'd staggered home drunk. Lucky for me, my neighbors didn't seem the curious type.) I caught my breath and took a half step back, waiting.

Ryan blinked when he opened the door, looking like an owl disturbed in the middle of the day. He sounded almost guilty when he said, "Rebecca? Is your lock sticking again?"

"No," I said, almost bouncing with excitement. "And call me Becca. That's what everyone calls me at work. And since you're about to spend a lot of time down at the Mercer…" I rushed on before he could get confused. "Congratulations, Ryan. *However Long* is going to fill our scheduling hole."

Good fortune strikes people in different ways. Some scream in happiness. Others start to cry. Still others stare in amazement, their jaws slack as they try to grasp the import of ordinary English words. I'd seen all those reactions and more, in all the years I'd watched actors read casting lists, discovering that they were going to be in the shows of their dreams.

Ryan, though? His reaction was totally new to me.

He hung his head, as if I were chastising him. He caught his lower lip between his teeth, sighing deeply, drawing out his exhale for so long that I actually worried he might grow light-headed.

"Ryan?" I finally said. "Are you okay?"

He ran a wiry hand through his hair as he looked up, fortifying himself with another one of those mammoth breaths. "Yeah," he said. "I'm fine…Becca. Thank you. Thanks for coming all the way over here to tell me."

Okay… So that hadn't been exactly the response I'd anticipated. But what did I know? What did I know about coming back to the States after two years abroad? About creating art based on that foreign experience, about building characters out of whole cloth, about relating the horrors and joys of real lives to an audience who had never even dreamed such people could exist?

So Ryan wasn't howling with joy. Why had I even expected such a boring, customary reaction, knowing the extraordinary story he had to tell in his play?

I pitched my voice low, almost as if I were comforting an injured animal. "You're welcome. I'm really looking forward to working on this show. *However Long* is just…amazing."

He raised his fingers to the neck of his shirt, tugging like a little boy made uncomfortable by his Sunday best. "Thanks," he said. "Um, would you like to come in?"

"That would be great." I felt a little awkward as he stepped aside, like I was back in elementary school, going to a birthday party at a classmate's home. We were like kids who had been coached on all the right words to say, but neither of us was actually comfortable with the social niceties.

Ryan's apartment was much smaller than my own. I found myself in a combination living room, dining room, and kitchen. A wooden workbench was pushed up against one wall, laden with potting soil and trowels beneath purple grow-lights. A folding screen cut off the other half the room, forcing a love seat and a rocking chair into close proximity. A twin bed peeked out from behind the screen, knotted sheets and blanket tangled on the floor at its foot, as if its occupant—Ryan, I assumed—had spent a restless night. A door to my right hinted at a bathroom; one to my left opened onto a single dim bedroom. The entire place was dark, even though the curtains were open, even though early-afternoon sun was shining on the street. A quick glance out the window confirmed that a brick wall was less than an arm's-length away.

So. This was how the Bentley looked for people who didn't have a genie at their beck and call. I supposed that I should be grateful Teel had swung her magic, getting me the river-view apartment I'd so greedily demanded. I felt vaguely guilty, though, as if I'd taken something that should have belonged to Ryan.

"Can I get you a cup of tea?" Ryan asked after my inspection spun out for a little too long.

"That would be great!" I could hear too much enthusiasm in my voice, and I warned myself to tone things down.

"English Breakfast all right?" Ryan asked, rummaging in the kitchen. "I have a pot made."

"That would be grand." I made a face at myself, because I sounded stupid. *Grand*. Who talked like that? Ryan pretended not to notice, though, turning his back to take a small carton of cream out of the well-stocked fridge.

I thought of my own kitchen, larger and brighter and much more bare—at least until I got my first post-Dean paycheck. "Thanks," I said, as Ryan passed me a mug. He gestured, and I followed him over to the tiny dining table in the common room. He took the seat closest to Dani's workbench.

"So," he said, adding cream to his own mug after waiting for me to do the same. "What do we do now?"

"We'll announce the new play on ShowTalk and in conventional media. Auditions are in nine days. After rehearsals start, Hal will want you there full-time. New plays develop better if everyone is totally committed from the start."

Gee. I made it sound as if I'd launched dozens of new plays before. The casual observer would never realize that I was making everything up as I went along. Except that bit about Hal wanting him there. Hal always wanted playwrights present. The Mercer would have done a lot more Shakespeare, if only Hal could have figured out a way to bring the Bard back from the beyond.

"So that's it?" Ryan sounded skeptical. "I just sit around for a week, waiting for things to get moving?"

I shook my head, and I fortified myself with a sip of tea before answering. "No, you'll need to meet Hal and the rest of the Mercer staff. Of course, you already know Jenn. And, um, me." I was delaying telling him the bad news. I was pretty sure that Ryan wouldn't be thrilled with his first true assignment, to get *However Long* on its path to production. "We *do* have one more real project, though, one we should get started on right away."

He stared at me, waiting for me to elaborate. His eyes seemed especially dark in the dim apartment; they glowed like melted charcoal briquettes. I'd already grown accustomed to his too-long hair; my fingers had almost—*almost*—forgotten that they wanted to brush it off the back of his neck. When I continued to hesitate, he said, "I'm not going to like this much, am I?"

"It's not terrible," I assured him. "It's actually one of my favorite parts of the job." I paused a moment, so that my enthusiasm could soften him up. "I'm going to need your help finding a sponsor for the show."

"A sponsor?" He sounded like a new arrival in America, a person just learning our language.

"We had one all lined up for *Crystal Dreams*. The Narcotics Awareness League was going to underwrite the entire production, make media buys, host the opening gala. But they won't support *However Long*." I saw him start to frown, so I turned up the wattage on my own smile. "Sponsors choose their shows really carefully. It's a huge financial commitment for them, and they want to make sure that they get as much good publicity as possible."

"Publicity! But they're *sponsors*. For the *arts!*"

I smiled wryly. I had been that naive once. Dean had trained that out of me, ladling his grim money management over my enthusiasm. I consciously set aside thoughts of everything else Dean had taught me, about business, about self-interest. I explained, "They still need to get something out of the deal for themselves. Our sponsors love the Mercer's upscale audiences." Ryan started to splutter, and I hurried on. "But they also want to feel good about what they're doing. That's why I want them to meet you. I want them to understand what you saw in Africa, what the Peace Corps taught you." He began to relax, lulled by my explanation. Chalk up another one for the dramaturg's inherent skills as psychologist. "I already have some great prospects lined up," I assured him. Well, I'd thought about a few possibilities. Okay, I'd thrown together a short mental list as I hurried over to tell him the good news.

"Like?" he asked.

I didn't want to get his hopes up too high. But he smiled— that sweet boyish smile that made a little part of me melt inside—and I couldn't refuse to answer. "Like the International Women's Union," I said.

"You think they'd be interested in *my* play?" His eyes grew large, and I resisted the urge to cross my fingers in hopes that I could make the sponsorship come together.

"We can't know until we ask," I said firmly. "And I have other ideas, as backups. So it's a deal? You'll do it? You'll go meet sponsors with me?"

He shook the hand that I extended. Once again, I felt the hint of calluses against my own pampered fingers, a silent reminder of the hard work that he'd put in half a world away. "It's a deal," he said.

Both our mugs were empty. I'd run out of excuses to stick

around. Reluctantly, I stood up. "I know you're going to jump online now," I said with a laugh. "Log in to ShowTalk and learn everything you can about the Mercer."

He looked up at me sideways, suddenly lapsed back to boyish shyness. "Actually, I already checked you out."

"You what!" Something about his tone said that he had checked *me* out. Not just the Mercer.

"I logged in to ShowTalk last night. After we talked." At his confession, one of my cursed blushes flooded my cheeks. I could just imagine what he'd typed after he'd helped me with my stubborn lock. I'd accepted bribes on the show, he would have told everyone. I'd stumbled home drunk. "Hey," he said, as I fumbled for something, anything to say. "Relax. There were just a few of us online that late."

Yeah. Like that made me feel any better. "It's just…last night, I was sort of… I…" What? I was just drinking myself into oblivion because my love life was in the toilet? Because my career was landing beside it? Because… Why *had* I been downing those Godmothers?

"You what?" He saved me from myself. "You had a really crappy day, starting out with an incredibly pushy playwright cornering you at the office to give you his play? And then you found out that your…your director of finance had walked off with a quarter of your theater's budget? And half of New York's theater community was writing about you on ShowTalk? And somewhere along the way, you learned that you had a gaping hole in your schedule because of some legal whatchamajig?" His gaze was serious, and his lips quirked in a sympathetic smile.

I decided to match that smile, so that I didn't cry. "What-chamajig," I said. "You've really got a way with words."

"Good thing I decided to write plays for a living."

I laughed at his disarming reply. "Thanks," I said. "For the tea and, um, everything."

"Anytime."

I thought about my empty kitchen. "You probably don't want to say that, with me living just across the hall."

He shook his head and crossed to the door with me. "And what are the odds of that?"

Of course, I couldn't tell him about Teel. My throat would close up, just as it had when I'd tried to tell Jenn about my genie. I shrugged, and muttered something inane about coincidence.

When Ryan reached across me to open the door, I could feel the heat of his body, rising through the sleeve of his sweater. For one crazy second, I pictured myself leaning closer to him, feeling that energy far more up close and personal.

Of course, I stopped myself. Getting involved with Ryan Thompson would be absolutely insane. He and I had to work together for two long months. Life would be crazy enough, bringing his play to fruition. Our relationship needed to stay strictly professional.

Nevertheless, Ryan seemed to have sensed my thoughts. He tumbled back into his awkwardness, hunching his shoulders and sliding his hands back into the pockets of his jeans. "Thanks for coming by, Becca. For giving me the good news in person," he said. "I appreciate it. Really."

"You're welcome," I said.

I thought about hugging him goodbye, but we really didn't know each other well enough for that. I would have offered to shake hands, but that seemed too much like the way to conclude a business meeting, too formal and distancing for the rapport we were going to need, so that we could build our production. I considered leaning in and kissing him on the cheek, but I wondered if he would try to kiss on both cheeks, if they even did that in Africa, like they did in Europe. I settled for coughing a little and saying, "You're welcome," again.

And then I scurried into my own apartment.

I should have gone straight back to the office. But it wouldn't hurt for me to take a short break at home, to see how the place looked in full daylight.

Just as I closed the door behind me, my cell phone rang. I fished it out of my bag and stared at an unfamiliar 212 phone number. Curious as to who'd be calling me in the middle of the workday, I hurried to answer before the call could go to my voice mail. "Hello?"

"Miss Morris, this is Detective Warren Ambrose. I've been assigned to the Dean Marcus case, and I wanted to follow up with you about a few things."

Great. Hal had told me that he'd given the police my phone number, but I'd hoped that they would never need to use it. I could hear Detective Ambrose swallowing a yawn before he continued, "Miss Morris, we're looking into some data that we found on Mr. Marcus's computer. What do you know about his plans to visit Russia?"

Russia. Dean had never *mentioned* Russia. As far as I knew, he might never have heard of the country. "Why would he go there?"

"Were you aware of his plane reservations, Miss Morris?"

"No, I—" All of the air was forced out of my lungs. "No," I repeated.

"Miss Morris, did you know that he obtained a visa to travel to Russia?"

"No," I said again. And suddenly I wondered how many other things I didn't know about the man I'd dated for the past three years. "But he's there now?"

"So it seems, Miss Morris."

"But why Russia? That doesn't make any sense at all."

"It does, Miss Morris, when you realize they don't have an extradition treaty with the United States."

The words settled into my belly like a frozen stone. Dean's theft from the Mercer wasn't some momentary lapse of judgment. He had planned this whole thing for a long time. He had completed the appropriate paperwork. He'd engineered the perfect escape. He'd never planned on coming back, never planned on explaining to me, never planned on telling me why he'd done everything that he'd done.

Ambrose tossed more questions at me, remaining completely formal, always saying "Miss Morris" this and "Miss Morris" that. I answered without really hearing myself.

Part of me was braced for truly difficult questions. How had I ended up with a condo in the Bentley, fully owned, one hundred percent paid up? How was I living in the lap of luxury when my bank account had been emptied by the guy who was now Russia's newest, biggest fan?

But those issues never came up. Apparently, Teel's magic protected me, covered for me, explained away the biggest gap in my changed state.

No, I just needed to tell Ambrose about how I had not had any idea that the man I'd dated for three and a half years was a lying, cheating, cowardly, thieving (even from me!) felon. Easy, peasy.

At last, Ambrose hung up, sighing and promising to call me again when he had more information.

I looked around the condo, the first permanent step I'd taken to separate myself from the lie I'd unwittingly shared. Ambrose didn't seem at all suspicious of my genie-gotten wealth. I was safe. This was my home. My life. I walked into the master bedroom, forcing myself to admire the view from the window. I turned around and threw open the closet doors, claiming them like Columbus staking out the New World.

And then I closed them. I didn't actually have anything *hanging* in the closets. That would have to wait until after my eagerly anticipated paycheck arrived. And the delay of that paycheck was going to cause a problem…

I couldn't visit potential Mercer sponsors wearing sweatpants or jeans. I needed something that looked professional. Something that said "Invest thousands of dollars with the Mercer, so that our businesses can grow together."

Sure, I worked in the theater. We artistic types could get away with a lot. We could combine colors and textures, accessorize with rampant creativity. But we couldn't ignore every last business rule with complete impunity. I had nine days to pin down a sponsor for *However Long*. I didn't have time to wait for payday.

Knowing what I had to do, I knelt beside the king-size bed. I reached beneath the 1000-count sheets, shouldering aside the lush duvet. For just a second, I worried that my treasure was missing, but then my sweeping fingers found the pillowcase that Kira had handed over the day before.

If the featherlight tattoos on my fingertips stood out sharply against the blue cloth, they positively *glowed* against the shiny brass of the lantern. I turned my thumb toward the window, marveling at the precision of those individual flames, at the perfect tattoo that had painlessly appeared on my flesh. Before I could lose my nerve, I pinched my finger and thumb together, saying in an overloud voice, "Teel!"

This time, I expected the fog to billow from the lamp. I expected the jangle of jewel-colored lights, dazzling my eyes as if I were the victim of too many paparazzi photographs. I expected the sudden coalescence of those lights into a human form.

I just wasn't prepared for the precise human form that emerged.

Apparently, Teel moonlighted for Con Ed when he wasn't hanging out in a courtroom or entertaining kids under the big top. He manifested as a burly man with a bad five o'clock shadow and no neck. His filthy coveralls looked like they'd been orange before he'd dragged them through every tunnel beneath Manhattan. His wide leather belt was heavy with wire cutters and pliers and tools that I couldn't even begin to name. His tattoo was clearly visible, though, blazing out between the wiry black hairs on his fat wrist. "You rang?" he said in a voice so thoroughly dipped in the Bronx that I almost laughed out loud.

Almost laughed, but for the fact that this genie, this Teel, was utterly unsuited to the wish I planned to make. Sure, he'd be great if I wanted a tour of underground Manhattan. Not so bad, if I wanted to figure out how to become an expert cat burglar, to break in somewhere and commandeer a public building. He'd be a charm, if I wanted to rewire a theater, to create an electrical superstructure that could handle multiple shows drawing from a single power supply.

But a new wardrobe? I didn't think so. "What are you doing dressed like that?" I asked.

"Youse got a problem with how I'm dressed?" He sounded like Bugs Bunny's more pugnacious brother. "I'm tellin' youse, a guy's gotta do what a guy's gotta do."

"And that means working for the utility company?"

"I don't ask what youse do with yer spare time." He had a point. But I wouldn't spend my time crawling around sewers. Or crawl-spaces. Or wherever Con Ed guys crawled. Teel grunted like a bull. "Got a wish?"

"Um, yeah." I twisted my fingers around each other. Quick. Think of something else. Think of a wish that this human wall could grant.

But that was ridiculous. Teel was Teel. Male, female, lawyer, clown—the genie was the same creature, no matter her appearance. His appearance. Whatever.

"Great," he growled. "Yer one of the six."

"Six?" I had no idea what he was talking about.

"Six out of ten. The ones who make yer second wish within twenty-four hours of yer first." That's right. He had spouted off that statistic. "We got a special goin', you know. If youse make three more wishes today, then I'll stay out of yer hair forever."

"Isn't that the deal, anyway? I make my wishes, and you move on to the next lucky person?"

He sighed like a whale surfacing from the vasty deep. "Always with the wise-guy stuff."

"I don't mean to be a…wise guy," I said primly.

He harrumphed, then nodded toward me with his bristly chin. "So? What'll it be?"

I was going to have to go through with this, Con Ed guy or no Con Ed guy. If my wish turned out to be an utter disaster, I'd still have two more to clean things up. "I need some new clothes," I said. "I have a lot of meetings to go to, business meetings, with important people. People who have money that I want to get, for the Mercer."

"Clothes, huh?" He scratched at his filthy coveralls.

"Can you do that? I mean, do you know the right type of clothes?" I nodded toward his current costume, arching my eyebrows in an expression that I hoped would convey that I wasn't *judging*. I was only asking questions. Like a responsible lamp-holder.

"My clothes ain't got nothing to do with yer wishes."

"Then it's okay? If I wish for something to wear?"

"Sure, lady. But youse still got to make yer request in the form of a wish."

Oh. I'd known I was forgetting something. I closed my eyes and tried to swallow the swooping feeling of distrust, the fear that I was making a huge mistake. "I wish that I had a new wardrobe, suitable for meeting with sponsors." I paused, but then I realized I had to give more details—for my peace of mind, if not for Teel's edification. "I'm sorry," I spluttered. "I really need everything. All my clothes are back at the old place, so I'm going to need everything from head to toe, you know, underwear and shoes, too. I'm going—"

The lineman rolled his eyes and raised one hairy hand to his ear. His tattoo flashed against his swarthy flesh, as if it were reminding me that appearances—all appearances—could be deceiving. He belched as he leaned forward into a grudging half bow. "As youse wish," he said. He tugged at his ear twice, and I was so disgusted by the burp that I almost forgot to brace myself for the flash of magic, for the tingle that swept over me from head to foot.

When the electric wave had passed, I breathed a quick

prayer to whatever god or goddess was in charge of Teel's handiwork. Setting my jaw against disappointment, I tugged open my closet door.

And I almost collapsed onto the thick carpet. The closet looked like a display piece in some designer showroom. Two dozen pairs of pants were draped over specialty hangers, marching in a subdued rainbow of earth tones. A quick glance confirmed variations in fabric and styling, but every piece looked like it had been tailored just for me. Lower closet rods displayed a forest of tops—the same earth tones, enriched with hints of deep, jewel-like color. Some had subtle patterns woven into the fabric; others were stark and perfect in their simplicity. A few had sequins, making them ideal for a gala opening night. Dresses hung from their own rod, spanning the options from casual to formal.

Shelves had magically appeared in the closet, and they were filled with accessories. I saw three shawls, each a different weave, a different weight. A jewelry box was open, displaying a dozen necklaces, complete with matching earrings. Shoes marched across the front of the closet, neat pairs that were sleek and sophisticated without shouting out trendy soon-to-be-passé designer names.

"I put yer lingerie in the dresser," Teel grunted. The French word sounded bizarre in his New York twang. I suddenly remembered to breathe.

"Um, thanks," I said. "I'm sure it's perfect. All of it is. It's just…incredible."

"Yeah, yeah." He settled a hammy fist over his tool belt and sighed. "As long as we're talkin', lady, are youse ready to make yer other wishes?"

"Not yet," I murmured, resisting the urge to slip a cashmere dress off its hanger, then and there.

"Youse saw the Garden, right? Youse understand what yer makin' me wait on?"

"Yes, Teel. I saw your Garden." Eye contact always made lies easier to sell. I remembered Kira's warning, and I steeled myself to challenge our genie. "I saw it, but I'm not going to rush my wishes just to get you in faster."

Again, that exasperated sigh, like a hippo discovering its mud wallow had gone dry. "Yer delay is leavin' me with a lot of downtime, lady. I can only read so many girlie mags in one incarnation."

That was an image I could have lived without forever. I bristled. "In all of Manhattan, you can't find some better way to pass the time?"

"It's not that simple, lady. I gotta be ready for whenever youse decide to call me. I can't be sitting in no bar, or talking to no cute girls. I can't just disappear into thin air, in front o' other people." Yeah, I suppose that might have been a problem. Disappearing barflies can really be bad for business. "You could do something, though," Teel said, and his bass voice dropped into a register that I was probably supposed to find seductive.

"What's that?"

"Take me to work with you. Youse got all these meetings…" He nodded at my wardrobe.

"I can't take a Con Ed lineman into meetings with potential sponsors!"

In a flash, that hairy wrist flew up to his ear, tugging so hard that I feared for his aural health. Suddenly, a pimply teenager stood in front of me, gawky, awkward, wearing a suit that was a full size too large, and a tie that had come pre-knotted. His voice broke as he said, "What about this?" He cleared his throat and started again. "What about an intern?"

I stared, dumbfounded, and he tugged at his ear again. A young woman stood in place of Zit Boy, her ample figure filling out a Fair Isle sweater. "Or an assistant?"

"I've already got an assistant," I said automatically, loyal to Jenn.

Another ear-tug. "Then a clerk from the accounting department." The middle-aged man had combed his hair across his balding skull. His cardigan sweater was buttoned up as if he were channeling Mr. Rogers.

"We're not that sort of company! We don't have accounting clerks."

Teel's watery eyes blinked. "Then you tell me," he said adenoidally. "Thirteen out of twenty wishers bring their genie to work. I want to count you with the thirteen. Who would go to a meeting with you? I'll be that person, anyone!"

I hovered indecisively. On the one hand, bringing Teel along could throw a definite wrench into things. I didn't know him, didn't know exactly what he might do, how he would behave. On the other hand, though, I owed the genie something. My delay was the only reason he wasn't rushing toward his Garden with open arms. Another little thought uncurled at the back of my mind: Teel would be a ready-made chaperone. No one—myself included—could accuse me of acting inappropriately, dramaturg to playwright, if Ryan and I had a constant traveling companion.

"You can be a student," I said at last. "Visiting from Yale. A woman who is shadowing me for a week, to see what dramaturgs do. The university sets up externships all the time. That would make sense."

The accountant nodded vehemently. "Woman. Yale. Student. Got it."

Something about the enthusiastic reply made me wary. "Let me see her," I said.

Teel sighed, as if he bore all the weight of the world, but he tugged at his ear again. A woman stood in front of me—medium height, probably ten pounds heavier than she should be. Her shoulder-length hair was straight; she hadn't bothered with barrettes or hair bands. Her olive skin bore the faintest hint of makeup—a touch of blush, a light dash of mascara, some lip gloss. She wore a black turtleneck and khakis, perfectly logical attire, given the early-spring weather outside. Her flame tattoo was hidden under the cuff of her sweater.

"Okay," I said, nodding slowly. "You can come with us. But you'll have to keep that ink hidden. A lot of people still don't accept tattoos in business meetings."

"Not a problem," she said, her tone perfectly reasonable.

"It'll take me a day or two to set up the meetings. I'll let you know as soon as we're ready."

The young woman flashed me a grin. Her teeth were perfect; she could have modeled for any dentist in the country, if her so-called dramaturgy career ever fell apart. "Thanks," she said. Her voice was deep, throaty. Confident.

"Don't mention it," I said. "Now, if I can just find the perfect sponsors…"

"Is that a wish?" Teel leaped to attention, fingertips already settling on her lobe.

"No! I'll tell you when I'm ready to make my next wish!"

She sighed. "Just don't wait too long, okay?"

I shook my head. "I'll wait as long as I need to." Two wishes were all that I had left. I wasn't about to make one on a whim. "Stop pouting! You'll have enough to entertain you, going to meetings with Ryan and me."

Alas, truer words were never spoken.

CHAPTER 8

I SHOULD HAVE KNOWN BETTER THAN TO TRUST A GENIE.

I'd had ample warning. Kira had rolled her eyes enough as she'd told me her own experiences with Teel. She'd hinted at the havoc that one supposedly innocent genie could wreak on a perfectly normal social interaction. I'd seen a bit of it myself—I mean, any creature who was willing to pull totally innocent human beings into an invisible, silent, absolutely unable-to-be-detected hallucination of a Garden…

But despite everything I knew, I felt sorry for Teel. I felt guilty for abandoning him. I felt responsible for his relying on dirty magazines to pass the day, at least in his Con Ed guise. And so, four days later, Ryan and I found ourselves waiting for my genie in a coffee shop, just around the corner from the International Women's Union headquarters.

We were sitting in a booth. Both of us had set aside the gigantic menus that were typical of a New York coffee shop—pages and pages of breakfast, of sandwiches, of salads and massive entrées, a hodge-podge of foods that vaguely declared an allegiance to Greece, by way of an American deep fat fryer.

Nope, at ten-thirty in the morning, coffee was all we needed. After all, we were just using the restaurant to kill time. To kill time and to organize our offensive. I tapped the folder I'd brought with me. "So, I'll take the lead, explaining why the Mercer thinks your play is a story that needs to be told, why we chose it now."

Ryan nodded. He'd updated his geek-boy wardrobe for our meeting, managing a tie and an oxford cloth shirt beneath a bulky brown sweater that I suspected earth-mother Dani might have knit. Unfortunately, his hair was already beginning to rebel against the combing that he'd given it. My fingers longed to reach across the table, to smooth it back into place, but I knew that my fussing would only make him more nervous.

He made the issue moot by running his own hands through his hair as he sneaked out an anxious laugh. Glancing at his watch, he pounced on his coffee cup, ignoring the fact that the liquid was the approximate temperature of a nuclear power plant core as he gulped a healthy swig.

"Relax," I said, purposely lowering my voice to an intimate sing-song. "This is going to be fine."

"Easy for you to say. You take these meetings all the time. This is the first one I've gone to since interviewing for my Peace Corps post."

I contemplated telling him that I hadn't attended a single outside meeting since taking over the Mercer's dramaturgy position six months before. Oh, I had *planned* some meetings, all for the coming season. And Hal had designated me the chief correspondent for our ill-fated *Crystal Dreams;* that would have resulted in lots of meetings. And I'd studied the science and art of meetings in school, sitting through incredibly boring classes on finance, so that I knew all the right words to use, the correct phrases to dangle, the way to sound like a trustworthy businesswoman.

But actually presenting a case, arguing that my theater company was worth the investment of a donor's hard-earned money? That was all new to me. Newer than the Eileen Fisher cardigan sweater I'd draped over a silk turtleneck that morning, tying the cashmere belt with a casual twist, as if I always wore designer clothes.

No. Ryan and I would both be better off if I didn't share just how nervous I was.

I glanced at my own watch. T minus fifteen minutes, and still no sign of Teel. I wondered if I should excuse myself, head to the bathroom. I could lock myself in a stall and press my tattooed fingers together, summon my genie from wherever she'd gotten to.

My eyes darted around the restaurant. Was she playing some game, hiding out in one of the booths, masquerading in a form unknown to me? From my current vantage point, I couldn't begin to make out the wrists of every single customer, couldn't spy the flames that would be Teel's dead giveaway. Any single person—male or female, young or old— could have been my genie. Watching. Waiting. Amused, no doubt, at my expense.

Yet another glance at my watch. Another wince as Ryan scalded his throat with coffee.

And then Teel swept in.

It was the teeth that gave her away. Those perfect teeth,

flashing against a slick of lip gloss. Lip gloss, and a tawny foundation that made her look like she'd just returned from a month-long stay at a beach resort.

And mascara. Lots and lots and lots of mascara.

Did I mention the mascara?

None of which would have been a big deal, really, if Teel had dressed the way she had in my bedroom a few days before. Somehow, though, she'd misunderstood when I'd given her notice of the meeting, when I'd told her we were going to the International Women's Union. She must have thought I'd said *Hookers'* Union.

It had never crossed my mind that a real woman might actually wear fishnet stockings, especially in the first week of March. *I* certainly wouldn't have risked them, rubbing between my toes inside my thigh-high leather boots. They couldn't provide her with any actual warmth, any insulation at all beneath her tiny plaid, schoolgirl miniskirt.

At least she'd worn a blouse with long sleeves, as I'd demanded. Her tattoo was completely invisible. Foolish me, though. I had completely forgotten to mention that a bra was a required undergarment. And it had never crossed my mind that scarlet might be considered an appropriate fashion statement for the boardroom.

What had happened to my conservative little dramaturgy student? Where had the demure khakis-and-sweater woman gone?

This meeting was going to be a disaster.

"There you are!" Great. In addition to raiding the closet at Slutwear United, my genie had adopted a bubble voice that would have put Marilyn Monroe to shame.

She sailed over to our table. Ryan started to stand out of

polite reflex, but she settled him back in the booth with crimson talons on his shoulder. "Please! Don't get up!"

I was ashamed for all Yale dramaturgy students everywhere, real and imagined.

Teel slid in beside me, looking expectantly at Ryan. "Um, Ryan Thompson," I said, by way of introduction. "This is Teel—" I didn't know my genie's last name. I didn't even know if my genie *had* a last name. "Daugherty," I tossed out, silently remonstrating with myself to remember her made-up name for the rest of the day.

"Charmed," she said, offering her hand across the table. It was almost an accident when her winter-white flesh came dangerously close to tumbling out of her blouse.

"This is the student I told you about," I said to Ryan, hoping to deflate his goggle eyes. "She's in the same program that I graduated from last year, taking courses in *professional* dramaturgy." I emphasized the penultimate word, barely resisting the urge to pinch her leg beneath the table. Hard.

"Eleven out of twelve dramaturgy students complete externships," Teel breathed.

"Um, of course," Ryan said, but the three words sounded like a question. A mighty confused question. An absolutely uncertain, Becca-have-you-taken-leave-of-your-senses question.

I sighed. "We'd better get going." I added to Teel through set teeth, "Don't you have a coat? It's freezing out there!"

"Oh, no." She batted those painted lashes at me. "I'm actually quite hot."

Ryan blushed.

I took the opportunity to elbow Teel as I slid out of the booth. "Quit it!" I whispered as loudly as I dared. She pretended not to hear me.

Things didn't get better as we made our way to the Union. Or as we waited in the reception area. Or as we sat down in a conference room opposite Ms. Eleanor Samuelson, the vice president in charge of community relations.

I fervently wished that Ryan and I had been accompanied by the first Teel I'd ever met. Lawyer-Teel and Ms. Samuelson would have had a lot in common, starting with their conservative navy suits. Ms. Samuelson inspected my current genie's incarnation over the top of her eyeglasses, raising a single haughty eyebrow in silent summary of her evaluation. Somehow, though, we made it through the introductory phase of the meeting. I explained what the Mercer was all about. Ryan delivered his elevator pitch for *However Long,* reducing the power of his play to about three minutes.

Ms. Samuelson leaned back in her chair, tapping the eraser of her needle-sharp pencil against the wooden table. "I have to tell you, the Union has never undertaken this kind of sponsorship before. I wouldn't even be talking to you, if it weren't for a new initiative that we're launching. We've declared this to be the Year of the Young Woman. We want to build our membership from the ground up, increase the number of women that we reach. Some of my colleagues think that contemporary theater might be a way to do that."

Some of her colleagues. But not Ms. Samuelson, I was willing to bet. Nevertheless, I smiled encouragingly, ready to explain that our missions could mesh well. Before I could speak, though, Teel leaned forward, stopping just short of cascading out of her blouse entirely. "If I could address that?" She cooed, "Since only one out of four of us *is* a young woman?"

What the hell did she think I was? A patient on the geriatric ward? I glared at her. Her job—her *entire* job—was to sit still and keep her mouth shut.

Before I could figure out a way to take back control, Teel pursed her glossy lips and bubbled, "Young women want challenges. We want excitement, for excitement's sake. We aren't dried up and boring and *old.*"

From across the table, I could see a fine sheen of sweat break out on Ryan's upper lip. I couldn't tell if he was reacting to Teel's seductive wriggling, or if he feared our source of potential funding was about to evaporate before our very eyes.

Ms. Samuelson straightened in her chair, and hard lines deepened from her flared nostrils to the corners of her mouth. "Here at the Union, Ms. Daugherty, we believe that young women want to be recognized for their ability. For what they contribute to the world around them."

"And that is why—" I started to say, but I was silenced by Teel's hyena laugh, a shocking bray that seemed especially loud after her floating voice of mock-innocence.

"Blah-de-blah-de-blah, blah, blah," she said. "All your fancy words don't add up to one single woman's real experience. One single *young* woman, anyway."

"Teel!" I gasped.

Ms. Samuelson pursed her lips and said, "I can assure you that we've commissioned some of the country's finest academics to study this problem for us. We're not *improvising* answers, Ms. Daugherty. We're studying them. We're committing to them."

Teel yawned, opening her mouth and curling her tongue with the complete dedication to the task that only a sleepy, fireside cat could demonstrate. Before she could say one more word, I grabbed her arm and tugged her out of her chair, out of the conference room, into the hallway.

"What the hell do you think you're doing?" I muttered.

"Trust me," she whispered. And then she giggled, like Gidget's flightier younger sister.

"You are destroying this meeting!"

"I'm making it more interesting." She took advantage of the glass on a framed print commemorating the Seneca Falls Convention to reapply her lip gloss.

"We don't want 'interesting,' Teel! We want professional! We want boring and mundane and staid and trustworthy! We want *money!*"

My voice had risen as I berated my genie. My vocal cords tightened as my anger spiked, each word becoming a little more shrill than the one before, until I sounded like a very loud, very hyper Minnie Mouse. On helium.

I glanced over my shoulder. In my rush to extricate Teel, I hadn't closed the conference room door.

I swore. "Stay here," I said. She started to answer, and I snapped, "No!" She drew another breath and I glared. "Not. One. More. Word."

I went back into the conference room. Ryan was doing an excellent impression of an arborist, studying the table as if it held the secret to all known tree life. Dani would be proud of him. She might even be able to use his acquired knowledge for her guerilla gardening.

Ms. Samuelson was staring daggers at him, but she transferred her gaze to me as soon as I crossed the threshold.

"Ms. Morris, contrary to your apparent expectation, the International Women's Union is not a bank." She spat out the last word. "We build partnerships with organizations. We work with like-minded groups to advance the cause of women. All women. If the only thing you desire is *money*—"

the word had never sounded so absolutely, completely filthy "—then I can assure you this meeting is done."

"I'm sorry," I said, loading my words with all the emotion I truly felt. "We've gotten off on the wrong foot."

My mind raced as I tried to think of something, anything, that could redeem us. Before I found my words, though, Teel laughed from the hallway. Each of us heard her coo to an unknown person, "Have you heard the one about the lap-dancer and the rabbi—"

"Teel!" I screamed.

"We'll be going now," Ryan said, standing stiffly.

"I think that would be best," Ms. Samuelson answered. The old expression "If looks could kill" was seared into my brain.

"Thank you for your time," I whispered. I don't think Ms. Samuelson heard me, though. Teel's bray sucked every last molecule of air from the building. We saw ourselves out.

"I am so sorry."

"You said that before." Ryan's voice was tight, and he refused to meet my eyes. Instead, he found the mottled work-bench in front of us fascinating, nearly as enthralling as the purple grow-lights that gave us both a ghastly pallor.

Dani emerged from her bedroom, frowning as she carried a stack of gray cups that looked like moldy rejects from the Dixie factory. She kept her voice completely neutral as she said, "Yes, she did, Ry. At least twice since I got here. I think she's waiting for you to accept her apology."

I had sent Teel away as soon as we all escaped from the International Women's Union. I'd reminded my genie that she had a "train" to catch, to get back to a "class" in "New Haven." I'd been so furious that I'd considered blowing her cover entirely, but even in my rage, I'd been pretty sure that she'd find a way to close off my throat, to knock me silent even as I blasted her. She'd make me look like an even bigger idiot in front of Ryan, in front of all of New York City.

With Teel gone, I'd apologized to Ryan for the first time. He'd only shaken his head and started the trek back home to the Bentley. The wind had been brisk in our faces, and I'd thought about hailing a cab, but I was reluctant to spend the Mercer's money in light of my utter failure to score a sponsor for the play. After about six blocks, though, I'd considered spending my own severely limited funds. It was *cold* out there. Alas, when I looked around, there wasn't a single cab to be found.

Ryan and I had trudged on, our silence growing heavier with every passing block. Only when we'd made it to our respective front doors on the Bentley's eighth floor did I manage to apologize again, stammering out an absurd-sounding explanation about how Teel had seemed totally reasonable when I'd met her before, when she'd approached me about her externship.

Before Ryan could respond, Dani had alighted from the elevator, balancing a bag of potting soil across a granny cart that rattled in the carpeted hallway. "What a day!" she'd exclaimed, waving a piece of paper in front of her.

Desperate for a break from genie-induced misery, I had sprung to my neighbor's assistance. The piece of paper turned out to be a citation she'd received from one of New York City's finest. Despite the bitter wind blowing outside, Dani had decided to turn the earth around four trees on our block, getting them ready for some secret guerilla midnight planting, once the danger of frost was past. It was just bad luck that a tired, bored, cold cop had stopped her, demanding to know what she was doing. Her behavior must have seemed especially strange, given the bite in the air.

In the end, he'd issued a written citation for trespassing. It wouldn't amount to much, so long as she wasn't stopped again in the next year. Nevertheless, Dani had seemed particularly peeved, especially because she'd been stopped on her way out to the hardware store to purchase the potting soil she needed for some secretive guerilla exploit.

I'd made consoling noises as I helped her balance the dirt on top of her wheeled metal cart. Before I could extricate myself from the situation, though, with whatever limited grace I could still command after Teel's destructive interference, Dani had ushered me into her living room, telling me to take off my delicate cashmere wrap-around sweater. Barely taking time to greet her own son, Dani had handed me a work smock to put over my turtleneck. She'd added a pair of heavy leather gloves, promising that I was about to get my first lesson in guerilla gardening.

Ryan, far more accustomed to his mother's green thumb ventures than I, had ducked behind the screen in the living room, emerging seconds later in torn jeans and a bleach-stained sweatshirt. He'd completed the transition from petitioning playwright to grubby greensman so quickly that I wondered if he was some sort of closet superhero.

Garden-Man to the rescue!

Yeah. Like Garden-Man could do anything to redeem the disaster of the meeting we'd just fled.

Dani seemed oblivious to the tension between Ryan and me. I couldn't help but think how different Dani was from my own mother. Mom would have zeroed in on my frustration from a mile off. She would have initiated a spirited game of Twenty Questions until she'd dug out precisely what had gone wrong in my morning meeting. After half an hour, I would have known exactly how my mother would have resolved the situation, complete with simple, easy-to-quote statements that I should have used in the heat of our Union encounter.

It wasn't that my mother didn't trust me to come up with solutions on my own. It was just that hers were so much better. Or so it was easier for everyone to believe. I really did love her, but there was a reason I kept an entire continent between my mother and me most of the time. Especially when my problems were related to theater, to dramaturgy, something she knew nothing about.

Dani, on the other hand, pretended that there wasn't anything massively wrong between Ryan and me. She talked about herself, babbling easily about the Gray Guerillas' latest project. She apparently never noticed that Ryan and I weren't speaking—not to her and not to each other. I shrugged. As long as I was a captive of the green army, I decided to take an interest in their work. It was better than apologizing to Ryan. Again.

Just as I reached that conclusion, my cell phone rang. I dragged it out of my pocket, frowning at the screen. The number was vaguely familiar. 212— That was it. Detective Ambrose. The policeman investigating Dean's disappearance.

I mouthed an excuse to Dani and Ryan and answered the call. "Rebecca Morris."

"Miss Morris." A gusty sigh. "Detective Ambrose here."

I wondered if the guy ever hyperventilated, sighing so deeply. He sounded so despondent, I felt my own shoulders sag in sympathy. "Yes, Detective?" I saw both Dani and Ryan perk up, paying closer attention to my call.

"Miss Morris, can you tell me the significance of the number one-nine-zero-eight?"

My voice hardened. "Nineteen-oh-eight. The last year the Chicago Cubs won the World Series. Dean was a big Cubs fan. We used 1908 as our PIN for our shared bank account."

If I hadn't heard the clicking on Ambrose's computer keyboard, I would have thought that he hadn't heard me. After an eternity, he said, "And, Miss Morris, the word *Puffpuff?*"

That question knocked the wind out of me. I actually staggered back a couple of steps, had to reach out to steady myself on the back of the living room couch. Dani looked concerned; she reached for my phone as if she were going to make the prying detective go away. I set my jaw, though, and shook my head. "Puffpuff is a stuffed animal, Detective."

"Miss Morris?" I'd caught him by surprise there. The sound of clacking computer keys disappeared.

"It's a stuffed dog I've had since I was a baby. Puffpuff. I kept her on our…" My throat closed over the next word, and I was suddenly furious with myself that I'd taken this call here, in front of Dani. In front of Ryan. "Bed," I whispered.

Ambrose sighed, as if he'd already expected such a sordid detail. Or was that just his usual, everyday tragic sigh? I couldn't be sure. "Miss Morris, did you use *Puffpuff* as a password on any of your computer accounts with Mr. Marcus?"

His formality, his constantly using my name in questions was grating on me. I wanted to tell him to call me Becca, to talk to me as if we were friends. But we weren't friends, of course. We never would be.

"Puffpuff. No."

"And, Miss Morris, did you ever use 1908 as a password?"

"No," I said again. "Just that one PIN."

"But, Miss Morris, it would not surprise you to learn that Mr. Marcus used those words, separately, or together, as a password on multiple bank accounts, both in the United States and abroad?"

"No," I whispered. I cleared my throat. "No, I wouldn't be surprised. Can you tell me exactly what sort of accounts? What is this about?"

"I'm not at liberty to say anything more, Miss Morris." Another one of those gusty sighs, as if his heart were breaking. Or as if he were about to fall asleep. "I'll be back in touch, Miss Morris, as we need more information."

He hung up before I could ask anything else. Like how they'd figured out the passwords. Like whether I was implicated, because Dean had used my stuffed animal's name. Like whether they were any closer to tracking Dean down in Russia.

I shuddered. Dean's using Puffpuff's name made me feel filthy, as if he'd purposely dragged me into his cruel, manipulative games. I supposed that I should feel lucky that Ambrose had been content with letting me go after such a quick telephonic questioning. I didn't feel lucky, though. I felt as if the entire world was closing in around me. Was stacked against me. Was laughing cruelly as I failed yet again.

Shoving my phone back into my bag, I surprised myself by brushing a few angry tears off my cheeks. I could only hope that my eyes were clear by the time I looked up at Dani and Ryan.

"Well?" I said, more brusquely than I intended. "Are we going to get started with this?"

A plastic sheet covered the floor in front of the workbench, apparently Dani's one concession to stodgy notions of traditional property value. Stepping onto the plastic carefully, Dani made sure that her Birkenstocks had a solid grip before she started to set out her gray cups in neat, expectant rows. They turned out to be made from pressed peat moss, as sturdy as paper, but clearly more friendly to green, growing things.

Dani dropped the cups into rows with the timing and precision of a competitive speed-stacker. Watching her practiced fingers, I was pretty sure that any Atlantic City casino would offer her a job as a blackjack dealer, if she ever decided to give up her life of ecological warfare and go legitimate.

"Ready?" she asked brightly, when the entire array was spread in front of us. "Now, Ry, I'm sure you remember how to do this."

He grunted. Dani smiled as if he had started whistling a tune happy enough to rival one of Snow White's dwarves.

She elaborated for my benefit. "We take that plastic tub, and we fill it with one small bag of potting soil and a bucket of compost." Ryan tore open the former with a ferocity that made me truly fear for Teel's safety if he ever saw her in her hooker garb again. Dani stared at him for a moment, but then she turned to me with a placid smile, offering a plastic pail, as if I were a child playing on a sandy beach. "The compost is in the kitchen."

"How can you keep it there?" I asked, intrigued despite myself. "Doesn't it stink?"

"Not if it's kept balanced. I've had that system stable for…what has it been, Ry? Five years?"

He grunted again. Dani's attempts at healing through conversation were failing. Miserably.

"Aren't there worms?" I asked. Nevertheless, I took the bucket like I gardened inside a Manhattan apartment every day. Anything was better than staying around Ryan's grim silence. "Will I hurt them?"

Dani laughed. "I sifted the whole thing earlier today. I set the worms aside, knowing that I'd be working this afternoon. I'll add them back in when I'm done." She glanced at both of us. "When *we're* done. I wasn't expecting so much help."

Yet another grunt from Ryan. Maybe this return to a Peace Corps environment of working with his hands had made him forget how to speak English.

Or else Teel had. Teel and her stupid, bored-little-magic-girl tricks.

Reciting another tirade against my genie in my head, I went into the kitchen and filled the pail with compost. Dani was smiling gently when I returned. "There you go! Mix it up in the plastic bin."

Ryan stepped aside to make room for me at the workbench. His action was exaggerated, as if he were afraid I'd give him girl cooties. "I'm sorry," I said again, knowing that I wasn't really talking about where we were standing.

After hesitating a moment, Ryan said, "That's okay." He cleared his throat. "I know that you didn't mean to let things get out of hand back there."

Progress!

I dumped the compost into the bin, and we started to mix the soils together. Despite Dani's reassurance, I expected the stuff from the kitchen to stink, but it really didn't. It just smelled like fresh earth, warm after a summer rain shower. I trailed my hands through the bin, watching the different shades of brown combine.

"We've got other chances," I said, forcing my voice to sound natural. "I have ideas for other sponsors."

Ryan swallowed hard. "It's just that the *International Women's Union*…"

"I know," I said. "But other people are going to understand what we're doing. Other people are going to get your play. I promise."

He sighed. "The Mercer shouldn't even be doing *However Long*."

"What do you mean?" I was shocked. "I'm thrilled that we get to produce it."

He shook his head, refusing to meet my eyes. "It just isn't right. There have to be other authors, other plays that you've considered for so much longer.…"

I started to understand why he was so upset. Success was scary—especially in a field as competitive as the one he'd chosen. I'd spoken to other playwrights before. I recognized the emotional struggle Ryan was going through. On the one hand, he had to make himself believe that his play was brilliant, that it was perfect, that it was going to succeed against all odds. On the other hand, though, he knew the pain and suffering that he'd poured into creating it. He knew the long hours spent agonizing over individual words, the endless emotion that he'd crafted into the scenes. He knew every single trouble spot, every rough patch that had cost him countless sleepless nights. He knew what flaws would be revealed to the public at large.

"Ryan," I said. "We chose *However Long* because it's what we need. What we want. What our audiences are going to love. Trust me. We are going to find a sponsor. It'll just take a little more time than I hoped."

I didn't convince him. Rather than argue, though, he started to fill Dani's peat cups with the dirt we'd just combined. I watched his hands move, smoothly, economically. All traces of the socially awkward playwright I'd first met in Ryan's body had disappeared. Now, he moved with the confidence of a man who knew his job, who had excelled at his work in the past.

I picked up a cup and followed suit, sifting the rich earth between the fingers of my leather work gloves. When I'd finished, I reached across his forearm to deposit the container in the dark plastic bin that awaited all of our handiwork. Ryan eased the cup into its proper place as I worked on filling the next one, and it took us only a few moments to settle into a routine. He completed two cups for every one that I managed.

Lather, rinse, repeat.

Halfway through the task, Ryan chuckled. The sound was surprisingly warm in the close space by the workbench. When I gave him a questioning look, he said, "Eleanor Samuelson probably would have made us join the union before she'd sponsor us."

Despite our earlier tension, I grinned. "Dues could be a nightmare."

"I'd have a hard time explaining what I was doing as a card-carrying member of the Women's Union. They'd revoke all my Man Points."

I pictured Ms. Samuelson's stern demeanor. "I bet that woman knows where Jimmy Hoffa's buried, though. All the best union leaders do—it's part of their secret initiation."

He actually laughed out loud.

"That sounds better!" We both looked up. I think that Ryan was as surprised as I was to see Dani emerging from her bedroom. Neither of us had noticed her departure. She brandished seed packets at us. "Here we are! Golden Acre!"

"What's that?" I asked. It sounded like a retirement home.

"Cabbage!" Dani's enthusiasm was the sort that most women reserve for chocolate. Dark chocolate. Imported. With truffle filling. As if to explain her joy, Dani said, "It's an early variety, great for small spaces."

I looked at Ryan, to see if he thought his mother had taken leave of her senses, but he only shrugged and pulled the peat pots to the center of the workbench.

"Excellent," Dani said. She handed over the paper packets and said, "You two get started with these. I want to see if I can find the Self Blanche."

I waited until she'd disappeared again into the magic cavern of her bedroom. "Self Blanche?" I asked Ryan.

"Cauliflower." He made a face. "She always starts way too much of it." Despite his criticism, he picked up a dull pencil and started poking shallow holes into the smooth tops of our dirt cups. It took him less than a minute to do the entire tray. "Ready?" he asked, handing me a trowel.

"I guess," I said. I had never planted anything, anywhere.

He ripped open the seed envelope and gestured for me to hold the trowel horizontally. When I complied, he tipped the packet upside down, spilling several dozen tiny white seeds into the center of the miniature shovel. "There you go. Just tip five or six into each hole."

I caught my tongue between my teeth. I thought I was being cautious, but I held the trowel at too steep an angle over the first one. A score of seeds flooded across the top of the dirt.

"Easy!" Ryan said. He tugged off his work gloves, needing

finer motor control than they permitted to gather up everything I'd spilled.

"I'm sorry!" Even though I hadn't meant it that way, it sounded like I was back to apologizing for Teel again.

Ryan looked at me quickly before bending back to the task at hand. "Why don't we just set aside those two words, all right? You won't say you're sorry anymore, and I won't hold anything against you."

I knew a good deal when I heard it. I nodded and said, "Deal."

He tipped the reclaimed seeds back into the trowel and said, "All right, now. Just five or six."

I started to tilt my wrist, but quickly realized that the angle was still too steep. I stopped myself just before I dumped the entire lot into a new, unsuspecting pot. "I'm s—" I started to say, but I caught myself just in time.

Ryan nodded. "It gets easier the more you've done it. You'll get the right feel eventually. Here. Let's try this." He set his fingers around my wrist.

His skin was warm against mine as he applied just enough pressure to bring my hand over the cups. He used his fingers to tap against my wrist, jiggling the trowel so that five tiny seeds rolled off the lip into the fresh earth that we'd prepared. His subtle guidance brought the trowel over the next cup, completing the task smoothly, calmly, without disaster.

Ryan Thompson might dress like a geek. He might grin like a bashful schoolboy. He might be unsure and uncertain in challenging social situations. But he knew a thing or two about teaching, about reaching out to people, showing them how to help themselves.

I shouldn't have been surprised. I'd read *However Long*. I

knew the passion and vehemence that he'd brought to his job in Africa, that he'd carried home from the Peace Corps.

As I looked at the cups we'd successfully completed, the tiny bones in my wrist seemed to heat up. Irrationally, my heart started pounding in my ears. I felt like I'd accomplished something heroic, something magnificent, something infinitely more significant than placing some cabbage seeds in dirt. My flesh thrummed beneath Ryan's hand, as if he'd crushed lush velvet against me. I wondered if he felt my surprised start, and that wondering raised a blush on my cheeks, a hot wash of color that only an idiot could have missed.

Ryan Thompson was no idiot.

He stepped closer to me, and I forced myself to relax my wrist. I ordered my hand to yield to his. I reminded my lungs to breathe; I willed my sudden flaming blush to fade.

And Ryan led me through filling the rest of the peat pots perfectly. Five seeds in each cup. No spills. No disasters.

When we were done, I said, "Thank you."

He looked at me for a long time. I felt him shift toward me again, a subtle movement, barely perceptible in the purple glow of the grow-lights. I saw him measure the new intensity behind my gaze, calibrate the tension as I froze beside him.

And I saw him remember that we were working together. Professionally. At the Mercer.

Not to mention the fact that his mother—his mother!—was somewhere nearby. He stepped back and dusted potting soil from his hands. "You're welcome," he said.

Before I could say anything else, before I could rekindle the moment, the hope, the expectation that had sparked between us, there was a shuffle of footsteps, and Dani emerged from her bedroom. For the first time since I'd met her, she seemed depressed. Defeated. She displayed her empty hands as she crossed over to look at our work. "Lucky for you," she said to Ryan, with a rueful smile. "I can't find the cauliflower seeds anywhere."

"Lucky for me," Ryan repeated. But he kept his eyes on me as he said the words.

CHAPTER 9

I WAS STILL THINKING OF THAT MOMENT—THE SOUND of his voice, the piercing quality of his gaze—as I stood in front of my own door, fumbling once again with my key in the lower lock. As always, the top one and the middle one had slid back without a problem. It was just…this…last…one that refused to budge. I gasped in exasperation and threw my key onto the carpet, knowing that I was acting like a baby, but needing to indulge a momentary temper tantrum.

"If I could be of assistance?"

I whirled around, half expecting to find Ryan standing behind me. Even as I turned, though, I realized that the voice had not been his. The timbre was too low. It was the rumble of a giant cat, and the words were iced with the faintest hint of a British accent.

I would have heard Ryan approach, anyway, would have heard his door open. Startled by the newcomer who had somehow appeared from nowhere, I started to scream, but I caught the sound at the back of my throat as the man held up his hands in a disarming, reassuring gesture. He took a slight step away, adding a soothing smile to his lips.

He was dressed in a perfectly tailored tuxedo. The satin stripe down the side of his pants glinted mellowly in the hallway light. His pleated shirt gleamed white, sharp, stark against his flawless cummerbund. Onyx studs marched down his chest, echoing the glint of his perfectly knotted bow tie.

As if he'd consciously chosen to dilute his unmarred image, the man's dirty-blond hair was ruffled; it looked like he'd just fought his way through a gale. His glacial eyes watched me with some amusement.

"I'm rather good with locks. Perhaps I can help?"

He extended one sinewy hand, palm up, and that's when I saw it. Brilliant gold flames, picked out in shimmering black ink. The tattoo looked as if it had come to life, like it was gathering in all the light in the hallway, transforming the very air around us into sunshine cast back at my dazed eyes.

"Teel!"

He cracked a self-deprecating smile. "You were expecting James Bond?"

I clutched my keys like a lifesaver. "Go away."

"Don't be like that," he purred.

"I don't want to talk to you."

"You don't mean that."

"I do. I really, truly do." I gaped at him, though, amazed by the transformation he had worked on his own body. A subtle energy vibrated off him, drifting toward me like musk. I remembered the way Ryan had originally reacted to the Marilyn Monroe monstrosity who had met us in the coffee shop. Was this what he had felt? Was this how Teel's manifestation had seemed to him—compelling? Alluring?

As I stared, Teel raised his hand toward his earlobe. His fingers were blunt against his coarse hair as he tightened his grip and tugged.

The metal key in my hand jangled, as if it had passed through an electrical field. I felt the motion, knew that something was changing, but I felt no actual pain. At the same time, my door whispered open, as if someone had actually taken the time to fit my new key into the stubborn lock.

"How did you do that?"

"Magic," he said with a self-deprecating shrug. "Consider it an apology. A peace offering. A wish I've granted for you, even though you didn't ask." He extended his arm, inviting me into my own home. "You'll find the lock won't give you any trouble now. I fixed it permanently."

A little stunned by how easily he'd made the repair, I walked into my living room. The late-afternoon sun streamed through the tall windows, painting the couch and love seat with great swaths of buttery yellow. At any other time, I would have been floored by the beauty of the scene. I would have felt indebted to the genie who had given me such a perfect home.

But I was still angry.

I closed the door and set my hands on my hips. "You can't do this," I said. "You can't just pretend that other incarnation never happened! You waltzed into my life and acted like an idiotic maniac, even after you told me, you *promised* me, that you'd appear as a student. An ordinary, everyday student. Teel, you can't go around sabotaging my job. This is my life—the only one I have—and you're ruining it!"

I drew a deep breath, ready to continue with my tirade. Before I could say another word, though, there was a flash of darkness, a sudden screen of black snapping down across my vision. I closed my eyes in reflex, flinching backward, and when I opened them I was nowhere.

Well, I was somewhere, but not anywhere that I could define. There was no floor below me, no ceiling above me. I looked to the left and to the right, but as far as I could see, there was only endless, featureless gray.

I was back in Teel's Garden.

I whirled around, and he was standing behind me. "I didn't give you permission to take me here!"

His sapphire eyes widened, and his jaw dropped, as if I'd tossed a perfectly shaken martini into his face. "I thought you liked it here!" He glanced longingly to his left, and I realized that the gate must be located there. The gate that only he could see. "I thought you loved it here as much as I did."

I couldn't exactly tell him I'd been lying. I was firmly ensconced on the moral high ground, and I intended to stay right there. "Even if I thought the Garden was the Taj Mahal and all that, I wouldn't want you just whisking me away without a word of warning!" At his crestfallen expression, I said, "Come on, Teel! This can't be news to you! Kira didn't want to be here, either! I heard her! She made you promise never to bring her here again!"

Teel took a step forward, curling his fingers around thin air, around the Garden's invisible fence. "But Kira couldn't see it, not the way you can. *None* of my humans has ever been able to see it. You're the only one."

Now he told me.

He raised his chin, and I could imagine that he was listening to some bird in the distance. For just a moment, I thought about Dani, about the gardens that she wanted to bring to the city. Maybe she worked so that some urban cave-dweller would get that same expression of perfect longing on his face. Maybe her guerilla gardens were a way of spreading light and joy, the same peace that Teel sought on this alternate plane.

When my genie spoke, his voice was soft, sing-song. "I thought that maybe I'd learned something at MAGIC. I thought that all of those seminars, all of those sessions, had finally taught me how to be a better genie. I thought that Jaze..."

"What's Jaze?"

He turned to me, his brilliant eyes haunted. "Not what. Who. Jaze is another genie, someone I met at MAGIC."

Wow. There were untold volumes behind that one sentence. I knew all about humans hooking up at trade shows, at out-of-town conferences. It had never occurred to me that genies might do the same thing. Truth be told, it had never occurred to me that Teel could have any sort of romantic life—not when he bounced back and forth from slick 007 look-alike to bimbo Slut of the Year to Con Ed lineman...

But there was no denying the longing in Teel's face. He stripped his bow tie open. "Jaze is in there now. He granted his last wish a few days ago. I want to join him before he's back out, back in his lamp for another full round."

Great. It wasn't like Teel was adding any pressure on me or anything. "Can you call him over to the gate? At least get a chance to talk while you're here?" I was taking a gamble, assuming that the other genie wasn't standing right in front of us. I'd see him, right? He wouldn't be invisible, like the Garden was.

Teel ran his hand through his rough-cut hair. "She's moved deeper inside, beyond the outer ranks."

"She?"

Teel shook his head, distracted. "Sorry. She. He. Jaze. You may have noticed that we genies aren't really tied to your human notions of gender."

I smiled wryly, thinking of my confusion when Kira had referred to my female genie lawyer by a male pronoun. "Yeah. I did notice that." Teel was barely listening to me, though. His eyes darted around—I was pretty sure he was checking out the shadows beneath trees, craning his neck to look beyond something that grew to shoulder height. "How long will she, uh, he, uh, Jaze be in there?"

With a visible effort, Teel stepped back from the gate. I could feel the power he put into looking away from the invisible Garden, into focusing on me. "Time flows differently for genies. I can't tell you precisely—part of it depends on how deeply he goes into the physical space, how much magic she uses to conjure other imaginaries to keep him company. To entertain her."

I shook my head, a bit dazzled by the rapid pronoun shifts. Apparently gender truly *was* immaterial to genies. "Are we talking a day, though? A year? A century? What's the ballpark?"

Teel shrugged. "Maybe as long as a year. Just possibly two. This isn't Jaze's first time inside. He's served at least two complete Fulfillment rounds in your human world. This is his third time in the Garden." Teel sighed. "I have no idea if she'll still be there when I get in. You still have two more wishes, and then I owe another four to someone."

He sounded so sad, so lonely.... Even though I was still angry with him about the Union, I couldn't help but take a step closer. I forced myself to ignore the strange feeling of moving through nothing, of trusting that there would be some floor beneath my feet when I set them down. "Teel…" I said, staring into the nothingness that hid the missing genie.

Teel sighed and clutched at his collar, working free the onyx stud at the bottom of his Adam's apple before he offered me a tired smile. "Of course, if you made your two wishes right away, made them now, I'd be that much closer to getting in."

"Dammit, Teel!" He might be a gorgeous guy in a tux, showing his emotional vulnerability, but he wasn't going to sway me that easily. "Is that what was going on this afternoon? Did you purposely screw things up at the International Women's Union so that I'd have to use an extra wish?"

"No!" To his credit, he looked horrified. "I would never do that! I *could* never do that—it would violate our contract!" I thought about asking which clause, but I knew he'd just rattle off an incomprehensible string of letters and numbers. Teel shook his head. "This afternoon wasn't about Jaze. I just thought it would be *fun,* to shake things up a little in the meeting. You humans are all so serious all the time. That Eleanor Samuelson could certainly use a laugh or two." I glared at him. "I'm sorry," he said, and he sounded sincere. "I'm really, truly sorry."

I thought about how many times I'd said those words to Ryan, just that afternoon. I thought about how much I had longed to hear him accept my apology, how much I had craved his accepting my mistake, forgiving it, letting us move on.

What was my real alternative here? I could remain angry with Teel from now until the day his brass lamp tarnished into a pile of metallic dust, but that wasn't going to change what had already happened.

I kept my voice perfectly even as I said, "I accept your apology."

The change in Teel was instantaneous. He jumped back from the unseen gate, clapping his hands once as if he'd just played a winning hand at baccarat. "We can fix things at the Mercer! You have two wishes left, and there's no time like the present to use them."

"Absolutely not!"

"Just one, then," he wheedled, glancing at the invisible Garden behind him. "Bring the theater into line, and you'll still have one wish left for whatever else your heart desires."

I crossed my arms over my chest, forbidding myself to think about Jaze waiting somewhere in the distance. My remaining wishes were too precious to waste, no matter how hard Teel tried to manipulate me. "No. And you can't make me."

"No. I can't." He sighed, but then he seemed to remember the guise he'd chosen for himself, the pure seduction that emanated from his suave incarnation. "But we could have some wicked fun while I tried." He pinned me with those gimlet eyes, and I felt myself buffeted by another wave of his subtle, magical compulsion. A tendril of naked lust curled around my belly. Or something lower.

With perfect clarity, I could imagine exactly what kind of wishes Teel would try to extract from me once he had me in a fully compromised position. "No, thank you," I said dryly.

He shrugged. "It was worth a try," he said, flipping the switch on his burning gaze. My heart fluttered as he released me; I felt like I'd had a few too many cups of coffee. My Casanova was suddenly a roguish little boy, hanging his head in mock shame.

"You are incorrigible!" I exclaimed.

"Isn't that what every girl wants her genie to be?" That slow smile spread across his rugged features and he waited just a beat, obviously hoping that I'd change my mind. Even if I'd been inclined to invite him into my bed—the very bed that he had given me less than one week before—I knew he'd only break my heart in the morning. That's what men did when they were as drop-dead gorgeous as Teel was pretending to be.

At least in my experience. And in the experience of every actor, stage manager, and other theater professional I'd ever spilled my heart to.

Teel sighed, finally abandoning his pretense of seduction entirely. "So? Who's up next on the sponsor list? Who are we meeting with tomorrow?"

"No one!" I answered so forcefully that I probably frightened off the nearest of the Garden's birds. "You are not meeting with any sponsors. You're not coming anywhere near the Mercer."

"Please?" he wheedled, stretching out the word like a child playing with chewing gum.

"No!"

"Even if I promise to be good?" Again, with the glowing eyes.

I ordered my body to ignore its immediate animal response. "You don't know the meaning of the word."

"You're probably right." He sighed and looked toward the Garden again, back to being the lovesick genie I pitied. "You know, I'd give you a bouquet of those wildflowers, if I could reach them through the fence."

I followed his gaze, acting as if I could see the blossoms. I pushed a little sympathy into my response. "And I'd take them from you. And enjoy every last one."

"Isn't the honeysuckle incredible?"

"I've never smelled anything like it," I said.

He sighed and filled his lungs so deeply that I thought his cummerbund would burst. "Time to get back to your real world, though, isn't it?"

"I think so."

He turned his back on the Garden I could only imagine. "Thank you, Rebecca. It helps sometimes, just to talk."

"I know," I said. "I understand."

I blinked, and I was suddenly back in my living room. The late-afternoon sunlight was blinding as I turned to ask Teel what he was going to do next. Alas, my genie was nowhere to be found.

Before I could worry about what mischief he was getting himself into, my phone rang. I glanced at the caller ID and battled a sudden wave of queasiness. "Hello, Pop-pop," I said after the third ring, forcing a smile into my voice. My grandfather had no idea that I'd lost his generous graduation gift.

"How's my favorite granddaughter doing in the big bad city?"

"As you know perfectly well, I'm your *only* granddaughter." The teasing felt old, familiar, like driftwood rubbed comfortably smooth by waves.

"How are things at work?"

"They're…fine." Damn. I'd let my voice hitch just a little. Maybe my grandfather wouldn't notice. Maybe he'd think it was just a hiccup in transmission through the phone.

"What's wrong?"

So much for that brilliant idea. I thought about everything

that was wrong. My genie was hounding me to make my last two wishes so that he could hook up with the imaginary creature he had a crush on. Yeah, I couldn't mention a word of that to Pop-pop, not without my throat slamming closed. My former boyfriend had taken off for Russia—Russia!—with every penny I'd ever earned. Right, like I was going to share that disaster. I needed to find a sponsor with thousands of dollars to pour into our emergency production of *However Long*.

Okay. I could talk about work, at least a little bit. "Things are just busy at the office." I gave him the thirty-second summary of our copyright woes, our rapid schedule change, and our funding needs.

"You'll work things out," he said, brimming with the absolute confidence that only unconditional grandfather love could create. "You just need to give yourself a little treat. Take some of that money I sent you and splurge on something for yourself—a day at the spa, or a nice dinner out with your young man."

My eyes welled up at the kindness in Pop-pop's voice. At the kindness, and at the all too real fact that I'd lost his money. I couldn't afford a bottle of nail polish at the corner drug store, much less an entire day of pampering.

As for dinner out with my young man… As soon as my grandfather said the words, I pictured Ryan Thompson. Not Dean, not the boyfriend that Pop-pop expected me to share with. Thinking of Ryan was absurd, though. No matter how smoothly he had planted cabbage seeds in peat cups, he hadn't conquered my heart. He wasn't boyfriend material. He *couldn't* be—we were working together. Until *However Long* was over, Ryan was strictly verboten, in any sort of dating sense. I couldn't even allow myself to think of getting involved with him.

No need to go into all of that with my grandfather, though. I forced a bright smile into my voice. "That's a great idea, Pop-pop."

"I won't keep you," he said. "I just wanted to hear your voice, doll."

Doll. That's what my grandmother had always called me, the woman Pop-pop had been married to for fifty-three years, before Alzheimer's cruelly stole her away. We said our goodbyes, and I headed into the kitchen to boil water for my chicken-flavored ramen noodles. As I sipped my salty yellow broth, I tried to imagine what it would be like to love someone for more than half a century.

Four days and seventeen meetings later, I was almost ready to summon Teel and take him up on his wish-granting offer. No, not his offer of flirtation and reckless abandon and probably mind-blowing sex. He was a genie—he'd leave me in the morning—or after I'd made my fourth wish. Whichever came first.

I was, though, seriously considering letting Teel fund *However Long*.

Ryan and I had sat in office after office, making our pitches. While I came to appreciate the responses that were quick and to the point—I'd always been one to just hold my nose and swallow my medicine—the sudden stab of disappointment never hurt less.

The African Connection was too deeply in debt themselves.

The Women's Empowerment Consortium refused to consider sponsoring a play written by a man.

The Better World Alliance wanted us to hand over e-mail addresses and phone numbers for every one of our patrons.

The Light in the Night Coalition demanded that we perform the show in their own grotty basement space, which could have used a few lights, or at least a couple hundred roach motels, before I'd even consider walking all the way to the back wall.

The Peace Fund, the World Understanding League, the New Voices Endowment, the New York Friendship Front— my list went on and on and on, but the bottom line was always the same. No one had any money. At least, not money for us. Not this close to production. Not without prior earmarks in the budget. Not, not, not, not, not.

Teel didn't make things any easier. Every night, he waited for me in my apartment, dragging me off to the Garden as soon as I closed the door behind me. I saw enough genie incarnations that I felt as though I was living in a real-world version of *Sesame Street*'s "Who Are the People in Your Neighborhood?"

Every single visit, he—or she; Teel was an equal-opportunity Garden recruiter—pointed out the amazing scenery, the delectable scents, the unparalleled sounds. And every single visit, I played along, oohing and aahing as if my senses had never been so stimulated. I couldn't admit the truth now, couldn't tell him that every prior visit had been a lie.

Fortunately, my dramaturg brain served me well in the midst of the nothingness that was Teel's private world. I was accustomed to taking notes on productions, to keeping track of endless details. Just from listening to my genie and watching the angle of his head, I learned which corner of the invisible Garden housed the roses, which contained the vast plots of wildflowers. I memorized where the nightingales tended to congregate, and I hardly ever forgot that the stream flowed from left to right, eddying into a pond just past the boxwood hedge.

But none of that knowledge got me any closer to my ultimate goal. Nothing about the Garden brought me funding for the Mercer.

When I'd learned about funding meetings in school, I'd never imagined how important they would be, here in my first professional job. I'd never dreamed how badly one poor victim-of-crime theater company like the Mercer could need funds, and how desperately one shamed dramaturg could pursue potential sponsors. We would have needed a corporate sponsor for any production that the Mercer undertook, but Dean's thievery made my mission for *However Long* infinitely more important than it would have been otherwise.

Matters weren't helped by the regular phone calls I got from Detective Ambrose. Once he called to ask if I, Miss Morris, had ever traveled to Alaska under an assumed name. No, Detective. Sorry.

Another time, he called to ask if I, Miss Morris, had ever met any of Dean's relatives face-to-face. No, Detective. Sorry.

Yet another time, he called to ask if I, Miss Morris, knew of any business associates of Dean's who specialized in international arbitrage. I barely knew what the phrase meant. No, Detective. Sorry.

Every time I spoke to the laconic investigator, I asked him if they were any closer to tracking Dean down, if they were tracing his movements in Russia, if they were able to rip free any of the millions he had embezzled from the Mercer and the thousands he'd taken from me.

Every time, Ambrose told me that no, Miss Morris, they were no closer to getting the funds. Sigh. But he promised, Miss Morris, that he'd let me know as soon as anything changed. Big, gusty sigh.

And so, after more than a week of the most frustrating conversations about money that I had ever had, Ryan and I found ourselves sitting in the office of Ronald J. Barton, a.k.a. the Popcorn King.

Barton was intent on doing for popcorn what Starbucks had done for Colombian roast. He envisioned one of his orange-and-yellow-themed stores on every block of every major city in the world. He had mastered the art of turning twenty cents worth of Iowa's finest corn into a five-dollar bag of crunchy snack food. His outlets featured a cornucopia of fine-grained sugars and salts, nearly endless flavor combinations that could be sprinkled over any of his three basic commodities: plain, cheddar, or caramel popcorn.

Somewhere along the way, Barton had heard that it was important to present a consistent marketing message to the world of potential customers. To that end, Barton lived inside a lemon-and-tangerine-colored kaleidoscope.

Ryan and I showed up for our appointment, wearing our by-now-customary begging clothes. After a week of dressing like a grown-up, I hadn't come anywhere near reaching the limits of my Teel-created wardrobe. I could continue to throw together one sober, responsible outfit after another—for another three months at least, if only there'd been a single prospective donor left on my list. If Ryan wondered at the source of my extensive collection of clothes, he didn't say anything. Instead, he'd shown up every morning in one of two hand-knit sweaters and clean khaki slacks. Neat, simple, and utterly, geekily boring.

We stood out in Ronald Barton's office like burnt popcorn kernels in a handful of white, fluffy perfection.

Barton's desk was covered in yellow Formica. Each of his office accessories had been molded out of orange plastic—a stapler the color of tiger lilies was poised on top of a stack of matching paper. Sticky notes blared their presence like freshly harvested pumpkins. The telephone looked like it had jumped out of a box of Crayola crayons. The computer monitor, the pencil holder, the pens, the scissors, the Kleenex box—each and every item assaulted my eyes with pure, un-diluted orange.

Barton himself wore a bright yellow sweater and matching slacks. His Popcorn King logo was picked out across his chest: a cheerful orange box with sloped sides, tilted to the right so that kernels of just-popped corn could cascade into a smile. Each puffy white cloud of crunchy goodness bore the initials P.K.

Ronald J. Barton didn't have anything to do with Africa. He had nothing to do with women's rights. He had, as far as I knew, never even heard of the Peace Corps.

But Barton had bought a half-page ad in the Mercer program for every single play we'd staged in the past two years. Like clockwork, his checks rolled in. Barton was dependable. Barton was reliable.

And Barton was rich.

"Come in! Come in!" he boomed. "Have a seat!" After a second's hesitation, I lowered myself into the yellow plastic chair across from his desk, letting Ryan take the orange one. With my red hair, I was going to look ghastly in either.

Before I could make polite conversation, Barton bellowed, "Now, now, now! Can I get you a snack? We're testing a new flavor combination this morning—Caramel Cactus!"

I managed to paste a smile on my lips. "Cactus?"

"Caramel corn!" Barton exclaimed. "With chipotle pepper salt!"

My stomach turned at the idea, but I knew I couldn't refuse. I glanced at Ryan, and he gave me the slightest shrug before saying, "That would be wonderful, Mr. Barton."

"Ronald! Call me Ronald!" As our host punched an intercom button on his desk console and shot orders at an assistant, I wondered if he ever spoke without an exclamation point.

Well, there was no time like the present, I told myself. Bracing myself, I launched into my by-now-familiar pitch. "Ronald, we really appreciate your taking the time to see us. As a long-term advertiser with the Mercer Project, you know—"

I was cut off by something that sounded like a hundred tiny explosions. Startled, I jumped back in my chair. Ronald, though, dove for his bright orange telephone. I realized that the Popcorn King had set his office ringtone to sound like popcorn fluffing to perfection in a stovetop pot.

"Pop off!" our potential sponsor snapped into his phone. Apparently, the person on the other end of the line was used to the greeting—a distorted voice immediately launched into some frantic argument, clearly audible across the desk. "I don't care what the lease says!" Ronald thundered. "Tell the lawyers they have to work out the language! That's their job! Call me when the deal is done!" He slammed the phone down and turned back to us with an expectant smile.

Gamely, I launched back into my spiel. "As a long-term advertiser with the Mercer Project you know and appreciate the reach that we have in our community. You understand—"

This time, I didn't back away when I heard the torrent of popping corn. Nevertheless, I cut off my pitch in response to Ronald's silencing palm. "Pop off!" he fired into the phone's mouthpiece. "Health inspectors can't enter the premises after business hours! They can show up on time or not at all! Tell them that, and don't take no for an answer!"

The phone slammed down, and I once again had Ronald's attention. I licked my lips and started anew. "Our theater holds just over a thousand patrons, and we sell out eight shows a week. Every one of those patrons—"

"Pop off!" This time, he'd caught the phone after a split second of the popping noise, almost as if he'd sensed the call before it arrived. Before I could hear the resolution of the current crisis, a harried-looking woman scampered into the room. She held three miniature boxes of popcorn, each one—no surprise—orange. Her smile was apologetic as she passed one to Ryan and one to me. She placed the third within reach of the Popcorn King himself.

Her lemon-colored dress combined with the dark circles under her eyes to make her look like a victim of the plague. Her lips were chapped, probably because she licked them constantly, as nervous as a lizard. She glanced at Ronald and then leaned closer to Ryan and me. "Cut to the chase," she whispered. "He'll be like this all day long."

"Thank you," I said in a normal voice, as if I'd never been happier to receive a sweet snack drenched in smoked jalapeño powder. She darted a smile toward me and scurried out of the room.

As soon as Ronald set down the phone, Ryan leaned forward. "Two hundred and fifty thousand dollars," he said.

I gaped at him. The figure was five times greater than we'd ever dreamed of receiving from a sponsor.

"What!" Ronald stopped with his fingers half-buried in his box of caramel-chipotle delight.

"Two hundred and fifty thousand, and you get your message in front of every Mercer patron for two straight months."

The sound of popping corn filled the office, but Ronald merely reached for his intercom. He pushed a button without looking and snapped, "Take a message!" And then he snapped at Ryan, "What about product! What about moving product!"

Ryan gave no sign that he'd been victorious. Instead, he said, "You can serve free samples during intermission."

"Advertising! What about advertising!"

I piped up. "Two full-page ads in the program. Four-color."

"Announcements! At the top of the show!"

Hal wasn't going to like that one. But we had months to figure out something tasteful. I said, "One prerecorded message."

"Actors! Appearing in my other ads! Tie-ins!"

We didn't even know who would be cast in the show. "Print ads only," I said. "One morning of shooting."

Ronald glared at me. When I didn't back down, he turned his squint on Ryan. The phone rang again, and the Popcorn King didn't bother to pick it up, didn't even order his assistant to act. When silence continued to reign, he filled it with, "Fifty thousand!"

Ryan shook his head. "Two hundred."

"One hundred! Take it or leave it!"

"One fifty. And you can insert coupons into every program."

I watched Ronald calculate the value of the package. I could almost see numbers stream across the register tape inside his head, yellow and orange figures drifting into infinity.

"One fifty! Paid in three installments!" he exclaimed at last. "You two drive a hard bargain!"

I extended a hand. Ronald's was gritty as he transferred chipotle powder onto my palm. He shook Ryan's hand, as well.

The sound of popping corn flooded the office again. "Talk to my assistant!" he barked at us. "She'll take care of the details! Pop off!" The last two words were directed into his telephone.

The nameless assistant was waiting outside the office door, a trash can in her hands, ready to receive our untouched Caramel Cactus.

"To the Popcorn King!" I said, raising my glass of Burgundy toward Ryan's.

"Pop off!" he said, clinking his goblet gently against mine.

I took a sip of the wine. It was the bottle that Jenn had given me, the one that had been intended to bribe me into choosing someone's manuscript. Somehow, it seemed like a complete exorcism of theatrical favoritism to share the wine with Ryan, to celebrate our good fortune together.

I sighed contentedly, collapsing back on the couch and watching the symphony of nighttime lights blinking on in the cityscape outside my windows. "Two hundred and fifty thousand dollars." I smirked at Ryan over the rim of my glass. "What made you start with that number?"

"I lived in Africa for two years," he said. "You learn a lot about haggling in the markets over there."

"I'll keep that in mind," I said, toasting him again. "What was it like there?" I asked.

"It was beautiful." He sounded wistful. "The sunlight has a quality that I've never seen anywhere else. For months at a time, there's no rain, and dust gets kicked up along the roads, picked up by the wind. Every sunset is gorgeous."

"Orange," I said dryly. "And yellow."

"Bite your tongue," he retorted, but he smiled. He took another sip of wine and then set his goblet on the table. "It was terrible, though, too. Entire families live for a year on what we Americans fritter away in a single week. It's bad for the kids, but the mothers have it worst. They gather whatever food they can, and they try to stretch their money in the marketplace. At home they serve their husband first. After he's eaten, the kids get what's left over. A lot of women survive on a handful of porridge a day."

He fell silent, and I knew that he was remembering specific women who had suffered for those they loved. I'd read his play. It had shown me the power structure, the religious framework, the social construct that forced generations into bittersweet roles.

But reading was one thing. Living was another.

Even though I'd brought up the topic, I wanted a distraction. I stood up from the couch and took my goblet to the window. The panes were well-insulated; I felt only a hint of a chill from the outdoors.

Nevertheless, I reached protectively toward the metal carts that stood next to the glass. Dani had rolled them in the day before, two metal frames, each with a solid shelf at knee height. Our cabbage seeds rested on one; onions waited on the other. I could just make out the tiniest fringe of green on the peat pots that Ryan had helped me to fill.

The tentative new growth made me smile. I had never

quite believed that the seeds would germinate, that actual, real vegetables could grow out of anything as tiny as those seeds.

Ryan came to look over my shoulder. "Ah," he said. "My mother has made another convert."

I laughed. "I know I shouldn't be amazed. Seeds, dirt, and water. That's the way people have been gardening forever, but it's new to me."

"That's how she lures folks in. It's new to a whole lot of people."

"But not you."

"No." He shook his head. "I've had a lifetime of too many cabbages. Just wait until she starts you on the peppers. And the zucchini. Hope that your guerilla plot never gives you space to plant zucchini." He shuddered in mock terror.

"How bad can it be?"

"Have you ever had zucchini chocolate cake?"

"That bad!" I said.

It felt good to laugh with him. Good to look at the seedlings we'd created. Good to bask in the glory of a job well done, both the gardening and our successful Popcorn King coup. The Ryan who had sat in that office today was a man I'd only glimpsed before. The Ryan who had confidently asked for thousands of dollars as if he were owed them, as if he *deserved* them. The Ryan who had bargained with the cool aplomb of a master.

Like a new-sprouted plant seeking out sunshine, I leaned back, feeling the heat of his chest through the back of my Lauren Hansen sweater dress, the latest of my Teel trophies to be worn into battle for the sponsor wars. Ryan's arms settled around me as if the motion was the most natural thing in the world, folding in the heat of our bodies.

His lips teased at the curve of my ear, nuzzling at my lobe with a delicate pressure that made me gasp in surprise. A laugh blossomed deep inside his chest, and he freed my goblet from my hand, settling it amid the cabbage peat pots, like it belonged there. The city lights danced off wine so dark it seemed black.

With both hands free, Ryan turned me around so that I was facing him. His deft fingers reached for the decorated chopstick I'd used to pin back my unruly hair. I shivered as the strawberry curls tumbled down the back of my neck. His palm cupped my jaw, and he drew me closer.

His lips were firm on mine, more demanding than I'd ever expected from the gawky guy I'd first met in the Mercer's Bullpen. There was nothing geeky or awkward about this Ryan Thompson, though. This man was supremely confident, absolutely sure of himself. This was the Ryan who had shown me how to plant seeds. This was the Ryan who had faced down the Popcorn King, who had secured a more profitable sponsorship for the Mercer than I'd ever imagined.

I pulled him closer, finally tangling my fingers in the unruly hair that I'd longed to touch since the morning I'd first met him. He made a sound deep in his throat, a harsh sigh that was equal parts need and desire. His lips found the sensitive hollow over the pulse point in my throat, and I clutched at his back as his tongue flicked over my heartbeat again and again.

My hands fisted in the heavy wool of his sweater, and I let myself fall back against the broad hand he'd spread across my back. My legs were trembling as if I'd run a marathon, and I gasped to catch a breath against the pleasure that shuddered down my spine.

He raised his lips from my throat for long enough to whisper, "Can't take that?"

"Mmm," I said, unable to remember actual English words. I seized the opportunity to guide him back to the sofa. My dress rode up around my hips as I edged back on the throw pillows. Ryan lay down beside me, returning his attention to my lips with a thoroughness that raised a whine in the back of my throat.

I shifted my weight a little to free my arm, to raise my hand so that I could tug at his clothes where they bunched between us. I wanted him out of his sweater, out of his careful white shirt. Out of whatever pair of anonymous khaki pants he'd worn as his uniform for the day's meeting.

The day's meeting. Our meeting with the Popcorn King. To get funding for *However Long*. For the play that he had written, that I was working on as the dramaturg. The professional dramaturg.

I froze.

He sensed the change immediately. His voice was husky as he whispered against my ear, "What, Becca?"

"I can't," I croaked.

He collapsed against me for just a moment, burying his face in the tangle of my hair. I caught my breath. My body wanted me to laugh. It wanted me to tell him I'd been kidding. I was game. I was more than ready.

But my mind knew I couldn't follow through.

We were professionals. We were working together on his play. On his first play, the first that would ever see production, the one that would cement his reputation forever. I was honor-bound to guide that production, to analyze it, to support it. I had to remain dispassionate. Separate. Apart.

He grunted as he pushed himself up to a sitting position. "What is it, Becca?" He waited as I flailed for an answer. "Is this about Dean? Is it too soon?"

"Yes. No." I hadn't thought about Dean romantically in weeks. But this *was* about him. This was about not wanting to make the same mistakes I'd made in the past. About not wanting to rush into a relationship, just because it felt good to be there. About not wanting to tangle my personal life with my career. "I don't know," I said. "I'm sorry. We're working together, and doing anything else, anything more, it just feels *wrong*." To my horror, my throat tightened, and tears burned in the corners of my eyes.

He rubbed one hand across the back of his neck, exhaling deeply. "I'm sorry," he said.

"I thought we'd agreed not to say that anymore." I managed to smile, even as a single tear snaked down my cheek.

He reached out with his thumb to wipe it away. Before he could touch me, though, my body flinched. I didn't intend to move; I didn't intend to react at all. But I jerked away by reflex.

"Right," he said. The bitterness that he ladled over the single word surprised me. He wiped his palms against his slacks. "Okay, then," he said, climbing to his feet.

"Ryan, I—"

"Don't worry about it," he said. "I think I just got carried away by our success today."

"Seriously, Ryan. I—"

He raised his chin and settled a broad smile across his lips. A goofy smile. The smile of a man who wasn't comfortable with who and what he was. "Auditions are tomorrow, right?" He didn't wait for me to nod. "I'll see you at the Mercer, then. Ten o'clock. Right?"

"Right," I whispered.

I knew that I should stand up. I should walk him to the door. I should thank him again for getting us the funding. I should smile and laugh and make everything all right between us. I knew how to do that. I was a trained professional.

But I stayed silent. I listened to his barely audible footsteps as he crossed the luxuriant carpet Teel had given me. I heard the click of the doorknob turning. I registered the whisper of the door snicking closed behind him.

Frozen in the amber of my own uncertainty, I stared at the blinking city lights outside my window. It was an hour before I even moved to collect my goblet from the seedlings—one full hour before I gathered up the bottle of Burgundy I was suddenly determined to finish on my own.

But those long minutes were nothing compared to the time I spent tossing and turning in my king-size bed that night. Alone. Cold. Waiting until the sun rose on auditions for *However Long*.

CHAPTER 10

THE NEXT MORNING, I WOKE WITH A SINKING FEELING in the pit of my stomach. Auditions were going to be awkward—Ryan and I were going to be stuck together for the entire day.

But I'd get through that. We were coworkers, after all. That was the entire reason I'd pulled back from…whatever I'd pulled back from. We were professionals. We were leading lights of contemporary theater. Or something like that.

Even given my ambivalence about Ryan, I was excited to participate in my first round of auditions at the Mercer. This was the first show that I would work on from beginning to end, the first where I would sit beside Hal in the audience seats, spread my paperwork across the rough table fashioned out of a sheet of plywood, the one that balanced carefully over a half-dozen red velvet chairs.

I ducked inside the theater door from the lobby, jumping into the gloom at the back of the house as I studied the lay of the land. Kira had already taken care of her responsibilities. As stage manager, she had run electrical cords to the worktable, set up a small lamp, plugged in Hal's laptop. She'd even taken care of creature comforts for all of us. I'd been thrilled to find hot coffee waiting in the rehearsal room (normal strength, not the legendary pure caffeine of Kira's preferred brew). Her frosted sugar cookies were a thoughtful touch (not that I needed anything to make my blood pound any faster).

Living up to her reputation as one of the finest stage managers in the city, Kira had even anticipated more obscure needs—she had provided an entire canister of Hal's precious Rollerball pens, and she'd laid in a solid supply of legal pads. A forest of freshly sharpened pencils waited, as well, their tips aligned like darts, waiting for some unseen bull's-eye to materialize out of the shadows.

I smoothed my hands down my charcoal wool trousers, grateful for the cool touch of the silk lining against my thighs. I resisted the urge to pluck at the knit shawl of my emerald sweater. I'd already spent fifteen minutes in front of my own bathroom mirror, making sure that the whisper-soft cashmere fell naturally. Easily. Gracefully. As if I were accustomed to owning a world-class wardrobe that complemented my green eyes perfectly.

Not that I'd taken any extra time to dress for Ryan. Not at all.

Thinking of the wish that had solved my sartorial problems so simply, I closed my eyes and brushed my thumb and forefinger against each other. It had been almost two weeks since Teel had first stormed into my life, but I still thought that I should be able to feel the tattoos dusted over my fingertips. I thought about what Teel had told me almost a week before, about his longing to join Jaze in the Garden. I had so much power embedded in my hands, the ability to summon my genie, to make my life complete. To make *his* life complete. If only I could decide how best to use it.

"Excuse me!"

Ryan's voice sent my heart skipping into the catwalks. My eyes flew open, and I clutched at the seat in front of me, suddenly unsteady on the heels of my perfectly sensible pumps. "Ryan," I said, trying to sound like I was bored. Or disinterested. Or…professional.

He jumped from my side into the aisle, shoving his hands into his pockets so quickly that I worried he would tear his pants. His tongue darted out over his lips, and he swallowed audibly. "I'm sorry," he said. "I didn't realize you'd be standing there! I just wanted to duck out of the way when I came in. I wanted to take a second to look at the stage. To let it sink in that these auditions are really happening. That my play is really going to be produced. I—" He finally stopped babbling for long enough to draw a breath. "I'm talking too much, aren't I?"

Despite the butterflies that were colonizing my esophagus, I smiled. "It's exciting, isn't it?"

Exciting. That was a bad word to use with him.

He didn't seem to notice, though. I tugged at my sweater, wondering how all the air could have been sucked out of so large a room. Even as my fingers clutched the soft wool, I wrinkled my nose, frustrated that I'd sabotaged the perfect neckline I'd smoothed into place with such care. I barely resisted the temptation to rake my fingers through my hair— my carefully casual chignon would never have withstood the attack.

"Becca!"

Saved by the shout. I jumped into the aisle, brushing past Ryan as I took a few giant steps toward the stage. Hal stood on a precisely taped X, shading his eyes from the overhead stage lights so that he could peer into the seats.

"I'm here," I said, closing the distance to the worktable with strides that would have made an Olympic speedwalker proud.

Hal craned his neck forward. "Are you okay, Becca? You look like crap."

"Thanks," I said, certain that my general appearance was only worsened by the crimson blush that immediately turned my cheeks into a mirror of my strawberry hair. "I'm fine."

"Okay," he said, practicality rinsing his words of any lingering shade of concern. He peered farther back into the house. "Ryan? Great to see you! Are you ready?"

"Absolutely."

Once again, Ryan surprised me by being closer than I expected. This time, he was standing behind me. When I started at his single word, my shoulders brushed against the dark brown cabling on his sweater. The sweater that he'd worn in my apartment, just the night before. The sweater that…

I leaped away from him, then tried to pretend that I was only counting the pencils Kira had left for us.

Hal jumped down easily from the stage and strode to meet us. If he suspected that anything strange was going on between Ryan and me, he gave no sign. Instead, he tapped a stack of pages against the plywood surface, lining up his papers with a precision that would have made the military proud. Before I could say anything, keep the conversation flowing about the theater, about the play, about anything other than my personal life, Kira poked her head out from the wings.

She shot all of us a quick smile and said, "Ready for the first round? Women reading for Fanta."

"Ready," Hal said, taking a seat between Ryan and me. I forced myself to lean back against the red velvet of the chair, to relax. I was grateful for Hal's electric presence, grateful for the distraction from Ryan.

Kira flipped a sheet of paper over the back of her clipboard and stepped toward the dressing room, where all the hopeful actors and actresses were waiting. She consulted her notes and then called out, "Patrice Leveque."

Automatically, I shuffled through my own scramble of pages, pulling out a resume. Hal had the hopeful actress's headshot displayed in front of him, a moody portrait in black and white that depicted a young woman with a tight-coiled sense of drama, a wild energy that vibrated off the slick page.

In person, the actress had even more energy as she bounded to the center of the stage. Despite the short notice about our choice of plays, Patrice had found time to embrace the African setting of *However Long*. Her long limbs were covered by a flowing robe, a silky garment that flashed intricately embroidered stripes of yellow and green and red. Her hair was bound up in an elaborate headscarf fashioned from the same material. The wild clothing contrasted dramatically with her dark skin; her features looked as if they were carved from ironwood.

She set her hands on her hips and proclaimed, "My name is Patrice Leveque. I'm doing a monologue from *Raisin in the Sun*."

Alas, Patrice had invested all of her energy in her appearance. Her voice turned shaky and weak as she recited her prepared piece. She had clearly memorized specific hand movements, taught herself to take one precise step *here,* another *there.* While she knew every word of the character's speech, her phrasing was off; she elided some words and drew out others, until I almost believed she was speaking a foreign language. Her recitation ran longer than the two permitted minutes, and Hal did not hesitate to snap out, "Thank you. Next!" when she'd reached her limit.

Once upon a time, I'd worried about actors who were shot down mid-audition. After all, these artists were baring their souls, showing everything that mattered to them, everything they cared about.

But I'd been hardened by my years of theater work. I'd learned that the vast majority of directors knew what they wanted within fifteen seconds of watching an actor onstage. A dozen heartbeats—maybe twenty, for the adrenaline-charged folks on display.

Hal, of course, was no different. He'd arrived at the auditions with a clear picture in his mind, a precise image of the cast he intended to harness to Ryan's play. And Patrice Leveque obviously had no place in that vision.

She wasn't the only actress to leave the stage disappointed. Rather, she was just the first.

We sat through an entire morning of auditions, a constant parade of hopeful talent. I settled into taking notes, jotting down a record of who performed which monologues, setting out my own opinions about how they'd executed their miniature roles. Occasionally, Hal left an aspiring performer standing center stage, covering his face with his clipboard as he asked me a question. Sometimes, he wanted clarification on the script, on issues that he'd already identified with specific scenes. Other times, he wanted to know if I was familiar with an actor's work, if I'd heard gossip from other theaters, from ShowTalk. A half-dozen times, he turned to Ryan, asking whether the playwright could envision one actor playing opposite another, if he had ever considered presenting certain characters in specific ways.

I settled into the rhythm easily, lapsing back into the tried and true, a process made familiar by years of amateur productions, by the half-dozen plays I'd shepherded through graduate school. Some of the actors were too overbearing. Some immediately conveyed that they were too precious, too difficult, not worth the inevitable investment of time, and special care, and hand-holding that they would require. Two people were absent when their names were called, overcome by stage fright or too-crowded schedules. One man forgot the lines of his monologue partway through. He crumpled in defeat and dragged himself off the stage before Hal could tell him to take a deep breath and start again. A woman insisted on embracing Kira as soon as she walked onstage, after she finished her monologue, before she walked away, each time ignoring the stage manager's silent but obvious desire to step away, to keep a physical distance.

Bit by bit, though, we pulled together a cast. Ryan's characters emerged in three vibrant dimensions as human variations spun across the stage. I hadn't realized that one of the daughters could be as old as the actress Hal favored, but as soon as he drew a solid line underneath her name on his pad of paper, I realized that she would bring a new gravity to the role, a solid certainty that I'd missed when I'd read the script.

Three women emerged as strong contenders for the lead, Fanta. Under Kira's able management, the actresses waited in the wings, came back onstage, delivered a second monologue and then a third. Hal had each of them perform with the indomitable daughter. He had them all read with the massive man he was considering for the husband. He asked everyone to improvise a scene, and he had them tell a personal story, about family, about lost chances at communication. (I steadfastly avoided looking at Ryan during that utterly ridiculous theatrical exercise.)

In the end, the cast seemed settled. Certain. Perfect—as if they'd been framed for their roles from the very beginning of time.

Except for one part: the grandmother. Anana had to be soft, gentle. But she also had to have a spine of iron, a solid will that taught her daughter, that guided future generations through hunger, through despair, through the challenges of a modernizing world where the old rules no longer worked, where new rules had yet to be defined.

Anana was only onstage for four short scenes, but those glimpses cemented all of the other characters, set everyone into the difficult lives that Ryan had crafted so delicately.

And we had no one to play Anana.

After reviewing his list for the fourth time, Hal stood up and balled his fists into the small of his back, stretching as he turned to face Ryan and me. "We could try going with Sheryl," he said, referring to one of the actresses who had been put through her paces for the better part of the morning. "We could work with her on the physicality of the role. Coach her to walk like an eighty-year-old village woman."

Ryan shook his head vigorously, oblivious to the way his hair brushed against his collar at the back of his neck. "I'm sorry. I know that you have more experience than I do. It's just that Anana has to be *real*. She's the core of tradition, of old Africa. In a lot of ways, she's even more important than Fanta."

Hal looked at me. "What do you think, Becca? Could Sheryl work?"

Great.

There I was, caught between my boss and my— What? Lover? Definitely not. Crush? I couldn't be certain. Neighbor? Yeah, but…

Oh. *Playwright.* That's what Ryan was to me. That's all that he could be, while we stood here in the darkened Mercer theater, trying to figure out who would embody his vision of Africa.

I braced myself and cast my professional lot with the man who knew the material best. "We shouldn't make a decision out of desperation, Hal. If we know that Sheryl's not right now, we can't count on her changing enough in just six weeks. The part's too important for us to hope she can get to where we need her to be."

Ryan flashed me a quick smile of gratitude. For just an instant, I felt like we were working together again, driving his vision forward, as we had done so successfully in the yellow-and-orange land of the Popcorn King. A sliver of heat uncurled in my belly, and I smiled without meaning to.

But that smile must have said too much. Must have reminded Ryan of how we'd celebrated our past alliance. Or not quite celebrated, as the awkward case might be. He glanced away, scrambling for one of Kira's needle-sharp pencils. As he bounced its perfect pink eraser against the table, doubt drowned whatever flicker of passion had considered awakening inside me.

Maybe that hadn't even been passion after all. Maybe I was just hungry, after the long hours of auditions.

"What about Maria Rodriguez?" I asked, less because I thought the actress would work as Anana and more because I needed to cover up the strange moment, needed to erase the bizarre tension between Ryan and me.

"Maria?" Ryan asked carefully.

Hal glanced at his pad of paper. "She's probably got the vocal range. She could age her voice. But I really see Maria as Lehana."

He had a point. Lehana was an auntie, an older woman who had power and control within the complicated family structure that Ryan had crafted. But Lehana was no grandmother, no matriarch for the ages. And neither was Maria. I sighed in frustration.

"Excuse me?" The voice came from behind us, from the back of the theater. A woman was speaking loudly, clearly, with just a hint of apology underneath her words. Hal was already facing the back doors, but Ryan and I turned at the same time to see the newcomer.

Kira spoke from the stage, keeping her voice polite as she shaded her eyes for a better view. "May I help you?"

The woman stepped into the theater, letting the lobby door close behind her. She blinked in the relatively dim light as she pulled herself to her full height—which wasn't much. I figured she was about a foot shorter than I was.

But she had me outpaced by a mile when it came to dignity.

As the newcomer approached us, she carried herself with a regal solemnity. Her spine was straight, rigid with a precision that spoke of a lifetime of pride. I could picture her raising her arm, waving to a crowd of onlookers, the Queen of England at a parade.

If the Queen of England just happened to be an elderly black woman.

She stopped halfway down the aisle, pausing to eye us with the patience and grace of an ancient lioness. "I apologize," she said, and the words flowed toward us like a stream of melted caramel. "I intended to be here at the start of auditions, but I was unavoidably detained." The woman offered up some papers—a resume and a headshot. "I beg your pardon. Is it possible for me to read for the part of Anana?"

Hal's excitement shimmered like a coil of heated wire. I followed his blue topaz gaze as he took in the new arrival's serious expression, as he measured the corona of tight gray curls that framed her earnest face. Ryan was staring at the woman, as well, his expression so rapt that I wondered if he'd even heard a single word she'd said. The pencil that he'd clutched as a defense against awkwardness, against me, clattered onto the table like a tree trunk toppling in a forest.

The woman spoke again. "I can assure you that my delay this afternoon is a complete anomaly. I'll not be late again. I know how important your time is, and I understand the demands of a theatrical production in a house as professional as the Mercer. May I read?"

Hal gestured toward the stage, his arm trembling as if he were King Lear. "Please," he said, and I think he just stopped himself from bowing. He and Ryan sank into their seats at the same time, excitement driving them to lean forward, as if they could pull perfect words out of the woman by force of will alone. I only barely kept myself from moving in the same inexorable pattern.

Kira jumped down to join us as the woman proclaimed, "I'm Felicia Halliday. My monologue is from *Richard III*."

She paused for a moment, her head bowed as if she were in some secret church. Her fingers curled into loose fists, and I could feel the energy that radiated out from her, pulsing across the theater.

"If ancient sorrow be most reverent, give mine the benefit of seniory and let my griefs frown on the upper hand."

The familiar lines of mournful Queen Margaret rolled over the seats. Felicia kept her voice low, but she spoke from her diaphragm, pulling every one of us to the literal edge of our seats. We could hear every single syllable that she pronounced, almost as if a cone of power magnified the force of her speech.

She set each word into the charged air of the theater, nestling her terrible images of death and loss into the air around us, as if every phrase were a delicate glass ornament. Every sentence settled into place with perfection, with the gravitas of a matriarch, with a terrifying hint of frailty, of vulnerability, of age. Felicia found Hal's eyes as she spoke, pinning him with her speech, pouring her emotion into his ears.

Despite my determination to avoid Ryan, to set myself apart from him, I heard him catch his breath. I saw him clutch his pencil. I watched him lean forward, drawn to Felicia like a thirsty man desperate for a fountain.

I felt the pull myself, a tug as urgent as undertow at the beach. I wanted to go with the actress. I wanted to travel wherever she would take me. I wanted to see her, to be with her, to stay forever in her presence.

She recited the last line of her speech, settled the last word into the theater's perfect silence. Her right hand relaxed by her side, loosening from the tight fist that had fueled her theatrical storm.

And that's when I saw it—the tiny hint of flame.

The tattoo was etched into her obsidian skin, woven into her midnight flesh so expertly that I nearly missed it entirely. But my fingers were attuned to that mark. My thumb and forefinger greeted "Felicia" with the slightest tingle, with the barest apprehension of power.

Teel, I wanted to shout.

Before I could say anything, though, Hal collapsed back in his chair, clearly overcome by the mastery we all had witnessed. He turned to Ryan, leaning close, but I heard his gleeful whisper clearly. "She's our Anana. She's perfect."

Before Ryan could agree, I sprang to my feet, brandishing my bottle of water like a woman bearing the Olympic torch through a crowd. "Thank you, Ms. Halliday," I said, and my voice sounded as false and hearty as a pitchman in a late-night infomercial. "Thank you very much for that reading!"

I leaped onto the stage, shoving my water into Teel's hand, as if the old woman had been threatening to collapse. I stepped in front of her to shield our conversation from everyone else, and then I muttered, "What the hell do you think you're doing?"

Teel looked up at me with ancient eyes, with eyes that knew a thousand ways to lie. "What do you mean?"

I glanced at her wrist, at the cuff that obscured all but a tiny flash of golden ink. "You can't do this! You can't be in our play!"

She turned her head to one side, a wise and curious raven. "Why not? I'll be available to you, whenever you're ready to make your last wishes. You won't forget about me, this way. You won't delay in making your wishes."

I wasn't about to apologize. I had every right to hold my two wishes in abeyance.

Teel grinned wickedly and twisted her rhetorical knife. "And this way, I'll stay out of trouble."

I bit my lip, struggling to superimpose the image of bubble-headed Marilyn Monroe over the diminutive but majestic creature who stood before me. I was only too certain that Teel could invent all new meanings for the word *trouble*— every day and in a million different ways. I seized her arm, hoping that no one else could see how tightly I was clutching her flesh. "You cannot ruin this show, Teel. It's too important. It means too much to Ryan. And to the Mercer. And—and to me."

She nodded toward the men and Kira, who were gathered into a tight knot. "*They* seem to think that I'd be perfect."

Of course, a little Marilyn Monroe flirtation wasn't the worst thing that could happen to Ryan's play. Losing its key actor in the middle of the run would be the greatest disaster. Realizing that I had one last big gun for the battle at hand, I hissed, "So help me, Teel, if you insist on being part of this cast, I won't make my final wish until the show is over."

"So you say," she said, apparently the voice of reason. "But if you found something worth wishing for, I'm sure you'd come around…"

"I wouldn't," I said, making my voice as firm as I could.

Before Teel could reply, Hal said, "Felicia?"

Teel stepped to one side, so that she could look at my boss directly. Her imperious shrug reminded me to release her arm. "Yes, Mr. Bernson?"

"I notice that you don't have an address on your papers. Are you living here in New York?"

"Oh, yes," Teel said. Standing this close to her, I could feel the spell that she cast through her tattoo, the ensnaring magic that she wafted toward the trio in the center of the theater. Kira frowned slightly; she must have sensed the genie magic, having been the beneficiary of Teel's spells in the past. Ryan looked disoriented, as well, uncertain. Or maybe I was just displacing some of my own feelings onto him.

Hal, though, was immediately ensnared by Teel's magic. He…settled into his place. I couldn't think of another word for it. He didn't move, not precisely. He didn't step out of the row of theater seats; his feet didn't shift at all. Rather, the set of his shoulders eased. Subtle lines on his face relaxed. He was comfortable. He was content. He was *home*.

Teel continued, as if there hadn't been a pause in her reply. "I was in transition, but I'm settled in the city now. I can give my address to your fine dramaturg here. Or to your stage manager, if you'd prefer."

I saw Kira *wake up,* shudder to attention as she realized exactly what was going on. I recognized the instant that she shook free from Teel's spell, the second that she pulled loose from our genie's hypnotic suggestion. She stared at the two of us in shock. I couldn't say if her expression was meant more for my benefit, or for the benefit of the creature at my side.

"Hal," she said, never taking her eyes from Teel. I watched her chase a half-dozen arguments to ground, fruitlessly. Neither one of us would be able to explain the full truth. Neither one of us could say the word *genie*.

As if to prove that Kira was no match for her, Teel boosted

her magic, the wave of her hypnotic control sparkling even higher. I found myself wondering why I was worried about having her join *However Long*. Why did I have any fear at all? Teel was a genie, after all. Teel was *my* genie. What could possibly go wrong, if she were cast as Anana? Who could ever make a better Anana than Teel?

I dug my fingers into the palms of my hands, forcing myself to toss off Teel's spell, just as Hal said, "We'd be pleased to have you join our production, Felicia."

Ryan spoke, as if someone had elbowed him in the ribs. "Yes," he said. "Pleased."

"Hal—" Kira started to say again, and I could read the struggle on her face, the pitched battle to remember why it was so important to warn him.

I shook my head in annoyance, fighting to clear my own thoughts so that I could bolster Kira's argument. Before I could speak, though, Teel coughed. The motion was enough to make me turn to face her. She reached out her knotted old-lady hands, folded them around my own fingers, clasping my water bottle between us. "Thank you, dear," she said, pitching her words just loud enough that the others could hear. As I let her take the bottle, she added something meant only for me. "Five out of ten public appearances by genies go exactly as expected. But you don't have to play the odds. You can just make your last two wishes. *Now*. Then, we'd all be happy."

Five out of ten. Fifty-fifty—*if* I believed a single statistic my genie had flung my way. I bit my lip and reached a decision. "Not now. I'm not ready to wish now."

"Then relax." Teel smiled serenely. "What could possibly go wrong?"

Even as she asked the question, I realized that Hal and

Ryan had come onstage. Both men were eager to greet our newest actress, to welcome her into the production. As Ryan shuffled in front of Teel, I turned and gazed out at the audience seats. Kira had collapsed beside the worktable, sinking into a chair and stretching out her legs, as if she were trying to melt into the floor. She stared at me, shaking her head slowly. I shrugged and mouthed, "What could I do?"

She rolled her eyes and sighed. I only hoped that we could work together to control our headstrong genie.

CHAPTER 11

ALL TOLD, THE AUDITIONS HAD GONE BETTER THAN I ever would have predicted.

Sure, I was worried about Teel being in the cast. I knew, firsthand, how destructive she could be. Moreover, I was concerned about what would happen to the show if I did make my last wish before the end of the play's run. Teel would go off to wherever genies go, and the Mercer would be left high and dry.

But I had seen the sheer emotional strength behind her audition monologue. I understood the acting ability that she broadcast every day, every second that she skated through the ordinary human world. I had no doubt that Teel was our Anana.

The rest of the cast had fallen into place, as well. The talent we'd accrued that Saturday morning had been stunning. *However Long* would be everything Hal and I had dreamed of; it would make the Mercer's reputation as a company that asked serious questions, posited real debates. We'd accomplish more with Ryan's work than we ever could have done with *Crystal Dreams.*

Ryan. It had been so awkward seeing him inside the theater first thing that Saturday morning. At least no one else had figured out what was going on between us. No one could have suspected that he'd almost ended up in my bed the night before. To any casual observer, we were the mature professionals we pretended to be. We were coworkers, diligently intent on creating a small theatrical miracle. We were colleagues, and I was determined to keep my distance, absolutely, completely, religiously. I vowed that I wouldn't talk to him unless we had someone else with us, a chaperone of sorts.

After nine straight days of work, I'd almost convinced myself that rule was working. (I know. A week should only have five workdays. Normal people rest for two days, recuperate over their weekends. But there was no rest for the weary—not with a production as far behind schedule as *However Long.* Through no fault of my own, of course. Through no fault of anyone—except, perhaps, an overzealous copyright lawyer named Elaine Harcourt.)

I'd kept myself busy for long hours, researching the political history of Burkina Faso, where Ryan had completed his Peace Corps service and where he'd set *However Long.* I'd prepared briefing books for Hal, for Kira, for the actors who would take on the play's lead roles. I'd read through reams of articles, peering at my computer screen until my eyes teared up with the strain.

Yeah. The strain of looking at endless electronic pixels. That's why my eyes were tearing. Really. It couldn't have anything to do with the mess I'd made of my personal life. Nothing to do with Dean or Ryan or anything else. Nothing at all.

Each night, I stumbled home to my apartment, feeling like a Marine conducting door-to-door fighting. My muscles were pulled tight, ready at any moment to jump back inside the elevator, to lunge for the emergency stairs. Anything to keep from running into Ryan by accident. Anything to keep from thinking about the heat that had soared between us. About the embarrassment that had crushed whatever fledgling emotions had tried to bloom that night in my apartment.

For good measure, I avoided Dani, too. I'd already seen the way that she could worm her way into my life. She'd enchanted me with her guerilla gardening, but I wasn't going to succumb to an attack of guerilla mothering. No matter how well she had seemed to understand me the night we planted the cabbage seeds. I wasn't going to let Dani drag me into a conversation about her son, about the man I'd almost…

That thought made another frustrated tear sketch its way down my cheek.

No. It was better to avoid Dani altogether. Twice, I'd started to open my apartment door, only to find that she was standing across the hall, juggling keys and potting soil, or gardening shears and a giant roll of heavy black plastic. The normal, sane woman who lived inside my body urged me to step out, to offer her a hand, to help like any ordinary neighbor would.

But the coward inside me whispered my door closed and counted to a hundred—twice—before venturing out.

I wasn't completely insane, though. I didn't kill the seedlings she'd entrusted to me. I kept them watered, turning the rolling rack every couple of days to maximize the delicate plants' exposure to sunlight. The green leaves continued to unfold, fragile as lace.

I managed to maintain my anti-Ryan vigilance for an entire week, until the Monday night of our second week of rehearsals. I'd spent most of the day in my office, researching the grim effects of starvation on mental processes. I was trying to create a window for Fanta, a way to help the actress see into her character's somber life.

I only felt a little guilty as I powered off my computer, as I collected the oversize purse that contained half my life. My life was so easy compared to Fanta's. Now that I'd received my first post-Dean paycheck, now that I'd broken my lease at the apartment we'd shared, left that part of my life behind forever, I was able to relax, just a little. In fact, I couldn't wait to get back to the Bentley. Tonight would be the perfect opportunity to shed my Teel wardrobe for my one pair of sweatpants, to pull my hair back into a loose ponytail, to watch the trashiest TV I could find while I used chopsticks to pick out the best tidbits of ordered-in Chinese food.

I was so intent on deciding between mu shu pork and Szechuan chicken that I forgot to keep an eye out for Ryan.

He was waiting right outside the theater's door, stepping out of the shadows just as I moved onto the sidewalk. He glided up beside me like some benevolent stalker. The collar of his coat was turned up, and he'd shoved his hands deep inside his pockets. "Ryan!" I said. "What are you doing here?"

I should have expected the goofy grin. "I work here. Remember?" He fell into step beside me, matching my stride step for step. "I wanted to wait for you," he said, then added deferentially, "As long as we're walking back to the same building."

I told myself that my breath caught in my throat because of our efficient, block-devouring Manhattan pace. At the same time, I racked my brain for something to say, for something meaningful to share with him. Okay, meaningful wasn't mandatory. I'd settle for something entertaining. All right, entertaining was a pretty high order for the day. I'd go with just about anything in English.

"Ryan—" I finally began, just as he said my name at the same time. "You go first," I said, grateful that I didn't have to improvise further.

He became unnaturally fascinated by the cornice on a building across the street. Directing his words to that marble molding instead of to me, he said, "Becca, I owe you an apology."

"You—" I started, but he cut me off.

"This is hard enough. Let me finish. I've been trying to figure out what to say all day." He stopped speed walking, pulling me to a halt with a gentle hand on my sleeve. "I'm sorry that I left that night."

"I threw you out!" I exclaimed, before I could think of something more demure to say.

He shook his head. "You told me to stop. You were right. We're working together. I shouldn't have confused things. I shouldn't have mixed our personal and professional lives. But when I did, when you stopped me, I should have stuck around. I mean, it didn't have to be—*doesn't* have to be just about the physical."

"It's okay," I said, because I needed to say something.

"No, it isn't. I thought it would be okay, because we got through auditions. But you've avoided me for the past week. I mean, I like Jenn well enough, but I can't spend the rest of the rehearsal process sending messages to you through your assistant."

"I am mentoring Jenn! I'm trying to give her more authority!"

His voice was very gentle, even though he continued to talk to the building across the street. "You're trying to avoid me. You shouldn't have to do that." He shrugged. "I was wrong. I shouldn't have run away that night."

As difficult as this conversation was, I was touched by the effort he was making. I was surprised by his willingness to put his feelings into words. I realized, though, that his eloquence shouldn't have surprised me. He was a playwright, after all. The words of *However Long* were what had drawn me into the play, well before I knew anything about the man behind them. "You didn't run away," I said. "You only did what I asked you to do."

He sighed ruefully. "Well then, I shouldn't have spent the past week poking my head around corners, making sure the path was clear before I ventured out of my own home."

I stifled a laugh. "Oh, come on! I can't imagine *anyone* doing that." I was relieved to see him grin in sudden understanding. Making a split-second decision to forge ahead with our New and Improved Work-Based Relationship, I cast off my dreams of a quiet evening alone, with only the Szechuan Gate for company. "Do you want to grab a drink at the Pharm? Half the Mercer will be there."

"I'd like that," he said. Even as he spoke, though, he stepped away from me. "But I can't. I promised my mother I'd help out with a project."

Without permission, my memory ducked back to the night we'd stood over Dani's workbench. I could feel Ryan's hands on mine, expertly guiding my trowel over the waiting peat cups. My cheeks flushed red, and I hoped the evening light was dim enough that he couldn't see. "What sort of project?" I asked.

"Seed bombs."

"What?" I don't know what I'd expected him to say, but *seed* and *bomb* were two words I'd never expected to find crouching in the same sentence.

He looked around before he repeated himself, as if he were a little embarrassed by the words. "Seed bombs. We mix flower seeds in soil, prepare 'bombs' that can be planted anywhere. It's warm enough now. The seed bombs are always the first major offensive of the year."

"'Major offensive'? I thought this 'guerilla' stuff was just a joke."

"It is, and it isn't. I mean, my mother isn't actually going to chain herself to a bus shelter so she can plant a few sunflowers, and she's not planning on blowing up any government buildings to make a point. But she's absolutely serious about our need to take back the streets. She's sworn to find beauty in New York, wherever it can be found. Just wait. Every year, once the vegetables are in the ground, she goes a bit crazy, protecting the seedlings until food can actually be harvested."

"I can't picture her actually going to war over a few plants."

"Some of the Gray Guerillas have been arrested, multiple times. But not Mom. Not yet, anyway." I tried to picture the gentle Dani shuffling into a courtroom wearing a prison jumpsuit, with chains looped around her hands and feet. I'd already seen the citation that policeman had issued, just because she was turning over the dirt outside our building.

I smiled at the notion of elderly saboteur gardeners gathering in the shadows. "And I thought the Bentley was such a prestigious address."

"You'd be surprised by what goes on there. The Grays are a particularly organized cell. Have you met Lorraine Feingold? In 3F? Let's just say you want her on your side in a battle." He shook his head with a laugh. "She's the Grays' webmaster. She keeps the whole website up, coordinating all the attacks, and she manages the e-mail list, the blog, all of it. Has an absolutely black thumb, kills every plant she comes near, but she doesn't want to be left out of the excitement, out of the subversive action. Besides, her son is a lawyer. He can bail her out if she ever gets dragged down to the police station." He caught my disbelieving stare. "What? You don't believe me?"

I laughed. "I just can't believe I never heard about all this before I moved in. Power to the gardeners!" I pumped my fist in a fake gesture of rebellion. "So, will you show me how to build a bomb?"

I expected an immediate answer, but I should have known better. Ryan thought things through, even if that meant he didn't come off like a smooth action hero. He was introspective. He contemplated the meaning of his actions, the impact that they'd have on others. He measured cause and effect before he did anything. "Sure," he said, meeting my eyes for the first time since our disastrous encounter on my couch. I hadn't realized how much I'd wanted that contact, that sign of trust. I hadn't realized how much I'd missed talking to him. He held my gaze as he said, "If that's what you want."

I remembered the way that Ryan had settled into his body when we had stood at Dani's workbench, the way he had relaxed into a calm, confident teacher as he showed me how to plant cabbage seeds. I thought about how much fun I'd had, planting the seeds. I remembered the satisfaction I'd felt as the first delicate plants unfurled in my living room. I imagined the flowers I'd see if I distributed a few seed bombs, or at least contributed toward making them.

I wondered what my mother would think, if I told her I was involved with an underground gardening group. She'd never understand, not in a million years. But Pop-pop might.

"That's what I want," I said.

I tried to tell myself that the guerilla gardening would help me as a dramaturg, that I would understand more about Ryan. I'd better comprehend the jagged-edged world he'd depicted in *However Long*. I could hardly pass up such an opportunity to discover more about my playwright, more about his work—my job practically *required* me to spend time with him. "That's what I want," I repeated.

We spent the last few blocks sharing our thoughts about the cast. Ryan raved about Teel, saying over and over again that she was exactly what he had imagined, that she was a dead ringer for the elderly women he had known in Africa. She *was* Anana, he said more than once, come to life.

I wanted to warn him. I wanted to tell him that she was the same bubble-headed bimbo who had sabotaged our meeting with the Union. I wanted to tell him that I didn't trust her, couldn't be certain that she wasn't going to find some new way to turn our entire production upside down.

But how could I explain that Teel had changed her shape? I could still remember how my throat had closed up when I tried to tell Jenn about the magic in my life.

Teel had been cast—she was the best Anana we'd seen.

There wasn't anything I could do about that now, nothing I could change. If I even wanted to change it. I just wasn't sure.

Besides, I was going to keep an eye on my genie. Kira was, too. We wouldn't let anything get out of hand. Everything would work out fine.

Yeah, I didn't totally believe that, either. But I couldn't share any more of my apprehensions with Ryan. Not without sounding like a raving lunatic.

Arriving home, I ducked into my apartment, taking the time to shed my Teel-wardrobe outfit, in favor of more comfortable jeans and a T-shirt. I stared at myself in my bathroom mirror, wondering what sort of idiotic mistake I was about to make. Why was I going across the hall? What exactly did I think I was going to gain by spending more time with Ryan?

I wasn't an idiot. I knew that I was inviting some sort of reaction, some sort of *interaction* by returning to the scene of our earlier crime, by volunteering to stand next to the workbench with him.

I was just going to have fun, though. I was going to do a bit of subversive gardening. Ryan was off-limits, and I was going to keep things that way. The success of *However Long* required me to keep things that way.

Anyway, it would be easy to keep my hands to myself. I'd seen what happened when I let myself get carried away. I'd just lived an entire week with the consequences of forgetting myself. I'd suffered the awkwardness of the wrong thing said, the improper things done. In fact, it was sort of a *good* thing that we'd let ourselves get a little carried away a week before. I'd recognize the danger signs now. I'd stop such contact well before anything else could develop.

Besides, tonight wasn't just about Ryan. I truly wanted to

work with Dani. I wanted to feel her potting soil beneath my hands. I wanted to build something, change something, make an impact on the concrete canyons of my adopted city home. I wove my hair into a loose braid, wrapping the end with a gray elastic. The rubber band was a sort of secret message, a silent alliance with Dani's organization. I squared my shoulders and set off to do warfare.

"Becca!" Dani exclaimed as I slipped through the open front door. "Ryan said you'd be able to join us—I'm so pleased! I ordered some Chinese food. You just missed the delivery man. I hope you like it spicy!"

"I love it spicy!" I said. Dani handed me a rice bowl and a pair of paper-wrapped chopsticks.

"Dig in!" she said, pointing to the bright red and gold containers of food. "There's Szechuan chicken and mu shu pork. And that should be lotus treasure, all vegetables. And rice, of course."

Szechuan chicken *and* mu shu pork. See? There were advantages to eating with others, to giving up my ideal of a quiet night at home, alone. As I breathed in the scent of chili oil, I asked, "How did you know I was going to join you?"

She looked nonplussed. "We're making seed bombs. Extra people always show up when we make seed bombs. It's guerilla ethics, or something."

"Mom always orders extra Chinese food," Ryan contradicted, stepping out from behind the screen that set aside his makeshift bedroom. "It reheats well."

"Don't you give away all of my secrets!" Dani chided, but she was smiling.

Ryan came and sat beside her on the couch. He had shed the sweater and khakis that passed for his work clothes. Now, he wore a stained T-shirt and jeans that were shredded across his knees. The outfit suited him. He looked like he had just walked in from some dusty dirt road, from stretching his legs, from surveying his domain.

"So?" Dani said. "How was rehearsal today? Are you pleased with how the show is developing?"

The finer details of plum sauce and rice pancakes kept me occupied while Ryan raved about Teel. I pretended that the mu shu pork needed my full attention. By the time Ryan loaded up his bowl with spicy chicken, we'd moved on to safer topics, to the other actors, to Hal's velvet-glove-and-iron-fist routine at the theater.

Ryan's enthusiasm was contagious. As he expertly worked his chopsticks, he asked me what I knew about the show's designers. He had grand ideas about the set—he wanted to re-create an actual Burkinabe hut, with a pounded-earth floor. He knew that it would have to be open, that it couldn't be completely accurate, but he hoped that the Mercer would remain as true to reality as possible.

"I haven't seen any plans yet," I said. "I know the general idea of how they meant to handle *Crystal Dreams,* but those designs all went out the window, of course. I'm sure Hal will keep you in the loop."

As we continued chatting, we all ate more Chinese food than anyone could say was strictly necessary. Dani finally collected our bowls and carried them into the kitchen. "Go ahead and get started," she said to Ryan. "As long as you have Becca to help you, I'm going to finish up my blog post."

"What are you writing about this time?" he asked, surrendering his chopsticks.

"How to avoid arrest if the police intervene in street action."

Ryan rolled his eyes, clicking his tongue in disapproval at Dani's placid smile. He turned to me as if he were cutting off an argument before it could begin and asked, "Ready?" He led the way over to the workbench.

Three buckets were already laid out on the table. Each was filled with a different substance. I recognized the dark brown of the compost, and white-flecked potting soil. The third container was filled with a variety of seeds. Some were tiny, scarcely larger than a crystal of salt. Others were larger, though; a few were the size of peas. They ranged in color from sand to mahogany.

As I rattled the seeds around their container, Ryan fished out two more buckets from beneath the workbench. "Watch," he said, "and learn from the master."

I laughed at his boast, pleased to see him so comfortable. He picked up a battered metal measuring cup, turning it in the purple-tinged glow of the grow-lights, as if it were a work of art. Using the cup, he scooped out equal amounts of potting soil and compost, five measures of each. With a showy flick of his wrist, he added a single cup of seeds.

"What are those?" I asked. "I mean, what type of plants?"

Ryan glanced at Dani, where she'd settled on the couch with her laptop. "Mixed wildflowers, I assume." She barely looked up from her computer and nodded. He explained, "We use different mixes for different seasons. By midsummer, we add in sunflowers. Those are my favorite."

"Sunflower seeds I would recognize."

Ryan plunged his hands into his bucket, sifting the earth between his fingers. His forearms clenched and unclenched as he worked the contents together, taking care to distribute the seeds evenly. The motion of his fingers was mesmerizing, the smooth, confident flow of his muscles as captivating as any tattoo sparkle that Teel could ever broadcast.

He spoke as he worked, his voice as relaxed as his physical stance. "The first seed bombs were thrown in the seventies. You know, radical gardeners, working to overthrow The Man. They built their bombs in old glass Christmas ornaments, or they used water balloons."

"Did they really *throw* them?"

"Oh, yeah." He grinned as he poured water into his mixture, working the resulting mud as if it were bread dough. "To hear Dani's old-time friends talk, an underhand lob worked best for the ornaments, but the balloons required substantial initial momentum."

"Initial momentum?"

"They threw them overhand. Hard. Like a baseball—splat!" I laughed, picturing the spray of subversive dirt and seeds and water. Ryan said, "Of course, no one wants to bother cleaning up glass shards or slivers of rubber balloons. Now we mold the bombs into dirt balls and dry them out. If we bomb the target on a rainy night, the seeds sprout in just a few days." He shaped some of his seed mixture into a sphere the size of an apricot and set the finished bomb on a waiting tray.

"Go ahead," he said. "Why don't you get started on your own."

I caught my lower lip between my teeth and picked up the dented measuring cup. Five scoops of potting soil. Five scoops of compost. One scoop of seeds. I only hesitated a second before plunging my hands into the mixture. It felt good between my fingers, warm and crumbly. I stretched my spine as I worked, hunching my shoulders up to my ears, and then relaxing them, taking a deep, satisfied breath.

The water was cold. The potting soil resisted absorbing it, but a little patience worked wonders. When the entire mixture was thoroughly combined, I rolled my first bomb. At first, it held together, but when I tried to transfer it to the tray, it crumbled back into the bucket.

I tried again, taking care not to make it too big. The soil compressed between my palms; the grit of the seeds rubbed against my skin. As soon as I tried to move the ball to the tray, though, it fell apart.

Ryan looked up from his last bomb. "You need more water," he said. He scooped some into my bucket, but my hands deflected the flow. I jerked to the side, barely avoiding creating a miniature cascade. My quick action saved the surface of the workbench, but it moved me precisely in front of Ryan. With a sudden heat, I felt the whole length of his torso against my back.

"Easy," he murmured, steadying my bucket with both hands. The motion brought his arms around me, pinning me between him and the worktable. My heart jackhammered in my throat, and I darted an embarrassed glance at Dani, certain that she must have heard my sudden intake of breath. Dani, though, was no longer sitting on the couch.

Ryan's lips were dangerously close to my ear. With my hair pulled into a plait, my neck felt exposed, vulnerable. I closed my eyes, overcome by a rush of memory from that night, from a week before. Ryan folded his hands over mine, ostensibly helping me to work the water into my seed mixture. The pressure of his fingers was steady. Deliberate.

And then, we both heard Dani emerge from her bedroom. One of her Birkenstocks caught on the doorsill as she joined us, and she clicked her tongue in patent exasperation. Ryan eased back half a step, his hands sliding away from mine in the bucket, his fingers automatically gathering up a ball of dirt, rolling it into a perfect, regular shape. My breath ragged, I followed his example.

"You two work fast," Dani said, as she approached the workbench to survey our creations.

"Any job worth doing," Ryan said, his voice perfectly normal. A quick glance, though, confirmed a shadow of a canary-eating cat grin.

"Is worth doing well," Dani finished. "I'm going to ask Lorraine to check out our computer router. The wireless signal in here was practically nonexistent. I was able to post from the bedroom, though." She set her laptop on the coffee table as she crossed to the workbench. "Those look perfect! They should only take a couple of days to dry. The next rainy night, we'll call a bombing party. You'll join us, Becca?"

I finished rolling the last of my bombs. "Absolutely. That is, if Hal doesn't schedule a rehearsal," I said. My voice shook a little more than usual, but Dani was apparently willing to accept that I was particularly fervent about theater. In the midst of my relief, I was surprised to catch a yawn against the back of my teeth. I glanced at my watch, startled to see that it was nearly ten o'clock.

Ryan followed my gaze. "Time flies when you're having fun." The words were innocent enough, but they sent my belly ski-jumping. "Let me walk you home."

I shot a meaningful glance toward Dani. "I think I can find the way."

Nevertheless, he washed his hands meticulously at the kitchen sink, drying them on a rough cotton towel that seemed to hang nearby for just that purpose. I followed suit, using the pure familiarity of the action to restore my emotional balance.

I turned to Dani and thanked her for dinner. "My pleasure, Becca," she said. "And thank *you* for all your help. Have a good night."

Ryan held the door for me as I stepped into the hallway. Like a consummate gentleman out of some 1950s movie, he took my keys from me. He turned all three locks easily, using the last motion to push open my front door. When he went to return my keys, though, he held them precisely between two fingers, letting them dangle from their leather fob.

They hung between us, like a mouse, caught by its tail.

I wasn't sure if the mouse was about to be freed forever, or if it was about to drop into the maw of a hungry snake.

When I hesitated, Ryan said, "Thank you."

"For what?"

"I could say, for helping with the seed bombs."

The tone of his voice implied all the other things that he could say instead. I wondered if his chest hurt as much as mine did, if his heart was pounding as brutally as mine. "Ryan, I—"

He stepped closer, raising his free hand to rub a thumb across the tip of my nose. "You had a smudge there," he said, without stepping back. "A hazard of guerilla activity."

The gesture was so simple. Disarming. Innocent. And yet the air crackled between us.

I was free to choose. I knew that. I could take my keys, say good-night, send him across the hall. We would never, ever have this conversation again. He would respect my choice. I knew he would.

But I could also choose to kiss him.

His ready arms closed around me, crushing me close. His

fingers traveled up my spine; one hand tugged gently at my braid. My lips opened, and his tongue was waiting, teasing, punctuating his silent argument with playful determination. I summoned every last molecule of logic in my naggingly mature brain to gasp, "We can't, Ryan. Dani."

"I'm a big boy, Bec. I can do whatever I want to do."

After a longer kiss than any theatrical director would dare depict onstage, I remembered the other reason we couldn't be doing this. "We can't," I said again. "The show."

His hands froze. Even though he didn't move, didn't take a step away, I felt him pull back, poised on the edge of letting me go. He said, "You're a big girl, Bec. You can do whatever you want to do." As if he weren't certain of the power of that line, he added, "We *can* make this work."

"But I… But you…" I knew all the arguments that were scrambling around inside my head. I was tired of all those arguments.

But there was another reason I should step away. Another reason I should forget about Ryan, leave him behind, for as long as we both worked in New York theater. That reason still hurt, though. That reason was still raw, still sharp-edged. "But Dean—"

Even as I whispered my ex's name, I sucked in my breath. I didn't want Ryan to misunderstand. I didn't want him to think that I was saying I still loved Dean, that I still wanted him, longed for him. In fact, I meant exactly the opposite. I'd seriously misjudged Dean Marcus, completely ignored all the warning signs, overlooked giant flashing signals of Right and Wrong. I never again wanted to lose myself in a man the way I'd lost myself in Dean. I never again wanted to forfeit my self-respect, to give away the core of my honor. I never again wanted to risk my job, my professional identity, just for a man.

"I'm not Dean. You're not the same person you were with him."

I should have known that Ryan would understand. We'd only known each other for a short time, but he really, truly *got* me. He understood people; he studied them. He used his intuition to figure out what they believed, why they did the things they did. That was the power that had drawn me into *However Long*. That was the power that lit his eyes now, that spread a scant blanket of patience over the fire that sparked there. That was the power that waited for me to decide.

Life was never easy. Sometimes, your boyfriend turned out to be an embezzler. Sometimes, your scheduled play turned out to be a legal minefield. Sometimes, your genie turned out to be a lead player in your hastily assembled cast.

But I could deal with all of that. I could make things work. I could do whatever *I* wanted to do.

I took Ryan's hand, weaving my fingers between his as I pulled him inside my apartment. The skyline of New York City sparkled all the way to the river. Our guerilla seedlings glinted in the moonlight, leaning toward the window with the instinctive yearning of all living things.

I pushed the door closed behind us, and the latch snicked home like a promise.

CHAPTER 12

A WEEK LATER, I WAS DESPERATELY TRYING TO REMEMBER what I'd been so worried about. Ryan had been right. We *could* meld our personal and professional lives. In fact, he made the balance seem easy.

First off, he handled the delicate nature of his living arrangements with a shrug and a smile. Sure, things might have been different if he'd been eighteen, if he'd never left his mother's home. But Ryan was twenty-eight years old. He had gone away to college. He had lived on his own when he worked as a consultant. He had traveled halfway around the world to serve in the Peace Corps.

He wasn't camping out in Dani's living room because he was a mama's boy. He wasn't so tied to Dani that he sought her approval for his every move, for his every thought, for his every emotional twinge. The cot in her living room was merely a matter of convenience, a resting place until he got back on his feet in the States.

I'd worried that Dani would be angry with me for taking

away her little boy. I'd feared that she would be disappointed in my wicked, carnal ways. But she remained her calm, easy-going self, always sweet, always preoccupied with her guerilla activities. She made it seem like I'd hooked up with a good friend's roommate, rather than with a mother's son.

Once, I tried to imagine how my own mother would have reacted under similar circumstances. The likelihood of a sane, logical response, though, was so remote that I immediately abandoned the attempt. I did, however, make a point of letting Mom know that Dean was out of my life. She was thrilled—she'd always hated the guy. I managed to make it sound as if Dean and I had come to a mutual agreement, that he'd found someone else, as I had. Things were simpler that way. For everyone.

Ryan also made things easy at work. A formal announce-ment of our relationship would have been strange under any circumstances, and it was absolutely unnecessary at the Mercer. If people noticed that we walked into rehearsal at the same time each morning, they didn't say anything. If they saw us leave together every night, they likely chalked that up to the fact that we lived in the same building. Of course, we paid attention to each other during the day—I was always subtly *aware* of where Ryan was standing, which seat he'd taken at our worktable, what errands he ran while his presence wasn't absolutely necessary to whatever we were working on. But I didn't track him like a lonely puppy. I didn't hover.

I didn't need to. Ryan gave me confidence in our relation-ship; he let me trust that he'd be there for me whenever I wanted him. Whenever I needed him. He surprised me con-stantly, making little gestures that salved my nervous soul.

My stomach flipped every time I walked by the costume shop, because I couldn't stop playing mental home movies about the morning Ryan had pulled me in there, crushing me against a rack of soft denim work shirts and worn jeans, detritus from the Sam Shepard plays. He'd laughed at my astonishment, his lips vibrating against my throat as the cloud of fabric closed around us, swallowed us up. He'd slipped a single sticky note into my hand, a folded square decorated with a sharp-edged heart.

And he'd openly invited me to sit beside him while the cast worked through the blocking of the complicated opening scene. We'd slouched in seats halfway back in the darkened theater, watching Hal set the placement for the actors. Ryan's script detailed the blocking to an unusual extent; it was extremely important to him where every character stood. He insisted that the staging was an extension of character development. When I listened to him explaining his thoughts on the subject, I understood, and I agreed.

Once the actors had their blocking down, Ryan relaxed a little. He hadn't felt the need to be as involved when Hal worked through the characters' actual lines, when he explored Fanta's opening words, which broke over the audience like shards of crystal, beautiful and dangerous. By the eleventh time the cast had worked through the scene, even I had been willing—eager, actually—to let Ryan's fingers distract me. I'd slunk low in my chair, resting my head against the back of the red velvet seat. I'd barely remembered to bite my lip to keep from mewing a protest as he played with the top button on my shirt, then the one below that, then the sweet lace panel at the top of my bra.

He'd laughed at me when the scene ended for the thirteenth or fourteenth time and Teel stepped to the front of the stage. My genie had shielded her eyes with her hand, peering out into the sea of seats with the crankiness of an old woman. When she finally discerned our shadowy shapes, she called out, "Becca? Could you pull together some information for us about these village markets? Some statistics maybe? What percentage of women barter, and what percentage pay outright?"

Teel and her statistics. I'd been certain she was tweaking me, fully aware of the…games Ryan and I had been playing. I'd swallowed hard, twice, before I'd trusted my voice to stay steady as I called back. "Of course, Felicia. I'll track that down right away." And I'd even resolved to do the research on my own, rather than to schedule a special study session with Ryan.

In fact, I ended up pulling together a three-ring binder specifically on the markets, printing out photos and news stories, journalistic summaries of the daily chaos that a woman like Fanta would face as she tried to stretch her limited household dollars. Ryan sat next to me, nodding in quiet approval as I spoke to the cast, as I tried to convey just how much haggling Fanta would do, just how frustrating it would be for her when the cost of cornmeal doubled each time that she managed to come to the marketplace with hard currency.

My explanation was apparently effective. The actors' eyes narrowed, all around the table. Several of them clenched their fists over their bellies. Hal watched, as well, nodding as he saw the bitter truth register. None of the Mercer cast had ever been turned away in a store, had ever watched prices spiral out of reach even as they waited in line to make their purchases. But all of them began to understand the unbearable weight of hopelessness, the frustration, the fear that this would be the first day when they didn't get to eat at all—not even a bite of corn mush—after their husbands had fed, after their children, after their honored elderly aunties.

The sober silence was broken by the sound of the lobby door crashing open. Kira leaped to her feet as daylight painted the theater aisle. "May I help you?" she called out.

In response, there was a series of loud popping sounds, like gunshots smothered by pillows. "Pop off!" came the rapid-fire response, and Ryan and I met each other's eyes in momentary horror.

The Popcorn King had come to the Mercer.

Kira and Hal, of course, both knew that we had secured Ronald J. Barton's sponsorship, but neither of them had had a chance to meet our benefactor. I rushed down the aisle to try to ease the encounter. "Ronald!" I exclaimed as he slammed his cell phone closed. I tried to sound like his visit was an unexpected pleasure. I hastened to take two huge orange shopping bags from him, narrowing my eyes a little to stop the color from vibrating against the yellow of his trousers.

"Thank you, Becca! I thought I should see the show I'm buying!" he said. Every actor's head swerved toward him, and more than one of the cast caught a breath in disapproving surprise. Ronald barely registered their shocked expressions as he bellowed, "Joke, people! That was a joke!"

"You know actors," I said, purposely pitching my voice low, hoping that he would reduce his volume to match.

No such luck. He pointed to one of the bags I now held, indicating a huge metal canister with splashes of tangerine and lemon paint across its lid. "I brought food! For the cast! No one should ever go hungry!"

I winced, knowing that Ronald had no way of understanding just how inappropriate his comment was, given the subject matter of our play, given the grim scene we had just worked through. "Thank you," I said, forcing out a smile. "I'm sure the cast will appreciate this very much."

"It's our newest flavor! Mousy Mocha Madness—cheddar popcorn with caffeinated chocolate sugar!"

"That sounds...wonderful."

"Mouse! Like cheese! Cheddar! Get it!"

"Absolutely," I said, and I added another, "Thank you."

By then, Kira had called a brief break in the rehearsal. Hal approached us like a bantam rooster; I could see him positioning himself to complain about the interruption to his cast's creative process. I attempted to smooth over the awkwardness by making introductions all around. "And you remember Ryan, of course," I concluded.

"Of course!" Ronald bellowed. "The man who gets things done!" He swallowed Ryan's hand in his own, pumping vigorously. "Pleased to meet you!" Ronald shouted at Hal. "Great things you do here, or so I'm told!"

Hal looked a little stunned as he took back his hand. His eyes traveled from Ronald's bright orange sweater to the soothing shadows at the back of the theater. "Yes," he said, and his voice was strangled. "We try." He shot a glance at me, one of open shock and disbelief.

"Don't have much time! But I wanted to bring shirts for everyone!" Ronald grabbed the second bag from me and pulled out two-dozen T-shirts. "There's more where these came from!"

The shirts in question would definitely come in handy if New York City experienced a blackout of epic proportions.

The brilliant orange and yellow swirls shimmered as if lit from within. In fact, the shirts could probably be used for medical experiments—I suspected they would induce seizures if innocent onlookers were forced to stare at them for longer than thirty seconds.

"Er, thank you," Hal said. I was pretty sure this was the first time I'd ever seen him at a loss for words. He nodded toward me to take the shirts from Ronald. I collected the shimmering mass, but I wasn't certain what to do with them, how to get them out of our immediate line of sight. Thankfully, Kira stepped forward like the ever-efficient stage manager she was and relieved me of the burden.

"I thought you could use them in the show! Those are supposed to be starving people onstage, right?"

"Some of them," Ryan said, when Hal was too bemused to reply.

"One or two should wear these shirts! You can add a line in the script! Something about a generous donor providing clothes for the village!"

"I don't think—" Ryan began.

"That can't be too much to ask! Not when I'm donating *one hundred and fifty thousand* dollars to your show!"

"But—" Ryan said.

"All right! You drive a hard bargain! I'll actually send some shirts to Africa! That'll make it real! Satisfy you theatrical types!"

"It's not a matter of making it real," Ryan protested. "It's just that the designers have a vision, a concept of how the play will look."

"One hundred and fifty thousand dollars!" Ronald's bellow must have been audible on the street. "If you can't use it here, I'll find a theater that can!"

Hal leaped forward. In his best artistic-director voice, he soothed, "Of course we can figure out some way to work in a T-shirt or two. Can't we, Ryan?"

I watched a battle play out on Ryan's face. He must be thinking of the Africa he knew, the real villages, the real people, the *truth* that he had brought out in his script.

But he was also thinking of his life now. Of New York. Of the Mercer. He was thinking of the career he wanted to build, the play he wanted to present, so that thousands of others could share his vision.

"They'll need to be toned down a little," Ryan said. "The family's clothes are patched. Mended. They're dusty."

Ronald glared at him, his eyes as hot as boiling butter-flavored oil. Ryan stood his ground, though, until Hal eased between the two men. "Dusty will be fine," Hal said. "The subliminal value will be even greater, when the audience doesn't immediately register the shirts as an advertisement."

Ronald barked out a laugh. "I like the way you think! Dusty it is, then!" Before he could say anything else, the theater was filled with the sound of popping corn. Ronald snapped into his phone, "Pop off!" He listened for a moment, then shook his head in frustration. "No! That's impossible! Absolutely not!" A squawk of a protest rose from whoever was on the other end of the line. "Because I said so! I'm the Popcorn King!" The caller, however, refused to give in. Ronald held the phone away from his head and bellowed, "Enjoy the shirts! I'll take this outside!"

The door closed behind him, muffling his shouts of "No!" and "Money talks!" He must have made his way through the lobby and out onto the street, because the sounds of big business finally faded away.

Hal looked at Ryan. Ryan looked at me. I looked at Kira and the neon pile of shirts that glared in the theater work lights. She grimaced and caught a straggling garment by its toxic sleeve. "I'll get these to the actors now," she said. "They can start wearing them today, washing them every chance they get. The colors might start to fade." She sounded doubtful, though.

Hal nodded. As Kira started to distribute her ill-gotten goods, my boss turned to Ryan. "Are you okay with this?"

Ryan sighed. "Am I happy that the Popcorn King is shaping the appearance of the play? Absolutely not." He raised his chin. "I understand, though. I know that theater is a co-operative art. I have to compromise. You don't have to worry about me."

Hal took him at his word, jumping back onstage and continuing with the scene that had been interrupted. But I'd heard the underlying uncertainty in Ryan's tone. I knew that he wasn't happy. I knew that he resented Ronald J. Barton, the Popcorn King. And I worried about Ryan for the rest of the day.

A week later, Teel was tugging at her tangerine and gold T-shirt, stretching the hem around her dark, wiry fingers. "Hal, I don't understand my motivation," she said. "I just don't think Anana would walk upstage there. There isn't justification in the lines."

This was our seventh try blocking this particular scene. The action occurred at the end of the first act; it was the emotional high point of the play's first hour. The audience had watched Fanta go to the market, had ached with her as she bargained for a scant bag of cornmeal. The show had demonstrated the strict family hierarchy at home, the way that Fanta's husband ate the lion's share of the meal, the way she fed her children next. There'd been the possibility that Fanta would enjoy the luxury of a full portion, enough food to silence her aching stomach, but then Auntie Lehana had arrived.

Fanta was left with a single palm-full of mush. Three bites, and the need to say that she was happy. That she was content. That she was loved and honored and respected.

Starving, exhausted, Fanta went to her mother, seeking counsel. Fanta had decided to run away, to make her way to Ouagadougou, the distant, mystical capital city of Burkina Faso, where she hoped to find a job, any job, even one that would shame her before her family, just so that she could earn enough money to eat.

Anana was supposed to protest. She was supposed to deny her daughter's dream. She was supposed to declare Fanta dead to her, if Fanta dared to leave the village.

But Teel had other goals in mind.

"In fact," she said, "this speech doesn't really make sense at all." Her dark eyes were serious beneath her crinkled cap of gray hair. The lines between her nose and mouth deepened as she shook her head. "Anana has never seen Ouagadougou. She could never talk about the streetcars. She'd never mention the Grand Mosque. She may be old and experienced and the voice of reason, but she's still a villager. She's still an innocent."

I glanced at Teel's wrist as she spoke. At my direct command, she was keeping her tattoo covered in rehearsal. I could sense, though, that she was still using its power. A minor hypnotic spell drifted over the room whenever she spoke aloud. That magic was part of what gave her performance so much power, but it also gave her an unfair advantage when she argued for more time onstage, or for different blocking, or for a change in the reading of her lines.

I sighed. At least the flames weren't glinting in the theater work lights. I didn't have to worry about some newcomer walking in, questioning what was going on, asking why an elderly African American woman had a wreath of fire tattooed around her wrist.

Hal pinched the bridge of his nose between his thumb and forefinger. The speech that Teel was questioning was the emotional linchpin for the entire first act. If audiences didn't buy her words, they'd never accept Fanta's ultimate choice, they'd never be drawn into the horrors of the second act, to the play's devastating catharsis and emotional finale.

"Becca?" Hal asked. "What do you think?"

The thing was, Teel had a point. Ryan had, by necessity, written his play from an outsider's perspective. As a white man, he had walked the broad streets of Ouagadougou. He had ridden in the city's green cabs. He had visited its museums, strolled through its university campuses.

The city was part of the magic he wove through his script. It held the shimmering seduction of the unknown, the unknowable. It symbolized change and advancement, even as it stood for loss and alienation.

But Anana would not know those things. Anana's strength came from her life in the village, from the decades that she had spent surrounded by tradition, by family, by the known and familiar.

I looked at Ryan as I answered, drawing out my reply by testing each word in my mind before I said it aloud. "I'm not certain that there *is* a textual basis for what Anana says. Nothing in the script tells us how she knows about the city."

Ryan protested, "She's heard about it since she was a little girl! Travelers come to the village all the time! They share stories!"

Teel replied before anyone else could. "But that's not what the words say. The words make Anana's experience much more immediate. Too real. Too personal."

Before Ryan could spit out a reply, Kira interrupted. "Sorry, folks. We're going to have to take a quick break here. The set designer has the theater reserved for an hour, to take some final measurements."

I flashed the stage manager a relieved smile. She met my gaze, barely shaking her head in a secret message. Teel's behavior was exactly what she'd warned me about, the precise type of interference that had nearly destroyed Kira's previous production. I needed to act quickly, to keep things from getting out of hand.

As Teel shuffled offstage, I hurried to her side, determined to buttonhole her before she could structure yet another round of argument. Out of the corner of my eye, I saw Ryan make a similar beeline to Hal, obviously starting to plead his own case.

Even as I reached out to tug at Teel's tangerine-colored sleeve, I couldn't help but watch Ryan. He was speaking too quietly for me to hear his precise words, but I recognized the tension that set his shoulders. I'd massaged those same shoulders the night before, doing my best to rub away a day's accumulated stress. My fingers had kneaded, probed, pushed deep into muscles set as firm as cement.

When a concerted half hour of uninterrupted attention

had done nothing to ease Ryan's body, we'd retreated to the couch in the living room. I'd collected a bottle of wine from the kitchen and poured two generous glasses. We'd sat at opposite ends of the sofa, our legs covered by a cashmere-soft blanket, and we'd talked. And talked and talked and talked.

I'd learned more about Ryan's life in one night than I had in all the previous time we'd spent together. I'd heard about how his father had died when he was eighteen. How he'd settled into being Dani's friend more than being her son. How he'd worked as a consultant to the finance industry, making plenty of money but never finding a second's fulfillment. How he'd spent his free time tinkering with computers, creating software that made his day job easier. How he'd realized he had to leave town, leave the country, join the Peace Corps and try to make the world a better place.

The night had felt more like a popcorn-and-pajamas overnight with a girlfriend than a soul-baring revelation from the man I was becoming (had become?) firmly, completely infatuated with. Well, it had felt like a girlfriend gossip night until Ryan had started to tickle the soles of my feet. Until I'd warned him to stop. Until he'd refused, letting his hands cascade over my calves, finding the sensitive hollows behind my knees. Until I'd had no option but to capture those hands, to put them to good use exploring other parts of my anatomy, until I'd dragged him back to my bedroom and thoroughly distracted him from his riotous inventory of everything that could make me squirm.

His shoulders had been a lot more relaxed after that. His shoulders, and every other inch of his body.

But the tension had returned. It radiated from his back, like a giant exclamation mark suspended over his body.

First things first, though. "Teel," I whispered harshly. "What the hell do you think you're doing?"

The old black woman in front of me blinked slowly, as if she couldn't believe I was asking my question. "I'm rehearsing the role of Anana."

"Why are you suggesting changes to the script? What do you care about the play, anyway? You're going to leave us as soon as I make my last two wishes."

My genie looked around, conspicuously making sure that no one could overhear us. "That doesn't seem likely to happen any time soon, now, does it? You've got *other* things to focus on."

"I—I've been busy," I said.

Teel's gaze cut across the room, dissecting Ryan as if he were a fetal pig pinned to a wax tray. "So I've noticed. Nine out of ten wishers delay wishes when they're involved in fulfilling physical relationships."

"Teel!"

"Hush!" The old woman pursed her lips in disapproval. "No one here knows me by that name. You're going to raise a lot of questions that you don't want to answer."

I wasn't in a mood to be lectured. "Is that your plan? Make my life so uncomfortable that I'll make my wishes just to get you to go away?"

Those placid coffee eyes hardened. "If I wanted to make your life uncomfortable, we wouldn't be chatting about it onstage." She drew herself to her full height, ignoring the fact that she was still a full head shorter than I was. "You make your decisions, and I make mine. I have decided to enjoy being an actress. I have decided to make Anana the strongest character I can. And making her strong means making her real. She wouldn't talk about Ouagadougou."

I hesitated. As much as I wanted to challenge my genie, as much as I knew part of her protest was a rebellion against my failure to complete my wishes, I also knew that she was right. I knew that an old village woman wouldn't speak the wistful poetry that Ryan had put into her mouth. She'd find other words, use other images, but the big city wouldn't be the core of her argument.

Nevertheless, I set my jaw. "You just watch yourself, Teel. I won't let you ruin this production."

"Have I done anything wrong yet?"

And she was right. She hadn't. She'd made the show better. If only I could make Ryan see that.

I turned away without answering. Dragging my feet, I approached Ryan and Hal, wedging my way between them as they huddled in the aisle. I set my weight carefully, leaning slightly toward Ryan, showing him the merest hint of favoritism. I didn't touch his side, but I could feel the heat of his body through his clothes. The same heat that had blazed against my Egyptian cotton sheets the night before…

I shook my head and thrust myself back into the present discussion. Hal helped, pinning me with his blue searchlight eyes. "So? What do you think, Becca? Does the speech make sense?"

"It's one of the most beautiful passages I've read, ever," I said. I felt Ryan relax a little, spinning out a tiny fraction of the frustration he'd been banking. "But I don't think it works for the play."

"What?" Ryan looked as if I'd trampled on his favorite guerilla seedlings.

"I just think that—" In my rush to explain myself, I couldn't remember Teel's assumed name, couldn't remember the lie that my genie had told in auditions. I stumbled over my words, anxious not to lose the thread of my argument. "I think that Anana is right. She wouldn't know those things. The power in this play comes from the compounding of simple images, the construction of simple thoughts."

Ryan answered with heat. "The power in this play comes from the facts! Villagers hear about life in the city!"

Hal said, "Maybe you can write another scene for us, something to give us that perspective. We can drop it into the first half hour. You can show us how the women talk, how they dream, what they know about Ouagadougou."

Ryan sighed in exasperation. "There isn't anyplace to put a scene like that. The entire first act is set up to separate Fanta, to show that she is alone, that she doesn't think the way the others do." I heard the anguish in his voice. The play was his child, his creation, and we were criticizing it, asking him to change it. I felt terrible.

And yet, I knew what I had to do, as dramaturg. I knew my responsibility to the production. "You're right," I said, taking care to keep my voice soft. Agreeable. My psychological training shone through; Ryan relaxed again. "But Hal's right, too. You can rework Anana's speech. You've built the images around the city. You can shift them a little. Show us the same themes, but use family as the anchor. Use Anana's character, as we've already seen it revealed."

His first instinct was to refuse. He shoved his hands deep into his pockets, hunched his shoulders, looking exactly like the nervous, awkward man who had first stood in the Mercer's offices, begging, hoping, praying that I'd look at his manuscript. I had to give him something more, some additional reassurance.

"You can do it, Ryan. I know you can. I know you can rework the scene, and it will be stronger than it already is. It will show us even more about the people, about the land."

"I—" He was going to refuse. But then he closed his eyes. He took three deep breaths, holding each for a solid count of five before exhaling. He took his hands out of his pockets, unfolded his fingers from his tight fists. He glanced at Hal, but when he spoke, he directed the words to me. "I'll try," he said. "I'll see what I can do."

"Wonderful," Hal said, clapping a hand on his shoulder. "That's all we're asking for."

Before he could say anything else, Kira called from the stage, asking Hal to check out some detail regarding the set design. Ryan barely watched him go, focusing instead on me.

"Are we okay?" I asked.

He managed a shaky grin. "Yeah," he said. "Of course we're okay. I'll figure out a way to rework the scene."

The wave of relief that crashed against me was terrifying.

Somehow, against all odds, Ryan and I managed to stay "okay."

The set started to take shape, rustic planks that formed the walls of Fanta's home, with a corrugated iron roof that slanted toward the audience, drawing onlookers into the dilapidated property. Ryan protested that he'd never seen a metal roof in the village where he'd worked. I pointed out, though, that iron castoffs were common in Burkina Faso, that the designer had used legitimate sources to structure the set, that the audience would be able to see and understand better, when the general design was familiar. Ryan gave in.

The Popcorn King stopped by again, surprising us all with

his explosive ringtone. He fell in love with the stage design, demanded that the roof sport the logo of his shops, etched in orange and lemon yellow. Hal shook his head at the idea, but Ronald reminded us that his second check still hadn't been delivered. Hal looked pointedly at Kira, ordering her to call an impromptu afternoon break in rehearsal. I took Ryan for a walk around the block, explaining that we could age the logo, make it look ancient, decrepit. The audience would hardly recognize the thing; it would be a subliminal message at most. And we could keep our funding. Ryan gave in.

The actress playing Fanta struggled with her West African accent, slipping out of the proper dialect into a Jamaican drawl with disconcerting ease. Hal began to tug at his beard, his frustration transparent. He considered performing the show without the verisimilitude of any accents at all. Ryan insisted that the rhythm of the speech was vital to the success of the play. He spent one night tossing restlessly in bed; both of us were yawning the next day. He spent the next night pacing in front of my windows, muttering lines of the play out loud, testing them in a legitimate accent, then repeating them in a nasal New York twang. The third night, he stayed at Dani's, giving me a chance to get some desperately needed sleep. I figured out a solution as soon as my mind was no longer tethered by exhaustion: I located an expert dialect coach and convinced Hal to free up some of the Popcorn King's largesse to pay for one-on-one tutoring for the cast. Ryan was relieved.

Everything should have been fine. Everything should have been easy. But a constant scoreboard flashed in my mind. I was always aware of the concessions that Ryan had made, the arguments that he'd lost.

I knew how to do my job. I knew how to shape a production. I knew how to measure a show, to adjust it, to make it appear more *true*.

But every tweak I suggested, every change Hal implemented, every modification the cast absorbed, echoed in my personal life. Every couple of days, Ryan left the theater frustrated, and I walked back to the Bentley alone. Every few nights, he helped Dani with guerilla gardening, making more seed bombs, distributing the cabbage and onion seedlings that had finally grown enough to leave the shelter of my sunny window.

I tried to talk to him. I tried to reassure him. I tried to tell him that every new play was modified, every production was worked and reworked and re-reworked.

But some things were too difficult to talk about, even with Ryan. Some things were easier left unsaid.

Unsaid, that was, except in conversations with my mother. Ever since she'd found out that Dean was out of my life, she'd been calling me regularly. Every other day, my cell announced her presence with the piano prelude to Christina Aguilera's "Oh Mother." Whenever I answered, I got a full dose of San Diego gossip. I spent the better part of each call, though, engaged in emotional fencing, squirming to avoid giving away too many details about my personal life.

I obviously mentioned Ryan once too often, though. My mother clicked her tongue in exasperation, and I could picture her rolling her eyes as she took a deep drag on her cigarette. "Becca, Becca, Becca," she said. "You just showed that Dean character the door, and you're already involved with someone else. Never could bear to be alone, could you? Never could stand not having a boyfriend."

"Mom, this is different."

"I'm certain that it is, dear."

I manufactured an excuse to get off the phone, and then I refused to answer the next three times that she called.

As if that weren't enough, Detective Ambrose continued to call on a regular basis, casting out his gloomy questions. Was I, Miss Morris, aware that Mr. Marcus had maintained a credit union account? Did I, Miss Morris, know about Mr. Marcus's disability insurance, about apparently fraudulent claims for some spinal injury? Was I, Miss Morris, aware of Mr. Marcus's failure to pay individual income taxes for the preceding three years?

Each of Ambrose's calls was a revelation. Each reminded me that I was well-served to be rid of Dean, personally and professionally. Each told me, in no uncertain terms, that losing my so-called then-boyfriend was the best thing that ever could have happened to me.

And if Ryan occasionally got a little moody about what we were doing to his play? That was nothing compared to Dean's legal transgressions. Nothing compared to the way that Dean had lied and cheated for the entire three and a half years I'd known him.

On the nights that Ryan needed his distance, Teel manifested, sometimes as Anana, but more often in another guise. One night she was a doorman, complete with gold braid and epaulets. Another, she was a theater usher, with a plush red jacket. Yet another, she was a rumpled taxi driver, chomping on a cigar.

She stayed just long enough to ask me if I'd decided on my last two wishes. Only once did she drag me to the Garden; I was so tired, I barely remembered to fake seeing the plants.

Instead, I regularly pleaded fatigue and creative exhaustion, and Teel generally took mercy on me, treating me to only a few rhapsodic recitations about the perfect, gender-indeterminate virtues of Jaze, virtues that could be explored much more completely and to far greater magical satisfaction once I finally finished my wishes and passed on the lantern to one more lucky soul.

During those nights when I slept alone, I rolled possibilities around in my mind, trying again and again to figure out what to ask Teel for, what to desire. And more often than not, I paced in front of my windows, resisting the urge to fling myself across my living room, to throw open my apartment door, to hurl myself across the hall and pound on Dani's door and force Ryan to talk to me. I wanted to beg him to tell me everything that he was thinking, so I could listen to exactly what he was feeling.

I restrained myself, though. He needed his space. He needed his independence.

We needed balance.

I'd known I was plowing a difficult field when I set my heart on a playwright I worked with. Now, I had to find a way to make things come together. I had to find a way to balance my personal and professional lives. I had to find a way to love Ryan, while still remaining true to Hal and the Mercer.

CHAPTER 13

IT WAS A DARK AND STORMY NIGHT.

Well, late afternoon, really, but I was tired of checking my watch to see if we could finally end rehearsal. With two weeks to go before we opened for previews, my patience was wearing thin with everyone and everything.

Desperate for a break from the Mercer, Ryan and I had promised to help Dani with a seed bombing as soon as it was dark enough to cover our guerilla tracks. Both of us felt guilty that she'd been forced to make so many of the grenades by herself. Ryan was particularly disappointed—the nicotiana and portulaca flowers in the midspring mix were some of his favorites. Rehearsals, though, had consumed every waking moment of the past week.

The dream sequence that formed the climax of the play was kicking our collective ass. The scene required three-dozen quick entrances and exits; actors needed to dash around backstage so that they could appear and reappear through various windows and doors on the fog-shrouded set. The rapid transitions were hampered by a massive wall that formed the major design element for the second act—it represented all of the barriers that Fanta faced when she went to the city, when she contemplated returning to her home. Kira had done her best to mark the backstage entrances with reflective tape, but the actors continued to have trouble hitting their marks—and not hitting their knees, elbows, and foreheads—on time.

"I don't know," Hal said to Ryan and me after the thirteenth consecutive attempt at running the scene cleanly. "Do you think we should reblock the whole thing?"

"We can't," Ryan said resolutely. "There's a specific sequence. A flow."

"Not when they're running into walls," Hal said reasonably. "Then there isn't any flow at all. What if Lehana makes all of her entrances upstage? Forget about the single line she says downstage left—just deliver it from the window there."

"That would completely ruin the balance." Ryan was shaking his head before the words were fully out of Hal's mouth. He held up his hands defensively. "I'm really not trying to be difficult! But you know these are the crucial stage directions for the entire play. The movement is modeled after a traditional village dance. It represents the heart and soul of Fanta, of all the women in her position. We can't give up on it just because it's difficult for actors to handle."

My boss turned to me, his raised eyebrows asking for my opinion. I knew that he wanted me to comment on Ryan's obsessive interest in blocking. Many, maybe even most, contemporary playwrights ignored stage directions altogether, content to let directors and actors develop the physical manifestation of a play through rehearsal. For Ryan, though, the blocking was paramount; we'd had more debates about where actors stood than about any other aspect of *However Long*.

Hal cleared his throat impatiently. This was the part of my job that I hated the most—I always felt trapped. After all, Hal knew what he was doing. He'd been directing for years, well before the first time I'd ever conceived of living my life in theater. He didn't need me to tell him whether the blocking was any good.

And yet that was one of the key things I'd learned in graduate school. Directors wanted reassurance. Dramaturgs gave it, over and over again, in a hundred and one different ways. The only thing no one had taught us in classes was how to take a diplomatic stand against the playwright when you planned on sleeping with the guy at the end of the day.

Oh. They did teach us that. In a course called "Ethics."

I cleared my throat. "I think the actors need to practice some more. This is the first day they've worked with the wall in place."

"They haven't come close to getting it right," Hal pointed out.

"We've still got some time," I soothed. "If they don't get it by the weekend, then we can think about changing things."

Hal looked at me for several heartbeats. I was pretty sure he'd figured out by now what was going on between Ryan and me. He wasn't a stupid man, after all. He made his living drawing out the most subtle nuances of human emotion onstage. Sighing, he glanced at his script, at the diagram that he'd slipped between his pages to outline his master plan for the climactic scene. "All right, Kira," he called out to the waiting stage manager. "Let's get everything reset. I want to try it one more time. From the top."

The actors moaned their dissatisfaction, but Ryan relaxed beside me. We'd won this round. That was, *he* had won the round. I'd merely been his accomplice.

Anxious to wrap up the stressful rehearsal, I glanced at my watch. The sooner we could finish working this scene, the sooner Ryan and I could escape, could get back to the Bentley and the Gray Guerillas and an easy relationship without conflict.

The Grays would be gathering in Dani's apartment about now. They were probably already sharing premission snacks, whole-wheat chips with a selection of organic dips. I pretended not to notice Ryan's frustrated grimace as the actors shuffled to their spots.

Kira made short work of resetting the windows and doors, of returning props to their appropriate places. "All right, everyone," she called out, her voice a perfect mask of efficient good humor. "Let's go from, 'I haven't slept in three nights.'"

Obediently, Fanta took her mark at center stage. Her voice echoed off the back wall of the theater as she proclaimed, "I haven't slept in three nights."

"That's Jamaican," Ryan muttered under his breath. "Not Burkinabe."

I brushed my hand over his, intending to convey sympathy. "She's meeting with the dialect coach tomorrow," I whispered. "I'll make sure they go over this scene."

"A lot of good that'll do." He stretched his legs out like a bored teenager, leaning his head against the back of his chair. In case neither Hal nor I recognized his level of frustration, he glanced ostentatiously at his watch.

I gritted my teeth. I understood the way he felt. I really

did. The rehearsal was boring and repetitive. The scene was important—the crux of the entire show—but it remained tantalizingly out of reach. Our Fanta was struggling, doing her best, but the performance we needed seemed beyond her ability. If she got the emotion right, she flubbed her lines. If she nailed the lines, her accent was off. If she scored a perfect ten on delivery, she messed up the blocking.

But I was confident that we would get to where we wanted to be. I'd worked on dozens of plays. I'd seen each of them pass through this gawky stage of adolescence. I'd seen most of them emerge as fully molded, beautiful adults. I had faith.

Ryan, alas, didn't have that level of experience. His nervousness had begun to rub off on the cast; he'd even made Hal question the validity of some of the company's more obscure interpretations of lines. Nevertheless, every time that tempers were completely frayed, every time that everyone was ready to walk away from the entire production, Ryan managed to step back. He managed to take a deep breath. He managed to find new words, new concepts, new ways of explaining to me, to Hal, to the entire cast, about what he'd seen in Africa. He talked about how he'd been changed, and what Burkina Faso meant to him. He talked about why he wrote Fanta's story. And the poetry of his words always brought us back, always reminded us that what we were doing was beautiful, meaningful, important.

Even if it was damned hard.

Throughout it all, I struggled to remain neutral, effectively invisible. I offered subtle reassurance to everyone when they came to me with questions. And I told myself over and over again that *However Long* would emerge from this crucible, fully annealed. It had to.

But not that evening. Lehana appeared downstage, delivering one line of her dream rhapsody. Then, she darted upstage, just hitting her mark for her next line. I caught my breath, waiting for her to dash stage right.

Crash! Boom! Bang.

"Crap!" Lehana shouted.

Kira sprang onto the stage, her first-aid kit already open. "What happened?"

"I tripped over the damn pots and pans." Lehana shook her wrist, irritably pushing away Kira's nursing. "Can't they be kept in the wings?"

"Not if we're going to get them onstage in time for Fanta's last line," Kira replied grimly.

Hal pretended not to hear Lehana swearing as he ordered, "Let's try it again, people."

Kira reset the props and ushered all of the actors to their appropriate corners. This time, though, Teel was the one who fell; she tripped over a doorsill as she delivered her very first line. I caught the faintest flash of her tattoo as she reached out to break her fall; I suspected that she used some magic to keep from suffering any lasting bodily harm. Half the cast gathered around, lifting her to her feet, dusting her off, making sure that all of her apparently elderly bones had survived the impact unbroken.

Hal stood up and walked to the front of the theater. "All right, people. Let's call it a day. I want each of you to review your blocking tonight. Think of it as choreography. This is a dance we're building, a ballet of the mind."

"This is impossible," Fanta mumbled. I think she got the accent right, but neither Hal nor Ryan was inclined to praise her for the sentiment.

Instead, our fearless director gave a pointed nod to Kira, who called out, "Okay, everyone. Back here at ten o'clock tomorrow." She started to collect the props, carefully ignoring the grumbling actors who cleared the stage.

Hal sighed and smoothed his hand over his beard as he turned to Ryan. "They'll get it. Sleeping on it is probably just the thing they need. We have to break, anyway, if you and I are going to get uptown on time."

"Uptown?" Ryan asked, darting a glance at me. His desire to escape the Mercer was clearly legible on his face.

"To the studio. It's up near Rockefeller Center."

"What studio?"

"What's his name, Ronald Barton? Your Popcorn King?"

Ryan laughed in disbelief. "I have no idea what you're talking about."

"We're going to be guests on the Pantry Channel? He called a week ago, said you'd already agreed to it. That was the only reason I agreed to go."

"The. Pantry. Channel." Ryan could have been talking about the Spanish Inquisition.

Hal grimaced. "I take it he never talked to you?"

Ryan shook his head. I could feel him shutting down. His shoulders slumped. He twitched away from my concerned hand, leaning against the far armrest of his chair. He sighed, as if the world were coming to an end. His frustration was obviously about more than missing the guerilla activity we'd planned for the evening. He was clearly questioning the wisdom of our ever accepting the Popcorn King's filthy lucre.

"Um, what's the Pantry Channel?" I asked, trying to buy a minute to work out some semblance of a solution.

Hal shrugged. "Some local cable thing. A bunch of people

who couldn't sell their shows to the Food Network. Every Wednesday night, they host a news show about local food trends, and tonight features the Popcorn King. He's going to hand over the second check to Ryan, right there, live and on air. He said something about our testing new popcorn flavors, too."

"I can't do it," Ryan said.

"Yeah, right." Hal shrugged on his leather jacket. "Maybe we can just pretend to eat the popcorn."

"I'm not kidding. I can't go." Ryan's voice ratcheted higher. He looked miserable. Miserable, but absolutely determined. My heart went out to him. He was trying to balance so much—making *However Long* into the best play it could be, juggling meetings with the Popcorn King, keeping his long-standing obligation to the Grays, building…whatever he was building with me.

Hal didn't have quite the same perspective. His laser eyes locked on Ryan. "Look, I'm pissed off about being manipulated, too. But this is actually a great opportunity for us. The Pantry Channel might only have a few thousand viewers, but those are people who've probably never even heard of the Mercer before."

Ryan appealed to me, looking as if I were a teacher who could write him a hall pass. Knowing he was going to be unhappy with me, I shoved honest regret into my voice as I said, "Hal's right. I know we were looking forward to the Grays. I know you promised Dani, but she does have lots of other people to help her."

I glanced at my boss, who gave me a satisfied nod. I was making the argument he wanted me to make, even if he didn't know anything about the Grays or Dani or any other details from my non-Mercer life with Ryan. "Look," Hal said. "I'm going to pick up some promotional brochures from my office. We can grab a cab in what, five minutes?"

He didn't wait for Ryan's confirmation before he strode off. I couldn't help but notice, though, that he did look back at *me* from the doorway. His hawk eyes watched to see if I continued to play my role properly. If I brought Ryan around. If I was the good dramaturg.

Instead of the good girlfriend.

"Ryan, we're almost through here," I cajoled. "We've only got two more weeks of rehearsal, and then your time will be your own again."

"I've been here day and night for a month. We were looking forward to this break tonight—both of us."

"Hey, I'm disappointed, too. But we'll do the next seed bombing together. I promise."

He pulled away from the hand that I put on his arm, the hand that I intended to be a symbol of comfort, of support. When he muttered a response, he sounded like a cross between a tortured artist and a spoiled five-year-old boy. "Do you really think that my appearance on some stupid local-access TV show is going to make a difference?"

"It can't hurt. Like Hal said, we need every bit of advertising we can get."

"Sure. Just like we need those idiotic T-shirts. Just like we need to slap that goddamn logo all over the set." He scrambled in his pocket for his cell phone. Flipping it open with enough force that I worried the device would snap in two, he snarled to an imaginary caller, "Pop off!"

"Ryan," I soothed. "You knew that staging your play would be a collaborative process."

"But I never expected you to drink the Kool-Aid, too! I never thought that you would sell out to the Popcorn King."

His words were so sharp I felt like I'd been slapped. Tears leaped to my eyes. "We didn't sell out, Ryan. The Mercer needed the funding."

"Not *we*, Becca. *You*. You, personally. Why exactly are the Mercer's finances so rocky? Why did you feel so responsible that you had to line up a sponsor no matter what, no matter who? That couldn't have had anything to do with the fact that your boyfriend emptied the coffers, could it?"

"That is not fair, Ryan! This doesn't have anything to do with Dean. You went to those funding meetings with me. You know how hard it was to get a commitment from anyone. We were lucky to get the Popcorn King. You know how hard I tried to find someone else."

"About as hard as you tried to get Hal to stick with my blocking this afternoon."

"Is that what this is all about?"

"This is about the mincemeat all of you are making out of my play. You're gutting it!"

"I can't help it if you wrote an impossible script!" The words were out of my mouth before I thought them through. Once they were free, though, I had to continue. "There's nothing wrong with our actors, Ryan. Your dream sequence just can't be done. No one could ever stage it the way you've written it. No one could ever make it work."

"It's not that complicated!" He leaped onto the stage with a speed I might have found admirable, under other circumstances. "Fanta stands here!" He darted upstage. "She moves here!" He ducked behind the wall. "She moves here!"

The crash was louder than anything I'd heard all afternoon.

My well-trained ears immediately identified the clatter of crockery scattering, followed by the heavy thud of a body hitting the floor. My heart leaped into my throat as I scrambled backstage.

"Ryan!"

He was lying on his stomach, his arms stretched in front of him, as if he'd tried to break his fall. I rushed to his side as he slowly pushed himself up onto all fours, his head hanging almost to the floor. He gaped like a goldfish out of water, unable to draw a full breath.

"Oh my God! Ryan!" I seized his shoulders, trying to ease him into a seated position. He held up one hand, effectively freezing me in place.

"I'm okay," he rasped. "Just…winded."

I fluttered my hands around his shoulders, unable to do anything to help. "I'm calling an ambulance."

"No," he choked out. "I'm fine." He celebrated that pronouncement by rolling onto his back. I watched his chest rise and fall as he finally managed to catch a handful of proper breaths.

"Just a second." I rushed into one of the dressing rooms. A collection of battered coffee mugs ringed the sink. I grabbed the one that seemed the least dirty, filled it with water, rushed back to the stage. "Here. Drink." I knelt beside him, carefully easing him up until he was half sitting, half leaning against my shoulder.

He folded his hands around the mug, downing one noisy swallow. He closed his eyes and pulled away from me, huddling into himself like a homeless man on some anonymous sidewalk. "Thank you," he said, settling the mug on the floor with a terrifying note of finality.

"Ryan, I—"

"Yeah," he said, and he sighed deeply before hauling himself to his feet.

"Wait here. I'll tell Hal that you can't go. We can take a cab home. We can talk about this some more."

He shook his head. "No. I'll go with Hal."

"But you were right—"

"No, Becca." He shoved his hands into his pockets. "*You* were right. The play isn't about me. We all have to do things to make it happen. We all have to make sacrifices."

"Let's talk about this, Ryan!"

His smile was sad. "We've talked enough. Hal's probably going insane out there, waiting for me. I've got to go."

"But we'll finish this conversation later, won't we? You'll come by when you get home?"

"I have to go." He eased himself off the stage gingerly. I waited until the door closed behind him, hoping that he would turn around, certain that he would say something else. Anything else. Even one single, solitary word.

The theater was very quiet when I stood alone.

When I'd run out of excuses for Ryan to come back, I forced myself to pick up the chipped coffee mug. I rinsed it out in the dressing room, holding it under the running water until my fingers started to pucker. I headed back onto the stage, stopping long enough to collect the pots, to stack them all for the next morning's rehearsal. I walked from stage left to stage right, trying to figure out a differ-ent configuration for the scene, a different way to have the actors move, so that they wouldn't kill themselves or each other, while still making their entrances at Ryan's speci-fied places.

And all the time, I tried to keep from hearing Ryan's quiet pronouncement: he had to go.

I should have been pleased. He was falling into line, helping the Mercer. He was sucking it up, meeting with the Popcorn King. How difficult could one little half-hour segment be, anyway? Ryan was being a man.

Ryan was being a man, but there was a part of me that wanted to chase after him, to beg him not to go, to plead with him to stay with me, to join me and the guerilla gardeners. But it was far too late for that.

I was halfway to the audience seats when the music started. R.E.M.'s *Gardening at Night*. For a second, I couldn't figure out what I was hearing, then I realized it must be Ryan's phone. He'd had it out, mimicking the Popcorn King. It must have gone flying when he'd tripped.

Michael Stipe reached the chorus as I rushed backstage, looking frantically for the device. I hadn't seen it when I picked up the pots; it must have skittered underneath— There! The phone was vibrating on the floor, lodged against the ominous wall.

Mom, the caller ID announced.

I flipped the phone open without thinking. "Dani, it's me. Becca."

"Thank God!" The connection sounded like it was coming from Mars. "I didn't think anyone was going to pick up."

"Where *are* you? It sounds like you're in a cave."

"Close enough," her voice echoed. "I'm at the police station. Is Ryan there?"

"No." I looked around in exasperation, as if I somehow expected him to reappear. "Why are you at the police station? Are you all right?"

"I've been arrested."

"You *what?*" I tried to picture Dani sitting in a jail cell. I couldn't reconcile the image of her Birkenstock sandals and her denim jumper behind bars. And yet, the Grays *had* been executing a raid…

"They're charging us with felony vandalism."

"Felony! What happened?"

"We got started early. The weather forecast said that the rain was going to start coming down hard after nine o'clock."

I wanted to rush her through her weather report, but my mind was reeling. Dani had been arrested, and she was obviously trying to reach Ryan with her one call. He was impossible to get hold of now; he must be deep in the heart of the Pantry Channel's television studio. I was going to have to take care of this myself.

"Becca?"

I shook my head to clear it. "Yeah, I'm here. But I don't understand. Why are they calling it a felony?"

"Lorraine Feingold was our mission commander tonight. That means she got to choose our target."

"What did she choose?"

"We seed-bombed Temple Beth Torah."

I shivered. Dani and the Grays were already skating on thin legal ice with their guerilla gardening. Half the members had received warnings in the past—Dani had shown me her own citation just a few weeks before. Even though I was afraid to know, I asked, "What happened?"

"We staged our attack from a little bodega, around the corner from the synagogue. Each of us brought our own grenades. We planned on carpet-bombing the side yard. We wanted to see it full of wildflowers by summer. There isn't anything but mud there now, and the children play outside on breaks from their classes."

Even though she couldn't see me, I nodded. I could imagine what had happened. The Grays had thrown their clods of dirt at the synagogue. A passing patrolman had witnessed the bombing. Or the bodega owner had reported them as suspicious characters. Or someone inside the synagogue had called in the attack.

Vandalism plus a hate crime. On top of the numerous warnings individuals had received, all spring long. The police would throw the book at them.

Dani's brave report was winding down, and I heard a quaver in her words. "They're keeping us here tonight, Becca. They say we'll be arraigned tomorrow. But if the judge decides we're a threat, he won't let us go. He'll hold us without bond!"

I wanted to reassure her, but I wasn't certain that I could. After all, actual hate crimes were serious things. And the Gray Guerillas *had* broken some laws. And they'd been warned before. Dani's own blog had listed tips for evading the police.

I'd watched enough *Law and Order* to predict what would happen. Some promising young district attorney would make a name for himself, prosecuting the Grays in the highly political, symbolic, never-ending battle for safe city streets.

"Okay, Dani," I said, trying to make my voice reassuring. "Let me make a couple of phone calls. I'll see what I can do."

"Becca, be careful when you go home tonight. They say they're going to raid our homes. They're going to collect evidence, find our 'implements of destruction.'"

My blood froze. I knew what it was like to have the police go through my home. I knew what it was like to be locked out of everything I knew, kept away from everything I owned, from everything that mattered to me.

There was no reason to think that the cops would cross the hall into my apartment. But they'd commandeer Dani's place. And Ryan's.

Ryan would be as powerless to protect his possessions as I had been.

I thought about the compost container in Dani's kitchen, the delicate ecological balance that she had nurtured for years. I pictured the purple grow-lights, suspended over the work-bench, the collection of buckets, the peat cups and seeds and all the other gardening supplies.

They'd all be confiscated. Ruined. Lost forever, even after Dani and her companions managed to explain away the absurd hate-crime charges.

Dani seemed to realize the same thing. The sound of her sobs echoed through Ryan's phone. "And Ryan—" Her voice broke, as if she were ashamed to tell her son what had happened.

"I'll fill him in. We'll see you tonight, if we can. If not, first thing tomorrow."

"Thank you, Becca. I—" She fought her tears into sub-mission. "Thank you."

I terminated the call and flipped the phone closed. I con-sidered hailing a cab, making my way uptown, interrupting the Popcorn King's grand television spectacle, so that I could deliver my bad news.

But I couldn't imagine what that would accomplish. Ryan was already furious with me—he might never talk to me again if the Popcorn King's cable extravaganza proved as obnox-ious as I expected it might be. Besides, Ryan couldn't work any miracles to free Dani from her police cell.

But I could.

I could work miracles.

I glanced around the theater, even though I was certain I was alone. The harsh work lights made my skin look pale, but when I raised my thumb and forefinger, I could still make out Teel's whorls.

I considered what I was about to do. I only had two wishes left. I'd been hoarding them, saving them for honest emergencies. Keeping them for the chance to change the world in some meaningful way, even if I couldn't solve poverty, couldn't eradicate hunger, couldn't "purchase" any of the big-ticket long-term Grand Wish items.

But that wasn't the same thing as saying that I couldn't have any impact at all on the world around me. That wasn't the same thing as saying that I couldn't do any good deeds at all.

I tugged at the neckline of my Eileen Fisher sweater. I loved my new wardrobe. It had given me the confidence to master my new job. But I couldn't exactly argue that a full closet was a great thing for mankind.

It was time to make a choice. A better choice. A more meaningful one. I pressed my thumb and forefinger together and said, "Teel!"

An electric shock jangled through my body, jolting me into perfect posture. All the hairs on my arms leaped to attention. The sudden pain made me flinch, and my eyes squinched shut. When I opened them, the stage was filled with opalescent fog, ruby and topaz and sapphire all glinting in a swirling mist. As I stared, the cloud cleared, resolving into a solid shape, into a man.

Tonight, Teel was a painter. He wore a long smock, a garment that had once been blue, but now it was slashed with a brilliant array of color. He balanced a classic wooden palette across his palm, his thumb poking through the hole near the edge. Daubs of paint glinted on the surface, and I immediately smelled the pungent bite of linseed oil.

"At last!" Teel said, pointing his paintbrush toward me with the vehemence of a witness accusing a murderer. As if to cement that image in my mind, the tips of the black bristles gleamed with crimson paint.

Teel had apparently chosen Salvador Dalí as his artistic role model. He sported an enormous mustache, waxed out to two perfect points. A jaunty emerald-green beret echoed his close-set eyes, but it made his swarthy skin seem almost sickly.

As I recovered from the burst of electricity that had brought my genie onto the stage, he circled around me, cocking his head at all sorts of unlikely angles. The hand that held the palette teetered dangerously, and I wondered if I'd have to clean up the floor after we finished our conversation. Teel held up his paintbrush the way some painters used their thumbs, squinting past its straight line and gauging me, all the while muttering about perspective.

Annoyed by the attention, I snapped, "How the hell did you have time to get set up as a painter? You were Anana an hour ago."

"Ve genies, ve vork in ze mysterious ways." His French accent was as thick as crème brûlée.

"I thought you had to stay quiet when we weren't together! How could you be painting someone?"

"Some*thing,* ma chère. I 'ave been, 'ow you say? Painting ze still deaths."

"Still lifes," I corrected automatically.

"All zose apples and oranges, and ze perfect silver knife. Boring, yes, but vat is a poor genie to do?"

He could start by choosing another pastime. But I hadn't summoned him to argue. "I'm ready to make my third wish."

"Enfin!" Teel started to clap his hands in excitement, only remembering his artistic encumbrances at the last possible second. "And vat is ze vish?"

"Guerilla gardening," I said. "Dani's group. I want to make it safe for them to work. I want them to get some positive recognition for all they've done. I want them out of jail." I sighed. "Teel, I don't even know what has to happen. I don't know how to make it right. Can you do the wish anyway?"

"Could Monet paint ze vater lilies? Phrase ze request in ze form of a vish."

"And you can—"

"Ze form of a vish!"

I took a shocked step backward as Teel jabbed his paintbrush toward me. He'd never been so forceful, not in any of our conversations, any of our discussions about magic, or the Garden, or Jaze, or even his—her—role of Anana. I realized just how much this wish meant to him. He'd finally be one giant step closer to completing his mission with me.

And the Mercer would be one giant step closer to losing one of our lead actresses, with the show already on shaky ground.

Well, there was time enough to worry about that later. I had Dani to think about now, and all the other Grays who were spending the night in uncomfortable jail cells. Dani was more important than any details about a play that still had two weeks before it was supposed to open. Dani, and the apartment she shared with Ryan, which might be being raided even as I delayed there in the Mercer.

I looked at Teel levelly and said, "I wish that New York

City recognized the value of guerilla gardening and created a supportive atmosphere for the Gray Guerillas. And other gardening groups. And individuals who garden. And…" I trailed off, realizing that I was babbling.

"Finis?"

"Um, yeah."

Teel thrust his paintbrush toward me. I took it awkwardly, turning my wrist to keep from getting crimson paint all over my hand. Once I was through fumbling, Teel raised his free fingers to his ear, edging his beret to the side. Eyeing me as if he suspected I might try to steal his art supplies, he enunciated, "As you vish." He tugged twice, hard, on his ear.

I'd forgotten to brace myself for the bolt of raw electricity, the power of magic changing the world. The shock felt like fire, darting from Teel's paintbrush all the way up my arm. My heart bucked from the charge, and I couldn't keep from shouting a wordless protest.

But the energy passed as quickly as it had come. I was left with only the memory of pain, only the recollection of power.

"That's it?" I asked, when Teel stayed silent.

"Ze vish 'as been granted."

I fished Ryan's phone out of my pocket, punching the keys to return Dani's call. The phone rang four times, then went to voice mail. I terminated the connection without leaving a message. "Are you sure?" I asked.

"'Ave I lied to you before?" I wasn't quite sure about the answer to that, but it hardly seemed politic to say so. Teel said, "Go 'ome. You vill learn about ze vish zere. Vith ze gardeners."

I sighed and tucked Ryan's phone back into my pocket. "Can't you just tell me?"

"I 'ave vork to do. Zose apples, zey do not paint zem-selves." He held out a demanding hand. "Ze paintbrush, *s'il vous plait?* Unless you are ready to make ze fourth vish after all?"

"No," I said, surrendering the brush. "I'm saving that one for a rainy day."

"Ze rain, she falls right now," Teel said. "Tonight is a perfect night for vishing."

"No," I said more firmly.

"Eight out of—"

"No! Go back to your painting, Teel, or whatever else you want to do. I'll see you at rehearsal tomorrow."

"You vill talk to 'Al? You vill change ze blocking for ze dream scene?"

I pictured Ryan sprawled across the floor, desperately fighting to regain his breath after his blocking had caught him by surprise. Even then, he hadn't admitted that the play wasn't working. Even then, he hadn't agreed to modify the script.

"I don't know, Teel. I don't think anything short of a wish will make that happen." He perked up, starting to pass me the paintbrush again. I held up my hand in the universal symbol for Stop. "And I'm not sure that even you are power-ful enough to change Ryan's mind. I'll see you tomorrow."

My genie was still grumbling to his artistic self as I ducked out the door to find out what, exactly, had happened to the Gray Guerillas.

CHAPTER 14

I STOOD IN FRONT OF THE DOOR TO DANI AND RYAN'S apartment, overcome with a feeling of déjà vu. Wait. It wasn't actual déjà vu. I *had* stood here before. I had carried out this exact same debate with myself, wondering whether I should knock, whether I should just make a phone call, whether I should resort to sending an e-mail message.

That was back when Ryan had just been an unknown geeky playwright who had insisted, in a rather underwhelming show of professional enthusiasm, that I take his script. Before I knew him. Before I knew Dani. Before I knew the first thing about the Gray Guerillas.

Before I'd made any of my wishes.

I had to know what Teel had done. With my other wishes, the results had been immediately clear. I'd received a phone call from that real estate agent. I'd seen a full wardrobe laid out in my bedroom closet. This time, though, I had no idea what was waiting for me. I had no idea what Teel had actually accomplished.

I raised my hand and knocked.

Nothing. Was Dani still in jail? Had Teel failed?

I knocked again, then placed my ear against the door. I could hear a faint shuffling inside, the distorted warble of a voice. Someone was in Dani's apartment. Ryan's apartment. Someone who wasn't answering my knock.

I pounded on the door again, using my fist this time. Even as the sound echoed in the hallway, I wondered who could have known that Dani and Ryan's apartment was unattended; who could have known that Dani had been arrested, had been kept down at the police station. There were people who monitored police-band radios, weren't there? People who could use the Grays' arrest to perpetrate their own crimes, breaking into premises when no one was home?

I fished Ryan's phone out of my pocket; it was faster to use his than to find my own. I flipped it open and pressed 9-1-1, scarcely bothering to register the irony that I wanted police to come investigate a possible crime in the home of a woman they were holding as a felon.

The first ring was interrupted by a cool, efficient voice. "Nine-one-one. What is the nature of your emergency?"

"My next-door neighbor—"

Before I could complete my report, though, Dani's door swung open. She held her own cell phone in one hand, and a wireless handset in the other. She raised her eyebrows in an exaggerated greeting when she saw me and ushered me inside, smiling broadly enough that I knew immediately that she was all right.

She said into her cell, "We need to get something out to all the members tonight. Right now. Tell them just to take their phones off the hook. I don't think this is going to stop anytime soon. I hope it doesn't. I've got to run—I've got another call."

Then, she turned to her household phone and said, "I'm so sorry to keep you waiting."

A voice squawked out of Ryan's cell, which I'd forgotten I was holding. "Ma'am! What is the nature of your emergency!"

I stammered, "I'm sorry. I must have been mistaken. My neighbor is fine. She just wasn't answering her door when I knocked."

The 9-1-1 operator asked a couple of follow-up questions, and I answered mechanically, half listening to Dani's own conversation. We both hung up at the same time.

She shook her head in amazement. "That was the television studio."

"Is Ryan okay?" I suddenly pictured him collapsed on the floor of the Pantry Channel's set. Maybe he'd hurt himself even worse than I'd thought when he fell at the Mercer. Maybe he'd been overcome with blind rage at the Popcorn King and attempted murder, or he'd been poisoned by some horrible combination of caramel corn and unknown salt.

"Isn't he with you?" Dani asked, concern digging a furrow between her eyebrows. Her phone started to ring again, but she didn't answer it. After four loud squawks, we were treated to a moment of silence.

"No, he went to the TV studio."

"How did they get to him so quickly?" Dani sounded completely confused.

"He had an appointment, with Hal."

"An appointment? But the mayor only issued his statement half an hour ago."

"A statement?" Now I was the one who had no idea what we were talking about. "Why does the mayor care about popcorn?"

"Popcorn? The mayor doesn't have anything to do with popcorn!" Dani's phone started to ring again, and she scowled as she waited for it to roll over to voice mail. "Wait. Go back to the beginning. Where is Ryan?"

"At some television studio, up near Rockefeller Center."

"Why is he there?"

"He's promoting *However Long*. With Hal and our sponsor, the Popcorn King."

"And what's the mayor doing there?"

"*I* never mentioned the mayor. *You* did!"

Dani shook her head vigorously, as if she were trying to toss confusion out of her ears. "Ryan's okay, though?"

"He was the last time I saw him. About two hours ago, before you phoned from the police station." I waited a second, to see if she was going to volunteer her own connection with television, the mayor, and just, possibly, popcorn. When she merely treated me to a bemused smile, though, I prompted, "Your turn. What happened to you? How did you get out of the police station? What happened to being held overnight until arraignment tomorrow?"

Again, the phone rang. Again, Dani waited it out. When she did answer me, she sounded vaguely astonished. "We were sitting in our holding cell, all of the Grays. And a policewoman came in. She said that we were being released, that there'd been some misunderstanding. Just like that, she opened up the door! At the end of the corridor, she stopped, and she told us to get ready, that there were already a lot of reporters there. We had no idea what she was talking about."

Without making any conscious movement, I realized that
I was rubbing my fingers together, the thumb and forefinger that were tattooed with Teel's flame markings. What had
my genie done? What magic had he worked at the police
station?

"We were astonished to find the mayor out there. Satel-
lite trucks were parked in front of the precinct, and lights,
you know, the ones on those tall poles?" She barely waited
for me to nod. "It was a press conference. Reporters were
pushing as close as they could—the mayor's security guards
had their hands full. But everyone went *crazy* when we
stepped outside."

If nothing else, I was impressed by how fast Teel had
worked. It was one thing to make a few clothes appear, that
just required tinkering with universal laws of matter and
energy. Even arranging for me to move into the Bentley had
just been a matter of paperwork. But to get the mayor down
to the police station? And all of those reporters? Astonished,
I asked, "What did the mayor say?"

"He introduced all of us, called us forward like we were
some sort of heroes. One of his staffers handed him a piece
of paper, and he read off each of our names, calling us one
by one to the podium so that we could each be recognized."

"Recognized? For what?"

"For guerilla gardening!" Dani sounded as amazed as I felt.
"The mayor said that he'd been on his way to the police
station to make a speech about the city's need for beautifica-
tion. He's been concerned about Manhattan's appearance for
a long time. He's determined to create and maintain a beautiful city, to make everyone's lives more enjoyable, and to drive
the tourist trade. He had a whole speech prepared, about the

dangers of graffiti, of vandalism. But when he got to the precinct house, the sergeant told him about the Grays, about what we've been doing. About why we'd been arrested. And he changed his mind, right there, on the spot."

"Changed his mind?" Even knowing that Teel had had a hand in matters, I was finding it difficult to believe the story Dani was telling.

"One of the mayor's staff members had an iPhone, and she was pulling information from the Grays' website even while he was talking to the reporters. It was amazing, Becca! The aide would pass a note to the mayor, and he barely looked at it—he just kept talking, folding in the new information, like he'd known about guerilla gardening forever. You wouldn't have believed it, if you'd seen it!"

I just might, though. Remembering the electric jangle that had shot through my entire body as Teel granted my third wish, I'd believe just about anything. "So, all of you were released on your own recognizance? Without any arraignment at all?"

Dani shrugged. "It didn't make sense to us, but we weren't about to argue. The mayor vouched for us personally. One of his aides said that the charges would be dropped in the next couple of days. It was like a miracle!"

Or magic, I thought, but I didn't interrupt.

Dani said, "The mayor announced that the Gray Guerillas should be a model for all neighborhood activists in the city. He asked me—me!—to write up some materials that he can distribute, from Battery Park to Harlem. He wants me to write about seed bombs and vegetables and—"

Her voice grew thick, and I could see that she was barely winning her fight against happy tears. I reached out to pat her shoulder, and she covered my hand with her own. "I never thought we'd see the day," she said. "I never thought we'd be officially recognized, that our work would ever be embraced by the mainstream. By the mayor himself!" And then she did start crying, hard sobs that had clearly grown out of years of frustrated hopes.

Her landline phone rang again. She sniffled and stared at it as if it were a living creature. "It hasn't stopped ringing since I got home. I answered the first few calls. People want me to appear on news shows. They want to interview me for the radio. Three different people called to offer their services as my agent. My agent!"

Wow. When Teel granted a wish, he really granted a wish.

Dani shook her head and shoved the phone under a cushion on the couch, muffling its continued ring. "But what were you saying about Ryan? He's on some television show himself?"

I told her about the Pantry Channel and the promotional gig that Hal had sprung on Ryan without warning. "He wasn't happy to go, and he'll be even less pleased to see me here if it turned out to be a disaster. I should leave before he gets back, so you can share your news with him."

"Oh!" Dani looked crestfallen. "You've been fighting."

Talk about a mother's intuition. Or maybe my emotions were just that transparent. I shrugged. "We were both a little…frustrated with rehearsal this afternoon. Okay," I amended at her skeptical frown, "a lot frustrated."

"Let me guess. Someone wants to change the play."

I stared at her. "Not the words. Just the blocking."

Dani sucked on her teeth. "That's even worse. I've told him over and over again that he's put too much of himself into that script."

"What do you mean?"

She sighed. "It's like none of it means anything, if even a single word changes. Nothing that happened in Africa, nothing that he accomplished with the Peace Corps. The play is some sort of…totem for him, some sort of protection against ever slipping back to where he was with Pam."

A cold hand clenched around my heart. "Pam?" I managed to say.

Dani froze, like a rabbit trapped outside its burrow. For just a moment, I thought she was going to deny having said the name, pretend that I'd imagined it completely. Instead, she said, "He hasn't told you about Pam? Nothing at all?"

I shook my head, not trusting myself to speak. Sure, there were a hundred and one innocent explanations for his forgetting to mention "Pam." She could have been a long-dead, much-beloved childhood pet. Or the girl who'd lived down the street when he was in elementary school. The resident advisor in his freshman-year dorm, or his aged mentor when he started his first consulting job.

But none of those roles justified the stark unease painted across Dani's face. None of them explained the tight shake of her head as she said, "I shouldn't have said anything. You have to ask him."

"You can't say that now! I can't just walk across the hall and go home like nothing's happened! You have to tell me the rest of the story."

She looked miserable, trapped. She dug beneath the sofa cushion to extract her phone, shaking it as if she could make a call come in, now that she'd welcome the interruption. She clicked her tongue in disappointment, but I didn't know if the emotion was meant for the phone, or for me, or for Ryan.

"I can't believe he hasn't told you," she finally said. "You know that Ry worked as a consultant, right?" I nodded. "And in his spare time, what little he had of it, Ry wrote a computer program."

I thought back to the night we'd sat on my couch, sharing a blanket and stories from our pasts. "He told me about that," I said, as much to reassure myself as to comfort Dani.

"Ry has wanted to be a playwright since he was in college, maybe even earlier. The program was a tool he originally created for himself, to plot out scenes, track blocking, that sort of thing. The busier he got at his consulting job, the more important the software became. He could work on it, even when he was too drained to work on his plays. It meant so much to him—it was everything he wanted to be, everything he wanted to do, for real. Outside his consulting job."

Ryan's obsession didn't surprise me. I'd seen the way he approached rehearsals of *However Long,* how he'd come to live and breathe the Mercer's production.

Dani's voice was clouded by pride as she said, "Ry *lived* for that code. He worked on it every night, every weekend. He reviewed every line, making sure it was as fast, as efficient, as perfect as humanly possible."

That was all well and good, but it didn't explain what I really wanted to know. Needed to know. "And Pam?"

Dani sighed. "When Ry became so obsessed with his program, I worried about him. I worried that he wasn't meeting anyone, wasn't spending time with people. Wasn't having any fun. But then he met Pam at work. He talked about her, more and more, and when he finally brought her over for dinner, I was thrilled." She darted a quick glance at me, as if she were ashamed of what she'd said. She hurried on. "It wasn't like they had a lot in common. If they hadn't worked together, I don't think they ever would have met. But he finally seemed happy. A mother wants her son to be happy."

I didn't want to ask, but I had to. "What happened to her? To them?"

Dani shook her head. "Pam's expertise was in marketing. It just seemed natural that she'd help Ry with the program, try to sell it. He was only too happy to have her work on it— he wanted as many playwrights as possible to have access to it. One of their coworkers suggested they make the arrangement official, form a legal partnership. They did, and three months later, she announced that she'd sold all of their rights to some huge computer company."

"Without asking him?"

"Without even mentioning the deal before it was final." Dani's lips were grim. "The buyers didn't want to help playwrights. They dropped the code into some home-renovation thing. They used Ry's blocking algorithm to lay out kitchens, to sell granite countertops and laminate flooring. They paid a huge amount for the exclusive right to the code."

Exclusive. As in, theater professionals would never get the benefit of Ryan's work.

I could only imagine how that blow had affected him. Ryan was a teacher at heart, a mentor, a guide. The thought of his creation being exploited by some money-grubbing corporation would have cut deep. But the realization that other people, other *artists* wouldn't have the benefit of what he'd done… That would have been the real blow.

"He was devastated," Dani confirmed. "It wasn't just the sale. It was that Pam hadn't even thought to check with him first. She said she wanted to surprise him. She thought he'd be thrilled. But she never really understood what the program meant to him. Better for them both to find out, really, before they got married."

Married. If I'd had any teeny, tiny, lingering doubt about how serious Ryan and Pam had been, Dani had just destroyed it.

A lance shot through my heart. I certainly hadn't expected Ryan to arrive in my life without some history, without some romantic past. But he'd never mentioned Pam. Not once. He'd never told me about a woman he'd considered spending the rest of his life with.

Either Dani didn't register my distress, or she felt as if she couldn't respond. Instead, she spread her fingers wide, the gesture conveying loss, concern, fear for her son, sorrow for his lost happiness. "He was just shattered. He applied for the Peace Corps the night he moved out of their apartment, and he was in Africa two weeks later."

Their apartment.

Wow.

Two weeks, and the entire world Ryan had ever known was left behind. But Burkina Faso had been a whole new life for him. A new world, where he could excel on his own. Without the interference of colleagues. Of lovers. Of liars.

I was willing to bet my entire Mercer salary that he'd written *However Long* with the program he'd created. He'd used his own software to monitor the incredibly complex story, to work out the blocking for the devastating second act, to track all the individual threads that added up to the astonishing whole. The Mercer's production of *However Long* must be an exorcism for him, freeing him forever from Pam's betrayal. But like any ritual, Ryan needed it to be performed precisely, exactly, without any variation from the perfection he'd created.

Even when the Mercer insisted on changes. When Hal insisted. When I did.

But we couldn't mount a flawed play, a play with impossible blocking, just because it meant a lot to its author. If only I had known about all this, I could have figured out ways to work around Ryan's needs. I could have figured out ways to help him understand, even as we solved the problems of his stagecraft.

But I hadn't known. Ryan hadn't told me.

Dani chewed on her lower lip. "I'm sorry, Becca. I just assumed that Ry had told you all this. I thought—" She cut herself off, but I knew what she was going to say. She thought that if Ryan was sharing my bed, the least he would have done was share his past.

I stood up and wiped my palms against my thighs. "Don't worry about it," I said. "I'm sure that he…"

That he what? That he'd meant to tell me before now? That he'd planned on telling me soon? When? Before I could figure out a way to finish off the lie, a key slid into the front-door lock. My heart bucked in my chest—it *had* to be Ryan.

He was talking before he even crossed the threshold. "You would not believe what a madhouse it is down there! Reporters are camped out on the entire block—someone famous must have moved in!" He finally realized that Dani wasn't alone. "Oh," he said when he saw me, and all the tension we'd shared before he stalked out of the Mercer came flooding back.

"Oh," I echoed.

"I'm the someone famous," Dani answered, her tone so

bright, so fake that Ryan stopped staring at me and turned to gape at his mother. Dani sparkled. "It's a long story, but the Gray Guerillas have become the mayor's pet project!"

"The mayor's—" He looked from her to me. I couldn't meet his gaze, though. Couldn't think past everything Dani had just told me.

Thankfully, Dani rushed on, filling the conversational void. "Becca tells me that *you've* been on TV! How was the show? The Cupboard Channel, was it?"

"Pantry," he corrected. "It was fine."

"What happened? What did you do?"

"I ate popcorn."

Ryan looked like he wasn't going to say more, like he was going to press me to pick up our earlier conversation, but Dani asked, "You ate popcorn?"

"Yeah. The way nature never intended it to be. Deli Dill Caramel. Vermont Maple Cheddar. Breakfast in a Bag. That last one is plain with powdered egg and bacon flakes."

My stomach turned over, but Dani was the one who said, "Those sound disgusting."

"Let's just say I didn't bring any home for you." He offered his mother a faint grin before casting another opaque look at me. "But I didn't realize both of you would be here. What were you talking about?"

"The Grays," Dani said brightly.

At the same time, I said, "The Mercer." I watched Ryan's expression turn quizzical. I stammered out, "The Grays and the Mercer. Both. Dani will tell you. I—I have to go. I have to—" I didn't have an excuse. I didn't have an explanation. I just wanted to get out of there. I wanted time to think. I caught myself short and repeated, "I have to go."

Fortunately for me, Dani's phone chose that moment to ring again, and I ducked out before Ryan could press for a clarification. Certainly before he could decide to walk me across the hallway. Before we needed to face the rest of the fight, er, discussion that we'd started back in the theater.

Safe in my apartment, I sank onto my couch, consciously pushing aside the memory of sharing its cushions with Ryan.

Teel. Teel was a safe topic. I'd think about Teel instead. About what an incredible job my genie had done granting my third wish.

I had to give him credit. When he worked a miracle, he really worked a miracle. Dani's guerilla activities had not only become legal, they'd become the talk of the town. I'd have to send Pop-pop information about the Grays. Maybe he could start a San Diego chapter on his own. He'd be good at that. He'd enjoy the camaraderie. The subversive activity.

There. That was about all I had to say about the Grays. All that I could force myself to think about my genie.

That left me with Ryan. With a man who'd never thought to mention the transforming event of his entire adult life. Who'd never thought to mention the woman he'd almost married.

I rubbed my thumb and forefinger together and wondered if Teel could straighten out my love life as easily as he'd straightened out Dani's life of so-called crime. And then I wondered if I'd want my genie to get involved. Was Ryan worth my fourth and final wish? Was Ryan worth all the time and energy and emotion that I'd poured into him already?

I was terrified that the answer was yes. But even more terrified that it might be no. And by the time the sun rose, I was no closer to finding an answer.

★ ★ ★

In fact, five days later, I still didn't have any idea what I should do.

Jenn stormed into my office, ignoring the fact that my door had been closed. "I assume you're getting all the e-mails I'm forwarding, and you've just decided to ignore me?"

I glanced from my assistant to my computer. "I turned off e-mail about an hour ago. I couldn't keep up with the flow."

"That man is driving me crazy. Completely, utterly, one hundred percent insane. He makes my cockatiels look like Mensa candidates." She shoved a pile of books off my guest chair and collapsed onto the furniture as if she could no longer breathe.

I didn't have to ask who she meant. Three days earlier, I'd officially designated Jenn to be Speaker to Popcorn—she was in charge of corralling Ronald J. Barton. I wasn't totally heartless—I'd warned her not to give out her home telephone number, or her cell phone, or her personal e-mail address. Unfortunately, though, Jenn had thought it would be faster to IM the Popcorn King with one quick question about the wording for ads in the program. He'd been stalking her online for the past seventy-two hours.

Stalking her online, and by the conventional office phone. And I'd heard his ridiculous ring tone at least three times over the weekend, as he roamed the Mercer's hallways looking for anyone who would give him the time of day. Ronald J. Barton might be New York City's busiest food entrepreneur, but he clearly had too much time on his hands. If Jenn had to field one more phone call, I was afraid she would quit. I sighed. "Okay. What is it now?"

"He's created new flavors. To launch when the play opens."

She actually sounded like she was going to cry. I forced myself to set aside the program notes I was reviewing—one last pass before they went off to the printer, before any existing errors were enshrined forever on slick glossy paper.

"What are they?" I asked with a sort of fascinated dread.

Wordlessly, she handed me a sheet of paper, the printout of an e-mail that probably lurked unread in the bowels of my own computer. I skimmed it with a growing sense of horror and then I gaped at her. "He can't."

"He's going to. He's shipping some over tomorrow, along with newer, bigger orange and yellow signs announcing the names. He wants the cast photographed in front of them. To advertise in every store in Manhattan."

"The cast can't promote this stuff. They'd quit if we asked them to."

"He said that you agreed—"

I remembered sitting in his office, listening to Ryan bargain with the master himself. The cast would sit for one day of publicity photos. I'd thought that with only a week and a half before previews began, we were out of the danger zone on that promise. I'd figured that Ronald had forgotten his original demands. I was an idiot.

"We agreed that the cast would pose for publicity shots," I explained to Jenn. "But I can't ask the cast to eat those flavors. Well, the last one, sure, they can eat it, but if I even read them his description, they'll walk out in protest."

"What are you going to do?"

What was *I* going to do? I thought for a second. For the past five days, I'd holed up in my office. I'd told Hal that I was too busy to sit in on rehearsals. I was researching and writing my program notes, perfecting the flyers that we were going to insert in the programs, the ones that told the audience about charities where they could help women like Fanta.

I'd argued that Jenn needed the experience sitting in on the actual rehearsals. That was it. I was *mentoring*. I wasn't shirking my own responsibilities. I wasn't doing my best to avoid the man who had been my boyfriend, who had been my lover, who had been the playwright I was assisting as he brought his dreams to life.

No, I couldn't possibly be doing all that.

It was just coincidence that I'd seen Ryan for a total of fifteen minutes in the past five days.

But even *I* couldn't justify staying locked up in my little office, now that I saw the horror that Ronald J. Barton, Popcorn King, intended to perpetrate on our production. "Don't worry," I said to Jenn. "I'll take care of it."

"How?"

"I don't know."

She followed me through the hallways, absolutely silent as I clutched the printed e-mail in my fist. We ducked into the back of the theater, taking care to close the door behind us silently. I immediately recognized the scene from the middle of the first act—Fanta was sweeping the dirt floor of her hut as she calculated how many francs she had to last the rest of the week.

The set was nearly finished. Dull red earth had been carted in by the barrowful. Fine dust had sifted over every surface, despite Kira's best efforts to control the environment. I knew that she was wetting down the dirt every morning and every evening, but I'd heard the actors complaining about how the grit got into their hair, settled at the back of their throats.

As if to emphasize that complaint, Fanta started coughing in the middle of a line. It was a dry cough, a racking one, almost as painful for me to hear as it must have been for her to produce. "Dammit," she said, when she finally managed to clear whatever dust had settled deep in her lungs. At least she maintained her perfect Burkinabe accent. "Where were we? Line?"

Kira called out from the front of the house, "If the wee ones share—"

"If the wee ones share their morning portion, then I can buy a bite or two of goat tomorrow. I'm not hungry today. No need for me to eat." Fanta glanced overhead at the supposed sun, realized that she was late heading to the market. She rushed to place her broom inside her home. As she spun upstage, ready to dart into the wings, her crocheted shawl caught on something, and the sound of ripping fabric was drowned out by her curse.

The actress dropped out of character immediately. "Hal, I can't get the broom back there if I'm going to exit before the children come on." She froze as the costume designer hurried onstage, shaking his head in frustration over the damaged shawl.

With Jenn still clinging to me like a barnacle, I strode down the aisle. As long as the rehearsal was interrupted, I might as well deliver my news. "Hal?" I said, approaching his seat on the aisle.

He held up a commanding hand, and I stopped, fidgeting with impatience. I hadn't realized Ryan was speaking to him, hadn't even seen Ryan crouching beside him. Now, though, I heard the heated words: "Hal, we can't change the scene. Her entire life *would* be sweeping the floor. That's what she does. That's why she has nothing else to turn to, nowhere else to go. She's just got to practice the blocking—it shouldn't be this difficult."

Now, I understood his argument. With the background that Dani had given me, I knew why Ryan cared so much about the staging, why it was so much more important to him than it had been to any other playwright I'd ever met.

Hal tried to sound conciliatory. "But we really haven't given her much to work with. You've already insisted that the children come on from both sides of the stage. I understand the symbolism in that approach, really I do. But Fanta has to have room to exit. She has to have room to move."

"She just needs to move faster," Ryan said stubbornly.

Annoyed, Hal slammed his notebook shut. "She can't. Ryan, this just isn't worth fighting over. She can walk upstage and exit there, without ever getting involved with the children."

"You don't understand! You can't change it now!" Ryan was stubborn.

"Kira!" Hal hollered. "Five minutes!"

"Five-minute break, everyone. Back to your places in five minutes." Kira's voice was a masterpiece of calm. She jumped onto the stage to calm the costume designer, then ran her fingers over the offending nail that had caused the damage in the first place.

I stepped forward before Hal and Ryan could come to fist-icuffs over the blocking. "I've got to talk to both of you. Now."

"What is it?" Hal snapped. Jenn flinched beside me, but I clutched at her arm, keeping her close. For moral support. Or, er, to further her training.

"The Popcorn King," I said. Both men sighed with equal disgust. "Now, Jenn has been dealing with him, and she's managed to rein in a lot of his ideas. But we're in trouble now."

"What is it this time?" Hal asked. He was used to dealing with demanding sponsors. He was used to applying carefully chosen compliments, to soothing moneyed brows. He would understand the delicate diplomacy we needed to finesse this most recent disaster.

"Sample popcorn," I said earnestly.

"And why do I give a good goddamn about sample popcorn?" Okay. So Hal wasn't used to *all* the challenging issues that came up with Mercer sponsors.

"Weeks ago, Ryan and I agreed that the Popcorn King could provide free samples of popcorn to all of our patrons, before the show and during intermission."

Hal shrugged. "So what? It's free. If they hate it, um, *when* they hate it, they don't have to eat it. That's his problem, not ours. Come on, Becca. We've got bigger fish to fry here. Which you'd know, if you'd set foot inside the theater for the past week."

Ouch. It was five days, not a full week. But I didn't think Hal would appreciate the contradiction.

In any case, Ryan seemed to understand that more was at stake than a few free snacks. His eyes reflected the stage lights dramatically as he asked, "What are the flavors?"

"Caramel Curry Karma."

"Curry?" Hal asked.

I glanced at Jenn, indicated that she should reply. She nodded with professional vigor and explained, "He insists there are African curries. He says it's a novel combination that's perfect for our show."

Ryan sighed. "I ate curry there. It's not native to the region, but with enough money you can get it."

"What else?" Hal asked.

"Cheddar Kola Chew," I announced.

Hal exclaimed, "Cola? Chew? Who chews cola?"

A glance from me, and Jenn hurried to clarify. "It's not *cola,* like you're thinking, like the soda. It's *kola,* with a *k.* Like the nut."

"Kola nut?" Hal asked, still perplexed.

Ryan shook his head. "They chew it in West Africa. It's bitter, and it eases hunger pangs. I can't imagine that it would be any good with cheddar popcorn, but it's more authentic than the curry."

Hal shrugged and said to me, "Fine. We can live with it. Is that all?"

"No," I said. I didn't want to name the last flavor. It was a bad joke, like someone trying to do a stand-up comedy routine the day after a horrendous natural disaster. I looked at Jenn, but she shook her head, obviously tossing the proverbial ball back into my court. I gritted my teeth and blurted out, "He wants to serve plain popcorn. No salt. No sugar. No flavor. And he wants to call it Plain Starvation."

"What?" Ryan and Hal bellowed together.

The cast had been standing around onstage, ready to resume their rehearsal. At the combined shout of anger and disgust, though, everyone turned to stare at us. They were actors, after all. They knew when good drama was staring them in the face.

"What sort of egomaniac takes the starvation of hundreds, of thousands of women and turns it into some sort of promotional opportunity?" Ryan was furious, angrier than I'd ever seen him.

"Jenn tried talking to him, but he absolutely refuses to give in."

"Jenn!" Ryan responded. "Why is Jenn dealing with that idiot? Isn't that your job?"

My voice froze. "I beg your pardon?"

"Well, you've been too busy to come to rehearsal! I just assumed that you were off doing important 'dramaturg' things." I could almost see the air quotes that he put around my title. "I should have realized you were making your assistant do your dirty work."

"Don't you *dare* tell me how to do my job!"

The cast moved toward us like a pack of hyenas closing in around a pair of dueling wildebeests. Hal cleared his throat pointedly, his icy eyes flashing a warning to me, to both of us, demanding that we calm down. He said, "Ryan wasn't—"

"Don't try to defend him, Hal. We've bent over backwards to make this play what he wants it to be. We kept his impossible blocking. We reworked the sets. We brought in costume consultants from the African Art Museum. We dragged in language and accent coaches. We've done everything we possibly could to make this show real. To make it true. Ryan should know by now that we're on his side. He should understand that. We. Know. How. To. Do. Our. Jobs."

Ryan's fingers folded into fists. He refused to look at me, refused to acknowledge my rage. Instead, he turned to my assistant. "I'm sorry, Jenn," he said, in a voice so low that, against my will, I stepped closer to hear. "I didn't mean to imply that you weren't capable of dealing with Ronald. I only meant to say that you shouldn't be required to work with that maniac."

Jenn? Why was he apologizing to Jenn? *I* was the one he had insulted!

Anger erupted inside me, flinging a white-hot curtain

across my eyes. I knew that there were words—scores of them, hundreds of them—words that I could use to express myself with perfect eloquence and precision. But I didn't want any of them. I didn't want to modulate my voice. I didn't want to be demure and ladylike and polite.

I wanted to blast Ryan out of the room.

"Don't talk to Jenn!" I shrieked. "Talk to me! Explain to *me!*" The cast was close now; I could sense some of them standing directly behind me. The tide of my fury was too high, though, to cut short my tirade. The force of my rage ripped through me, releasing the tension of the past month, cutting away the tightrope I'd balanced on for weeks as I tried to be the perfect dramaturg *and* the perfect girlfriend. "Ryan, you owe me that much! You owe me more! Tell me about the computer program you wrote! Tell me about Pam! Tell me about how Africa gave you back your life! You owe me—"

And everything disappeared.

Suddenly, I was no place. Nowhere. There wasn't a roof above me. There weren't orderly rows of red velvet chairs around me. There wasn't a group of people, dozens of cast members, pressing in against my back.

There was just an endless sea of gray.

Gray. And Teel, dressed in her Anana costume, holding on to her old woman form.

"What did you do?" I asked, and my voice sounded very, very small.

"I figured I'd better get you out of there, before you said anything else you were going to regret. I thought it might be helpful if the two of you finished your conversation on neutral ground."

"Two—" Before I could finish the question, though, Teel jutted her chin toward my shoulder, sweeping her wrinkled hands before her in a grand gesture of welcoming. My breath froze in my throat, and I barely managed to turn around.

Ryan was staring at me, his own jaw slack with disbelief. "You have a genie, too?" he asked.

CHAPTER 15

"TOO?" I ASKED, SO SHOCKED THAT I COULDN'T PUT
together a true sentence, couldn't express the utter confusion
that buffeted me.

Ryan asked, "Anana is your genie?"

"Teel," the meddling old creature said by way of self-intro-
duction. She extended her hand to shake his, letting her
sleeve creep up to reveal her flame tattoo. The individual
tongues of fire wove back and forth, twisting around themselves as if they were excited by their proximity to the Garden.
Ryan's attention was snagged, stolen by their hypnotic spell.

Irritated by the feeling that everyone else knew what was
going on except for me, I clapped my hands to get Ryan's
attention. The brief sting of my palms fed the block of ice
that was settling in my belly, freezing my anger into a righ-
teous ballast. "Hello! 'You have a genie, *too?*' So you're
saying that you've got one? And you never told me?" As
Ryan spluttered a nonresponse, I rounded on Teel. "And
what the hell are the odds on *that?*" Teel whistled tunelessly,

a snatch of song that her character sang in the first scene of *However Long*. "You had to know! Don't give me that innocent act!"

She pouted. "Well, I did tell you about Jaze, didn't I? That I was hoping to share my time in the Garden with someone special?"

Yeah, she'd told me. Over and over again—but I'd always assumed that Teel's romantic dreams were just a touch of added drama, cheap manipulation to get me to speed up my wish-making. "Jaze is Ryan's genie? And you've known that all along? Without telling me? Telling us?"

Teel raised one lined hand. "Guilty as charged." She shrugged, her shoulders moving as if she were a much younger woman. "What can I say? MAGIC fired us up. The Decadium got us all excited to get into the Garden. It made your human world seem…boring. But Jaze and I thought it might be entertaining to see what happened when two of our humans got together. We wondered how long it would take for the two of you to figure it out. You really weren't very clever, were you?" Teel must have recognized the look of fury on my face. She blurted out, "It was all Jaze's idea."

"I don't believe it," I shouted. "You've been manipulating me—manipulating *us*—from day one!"

"You got your wishes," Teel said sullenly.

Before I could retort, Ryan finally succeeded in dragging his eyes away from Teel's wrist. The expression on his face was so dazed, though, so confused, that I half expected his eyes to swirl like pinwheels when he looked at me. "I never dreamed you had a genie, too."

I whirled back to Teel. "So let me get this straight. You and Jaze purposely brought Ryan and me together, just to see what would happen? Like we were some sort of experiment? Some sort of rats in a maze?"

Teel said, "Not exactly. Or not completely." She looked at Ryan and prompted, "Aren't you going to say anything?"

When he didn't answer, I snapped, "Ryan! Did you know about this? Did you just forget to mention it, like you forgot to mention Pam? Like you forgot to mention your software project?"

"No!" The vehemence of his reply chased away the last of his hypnotized response to my genie. "I never knew you had…Teel," he said. "And I didn't think I could tell you about Jaze. I thought the words would just get stuck in my throat. You know, the whole silence thing?" he said.

Yeah. The silence thing. Like he'd been silent about Pam, about his past.

I let some of the ice inside me freeze my words as I glared at Teel. "Could you give us a minute alone?" I waved my hand, indicating the general direction of the Garden. "Can't you go watch the birds fly, or something? Spend some time smelling flowers through the gate?" Teel's eyebrows drew together in consternation, and I thought that she was going to refuse my request. "That's why you brought us here, right? You wanted to give us a chance to talk?"

"I thought that was what *you* wanted." Teel's old woman voice was stretched tight with a curious haughtiness. "I thought that *you* wanted to discuss lies, and the type of person who tells them. You know, to supposed friends."

Even as I tried to parse those words, tried to figure out what I could possibly have done to earn Teel's scorn, my genie pulled herself up to her full, if diminutive, height. Her silver hair gave her a halo of dignity as she stepped toward me.

Stepped toward me, then glided around Ryan, then took several steps away into the gray distance.

Only when she raised her hands, curling her fingers around invisible iron bars, did I realize that I'd completely mislocated the Garden. In my frustration with Ryan, in my absolute surprise to find him there, I'd forgotten to wait for Teel's cues, forgotten to stall while she let me know exactly where the Garden was, exactly what she was seeing.

I was totally busted.

But first things first. I clenched my arms around my frozen core and turned back to Ryan. "Go ahead," I said. "What other things did you forget to tell me? Let me guess. You're actually a government spy from a supersecret agency, and you've got a license to kill? No! Wait! You're the heir to an Eastern European throne, with millions of dollars locked up in Swiss bank accounts. No! Better! You never actually wrote *However Long,* you just found the manuscript on a table in a coffee shop, and you decided to pretend that it was yours!"

The disappointment on my tongue turned my words as bitter as kola nut—with or without cheddar popcorn. "That's not fair," Ryan said. "Becca, I know this must be a shock, finding out about Jaze, but there was no way for me to tell you about her. At least, I didn't think there was, since I didn't know you had your own genie."

His words pricked my conscience with enough guilt that I recalled my own efforts to talk about my magical encounters. I thought about that day, weeks ago, when I'd tried to talk to Jenn, when I'd tried to tell her about the bizarre gift that Kira had left for me. I remembered the way my throat had closed up, the way the words had just stopped.

Okay. So, he had a point. About the genie. "But what

about Pam? Oh, I know! *She* had supernatural powers, too! She made you go silent whenever you tried to say *her* name!"

He sucked in a quick breath, and I knew I'd scored a point. I also knew that he was going to run his fingers through his hair, ending with the curls that were just a little too long, the ones that brushed against the back collar of his shirt. I knew that he was going to hunch his shoulders and sigh. I knew that he was going to look up at me through his eyelashes.

I knew Ryan.

Except, I didn't.

I knew all those superficial things, all those mannerisms, all those actions that anyone in the world could see, if they only watched him long enough. But I didn't know his thoughts. I didn't know the way his mind really worked, the way he chose what to share and what to keep buried inside forever. I didn't know the real, true him. Just like I hadn't known Dean.

"Pam…" he started, but he trailed off as if he were searching for an answer. Well, he could stare off into the nonexistent scenery all day long, but he wasn't going to find any guidance there.

He squared his shoulders and tried again. "Pam was part of my past. A part that I'm not proud of. I let myself get sucked into the world I thought that we—that she and I— shared. I let myself believe we had a future together, that we had a real relationship. But it wasn't based on anything. Not anything real. And when she sold the software, when I finally realized…" He shook his head as he trailed off. "Something just broke inside me. I started to question everything I'd ever done, everything I was." His hands worked, clenching and unclenching. "Becca, I needed to build a whole new life for myself. I know you'll never understand, but I needed to start from ground zero."

But he was wrong. I did understand. At least a little bit.

When Dean disappeared, he tore down the ramparts of both my professional and my personal life. His embezzlement revealed his true colors, but money wasn't all he'd stolen. He'd taken my confidence. My faith in myself.

And I'd selected *However Long* as my path back. My method of rebuilding my own identity.

The brick of ice in my belly started to melt, especially when I thought about how little I'd told Ryan about Dean. Not that I'd really needed to share that dirty laundry. There was plenty of gossip about Dean and me posted on ShowTalk. I said to Ryan, "Okay, so maybe I can understand your need to separate the past from the present. But to never even *mention* her? To wall off a part of you that is so important, that made you who you are today?"

He caught my gaze and held it. "You're right. I should have told you about Pam."

The admission was so honest, so frank, that I caught my breath in astonishment. Unable to let the argument drop so suddenly, though, I said, "I was embarrassed to hear about her from your *mother*."

"I understand," he said. "That must have been really awkward."

I continued the debate, even though he wasn't engaging. "I mean, Dani hardly seems like your mother, like *anyone's* mother, but she thought I knew, and I had no idea, and it was so uncomfortable for both of us—"

"You're right," he said for a third time. The chunk of ice inside me splintered, shards of bitter cold breaking away like an iceberg calving into the ocean. At least until he said, "But there's more I need to tell you. More that you should know, more that I think you'll understand, since you have…Teel."

I didn't want Ryan to tell me more. I didn't want to hear anything else that might break my heart. But we'd had enough of supposedly protective silence between us. I braced myself and said, "Go ahead."

"You need to know about my wishes. I found Jaze's lamp in a used bookstore, four, almost five years ago. My first wish was to make Pam, um, love me."

Love him. Somehow, I couldn't picture a guy making that wish—it was too princess-and-pony, too dream-date-for-the-prom. "Sure," I said. "Love."

He blushed. "Okay. I wanted her to…want me." He shot another look at me from under those eyelashes. For a man who made his living by words, he seemed completely uncomfortable with the ones he was choosing right now. "That was part of the problem between Pam and me," he wobbled on. "I started things under…under false pretenses. And when I thought I really loved her, she wasn't interested. Had never been interested. Had only been caught by Jaze."

Ouch. I decided to let him off the hook about word choice. "So what was your second wish?"

"I wanted to sell the writing software." I nodded in sudden understanding as Ryan went on. "The way it all played out, I was furious with myself for not making my true wish clearer. I blamed Jaze for playing tricks on me. I blamed Pam. If she'd just told me about the deal before making it final, if she'd warned me about the exclusivity clause, I probably could have fixed things. But she didn't, and everything just collapsed around me. Around us." He shook his head. "She was so proud of herself for making the sale. And I was so angry with her. And she was still being driven by…manipulated by…my first wish, so we ended up hurting each other even more, understanding each other even less." He closed his eyes against the old emotions. When he continued speaking, his voice was very soft. "I'd made huge mistakes, with both my wishes."

His hurt was so obviously raw that I settled my palm against his arm, trying to soothe him. He jumped a little at my touch, and his eyes flew open. I held his gaze and said, "And your third wish?"

"The Peace Corps. I'd thought about it before. I'd imagined the things that I could do, the places I could go. I came back to it seriously, though, when I realized what a mess I'd made of everything in New York, everything with Pam. I thought I could…redeem myself by going to Africa."

I heard the doubt in his voice, the judgment he was casting on himself. "But?" I prompted.

"But using the wish was cheating. I mean, people apply to the Peace Corps and then wait months, even years for placement. I just spoke to Jaze, and bam! I was heading to Burkina Faso in two weeks, job, visa, inoculations, all in order."

"But you *did* do great things while you were there! You helped people. And you wrote *However Long*. Your work was good enough that we picked it up, even though you came to us outside our usual process."

He took a deep breath and stepped away from me. My fingers curled into the empty space where they'd been touching his sleeve. "That's the thing," he said. "*However Long*. That was my fourth wish. To have the Mercer produce my play."

I felt like he'd punched me in my stomach.

His play. His amazing play. The one I'd read, the one I'd championed, the one I'd moved heaven and Hal to produce… All because of a wish? All because of a genie's manipulation?

He had to be lying. I didn't know why yet, but he had to be making up a story.

But I remembered waking up with a sudden compulsion to read *However Long*. I remembered knowing that it was perfect, that Hal had to select it. I remembered knocking on Ryan's door to share my good news, our good news, to tell him that we'd selected his play. And I remembered his strange reaction, the way he'd taken two deep breaths, as if he were ashamed.

As if he were guilty.

As if he'd used magic to achieve his fourth and final dream.

Sudden tears pricked the backs of my eyes. I *had* to be a better judge of theater than that! I had years of education behind me, countless hours spent reading endless scripts…. I knew a good play when I read it. I couldn't have been fooled by Jaze, by Ryan, by a stupid, idiotic wish.

Nausea twisted through my gut, and I forced myself to take deep breaths. This wasn't happening to me. This couldn't be real. My first solo choice as a dramaturg, my first declaration of independence from Dean Marcus, couldn't have been because I'd been manipulated by someone else's magic.

I remembered that night at the Pharm, the night that Jenn had handed over the bribes from other playwrights. I'd spent so much time convincing myself that I'd been right, that I'd been fair. That I'd followed all the rules.

And all that time, it had never occurred to me that I was being manipulated in a far more subtle way. I'd been dragged through ethical breaches I hadn't even imagined existed. Ryan's wish had forced me to forfeit every moral standard I'd ever worried about as a dramaturg.

But then, as clear as the nightingale song that I couldn't hear in the Garden, I realized something. *However Long* was a good play. The story was strong. The characters were unique. The language was pure poetry.

Ryan may have wished his play into rapid production, but he'd only expedited his success. In the ordinary course of business, I would have eventually gotten around to reading his manuscript, eventually plucked it out of the pile on my desk. I would have recognized the script's inherent power. I would have suggested it to Hal, worked to bring it into the Mercer.

All of that would have just happened a few years further down the line.

Even as I took comfort in my realization, a tiny part of me was struck by the absurd irony of the situation. If Ryan hadn't wasted his last wish on getting my attention, *However Long* might have been in a stronger position to debut. A year from now, two years from now, Dean's theft would be ancient history. The Mercer would have rebuilt its ties with its traditional sponsors. We'd never have become indebted to the Popcorn King. I never would have stormed into rehearsal, ranting about Ronald's insulting popcorn flavors. I never would have started screaming at Ryan like a madwoman, and Teel never would have intervened by taking us away, taking us both to the Garden.

I never would have known that Ryan had a genie, too.

"Okay," I said, realizing that Ryan was still standing in front of me. I could read the agony on his face, the absolute certainty that I could never forgive his manipulation, his turning me into the object of his fourth and final wish. It was time for me to speak. "I understand."

"Really?" The tiniest spark of hope brightened his face. "And you don't hate me?"

"I don't hate you. Any more than you should hate me, for moving in across the hall."

I watched him process that. "One of your wishes?"

"Not specifically. I mean, not across the hall from *you*. But after I realized Dean had left me with no place to live, I had to do something. My first wish was for a place to live. Teel stole your address from the copy of *However Long* that was on my desk. She and Jaze must have loved that opportunity to mess with our minds."

"And your second wish?"

"For clothes, back when I didn't have anything. When all of my possessions were still wrapped up in Dean's police investigation. I wished for the wardrobe that got us through all those business meetings. And my third was for the Gray Guerillas."

"You used a wish to help my mother?"

I nodded. "After I saw what the Grays were doing, after you showed me how to plant the seeds, and I watched those little plants sprout… I had to do something when Dani was arrested. Had to let others have the same experience. I mean, I didn't plan on getting the *mayor* involved, but…"

"So, you have one wish left?"

"And I'm saving it for a rainy day." I think that the old cliché made us both think of seed bombs, of the type of dark and stormy night that was perfect for guerilla attacks. We smiled at each other.

"Hey," I said. "What did you do with your lamp? After you made your last wish?"

"I packaged it up and sent it to Burkina Faso. To a woman in the village where I was stationed, the model for Fanta. I knew that she'd be able to use the wishes, and I liked the idea of putting a genie in circulation there."

I liked that idea, too. I wasn't sure how Jaze would fit in to African village life, once her sabbatical was over in the Garden. But one thing was for sure. She'd be appreciated. Probably more than I could ever imagine.

Ryan cleared his throat. "Becca, I'm not even sure what we were fighting about back there, in the theater. I mean, I know I was furious with Ronald, but I never should have taken it out on you. Or on Jenn. Or on you about Jenn."

I didn't know what to say. I wasn't used to guys apologizing to me. I wasn't used to the sudden rush of pleasure that his words brought, wasn't used to the realization that *he* was reaching out to *me*. "I was wrong, too," I finally said, amazed at how easily the words came once I started. "I mean, it's not my fault that the Popcorn King is a jerk, but I shouldn't have gotten as upset as I did. I think I was mostly embarrassed. I'd been avoiding you, and it was hard to come in there, with that news, with yet another disaster."

"And you were avoiding me because of Pam?"

I tried to put my thoughts into words. "Not exactly. I mean, I know you dated other women before me. But I was upset that you'd never mentioned her to me, that you'd barely even mentioned the software. When Dani told me, I understood why the blocking was so important to you, and I just wished that you had told me yourself. I could have helped. I mean, helped you *and* the show."

"I can see that now."

Wow. This was how adults talked through their problems. This was how two grown-ups explained their misunderstandings to each other.

All of a sudden, I thought back to that night in Dani's apartment, the night that Ryan had shown me how to plant cabbage seeds. I'd realized then that he was an excellent teacher, that I could learn from him. And here was another lesson he was handing over to me, wrapped up, with the proverbial bow on top.

I caught myself grinning awkwardly. Like he used to do. Like he used to do, when he was gangly and uncomfortable, when he'd first appeared in my office, and I'd nearly dismissed him as some sort of mis-socialized geek.

I was glad I'd taken the time to get to know him better.

"I'm sorry," he said. Before I could respond to his apology, before I could formulate any sort of suave, adult reply, he closed the distance between us. His fingers were warm against my cheek as he leaned in for a kiss, but his lips were soft, tentative.

That sweet uncertainty awakened the beast that had been frozen in my belly. Heat uncurled inside me, reaching out tendrils to steal my breath, to make my pulse pound hard. He must have felt my response, must have recognized it for what it was. His hand slid to the back of my head, and his fingers twined in my hair. His kiss became more urgent, more demanding.

My own hands made themselves busy, clutching at his back, pulling him closer. I tugged at his shirt, ready to free it from its waistband.

And that's when I heard the cough.

A polite little "ahem," delivered against a wrinkled palm. A prim reprimand, like the chastisement of a grandmother. A deferential reminder that someone disapproved of my behavior.

Teel.

Ryan froze at the same time I did. When he stepped back, he slid his hands down to my elbows. The motion effectively kept him between my genie and me, giving me a much-needed moment to catch my breath, to collect my composure. There was nothing I could do about the tingle in my lips, though. Bracing myself, I stepped to the side and confronted my judgmental genie's ebony gaze.

"*If* you two are quite through, we can go back to rehearsal." Teel-as-Anana's disapproval shattered against the gray nothingness. "You seem to have finished your discussion, and you *obviously* don't need to look at the Garden."

Ryan glanced at me. "You can actually see it?"

Great. Even if I'd wanted to continue lying to Teel, wanted to spin out some elaborate story to cover my earlier confusion over the gate's location, I couldn't do that now. Not with Ryan asking me a question, point-blank.

"Not exactly," I said. Teel harrumphed, and the cap of her silver hair trembled like a high-strung horse's mane. I swallowed hard and forced myself to explain. "But I pretended that I could. Before. When it was just Teel and me."

Teel's old-lady voice was raspy. "I thought that you were a Perceptive. One of the very few humans who can truly see the Garden. One who can understand."

I twisted my hands in front of me, honestly miserable. "The first time you brought me here, I thought that *I* was the strange one. The way you went on and on about how wonderful it was, I thought that everyone else had to be able to see it. I didn't want to disappoint you. I didn't want you to give up on me, to take away my wishes because I was defective, or something."

"But I *believed* you! I shared my secrets with you!" Her words trembled, and an actual tear carved a valley down her cheek.

"Teel! Don't cry!" I rushed over to her, folded her hands between mine. It was hard to believe that this was my genie, this pitiable old woman whom I'd inadvertently hurt....

She was also the Con Ed line worker. She was the debonair man in a tuxedo. She was the painter and the bombshell who had ruined my hopes of soliciting money from the International Women's Union, and she was the clown and the lawyer. I couldn't picture any of those personas crying. I couldn't imagine any of them caring enough, any of them being influenced at all by who I was, by what I said, by what I did.

And yet they were all one and the same. They were all, at their core, the same creature. The same magical being who had been there for me each time I thought my life couldn't get any worse.

Sure, Teel could be annoying. She purposely got a few wish details wrong, just to spice up her magical life. She sparked each week of her life with more drama than most humans would pack into a lifetime.

But she didn't deserve being lied to.

"I'm sorry," I said, applying the lesson I'd just learned from Ryan. "I shouldn't have lied. I thought that I'd be making things better for you, not worse."

The old woman sniffled before she pulled her hands away from mine. She tilted her head to one side, squinting her eyes as if she were measuring the actual dimensions of my apology. I hung my head, trying to convey the full extent of my remorse.

"There *is* one thing that would make me feel better," she said.

"What?"

"Make your fourth wish, now." She struck like a cobra.

"Teel!" When I looked closer, her eyes were completely dry; her tears had faded as soon as she revealed her true purpose.

She shrugged. "It was worth a try." She cocked her head, taking in Ryan. "So, are you two ready to go back?"

I thought about the argument we'd had back at the Mercer, the frantic escalation of our emotions. I didn't want to yell anymore. I didn't want to fight. "Do we have to?"

"It's that, or stay here forever," she said.

Ryan stepped up beside me. "We'll go back." I heard the fervent desire in his voice. He must really dislike the Garden space, as much as Kira did.

"But what about everyone else? They're going to realize something's wrong, if Ryan and I aren't screaming like magpies."

Teel rolled her eyes. "You were the one doing the screaming. He kept his voice down the entire time."

"Great. Thanks for reminding me."

Gallantly, Ryan got us off the subject. "Seriously, though. What are we going to do? We can't explain to anyone what's happened. Your magic would just knock us silent, won't it?"

"Silence won't be a problem," Teel said. "I promise."

Before we could ask for an explanation, she raised her mahogany fingers to her ear. The wrinkles across her knuckles were deep, mesmerizing, and I almost forgot to grab a breath before we translated through the gray nothingness.

I stumbled just a little as I came back to the Mercer. Ryan shot out a hand to steady me, leaving his fingers on my forearm. I glanced at him, hoping that he had an idea, that he could figure out something on the spot to explain to everyone why we weren't fighting anymore.

And then I heard the sound of popping corn, and I knew why no explanation would be necessary.

"Pop off!" exclaimed Ronald as he rolled through the theater door.

Hal still held the printout of Jenn's e-mail in his hand. The cast still thrummed with outrage about Plain Starvation. And everyone was waiting for me to take the lead, for me to respond to the rampaging Popcorn King.

I swallowed hard and stepped forward. I waited until Ronald slapped his cell phone shut, and then I said his name by way of greeting, keeping my voice perfectly level.

"I got tired of talking to your assistant! Sweet girl! But can't make a decision to save her life!"

I heard Jenn splutter behind me. I said, "I have absolute faith in Jenn's ability to make up her mind, Ronald."

"No! Not her! I gave her a simple list of product names! But she couldn't approve them!"

"I think you misunderstood." I tried to paint a coat of sympathy over my words, but I didn't waste a lot of time getting the sound exactly right. For someone as tone deaf as Ronald, nuance wasn't worth the extra effort. "Jenn didn't say she *couldn't* approve them. She said she *wouldn't* approve them."

Ronald stopped dead in his tracks. "What?" His roar must have been audible back in his own office.

In another place, in another time, I would have found a way to be conciliatory. I would have woven the necessary lies. I would have placated. I would have soothed. I would have applied every last trick in my bag of dramaturgical training.

But not now. Not when I had just learned how dangerous silence could be.

My goal as dramaturg wasn't to make every single person in the Mercer love every other person. It wasn't to smooth over conflict solely for the purpose of smothering negative feelings. My goal was to make the best play possible.

And Ronald J. Barton, Popcorn King, wasn't part of that vision.

I could feel Ryan behind me, his support as solid as the painted metal roof on Fanta's hut. The cast murmured beyond him. Some of the actors had never before laid eyes on Ronald J. Barton. They hadn't had the opportunity to view his fashion sense firsthand. They hadn't had the pleasure of listening to his foghorn bellow.

Hal knew what we were up against, though. I glanced at him, made sure that he was on board. He gave me the tiniest of nods, the slightest visual sign of his approval.

Taking another step forward, knowing that I had to stand alone, I raised my chin. I spoke clearly, precisely, never raising my voice but using every last shred of my theatrical experience to make sure that Ronald could hear each syllable of my reply. "Ronald, we will not use your flavors. They, and their names, are insensitive and insulting. We will not devalue our audience or this production, just to help you sell more popcorn."

Ronald's eyes bulged. His face flushed crimson, contrasting violently with his lemon-yellow sweater. His hands curled into fists so tight that I feared for the structural integrity of his cell phone. "We have a contract!"

I exploited his shout, lowering my own voice for greater contrast. "I am well aware of that."

"You'll never see a penny of my third check!"

"We don't expect to."

"I'll sue!"

"And I'll accept service of your complaint, right here."

Hal stepped forward. "Or I will."

Ryan wasn't about to be outdone. "Or I."

We stood there, like the Three Musketeers. Out of the corners of my eyes, I could see the cast gather closer. A few actually wore their Popcorn King T-shirts, and the fluorescent colors almost threatened to steal my attention from the apoplectic man before me. Almost.

"I—!" he shouted. "You—! They—! We are through here! You'll never see another penny from me! And I intend to see you repay every single cent I've given you so far!"

Ronald J. Barton, the Popcorn King, turned on his tangerine-clad heel. He slammed the theater doors behind him and, by the sound of things, crashed through the lobby doors, as well.

Shaking, I turned to look at Hal. His lips were stretched thin, his jaw practically wired shut. I only realized then how much he had longed to speak out, to interrupt Ronald's tirade, to berate the Popcorn King himself. He spared me a single nod, a tight, incontrovertible gesture of approval.

When I looked at Ryan, he was smiling. He raised his hands in front of him. He clapped once. Twice. And then the entire company joined in, filling the Mercer with the sound of applause.

I barely resisted the urge to take a bow.

CHAPTER 16

NO ONE WOULD HAVE CLAPPED IF THEY'D REALIZED how much work it would be to cut loose the tentacles that the Popcorn King had wrapped around our production. Sets, costumes, programs, lobby—just about every aspect of the Mercer had been co-opted by our unholy alliance with Ronald J. Barton.

The first thing Hal ordered was for the set to be repainted. It took four coats of gray to block out the fluorescent glow of yellow on the corrugated roof of Fanta's hut, but everyone agreed that the change was for the better. Even if we needed to adjust the lighting levels to account for the darker color, nudging everything up a notch or two. Even if the shift in lighting made it more obvious when the actors missed their precise marks for those tightly choreographed scenes in the second act. Even if the brighter lighting required a change in makeup design, so that everyone's wrinkles and fatigue appeared more realistic.

It was worth it, just to be free from the all-smothering logo of the Popcorn King.

Similarly, it was worth the effort to rework costumes for the players who had been slated to wear orange and yellow souvenir T-shirts. Of course, Ronald's fluorescent dyes had never faded as we'd hoped; his hideous advertisements had remained brilliant despite our best efforts to camouflage them into submission. Now, we threw out the promotional garbage, but we stuck with the same general concept in our costume redesign—the characters lived in rags, in donations from benefactors they'd never met. The new costumes were more subdued, defeated, grim, like the living conditions we showed throughout the play.

Everyone was grateful that we no longer risked migraines from staring at the mix of never-appropriate, brightly colored American ultimate-symbol-of-consumerism shirts.

Cleansing Ronald's influence from our brochures and programs posed a bit more of a problem. We'd already laid out the written materials to include the Popcorn King's two bargained-for ads. We were up against a tight deadline as it was, getting everything to the printer on time. I spent one entire sleepless night updating the programs, scrubbing every last reference to our supposed benefactor.

I was yawning the next day, but it was worth it to have everything correct.

We had a substantially easier time jettisoning the massive advertisements that Ronald had created for our lobby. Everyone breathed a little more freely when we were no longer assaulted by raging yellow and orange billboards every time we walked into the theater.

The transition wasn't one hundred percent painless. The house manager had to scramble to rebuild our traditional lobby display for the actors' headshots. She had to remove the performers' staid black-and-white photographs from the riotous, circuslike foam-board frames that Ronald had provided. She restored them to the traditional, boring, easy-to-view white background that had served well enough for every other production the Mercer had ever hosted.

The dim burgundy and navy lobby might be boring, but it was familiar. It was home.

Kira even saved the day when it came to the refreshments we intended to serve before the show and during intermission. Weeks earlier, she had placed a triple order for soft drinks, recognizing that our patrons would likely consume more than usual—a lot more—as they attempted to wash down the Popcorn King's heinous flavor combinations. Kira remembered the unusual order early enough to cancel it with a simple phone call to our supplier, reverting to our usual purchasing. At the same time, she arranged for candy bars, mints, oversize cookies—the usual snacks that our audiences expected.

Those treats might be boring, but at least we wouldn't have to worry about patrons getting sick on cruel and unusual flavors.

The last phase of de-popcorn-ification was the trickiest. We needed to review our accounting books to determine precisely how much of Ronald's money we had already spent, and how much we could return to him. We combed through columns of assets and liabilities, through checkbooks and credit-card statements, investing more attention to fiscal detail than Dean had likely spent during his entire tenure at the Mercer.

One calculation was simple: the Popcorn King's entire third payment, the $50,000 we hadn't yet received, was earmarked for advertising and promotion. With a few minor penalties, we canceled all of our radio spots, withdrew the splashy print ads that we had hoped would catapult the Mercer into the top tier of New York theaters.

Even so, our financial numbers were grim enough that I lost another few nights of sleep. A lot of Ronald's money had been used for the theater's day-to-day expenses. The Popcorn King had paid salaries for cast and crew. He had kept the heat and lights on. He'd covered the accent coach who had finally brought Fanta in line, after so many weeks of inappropriate Jamaican sojourns. Ronald's funds had been invested in costumes, in the set, in the fine, dry earth that drifted over the entire theater, despite Kira's best efforts to contain it.

Nevertheless, we juggled the numbers as best we could. Hal called an emergency board meeting, tapping into the directors' pockets for donations that each was likely to make at *some* point during the year. He met with our banker. He convinced the cast and crew to take a ten percent cut in pay for the rest of the rehearsal period, for the entire run of the show. He called in the directors for the remaining three plays in the Mercer's season, bargaining with them until they donated some of their shows' funding to ours.

Ultimately, we wrote a check to Ronald for $75,000. We owed the man another twenty-five, but we were temporarily out of fundraising ideas.

With three days to go before preview performances, we'd exorcised the Popcorn King as best we could. Everyone in the company was happier. Jenn still thanked me morning, noon, and night for sparing her from Ronald's constant phone calls and e-mails. The Mercer's flirtation with orange and yellow was safely in the past, a nightmare that rapidly lost its hold as each of us came fully awake.

Throughout all of the changes, Ryan and I worked side by side, happily united in our common goal of expunging Ronald J. Barton from *However Long*. We also did our best to adapt the troublesome blocking, however belatedly. Ryan continued to be pained by every single change that Hal proposed; twice he absolutely refused to modify particularly poignant choices that he'd enshrined in his script. In the end, no one was totally happy. Ryan felt that the soft underbelly of his play had been ripped out. The actors felt that they were being asked to do the impossible. I tried to shrug off the ongoing conflict. Even the world's best dramaturg couldn't solve every problem in a production.

At least we didn't bring the conflict home with us. Every night, Dani followed our theatrical exploits with interest. Ryan and I stopped by her apartment after rehearsal, and the three of us ate late dinners, sharing stories about our respective days.

Dani was busier than ever. She had become the official spokesperson for the Gray Guerillas, and her presence was in great demand. She had speaking engagements at schools, at churches, at office buildings throughout Manhattan. Overnight, guerilla chapters had become trendy; many had their own pages on Facebook and MySpace and a dozen other social networks. Page Six posted daily updates of celebrities who engaged in their own green guerilla stunts.

In light of Dani's busy schedule, I was astonished to find her on the sidewalk outside the Mercer when Ryan and I took a lunch break one Tuesday afternoon. We'd spent the entire morning hashing through the tech rehearsal for the first act, adding in all the light cues, all the sound cues, all the final technical details that would bring our show fully to life. Although the work was absolutely necessary, it was tiresome, and there were many starts and stops. When Kira announced an hour break for lunch, I heard the siren call of a spinach and feta omelet singing my name, loud and clear from the coffee shop down the street.

I was so intent on procuring that lunch, complete with steaming hot French fries, that I actually ran into Ryan when he stopped dead on the sidewalk, a scant three feet outside the Mercer's front door. "What—" I started to ask, but then I saw what had brought him to a halt.

Crocuses. A carpet of them, yellow and purple, nestled around the plane tree that grew in the grotty patch of earth between the sidewalk and the street. I glanced to my right. More crocuses, surrounding the next three trees. I turned to my left. Still more.

They were gorgeous in the spring sunshine, vibrant, defiantly challenging the grim tree trunk, the gray cement ocean around them. Only when Dani stepped out from behind the parked cars in the street did I realize what had happened. "Us?" I said, laughing. "The Mercer has been targeted by guerillas?"

She chuckled. "We figured it was the least we could do to help our favorite theatrical production. We wanted to spruce things up a little before preview audiences arrive on Friday. You know, since the theater itself is so drab these days."

We laughed, all of us grateful for "drab" because that meant the Popcorn King's orange and yellow had been vanquished. Ryan shook his head in amazement. "But they're bulbs! They must have taken you forever to plant!"

Dani grinned like the Mona Lisa. "Ah, the wonders of peat trays."

"Dani, they're beautiful!" I said, truly touched.

Before I could continue, a man's voice said, "Rebecca Morris?"

"Yes?" I turned around, half expecting to see a film crew on the sidewalk, someone who had been tracking Dani and the Grays and wanted to capture my reaction to their largesse.

A short man in a fawn-colored trench coat stepped forward. "Ryan Thompson?" he asked without responding to me directly. The fresh spring breeze ruffled the guy's mousy hair as Ryan nodded. Through some sleight of hand, he produced two envelopes, touching each of us with a sharp paper corner. He avoided meeting our eyes as he said, "You've been served."

A curse rose in my throat, and I took my envelope by reflex, ripping it open as Ryan fumbled with his. The process server disappeared down the sidewalk, not even sparing a glance for the riot of crocuses.

Ronald J. Barton… Popcorn King… Rebecca Morris… Ryan Thompson… Harold Bernson… The Mercer Theater… Temporary restraining order… Breach of contract… Conversion… Defamation… Slander… Intentional infliction of emotional distress… $25,000 in actual damages… Five million dollars in punitive damages…

"Five million dollars," I stammered.

"That's impossible!" Ryan protested, but after turning a few more pages, he agreed in a disbelieving voice. "Five million dollars."

Dani shook her head angrily. "He'll never get it! Not after what he put you through!"

I swallowed hard. "Even if we end up winning, it'll cost a fortune to fight this. We'll have to hire lawyers, both of us. And Hal and the Mercer, too."

Ryan had read further into his sheaf of papers. "It's not just the money. He says he'll be irreparably harmed if we do the play without his sponsorship. He says his reputation's on the line."

"*His* reputation!" I almost choked.

Ryan's face was chalk-white. "He got a judge to sign off on it. He got a temporary restraining order. We've been shut down, effective immediately."

Dani's brilliant crocuses seemed to fade as I struggled for something to say. I stared at the papers in my hand, as if I could will them into some transformation. I struggled to read the words, but they defiantly danced around the page.

I heard Ryan say something to Dani, thank her for the flowers, for the guerilla action on our behalf. Then he sent her on her way so that we could start slicing through our legal emergency. "We've got to find Hal," I said, fumbling my way back into the theater. Ryan stayed by my side as I ran through the lobby.

The stage was empty, though. Everyone had rushed out for lunch, eager for a break after the grueling rehearsal. Without a lot of hope, I said, "Maybe he's in his office." I led the way backstage, down the stairs, through the passage that led to the business side of the Mercer.

Jenn's computer was on in the Bullpen, her cockatiel screensaver mocking me with its cheerful colors, but she was nowhere to be seen. I knocked on Hal's door, simultaneously pushing it open. He wasn't there. Frantic, I darted into the conference room, poked my head into every single office down the long corridor.

Only when we got to my office did I accept that Ryan and I were truly alone. We had to grapple with this disaster without any help, without any guidance. I closed the door and threw my summons onto my desk, glaring at the ruffled pages.

Five million dollars.

That was more money than I could imagine earning in a lifetime. It was more than Dean had stolen. And a judge had already said we couldn't do the show? Without even holding a hearing?

I tried to remember to breathe.

"I don't know who to call," I muttered, longing to pace, but hemmed in by the stacks of books and boxes that filled my office. "Do you have a lawyer? Maybe Dani has one?" I fumbled through the stack of business cards piled by my computer monitor, as if legal counsel would magically appear. Ryan made a few negative noises, but he didn't bother explaining that he didn't keep a consigliere on call. He didn't need to.

Hal was going to be furious. Sure, he'd stood by me when my (now ex-, thank God) boyfriend embezzled funds. He'd put up with Ryan's pickiness over the staging. He'd embraced all the challenges of producing *However Long*. But having our show shut down before we started? All because I'd recruited the wrong sponsor? Because I'd let myself lose my temper with the Popcorn King? Because I'd abandoned every precept of dramaturgy when I read Ronald J. Barton the riot act in front of the Mercer's cast and crew?

Hal was going to fire me.

And the worst part of it was, he'd be right to do so. I had ruined our production. I had totally and completely screwed up.

The towering stack of plays on my desk mocked me. Someone else would inherit them. Someone who was more organized. Someone who could track all the details of this job neatly. Someone who was a better judge of character than I.

I couldn't help it. I started to cry.

Ryan was beside me instantly. His arms around me should have been comforting. They should have felt like protection, like a bulwark against all the tumbling chaos. Instead, though, they reminded me of everything I'd had, of everything I'd lost.

"Hush," he murmured as my sobs crescendoed. He brushed his lips against the top of my head. That tenderness broke something inside me. I hadn't just disappointed Hal, hadn't just let down the Mercer. Ryan was losing, too. Ryan's first play, his debut in New York—destroyed, because I had misplayed my cards with the Popcorn King. My tears turned to hysterical waves of desperate sorrow, of loss, of hopelessness.

Throughout the torrent, Ryan stood fast. He held on to me, became my only anchor in that forlorn sea. Just when I thought my sobs would tear me apart completely, he tightened his arms around me, pulled me even closer, supported me even more.

That sort of breakdown couldn't continue forever. I needed to catch my breath. I needed to blow my nose. My racking sobs faded to gasps, drifted away to hiccups. I could hear Ryan's heart, pounding through the drenched fabric of his shirt. Ducking my head, I slipped out of his embrace and stumbled to my desk, flailing around until I found a box of Kleenex.

I kept my back to him as I blew my nose. Great. With my waterlogged face, I was going to look like some alien monster. Embarrassed to face him, I fumbled for another Kleenex. I missed the box, though, sent it skittering across my desk. Ryan rescued it and plucked a tissue, which he pressed into my seeking hand.

I took another minute before I trusted myself to speak. "Well," I said, not certain what other words to add.

"Well," he agreed. "That was a long time coming."

I nodded, even though he couldn't see my face. Sure, I'd been crying about the lawsuit. But I'd been crying about so much more—the endless tension in bringing the play to completion, the loss of Dean, of my first home in New York, of my silly, schoolgirl dreams.

I took a fortifying breath and exhaled slowly, collecting the tattered shreds of my tissue and my dignity before turning to face Ryan.

He didn't flinch at my tear-mottled face, at my swollen eyes and runny nose. He didn't fling a hand over his eyes, didn't scream that I was a hideous monster, a gross, distorted alien. Instead, he reached out one hand and tucked a wayward strand of my strawberry hair behind my ear.

I forced myself to meet his gaze. "I think today is a rainy day."

He didn't pretend to misunderstand me. "Are you sure? It's your last wish. I don't want you to waste it."

"It's not a waste," I said. "It's a necessity." With stolid determination, I raised my tattooed fingers between us. I turned my wrist slightly, watching the near-invisible flames fracture the light, send it back to us in rainbows. Matching my thumb to my forefinger, I pressed hard and said, "Teel!"

Even though I was braced for the electric shock, it still surprised me. It caught Ryan, too; I saw him jerk once, as if he'd been suddenly awakened from a sound sleep. My entire office was filled with a kaleidoscope of lights, jeweled motes that coalesced in the air, that solidified on every surface. The brilliant dust swirled toward me, ruby and cobalt and emerald and topaz, all glinting like fireworks on a dark summer night. Each individual spark blazed brighter for a single, unified heartbeat, and then they all collapsed inward, solidifying into one dark shape.

A man. A policeman.

His navy blue uniform seemed molded to his body. The knife edges ironed into his shirtsleeves looked sharp enough to draw blood. His black belt was tight around his trim waist, and his nightstick and gun looked ready to jump into his confident hands. His strong jaw and deep-set chestnut eyes made me absolutely certain that he had graduated first in his class at the academy. Only the tattoo blazing on his wrist marked him as a man who'd never set foot inside a traditional police station.

I stepped forward and raised my chin. "I'm ready to make my fourth wish."

"I observed your intention as I exited the transition plane, ma'am," he said. He sounded like he was testifying in a court of law about some crime that he had foiled through hard work, long hours, and unquestioned diligence. His voice rumbled with an authority that could have stopped a bank robber midheist. Sparing a tight nod for Ryan, he said, "I take it, sir, that you've been included in the preparations for this wish transaction?"

Ryan straightened his shoulders and answered with resigned acceptance. "Yes."

I took a deep breath. "Teel, we need to erase Ronald J. Barton's lawsuit against us. Against Hal and the Mercer, too. We need to get rid of the order that the court issued this morning, eliminate any chance that we could owe damages."

The policeman's jaw clenched, as if his teeth were working steel chewing gum. He plucked a notepad from his belt, flipped back its leather cover. Grasping a pen between his iron fingers, he jotted something on a form, checking a couple of boxes, and reviewing the entire document before he scribbled his name across the bottom.

"What's that?" I asked as he tore out the page and gave it to me.

"Prior written notification of a time variance stemming from a high E.I.Q. pursuant to the original contract that you signed." His eyes narrowed as he pointed to one square on the form. "Your request will take two weeks to grant."

"What?" I was astonished. My wish was a simple request, not something like world peace. "I just want the Popcorn King off my back!"

Teel recited, "Applying the standards set forth at the most recent Decadium—"

"Yeah, yeah," I said, cutting off a lecture that sounded as exciting as a Miranda warning. "You have to warn me if you can't do the wish right away. But what's the problem? Why will this one take so long to fulfill?"

The cop brought his blunt fingers to rest on the grip of his gun, as if he wanted a reminder of his position of authority. His fingers curved easily around the textured metal, and his voice was professionally cool as he said, "Applying the standards set forth at the most recent Decadium, your request generates an E.I.Q. of one hundred and seven. All fourth wishes generating an E.I.Q. greater than one hundred require a two-week holding period."

"E.I.Q.?" Ryan asked.

"Ethical Interference Quotient." Teel nodded once, as if he were responding to roll call in the patrol room. "Paragraph seventeen point K point twenty-seven point A sub three. It's all there in the contract you signed. Ma'am."

Yeah. The contract I'd barely skimmed through. I vaguely remembered the lawyer-Teel mentioning a handful of special circumstances, of wishes that could cause a delay in fulfillment. "Um, could you refresh my memory?"

"Your requested action involves the modification of an order issued by a legally constituted court of law."

"So what?" My frustration shortened my temper. Two weeks of delay might as well be forever. Two weeks would keep Ronald's restraining order in place through what should have been *However Long*'s previews, into the first full week of performances. We'd still have to hire a lawyer to secure the right to open the show, and we'd still be on the hook for five million dollars if Ronald actually managed to prove that our play had irreparably harmed his reputation.

Teel didn't bother reacting to my tone. Instead, he shifted his feet until they were shoulder-width apart. He linked his fingers behind his back, as if someone had barked out the parade rest command. With a grim nod, he recited, "Nine out of ten wishers who interfere with a court's decision require additional wishes to achieve their ultimate objectives."

Again with the statistics! "But I've only got four wishes, Teel. If I screw things up, that's my problem, not yours!"

"Seventeen out of twenty people who use their fourth

wish on high E.I.Q. wishes attempt to manipulate the person who next receives their lamp."

Seventeen out of twenty. Wow. That number seemed unbelievably high.

So the E.I.Q. functioned as a rough gauge of morals, of ethics. People who cast high E.I.Q. wishes were willing to engage in ethically risky behavior, ducking out from under punishments that had already been determined by a court of law. Sure, there were plenty of reasons someone might deserve to escape justice—Ryan and I were a perfect case in point—but I could see that most people in my position were a little on the shady side.

Okay. A lot on the shady side.

And if things didn't work out the way I'd planned? Once I'd already crossed that first ethical bridge? What was to keep me from giving the lamp to someone I knew I could control? Someone who would effectively give me another four wishes to play with?

But that wasn't me. That wasn't my situation. "I'm not just any wisher, Teel! You know me! You're in the show. You know why I need this!"

Teel shook his head, staring me down like a patrolman at a D.U.I. random stop. "The two-week hold permits both MAGIC and persons of interest to evaluate their choices more completely."

Persons of interest? He made me sound like a suspect in some case. Some very nasty case.

"Becca." Ryan's voice was so soft I almost didn't hear him. "You're going to have to make another wish."

"Another—?"

"Wish away the production." He turned to the policeman,

who was eyeing us as if we were security risks at an open-air presidential rally. "That would work, wouldn't it? If Becca wishes that the Mercer had never staged *However Long*?"

A dull ache started to pound between my eyes. If we'd never staged the show, then we never would have approached Ronald for money. If he'd never donated funds to us, then he couldn't sue us. But we *had* approached him, and he *had* sued, so didn't we still run into the E.I.Q. problem?

But who was I to say how magic worked? Teel spared us another haughty nod before he testified, "Without an Ethical Interference Quotient over one hundred, I can grant your wish instantly."

I said, "I can't do that! I can't kill the play."

Ryan reached toward me, cupping my cheek with fingers so cold a tremor rippled down my spine. "It's all you *can* do, Becca."

It wasn't fair. I couldn't wish *However Long* out of existence. I couldn't erase all the progress that we'd made, all the things we'd learned about the script, all the art that we'd created together. I couldn't peel back time so that our show had never existed.

And might well never exist in the future.

Oh, sure. If we wiped out the production, I could still "discover" Ryan's play in the stack on my desk. I could bring it to Hal. I could suggest that we produce it in a future season, that we bring it into a new and healthy full-fledged existence, with proper planning, with appropriate sponsors.

But everything would be different. Hal might push the show toward a different director. Our designers might be busy with other projects. The cast might be committed to other roles.

The cast.

We'd never have Teel to play Anana. I couldn't imagine another actress in that role. I couldn't imagine anyone else speaking reason to Fanta, explaining life's bitter truths.

Bitter truths. Like the one before me: the only way to avoid the Popcorn King's suit was to wish away *However Long*.

I stared at Ryan, fresh tears in my eyes. He sighed, looking like he'd aged twenty years in the time it had taken me to catch up to him, to realize that we truly had no other option. I took his fingers in mine, squeezing gently.

"It's okay," he said. "You don't have any other choice."

As I squared my shoulders, Teel announced with perfect, Academy-trained respect, "I'm sorry for your loss, ma'am."

The finality of his words made me tremble. All of a sudden, I had a terrible thought. "Will everything else disappear? I mean, after you're gone, will they take away the condo? My clothes?"

The policeman shook his head, one firm, confident gesture of negation. "No, ma'am!" He might have been re-porting on the police parade ground, for all the force that he shot into his reply. "Once wishes are granted, they cannot be withdrawn. Your domicile will remain secure."

Well, that was one tiny thing to be grateful for, I supposed.

"Thank you," I stammered, and then I pushed a memory of certainty into my voice. This was it. This was what I had to do. And after I made my fourth wish, Teel would disap-pear forever. "Thank you," I said again, "for all of my wishes. I can't say they turned out the way I expected them to, but I appreciate your giving me every one."

"One hundred percent of wishers are surprised by the results of their wishes," he said, and then he added a defer-ential, "Ma'am."

"Good luck with your next wisher. I hope…I hope they get through their four quickly. I hope you get to the Garden in time, that Jaze is there for you."

He tipped his hat at me, the very image of a respectful peace officer. "Thank you, ma'am."

I glanced at Ryan and tried to think of something else to say, some explanation, some excuse, some way not to undo everything we'd built together. But there wasn't any choice. There weren't any words. We'd run out of alternatives.

I held his gaze as I spoke the words. "I wish that our production of *However Long* had never been."

The policeman's eyes blazed in fierce triumph, as if he'd just brought down the leading drug kingpin in Manhattan. He lifted one strong hand toward the bill of his dark blue hat, and I thought that he was saluting me. The flames that looped around his wrist blazed high with light, yellow and gold flaring free from their black boundaries. Teel settled his blunt fingers on his earlobe. "As you wish, ma'am," he barked, tugging twice with firm authority.

A blaze of electricity rolled in waves off his uniform, sparking power that knocked me back three steps. Ryan was assaulted too; I saw him stagger until the backs of his legs touched my desk. My breath seared my lungs, too hot to breathe in, too hot to exhale. A cry rose in the back of my throat, and the jangle of power zipped down my spine, through my legs, into the carpet and away.

And then the policeman was gone.

No trace remained—not his uniform cap, not his tool belt with its nightstick and gun, not a loop of handcuffs, nothing. I held up my hand, turning my thumb and forefingers in the light. The rainbow tracery had completely disappeared; my flesh had no record whatsoever of the flames that had lurked just out of sight for the better part of two months.

"He's gone," I whispered, and the unnecessary words sounded like a shout in my tingling ears.

Ryan nodded, and then he pointed toward my desk. "And so is the summons. It looks like your wish came true."

CHAPTER 17

THE SUMMONS WASN'T THE ONLY THING MISSING.
Stacks of books had disappeared from my guest chair, from
the floor, from my desk. I'd had at least seven different
volumes on native dress in Burkina Faso—I'd borrowed them
from the Fashion Institute of Technology to assist our
costume designer.

Er, former costume designer.

Similarly, the books I'd collected on subsistence farming
were nowhere to be seen. Photo essays on African housing—
gone. Images of sunsets that I'd pulled for our lighting
designer—disappeared into genie-created smoke.

So much was missing. So much was gone.

And yet all of my memories were intact. I knew precisely
what we had created before the Popcorn King had forced us
to retreat. I knew what we'd held in our hands, what we'd
come so close to sharing with so many eager audience
members.

"Ryan…"

He sighed, like a man stepping off a merry-go-round at the end of a wild ride. "All's well that ends well, right?"

"I am so sorry," I said.

"I thought we agreed not to say that anymore."

He was right. We'd made that truce weeks before, after our initial disastrous rounds of fundraising for *However Long*.

I waved at the stacks of manuscripts on my desk. "So? Do you think it's lurking here, waiting for me to 'discover' it? I could bring it to Hal tonight. Get the ball rolling all over again."

He shrugged. "I don't see it. It must be buried really deep. How many of these things do you have sitting around here, anyway?"

He was trying to be brave. Trying to gauge his competition as we figured out how to promote *However Long* in the ordinary course of business. I grimaced. "You don't want to know."

And then, even though I was feeling miserable, even though my lungs felt like a twenty-pound of sack of flour was trying to compress them, even though I wanted to crawl beneath my comforter and sleep for a month, my stomach growled.

I never had gotten that feta and spinach omelet. I never got any lunch at all. "Should we get something to eat?" I asked Ryan. "Maybe things won't look so grim if we're not starving."

"I'm not hungry," he said.

"Pretend." I took his hand, laced my fingers between his. "At least keep me company."

Wordlessly, he gave in, taking a step toward my office

door. Before we could escape into the hallway, though, Jenn came rushing in, barely knocking before she threw the door open. "There you are! Hal's been looking for both of you! He wants to talk about that final scene one last time. He's still not satisfied with how we're representing the blocking."

I gaped. Jenn was talking to both of us. To me and to Ryan. To Ryan, whom she shouldn't have known, if we'd canceled our production of *However Long*. To Ryan, who certainly shouldn't have had a say in any final scene, in any representation of any blocking whatsoever, if my last wish had scrubbed his play from the Mercer's schedule. "Y-You know him? You know Ryan?" I stammered.

She tilted her head to one side, looking for all the world like one of her pet cockatiels. "Ha, ha, ha," she said. "So, I took an extra hour for lunch—I had to go home to feed the birds. Very funny—like I've been away from this place long enough to forget anything at all!"

"No," I said, rushing to fill the strange silence as Jenn looked to see if she really was in trouble. "That's fine. I just thought—" I glanced at Ryan, caught the barest shrug as he told me he had no idea what was going on. "Never mind," I trailed off.

It was Jenn's turn to give me a funny look. "So? Should I tell Hal you're on your way?"

"We'll come with you." Utterly confused, I followed my assistant down the hallway, trying to take some comfort from the touch of Ryan's palm, firm against the small of my back. Something had happened in that final wave of electric power. Teel had erased the production—that was the only reasonable explanation for the missing legal papers, the absent books. But whatever my policeman genie had accomplished with my final wish had not been quite what I expected...

The lobby was familiar, sedate in its classic burgundy and navy furnishings. Actors' head shots were displayed on one wall, all of the men and women who'd become familiar in the past two months. All but one, I quickly noted. Teel was missing, Teel as Anana.

A poster was displayed beside the photographs. The abstract design was eye-catching, shards of black and white and gray that just hinted at a coherent whole. *However Long,* announced bold type. By Ryan Thompson.

"What—?" I started to ask, but there wasn't anything to say, wasn't any way to pose my questions without sounding like an idiot. Or a madwoman.

I could hear Ryan's harsh breathing beside me. Without making any conscious decision, I raised my hand in front of me, stared at the whorls of my fingerprints.

No tattoos there. No trace of the flames that had summoned Teel so many times.

Jenn opened the door to the theater, utterly oblivious to our confusion. Curious despite myself, I stepped inside, telling my brain not to think, just to move forward, just to accept.

Hal and Kira stood onstage. A dozen chairs sat around them, loosely grouped in a semicircle. No set lurked upstage—no corrugated metal roof, no behemoth wall, no doors and windows marked with rolls and rolls of glow-in-the-dark tape.

Definitely no hint of the orange and yellow cacophony that had shouted from our set less than a week before.

The dirt floor that had plagued everyone's lungs and laundry for the past three weeks was gone, as well, without even a trace of dust on the audience seats. I glanced at the pipes above the stage. They were bare of lighting instruments. I could see the rolling metal racks that normally held costumes waiting in the wings, empty. The prop tables, which had held cauldrons, a walking stick, a torn sack of cornmeal, were bare.

"We're doing a reading," I breathed.

Jenn stared at me oddly. Ryan stepped forward, clearing his throat before he said, "Of course we're doing a reading. What did you think? Jenn was going to surprise us with a fully staged production, after an hour's lunch break?" I heard the false cheer in his voice, the note that everyone else was supposed to take as his gently teasing me. The note that I read as a warning, an admonition not to give away our secret, not to disclose the memories that only he and I shared. "That's exactly why Hal wants to talk about how we should handle the stage directions for the final scene."

As if my lines were printed on the air in front of me, I realized what I had to say. "I know those directions are important to you, Ryan. But I just don't think there's a way to convey them in this setting. They'll be there for the next company to use, though. When *However Long* is fully staged."

Somehow, I managed to sound normal enough to satisfy Jenn. She crossed to the foot of the stage, waiting until Kira gave her a nod, acknowledging that my assistant had done her duty by retrieving Ryan and me. Then Jenn turned back to the two of us. "Bec, if it's okay with you, I'm going to head back to my desk. I want to take a look at the stalking list before everyone heads over to the Pharm."

The stalking list. The online tangle of websites and blogs and discussion groups where Jenn had first found Ryan. Where she must be searching out another new playwright, another brilliant discovery for some future Mercer season.

"Sure," I said. "I'll see you later." I barely remembered to take the three-ring binder that she thrust into my hands. My copy of *However Long*. Annotated with my notes, from the weeks we'd spent rehearsing this staged reading.

I bit my tongue to keep from saying anything else until she was out of earshot. Then, I hissed in Ryan's ear, "Do you see what's happened?"

"I don't believe it," he said. A couple of actors wandered onto the stage, crossing to their chairs as if they'd been working on this show for weeks. Which, all genie interference aside, they had been.

Genie interference.

Sure, Teel had worked my wishes for me. He'd saved us from Ronald's restraining order, from expensive litigation and potentially crippling damages. But Ryan had made his own wishes; Jaze had been tasked with meeting his demands. My wishing us free from the Popcorn King's tyranny hadn't negated Ryan's own magical demands. At least, not entirely.

I clutched Ryan's arm. "What did you wish for?" I whispered, afraid of drawing too much attention from the group gathering onstage. "Your fourth wish! How exactly did you phrase it?"

"I don't know." His voice matched mine, urgent but suppressed. "I asked for…I *think* I asked for…" He shook his head. "I can't be certain now. It's been too long. But I probably said something about staging *However Long*. I asked Jaze to have the Mercer stage my play."

I nodded. "And we are. We're *staging* it. A staged reading."

It was so simple. A staged reading would fill the hole in the Mercer's production schedule. Sure, it was an unusual move; audiences would be surprised. But I was certain that

Hal had found a way to spin the decision, to make it a positive adventure. I'd seen him work a room of hostile board members. By comparison, it would be a breeze to convince eager theater-lovers that they wanted the novelty of watching a show in the very throes of creation.

The reading would bring Ryan's language into stark focus. At the same time, it would meet the Mercer's budget requirements—even the strict budget that Dean's misdeeds had thrown our way. With a staged reading, we didn't need to hire designers, didn't need to pay for sets, for costumes, for lighting, for makeup. We'd have no need for a sponsor, for the Popcorn King or anyone else.

But most important, a staged reading would meet Ryan's needs. His play would see the light of day. New York theater cognoscenti would be bound to take notice of a reading at the Mercer—the very unusualness of the venue would attract attention that might have been missing in smaller theaters. Producers from around the country could be invited to see the play.

I glanced down at my three-ring binder. I recognized my printing on the cover, my neat label with the play's name, with the dates of our abbreviated run. Catching my breath, half-fearful that the magic would buckle and I'd see only empty pages inside, I opened the cover.

However Long was there, sticky notes sprouting from almost every page. But there were other documents in the notebook, as well. Tucked into the front pocket was a guest list, a compilation of names and addresses. My own printed notes told me that I'd sent invitations to the Minneapolis Repertory Company, to the Lifewise New Plays Festival, to a dozen other theater companies that prided themselves on nurturing new playwrights. I clutched the notebook tighter when I saw the notations beside each name. Every one of our targets had accepted our invitation.

However Long was going to be seen by the movers and shakers at every leading theater company in the United States. I'd be astonished if it didn't receive a full staging within a year. Maybe two would pick it up, simultaneously. Or more.

I shoved the binder into Ryan's accepting hands, directing his gaze to the invitation list. I saw the precise instant that he realized what I was showing him, that he recognized our success.

His smile was brilliant, like sunflowers bursting into golden halos.

As he handed the notebook back to me, a postcard slipped free from the pages. I grabbed it before it could fall to the floor. The picture on the front showed a mother zebra and her foal, nuzzling each other against a backdrop of tall, bleached grass. I flipped the card over and saw that it was from the San Diego Zoo.

More important, it was from my mother. Her bold cursive filled the left half of the card. "Break a leg, darling. Wishing you and Ryan all the best for opening night. Dad and Pop-pop send their love. XOXO, Mom."

Tears welled up in my eyes. My mother had never sent me a card before, had never acknowledged one of my shows. Or, for that matter, one of my boyfriends. I wondered what I'd done to earn such a booster-wish from Teel. Maybe he'd felt guilty about manipulating Ryan and me, about using us to entertain himself and Jaze. Whatever the reason, I wasn't going to complain.

"Ryan," Hal called from the stage. I hastily tucked the

postcard back into my binder as my boss said, "Let's go through this one more time. We need to figure out once and for all what we're doing with the dream sequence stage directions."

Ryan grabbed my hand, making sure that I stayed beside him. Hal watched us approach, his brilliant blue eyes seeing everything, knowing nothing. Kira gave us a curious glance as we drew near, and for just a second, I thought that she must know the truth, she must be aware of the changes that Teel had wrought in the production. Whatever concerns she had, though, drifted away before she could say anything, as if she were forgetting some vague dream, even as she woke up. I suspected I was seeing the last demonstration of Teel's power.

Hal spoke with the diplomacy that had made him one of the most successful artistic directors in town. "Ryan, I know we've gone back and forth on this. I understand that the stage directions are important to you. They're part of the script, part of the play that you created. But I just don't see how to represent them for this reading. We've tried everything. When Kira reads them out loud, they sound flat against the fully interpreted dialogue. When an actor reads them, they sound fanciful. People aren't used to hearing stage directions at all. I'm afraid we're only going to confuse the audience, no matter what we do."

Ryan stared at the stage, at the stark wooden boards broken only by the scattering of chairs. The directions were the heart and soul of his script, the harvest that he'd sown with his software package, years ago, before he'd decided to go to Burkina Faso, before he'd ever dreamed of writing Fanta's story. The directions were the remnant of the time he'd spent with Pam, the time he'd spent creating his software masterpiece. They were the fruit of all his wishes.

But in the intervening years—and in the past ten minutes—Ryan had learned a valuable lesson. From his genie,
from mine, from the entire notion of a staged reading, he'd
learned the art of compromise.

"Let it go, Hal."

"But—" I couldn't help interrupting.

Ryan shook his head. "Let it go. Maybe Becca can write
something for the program, an insert that explains the traditional Burkinabe dances, describes their importance to Fanta
and her people. That way, the audience will know about
them, even in this setting. And when the play is fully staged,
other directors can draw on the specifics I put into the script."

Hal looked at me. "Becca? Can you write that?"

"Of course." Hal had asked the question, but I gave my
answer to Ryan. I wanted him to know that I understood the
concession that he was making. "We can work together to
come up with something appropriate."

Hal nodded tersely. "Okay, then. Kira, let's get everyone
onstage. Let's start from the top and make it perfect—those
Yale folks will be expecting a lot tomorrow."

Yale Drama. My alma mater. I wondered whom I'd invited
for the preview. There'd be time enough to find out later.

As Kira summoned everyone to their chairs, Ryan and I
moved to the center of the house. An expectant air drifted over
the theater as we took our seats. There was a shuffle of paper
as actors thumbed to the front of their scripts. I caught my breath
in the endless moment before Fanta delivered her first line.

"When I was a little girl, I thought I'd marry a king."

The accent was perfect. Fanta sounded like she'd lived her
life in Burkina Faso, like she'd never even heard of the island
of Jamaica.

I couldn't help myself. I turned my notebook pages as quietly as I could, searching for an explanation. It took me halfway through the script before I found what I was looking for. Again, my handwriting was familiar, was perfect, was mine. But I had no idea when I'd written the note. *Accent coach,* it said. And underneath that, *Teel.* And a 212 telephone number.

With a sad certainty, I knew the number would be disconnected if I phoned now.

But what did that matter? I'd obviously brought in the help that Fanta needed. Affordably, too. Without the need for a Popcorn King stipend.

I sat back and enjoyed the rest of Fanta's introductory lines. It wasn't until she reached the end of the first scene, though, that I realized Ryan had stiffened beside me. He was leaning forward in his chair. His fingers dug into his armrests, and he caught his lower lip between his teeth.

And then I understood what he feared.

Anana's first scene. I took an instant survey of the familiar actors' faces. There was someone new up there, someone I had overlooked in all of my surprise, in all of the changed events.

She was younger than Teel had been. Deep lines ran between her nose and her mouth, but her forehead remained smooth. Silver whispered at her temples, but she had no hint of my genie's regal halo. She held herself stiff in her chair, her backbone rigid, her neck proud.

And when she spoke, her commanding voice carried to the last row of the theater. She drew every eye in the house. She captured every ear.

She wasn't Teel. She didn't read Anana's lines with the

identical energy, with the exact same meaning, the by-now familiar grave vigor. Instead, she presented a new interpretation of a matriarch, a new view of Ryan's core vision.

She wasn't Teel, but she was superb. She was Anana.

I felt Ryan relax beside me. I heard him draw a full breath, and then another and another. I watched him sink back into his velvet chair, relax into the play, into the poetry of the lines, into the beauty of the reading.

The cast worked through the first act, then plunged directly into the second. The dream sequence was haunting, mysterious. What it lost through physical staging, it gained in the actors' careful attention to every single word. Ryan's lines resonated like ancient songs, thrumming deep inside my heart. When Fanta delivered her final, fractured words, I realized that I'd been holding my breath, poised on the jagged edge of creative perfection.

Hal held the silence for a full measure. Another. Another. And then he jumped to his feet. "Excellent, people! Excellent job! Ryan?"

I watched Ryan pull himself upright. He took his time, studying the entire cast, meeting the eyes of each actor in sequence. "Thank you," he finally said. "Thank you for giving voice to my words. Thank you for understanding what I was saying, for preparing to share it with others so perfectly."

There was a flurry of chatter after that. Hal delivered his inevitable notes. Kira reminded everyone to arrive early the next night for a round of group warm-ups. One actor asked Ryan about motivation for a single obscure line. Three women cornered me, wanting to know if I could do yet more research about haggling in African markets.

Before we knew it, though, everyone was collecting their

belongings. Scripts were shoved into backpacks. Empty coffee cups were tossed into trash cans. Laughing instructions were issued to the first people who left, requests to save tables, to order drinks. The Pharm would soon be filled with our boisterous cast.

As I watched order return from the controlled chaos of the reading, my cell phone rang. I excused myself from Ryan and stepped into the lobby to answer. With a sinking feeling, I recognized the phone number before I said, "Rebecca Morris."

"Ambrose," came the hangdog reply. I braced myself for more bad news, for more interference from Dean, for more deflating of my dreams, just when I thought everything was finally going perfectly.

"Good evening, Detective." I tried to sound professional.

"Miss Morris, I just wanted you to know that we're closing out our file on Mr. Marcus."

I stared at the phone, wondering if it had somehow been broken in the electric jangle of Teel's magic, if it had somehow been destroyed by the current that had passed through it, around it. "Excuse me?" I asked.

He sighed. "We've completed our investigation, Miss Morris. We're turning everything over to the prosecutor."

"Prosecutor? But what good will that do, if Dean is in Russia?"

Another one of those monumental sighs preceded Ambrose's announcement. "Miss Morris, Mr. Marcus is en route to the United States as we speak. My men are waiting to take him into custody as soon as his plane touches down at JFK." As if for good measure, he added a "Miss Morris."

"But why would Dean come home?" My head was

reeling. Was this something else my former, despicable boyfriend had somehow worked out, just to make me miserable? After all these months of my building my own life, of my working through the problems that Dean had left behind, was he coming back now, just to spite me? "What could he possibly want from me now?"

"Nothing like that, Miss Morris." Another gust from Ambrose, as if a hurricane were swelling in his chest. "Let's just say, Miss Morris, that once an embezzler, always an embezzler."

"Dean tried to steal from someone else?" I was incredulous. What could he need *more* money for? He had millions to spare, if he just kept a low profile and parceled it out on vodka, babushka women, and balalaika song.

"Miss Morris, we find that's often the case with criminals, especially when they spend as much time as Mr. Marcus did, structuring his theft from the Mercer." Ambrose sounded so sad that I actually wanted to comfort him, wanted to tell him that it would all turn out okay.

"But who did he steal from?" I was so confused. "And why is he coming back here?"

"Let's just say that the Russian mob is a lot less understanding than the U.S. court system. Sometimes even a prison starts to look like a good, safe place to be. For a thief."

For the first time ever, Ambrose forgot to call me Miss Morris. And for the first time ever, I heard a smile in his voice, just a grim hint of one.

Dean had bitten off more than he could chew—way more. I could only imagine the people he had made angry. I could only begin to picture shadowy underworld bosses, slinging back shots of vodka as they ordered Dean's head on a platter.

Dean was coming home. He was going to face the music here.

"Will he be forced to make restitution?" I asked, thinking of the Mercer, of all the trouble he had caused.

"Miss Morris, let's not get ahead of ourselves. We'll need you to testify against him."

We were back to our usual formality, I noted, but I could hardly care. My own smile threatened to make my cheeks ache. "With pleasure, Detective Ambrose. With extreme pleasure."

He told me more details, about Dean's flight, about how he would be taken into custody. Someone from the prosecutor's office would contact me. I'd likely provide a deposition, at least at first. There'd probably be a plea somewhere down the road, hopefully sooner, rather than later. Dean would definitely serve some jail time. And, yes, he would be required to make restitution, to the extent that he still had his ill-gotten gains.

I didn't absorb everything that Ambrose said, all the details of how the criminal justice system would work. All I knew was that at long last, I was vindicated. Dean Marcus would be brought to justice. He'd be forced to pay for what he'd done to me, to the Mercer.

As Ambrose hung up, I couldn't describe how I felt. Once upon a time, I'd been angry about Dean. And embarrassed. And deeply, terribly sad.

But now, I felt…relieved. I'd escaped Dean before he could truly, irrevocably hurt me. He was a thief and a liar and an idiot, too—he'd gotten greedy, and now he had to return home, to pay the piper.

For all practical purposes, I never needed to deal with Dean again. Ambrose and his ilk would dot i's and cross t's. And then Dean would be out of my life forever.

Forever.

I tested how that felt, rubbing my emotions across the discovery, like a tongue across a chipped tooth. It snagged a little, as I remembered how foolish I had been, how trusting, way back when. But I already knew I'd get over that. I'd forget it. I'd forget Dean. I practically had already.

Squaring my shoulders, I headed back into the theater.

Hal had already headed back to his office. There'd be time enough to tell him the good news, time enough to let him know that the Mercer's coffers would likely be restored, at least in part.

Kira was pulling the onstage chairs back to their proper places, preparing everything for the next night. Still a little dazed by Ambrose's call, I floated over to Ryan. He continued to be gripped by the play's spell, by the power of the reading we had witnessed.

I grasped his hand and led him out of the magic cave of the theater, into the lobby. Like a man waking from a dream, Ryan reached out and touched the stark poster for the show. For *his* show. *Our* show. "However long the night," he said, "the dawn will break."

I laughed, thinking how appropriate the words were, especially in light of Ambrose's call. Ryan's smile, when he turned to me, was brilliant. His fingers tangled in my hair as he pulled me close, and I felt his laughter through his chest, down his arms. His lips on mine were teasing, playful, and I lost myself in the sheer joy of success.

"We did it," he whispered. "We actually, finally did it."

"I know it's not what you planned," I said, when I could think coherent words past the distracting things his lips were doing to the pulse point in my throat.

"Plans," he murmured. "Who needs plans?"

"Especially when you've got a genie or two to pitch in." We both laughed at that, only to be startled into silence when the door to the theater opened.

"Okay, you two," Kira said. "Out of here. I need to lock up."

"Are you coming over to the Pharm?"

"I'll probably stop by later. John is going to meet me here in about ten minutes." John. Her husband. The man she'd met in Minneapolis, when Teel had been her genie.

I started to tell her what Teel had just done, how he'd shaped my last wish. But before the words were out of my mouth, I realized that they'd only lead to questions—questions about Ryan, about how I could discuss a genie in front of him, about Jaze, about the four wishes Ryan had spent before I knew him.

It was easier just to say good-night. Easier to take Ryan's hand in mine. Easier to walk out the door of the Mercer.

I stopped dead when I saw the carpet of crocuses underneath the plane trees. I'd forgotten about Dani's handiwork, about the Gray Guerillas. The purple and yellow flowers were just starting to close in the twilight. Seeing them reminded me that I never had gotten my omelet for lunch. I was suddenly starving. "I need something to eat before we head over to the Pharm."

"There's a Popcorn King on Fifth. I hear they have some great snacks."

"Bite your tongue!"

"Or we could just go home," Ryan said. "Order something in for dinner."

Head home. To my apartment, the perfect one with a

view of the river, with the sparkling lights of New York City displayed like candles on a cake. The one that had plenty of room for two people to share, for two people to build a life together in the chaotic, demanding, insane, perfect world of New York theater.

"What were you thinking?" I asked. "Chinese? Indian?"

He shrugged and wove his fingers between mine. His hands were warm, filled with promises, as we started the familiar walk back to the Bentley. "I don't care," he said. "You decide. Your wish is my command."

★ ★ ★ ★ ★

How long will the next four wishes take?
Find out in
TO WISH OR NOT TO WISH
Coming in October 2010!

ACKNOWLEDGMENTS

Creating a book is a lot like staging a play. Many people envision an author working in solitude, creating books without assistance from anyone else. In the real world, however, authors rely on dozens of people to transform the stories inside their heads into real, finished books.

In creating this volume of the As You Wish series, I am deeply indebted to a trio of dramaturgs who responded to my emergency plea for information about their daily jobs. Akiva Fox, Sarah Wallace, and Miriam Weisfeld went above and beyond the call of duty, sharing details of their working lives, offering advice on professional ethics in the theater, and telling entertaining story after entertaining story. The D.C. theater community is incredibly lucky to have these smart, funny, and dedicated dramaturgs. Any inaccuracies about real-world dramaturgy are my sole responsibility.

During the "rehearsal process" for this novel, Bruce Sundrud provided invaluable notes, pointing out linguistic and logical flaws, even though I forced him onto an impossibly tight timetable.

The "running crew" for this production included my agent, Richard Curtis, who continues to provide his unique blend of compassion and common sense, often at odd hours of the night and on weekends. As always, the incredible people at Harlequin/MIRA Books have been instrumental in the completion of this book: Mary-Theresa Hussey and Elizabeth Mazer lead the way, but they represent dozens of hard-working souls, including but by no means limited to Alana Burke, Valerie Gray, Mary Helms, Amy Jones, Tracey

Langmuir, Don Lucey, Margaret O'Neill Marbury, Linda McFall, Diane Mosher, Emily Ohanjanians, Marianna Ricciuto, Lola Speranza, Malle Vallik, Stacy Widdrington, Amy Wilkins, and Adam Wilson. Once again, I offer special thanks to Margie Miller, for her incredible work on the cover design for this series.

Additional backstage support came from my family, the ever-enthusiastic Klaskys, Fallons, Maddreys, and Timminses. My husband, Mark, deserves an Oscar, Tony, Emmy, and every other award I can think of, for his constant, unwavering support of me and my writing career.

Of course, no show is complete without an audience—the readers of this book. I look forward to corresponding with you through my website at www.mindyklasky.com.